SHELTERING YOU

WRIGHT HEROES OF MAINE
BOOK 4

ROBIN PATCHEN

JDO PUBLISHING

Published in Austin, TX.

Cover by Lynnette Bonner

Paperback ISBN: 978-1-950029-45-7

Large Print ISBN: 978-1-950029-46-4

Hard Cover ISBN: 978-1-950029-47-1

Library of Congress Control Number: 2024911711

For Malakai.
You are a joy and a delight.

CHAPTER ONE

His opportunity had finally arrived.

When word came from the cartel that ran this stretch of Mexico, Khalid Qasim gathered his things and trudged away from the crumbling hotel in the tiny town where he'd holed up.

The road was dusty and brown and ugly, but not empty. Hundreds of others were making their way north, and as they got nearer the border, those hundreds became thousands.

They spoke Spanish or Chinese or French or languages he didn't even recognize. Some spoke Qasim's native tongue, Arabic.

While the rest of the hopeful immigrants went in one direction, he and two Chinese men he'd not met before climbed onto the back of a truck, its driver a rough-looking Mexican who stank of sweat and last night's tequila.

They drove for hours, then waited in the middle of the desert for even longer, sitting beneath the only tree in sight and sipping lukewarm water. The Chinese men spoke to each other, but Qasim and the driver remained silent.

It was dusk when the driver's phone dinged. He read the text, then snapped, "In, in. It is time."

"How can you be sure?" Qasim asked the question in English, hoping the driver understood. The man had said almost nothing all day.

He pointed north into the pale sky. "Drone."

Qasim didn't see it, but a drone would explain how the cartel knew what was happening north of the border.

"They go to crowd," the driver said. "Here, nobody to see."

That made sense.

After a short ride, Qasim and the others were directed to go down a hill, cross a shallow river, and walk up the other side. "America, there," the driver said.

No fence, no guards. Nothing. Just a little bit of water.

The Chinese men were young. Before the driver stopped talking, they bolted.

Qasim was careful to watch where he put his feet on the rocky, uneven soil. He was in decent shape for a man of sixty-four, but he couldn't afford to fall. A delay would cost him, and a hospital visit could thwart his plans.

He needed strength for what he had to do. And he needed to stay hidden.

Two months after his second wife's escape, Khalid had finally gotten a whiff of her whereabouts. Somehow, she'd made her way to America, though where she'd landed in this vast country, he had no idea.

He'd find her. He had a plan, and she would walk right into his trap.

Qasim would return his second wife—his *Hagar*—to Iraq. And when she gave birth to his child—his little *Ishmael*—he would present the baby to Salwa, his treasured first wife, as the son she'd never been able to bear.

As for Yasamin...?

After running away from him, the little fool would suffer every pain she deserved.

CHAPTER TWO

There had to be a way out of the friend zone.

Derrick Wright had heard of this place, where women saw men as pals instead of prospects. He'd always thought it was the stuff of myths and legends. Nightmares, maybe. Because, really, how hard was it to just ask a woman out? Derrick had never had any trouble getting dates. The problems always came after the asking, when he had to suffer through the actual events, which usually included long-winded discussions about social media ad strategies, or the care and feeding of two-year-olds in a daycare, or—and this had been the worst—the step-by-step process of cleaning a dog's abscessed tooth.

He'd hardly been able to finish his lunch, sitting across from the veterinarian who'd gotten less and less attractive with every word.

Suffice it to say, though getting *first* dates wasn't a problem, Derrick hadn't had a lot of *second* dates in his life.

Being a pilot was a plus in the whole attracting-women thing, and when they learned he owned his own jet, they were usually keen to at least give it a go. Not that he ever shared how, after years in business, he still had months when he struggled to make the payment on said jet. Good thing his brother had financed it, and Sam wouldn't foreclose if Derrick missed a month. But Derrick sure didn't plan to take advantage of his brother's generosity.

Not only did Jasmine know Derrick was a pilot, but she'd ridden on his plane when he'd brought her and her sister to the US from Greece. It'd been a rescue mission. That should count for something, right?

Yet, here he sat, in Jasmine's friend zone.

Technically, he sat on Sam's couch, watching the woman of his dreams on the far side of the living room. A Christmas tree glittering with lights and shiny ornaments stood in the corner between a stacked-stone fireplace and a wall of windows. The star that topped the tree sparkled just centimeters below the twenty-foot ceiling. Presents already poked out from beneath it, though they were still weeks from the holiday. Other Christmas decorations filled almost every surface—Eliza's doing, no doubt.

Between the festive decor and all the family and friends, it was downright cramped. Eight women were gathered near the entrance, and Derrick's brothers and dad hovered around them like spotters at the gym, as if one of the females might swoon and need rescue.

Only Derrick held back, trying to be a casual observer. Trying not to stare.

Despite being the future bride's twin and the maid of honor, Jasmine stood apart from the rest of the bridal party as they prepared to go wedding gown shopping. She wore a shapeless dress that was too big for her slender, five-foot frame. She had straight, silky brown hair that reached past the middle of her back and the most gorgeous liquid-brown eyes he'd ever seen.

Right now, they were wide as she observed the crowd, an expression Derrick had seen often in the months since he'd met her. She was overwhelmed and nervous—but also delighted, as if being here were a blessing she couldn't wrap her mind around.

That was one of the reasons Derrick loved her—that beautiful wonder she saw in the world.

"You got a little drool"—Bryan plopped on the sofa beside him, tapping his chin—"right there."

"Shut up."

His brother grinned. "How's that coming along?" He tipped his head toward Jasmine as if there was no question of what he meant. All the brothers knew exactly how Derrick felt about Jasmine, who'd escaped with her sister from their tyrannical father in Iraq. He figured her twin, Leila, also guessed Derrick's feelings, though, unlike his brothers, she was too kind to tease him. Mom and Dad knew. If Derrick had to guess, all the sisters-in-law knew.

Everybody knew how Derrick felt about Jasmine—except Jasmine.

"It's fine," Derrick said. "Just great."

"You ever need some advice—"

"I'll ask someone who knows something about women."

"Which one of us has a girlfriend?" At the word, Bryan glanced at the curly-haired blonde who'd recently moved in with Leila and Jasmine. Sophie probably knew, too, come to think of it. She, like the twins, was hiding in Shadow Cove from terrorists. Because...yeah, his family had had a strange few months. Derrick wasn't privy to all the details, just enough to know there'd been danger and excitement—all of which he'd missed.

"I'll figure it out," Derrick said.

Bryan eyed him like one might eye roadkill. "You should get a haircut. Maybe Jasmine prefers her men to look like, you know, men."

"She likes it." Didn't she? She'd remarked on it once, her cheeks turning bright red about a second later. Derrick ran a hand through his shoulder-length hair. "You're just jealous."

"Yeah"—his voice was heavy with sarcasm—"that's it."

"Bryan," Sophie called from the middle of the throng. "Can you help me with something?"

He popped up and rushed to her as if he'd been summoned by the queen.

Derrick's gaze skimmed the women and, of course, landed on Jasmine again. She smiled that shy smile—lips closed but tipped up at the corners, chin dipped, eyes wide as she watched him from below those long eyelashes.

The expression was a hit to the solar plexus. It took everything in him not to act just like his brother, run to her and take her in his arms.

He was an idiot.

His phone rang in his pocket, and he wasn't sorry for the excuse to walk out. Heading toward the kitchen, he glanced at the number, then swiped to connect. "Derrick Wright."

"Hey, man." Chet Williams, Derrick's biggest client. "Hate to do this to you, but I gotta cancel. We had a last-minute change of plans."

Derrick's stomach swooped like he'd hit an air pocket. "Just tomorrow, or..."

"The whole week. Board's decided to have the meetings on Zoom to save money and stick close to home for the holidays. You know how it is." He lowered his voice. "Tell you the truth, I was hoping to get out of here. My mother-in-law's in town."

As if Derrick should feel bad for the guy. He'd been hired to fly Chet to North Carolina, then the entire board down to Florida for a few days of golf before returning everyone home.

He'd had it on his schedule for months.

He'd turned down other clients because of it—higher-paying clients.

And now he'd lose a week's worth of wages in the middle of the holidays.

Gaze downcast, he leaned against the kitchen counter, his heart pounding. "Thing is, Chet, I'm, uh... It's really late notice."

"Yeah, I know. Sorry about that. But we'll be sure to use you when we plan the Q2 board meeting."

"Right, but..." Derrick could do this. He *had to* do this. If he didn't start standing up for himself, his savings account would be empty. He'd miss payments, and what would that do to his relationship with Sam?

He'd have to sell the plane. He'd be bankrupt.

Footsteps told Derrick somebody had joined him in the kitchen, but he didn't look.

He took a breath for courage and forced the words out of his mouth. "I'll send you a bill for the late-cancellation fee." Which would be half what the company would've paid for the charter, but better than nothing.

Silence.

It ticked for seconds.

Derrick was pretty sure his heart was going to slam right out of his chest before Chet finally spoke.

"You're not serious. You really expect me to pay that?"

"You signed a contract."

"Here's the deal, Wright," Chet said. "You can either have your money now or you can have our business later. But you can't have both."

Derrick tapped the cell—was banged a better word?—

against his forehead. He needed the money. He needed the client more.

He returned the phone to his ear. "Quarter fee, then," he said. "And next time, I need at least two weeks' notice."

Another long silence, and then... "I hope the money's worth it." The three quick beeps told him his most loyal client—former client, maybe—had ended the call.

"Everything okay?"

Grant, brother number four, was staring at him over a giant cooler on the kitchen counter. He might not've been the tallest of the brothers, but he was definitely the biggest. Derrick figured he could hold his own in a fight against the rest of the Wrights, but Grant would squish him like a bug.

Not that he'd ever admit that. Especially considering, of all the brothers, this one felt the most distant. Their relationship had taken a hit after Bryan's accident, and it had never recovered. Derrick hated that, but he'd had no opportunity to fix it, considering he never spent time alone with him. "Thought you were fawning over the women like the rest of the guys."

"There's only so much of that"—Grant chin-pointed toward the chatter—"a man can take."

"No kidding."

A few twelve-packs of drinks sat on the floor by Derrick's feet. He grabbed one and started shifting cans into the cooler.

Grant did the same. "What was that about?"

"The call?" Stupid question, but he didn't want to say. He was trying to imagine anybody in the world treating his ex-Green Beret brother that way.

Grant didn't need words. His slightly raised eyebrows spoke loudly enough.

"Cancellation for tomorrow's trip."

"I take it he didn't want to pay the fee."

"I don't usually expect him to, but he does this to me a lot."

"Because you don't expect him to pay."

"Probably. I like to be good to my clients. I'm good to them, and they're good to me."

Still transferring cans into the cooler, Grant said, "Canceling a day before a trip is good?"

"Obviously not." Derrick couldn't keep the frustration out of his voice. He lifted the last box of soda from the floor and slammed it on the counter. "But neither is what just happened. I probably lost that client for good."

"You need better clients."

"Owning your own business isn't that simple."

Grant shrugged. "I wouldn't do business with people—do life with people—who think they can walk on me. Sometimes, you have to stand up for yourself. The people who matter will respect you for it. The people who don't respect you for it—they don't matter."

Easy for Grant to say. He wasn't an entrepreneur. He didn't have to kowtow to rich people to make ends meet.

Derrick grabbed a bag of ice from the freezer and dumped it on top of the cans and water bottles.

Not that the drinks wouldn't get cold enough just being outside today. It was December in Maine, after all. Probably wouldn't even hit thirty-five degrees.

"Thanks." Grant added a plastic bag that someone had packed for the snowmobiling excursion. Because as long as the women were off to do something fun, the men ought to as well.

Derrick had so few interactions with Grant. He hated that this one had been focused on his own deficiencies, especially when he had something far more important to talk about. "Can I ask you a question?"

His brother closed the cooler, then lifted the giant thing and set it by the door to the garage. He straightened and leaned against the countertop, nodding for Derrick to go ahead.

"You and Summer were friends for a long time before you were together, right?"

Grant nodded again. The man used words as if each one were as valuable as gold and he was low on cash.

"How'd you go from friends to...more?"

At that, his brother's lips tipped up at the corner. "Sure you want my advice?"

"You made it happen, so I think I do."

"Took seven years."

"From when you met? Or from when you realized you had feelings for her?"

"Yes."

Oh.

Not what Derrick wanted to hear.

"Summer wasn't ready," Grant said. "I had to be patient. But then I got to the point where it was too hard to be around her. I had to tell her the truth. Figured if she didn't feel anything for me by then, it was time to walk away."

"I'm not waiting seven years." And Derrick wasn't walking away either. That wasn't an option.

He was all-in with Jasmine. He'd had no say in the matter. One look and he was smitten like...like some stupid lovesick puppy.

Grant shrugged. "If I'd tried to rush Summer, she'd have pushed me away. Or slugged me—you never know with her." By the way his eyes lit, he seemed delighted by the prospect.

Before she'd opened the clothing boutique, his wife had been a bodyguard, like Grant, so Derrick figured she packed a punch.

"Seven years, though." Derrick ran a hand down his face. He couldn't imagine waiting so long. "And then you just told her, and she...what? Did she feel the same way? Everything was good after that?"

By the quirk of Grant's lips, that wasn't exactly how it happened. "She came around."

"You really know how to encourage a guy."

"Never been good at dancing around the truth. I can tell you this—Summer was worth the wait." Grant clamped a hand on Derrick's shoulder. "Considering nobody reads people like you do, I figure your girl must be too."

The compliment surprised him.

Before he could respond, Michael stepped in and looked between them. "I'm trying to escape the estrogen. Seems like I walked into more."

Grant dropped his arm. "Say that again. It's been a while since I've thumped someone."

Michael laughed. "I would, but I wouldn't want you to get in trouble with your wife."

Grinning, Grant nodded to the cooler. "You two see if you can wrestle that into my truck. Let me know if you need my help carrying it." He walked out, chuckling.

"Idiot," Michael called after him.

"Putz." Grant turned the corner toward the women, whose voices were fading.

"Are they finally leaving?" Derrick asked.

Michael glanced at his watch. "Only an hour late."

"What was the problem?"

"Mom had her plan. Summer had different plans. I guess she knows people. There were some tense negotiations." He crossed the kitchen to the cooler Grant had left and grabbed one of the handles.

Derrick gripped the other. "Does Leila have any say in the matter?"

"She doesn't know one store from another, so she doesn't care. She's just excited to try on wedding gowns, wherever they take her. Ready?"

They carried the cooler into the dark garage and set it by the door. Grant's truck was outside. The women's conversation carried from the driveway, along with the slamming of car doors. Derrick strained to hear Jasmine, but of course she wouldn't be talking, not in such a big crowd.

"Let's not open the door until they leave," Michael said. "I don't want to get sucked in." He headed back to the kitchen. "Anything new with Jasmine?"

"Why does everyone keep asking me that?" Derrick slammed the door.

Michael gave him a *don't be an idiot* look but said nothing.

"Grant told me to take it slow."

"Grant's right." Michael leaned a shoulder on the fridge and crossed his arms. "There's a lot about Jasmine you don't know."

"What do you mean?" He was careful not to let irritation seep into his tone. "Like what?"

"Her life hasn't been easy."

"I know that. She's told me a lot about her past." Well, not *a lot,* but enough that he understood she'd been imprisoned by her family. "Maybe she's already told me everything."

"She hasn't."

Michael's confidence ticked him off. He clamped his lips shut to keep his annoyance from escaping.

"Don't push her," Michael added. "She needs to heal."

"From?"

"If she wants to tell you, she will. If she does"—Michael's head dipped from side to side—"it's possible your feelings for her will change. I just want you to be prepared. She's great—I'm not saying she's not. Only that there are things you don't know. Until you do, you need to...hold back a little. Don't hand your heart over."

It was too late for that, and his feelings weren't going to

change. But Derrick didn't say those things because...because Michael knew something he didn't.

Whatever Jasmine hadn't told him wouldn't matter. Derrick had never been in love before, but the feelings he had for her weren't fleeting or disposable. He loved her. Ridiculous as it was, he loved her, and nothing—including whatever secret she'd yet to share—was going to change that.

CHAPTER THREE

Jasmine Fayad—Jasmine *French*, she reminded herself—had done her share of shopping since she'd arrived in the US. Just having the freedom to leave the house whenever she wanted was a thrill, so even though she didn't have much money to spend, she loved looking at all the pretty packages at the giant Target store and the small shops in downtown Shadow Cove. And now that it was Christmas season, everything was extra sparkly with pine trees and twinkle lights and shimmery holiday balls.

But she'd never been to a place like this.

The building was shaped like a little house on the outside with wreaths hanging in front of every window and garland around the front door. Only the round sign hanging over the entrance gave away that it was a shop. Inside, mannequins were displayed on pedestals all around, each wearing a different gown. Sleek and elegant—puffy shoulders and strapless and everything in between. There were colorful dresses, likely made for bridesmaids—reds and greens, which seemed the predominant colors for the holiday season—but most were white and pure and represented what marriage should be. They represented what her marriage was not and could never have been, even if she hadn't run.

The gowns represented everything Jasmine had lost and would never get back, no matter the freedom this country offered her.

Her shame felt heavier than any beaded and sequined dress could ever be.

"This place is amazing, is it not?" Leila broke off from the other women and linked her arm with Jasmine's, leaning close. "Which is your favorite?" Jasmine shrugged, but her twin pressed. "Please, I want to know."

As they perused the selection, Jasmine allowed herself to imagine how she'd look in the different styles, considering and then discarding each one.

And then she and her sister followed the other ladies around a corner, and a dress caught her eye.

The pure white satin bodice was covered with lace that rose to a bateau neckline, stretching from the shoulders across the base of the mannequin's neck. The lace continued down, forming long, elegant sleeves. The lace tapered over the full skirt, which fanned out behind the mannequin in a beautiful train.

"Yes." Leila studied the dress, reading Jasmine's mind. "It's exactly right. Modest and lovely, just like you."

Jasmine attempted to smile but couldn't pull it off. Leila was trying to be kind, but imagining the gown, imagining herself wearing the gown, brought a stab of grief and regret.

Why hope for things that could never be?

The store owner asked Leila to point out the styles she liked best. The rest of the bridal party crowded in.

Summer, the former-model-turned-fashionista, offered her opinion, as did Michael's mother. They both had good taste, but they didn't understand Leila's style.

Leila beckoned Jasmine through the crowd of women. "What do you think, sister?"

Jasmine took her time studying the gowns the other women had pointed out. "They will be lovely on you." But Leila didn't need a compliment—they were *identical* twins, after all. Across the showroom, she spied a style similar to one Leila had exclaimed over in a magazine. Off-the-shoulder with a modest neckline, it wasn't fussy with sequins and lace. The beauty would come from the woman who wore it. Jasmine gestured to it. "This one, I believe."

Leila gave her sister a grateful smile. It wasn't that she was shy—she'd always been the bolder sister. She didn't want to offend these women who would soon be her family.

The clerk promised to pull all the gowns the women had chosen and a few more and ushered Leila away.

Jasmine joined the other bridesmaids on sofas that faced a platform in front of mirrors, choosing a seat beside Eliza, Sam's wife. Sophie, who'd recently moved to Shadow Cove and was staying with Jasmine and Leila, took the spot on the adjacent sofa.

Peggy, Summer, and Camilla—wife of the oldest Wright brother, Daniel—chatted on the other sofas. Summer was expecting a baby, though she was barely showing. Jasmine figured her height—nearly a foot taller than Jasmine—was at least part of the reason she could hide her pregnancy so long.

Jasmine wouldn't be so lucky.

The women laughed and shared stories, and Jasmine tried to follow them, but she didn't contribute. She knew very little of this culture, and none of her stories would make them laugh.

Finally, Leila emerged wearing a lacy A-line dress.

It was beautiful, and the women exclaimed over it, but by the distaste in Leila's eyes in the mirror, she didn't care for it.

"I'm not sure." Jasmine's voice never carried far, and she was surprised when the women turned to her. She shrugged, feeling her cheeks warm with the attention. "It is not what I imagined you would choose, Leila."

"Yes, you're right, sister. It is lovely, though." She shot Jasmine a grateful smile and returned through the door to try another.

She'd only been gone a moment when Jasmine's cell phone vibrated in her pocket, sending a jolt of excitement through her.

She'd always wanted a cell phone. Baba had strictly forbidden it, and Khalid had only laughed when she'd asked. *"Who are you going to call? Everybody you know lives here."*

As if Khalid had ever known anything about her. Jasmine had had school friends in Baghdad. But after Leila escaped, after Mama died, Baba had hemmed Jasmine in, practically imprisoning her. He'd deemed all of Jasmine's friends bad influences, forcing her to sneak around like a criminal to have a simple cup of tea with a neighbor.

She didn't miss Iraq, but she did miss Basma, her dearest friend. But Basma, like Iraq, was lost to her now. She'd reached out to her, but Basma hadn't returned her messages in years.

Not that Jasmine would complain. She had new friends in Maine. She had freedom here. She was happy here. She was allowed to be happy. *Encouraged* to be happy.

So different from life in Iraq.

In America, she'd seen women ignore notifications on their phones, rolling their eyes as if it were a chore to have people who loved them. For Jasmine, every ding, every vibration, every little red dot reminded her of her freedom.

But it would be rude to take out her phone. Even when it buzzed again, she ignored it.

"Do you have a similar tradition in Iraq?" Eliza asked. "Shopping for a wedding dress?"

"Perhaps some families did." Jasmine shrugged. "Since the war, things have been very difficult. Nothing is as it was before."

"Oh." Eliza's brows lowered. "I didn't realize... The war was over a long time ago, wasn't it?"

"For America, yes. But there was a civil war after that, and the economy was difficult, and—"

"Here she comes!" The cheerful clerk hurried through the doorway, and Jasmine wasn't sorry to be interrupted. The last thing she wanted to do was explain Iraqi politics. Everything had fallen apart—in her country and in her family. They all needed Jesus. Until her people found the One True God, they would remain lost. And angry. And filled with hate.

There was no room for such ugly thoughts in this beautiful place.

Oh. Speaking of beautiful...

Leila wore the gown Jasmine had liked for herself. Leila didn't tell the other women that, and when they told her how gorgeous it was, she thanked them but caught Jasmine's eye in the mirror.

Jasmine couldn't think of a word to say. It was everything Jasmine had always wanted and would never have. It was the moon. Unspeakably lovely.

And as far from reach.

"That is beautiful," Peggy exclaimed. "I can't imagine you any lovelier."

Leila broke their eye contact and turned to her future mother-in-law. "Thank you. It is, but it's not mine." Without further explanation, she returned to the dressing room, leaving confused murmuring behind her.

"I really liked that one," Sophie said. "I guess she didn't, though."

"It wasn't her style." Jasmine swallowed the emotions trying to give her away. "She will find the perfect dress."

A few minutes later, Leila emerged wearing a slim-fitting sequined gown that flared at the bottom. A mermaid-cut, a dress Leila never would have picked out.

"That's striking," Summer said. "There aren't very many women who can wear that style, but it works on you. And see how it makes you seem taller?"

Peggy added, "And shows off your slim figure."

Leila angled this way and that, checking her reflection. "I'm not sure." When she caught Jasmine's gaze, Jasmine saw what she really meant. She hated it.

"I'm not sure it is quite right for you." It wasn't like Jasmine to be the contrary one, but she would do this for Leila. "It is a little...like the lights are blinking?"

"Flashy?" By the tone of Summer's word, she disagreed.

"Yes, that is a good word to describe, I think." Jasmine nodded at the intimidating blonde, then turned back to her sister. "It doesn't reflect who you are." It did reflect everything else in the room, though. It was like wearing a disco ball.

Leila nodded, her lips tipping up at the corners. "You are right, sister. Thank you." She stepped off the platform and back through the door, the clerk following.

Jasmine dared a peek at Summer, afraid she might be angry, but Summer only smiled. "You know her better than we do. I'm glad you're here."

"Yes. I am as well." The words, such small words, could never convey the depth of feeling that lay behind them. Even in her native tongue, she didn't have the words to express her gratitude for being there with her sister. Safe. Protected.

"They're all going to look amazing on her," Peggy said. "You'll help her find the one that suits her."

As girls, Jasmine and Leila used to dream of their future weddings. They'd both wanted Cinderella gowns then—wide skirt, fitted bodice, puffy shoulders. Recently, as they'd perused magazines, Leila had shown a preference for more modern, elegant cuts.

Jasmine still dreamed of the fairy tale, probably because that was all it would ever be for her.

A fairy tale. A fantasy.

Her phone vibrated again.

Eliza must've heard it because she asked, "Somebody important?"

"Probably Derrick."

"Really?" Eliza infused meaning into the word, though *what* meaning, Jasmine didn't know. "What's going on with him?"

"We are good friends. I've never had a man friend. In Iraq, it's not allowed." She was working on using her contractions. "I'm glad it's allowed in America."

"That's all it is?" Sophie asked on the other side. Jasmine turned to find the curly-haired blonde's eyebrows high on her forehead. "Friendship?"

"What else would it be?"

Sophie shrugged. "You don't think there's any chance he's interested?"

"He finds me interesting, I think. I find him interesting." By the way Sophie's head tilted to the side, that wasn't what she meant. This conversation was confusing. "Interested in what?"

Her eyes widened. "Uh..."

Before she could explain, Jasmine's phone vibrated again.

"Maybe you'd better see who it is," Eliza said. "Could be important."

Not that anybody would need Jasmine in an emergency, but she wasn't going to argue. She pulled the phone from her dress pocket and checked the screen, expecting to see a text notification. But it wasn't a text.

It was an email.

Basma was the only person who had the address to the

account Jasmine had opened years before and kept hidden from her father and, after the wedding, her husband. It'd been a long time since her old friend had written. Jasmine had sent her a message after she'd arrived in Maine to let her know where she was.

Finally, Basma had written back.

"Excuse me." She pushed up from the sofa and walked toward the windows at the front of the shop, reading what her friend had written.

> *Dear Yasamin,*
>
> *I rejoiced to read that you have escaped Khalid and reunited with your beloved sister. I could not be happier for you both. I'm sorry it's taken me so long to respond. And I'm sorry to respond with this message now, but I have no choice.*
>
> *I need your help.*
>
> *My little brother and I have been happy with my aunt and uncle since Baba passed, but my half brother has decided to return to Baghdad and expects Rabie and me to move in with him.*

Jasmine gasped. She'd met Basma's half brother, Dari, only once before, and just the memory of him had her shuddering.

She had spent years in the company of terrorists and murderers, men who treated women like slaves and children like pets. Her husband had been the worst of them.

But one glance from Dari, and Jasmine had felt as if scorpions crawled along her skin and in her hair. He wore darkness like a cloak.

Despite the warmth of the bridal shop, the festive decorations, and the sparkling gowns, she crossed her arms to stave off a chill that slid down her spine and returned her focus to the email.

> *Obviously, I cannot let this happen.*
>
> *Though I tried to convince Uncle that Dari would not be a suitable guardian, he brushed off my worries. Even if he wanted to help me, he feels he has no right to do so, as Dari is a closer relative than he. Auntie tries to understand how I feel, but she doesn't know Dari well, and even if she did, she holds little sway over Uncle.*
>
> *Perhaps to placate me, Uncle has surprised us with a trip. We have just landed in Washington, DC, where he is expected for an event. We will only be here for a few days.*
>
> *Please, you must come and help us escape from Uncle's security. We can take a train to Mama's cousin. She will welcome us.*
>
> *I know it is much to ask after everything you've been through. I wouldn't if not for Rabie, but I fear Dari will corrupt my little brother as he is corrupt.*
>
> *As soon as I know where we're staying, I'll email again.*
>
> *You are our only hope.*
>
> *Please, help.*
>
> *Your friend always.*
>
> *Basma*

Jasmine reread the email twice before she slipped her phone into her pocket, her hands shaking.

Basma, the only friend she'd had in the world after Leila ran away, needed her help. How could she turn her back on her?

But what could she do?

"Jasmine?" Sophie's voice came from a few feet away. "Everything okay?"

"Yes. Yes, thank you."

"Your sister has another dress to show us."

Jasmine peered past Sophie to where Leila stood on the platform, watching her with concern in her gaze. She was too far away to ask the question forming on her lips.

She wore the dress Jasmine had been certain she would like. It was satin with a pleated, off-the-shoulder bodice, a low waist, and a skirt that was neither too fitted nor too bell-shaped, just gracefully flared. It was exquisite and sophisticated and perfect for Leila, though she seemed more concerned with what had distracted Jasmine than she did with the gown.

Moving closer, Jasmine said, "You are stunning, my sister."

Leila faced the mirrors, giving them a view of the back of the dress, which draped low, showing off her flawless cappuccino skin.

Jasmine bent and spread out the long train, then stepped back to admire the image she saw in the mirror. A splendid gown for Leila, who was about to marry into an amazing family and start a glorious life.

Tears filled Jasmine's eyes. Happy tears, of course. Why wouldn't she be happy for the sister she adored?

Leila and Michael were well matched. They would marry and live in the lovely house in Shadow Cove and have sweet children and grow old together.

At least this time, Jasmine wouldn't be left too far behind. She'd live nearby...somewhere. In an apartment, she supposed. Their children would be cousins. Jasmine would babysit for Leila's little ones. She could cook for their family, and perhaps clean. Maybe, if she was very useful and very quiet, she would be invited to family functions.

Perhaps she wouldn't be forgotten.

"Oh, my word." Peggy sounded almost reverent. "That is gorgeous."

Jasmine stepped away, shaking off her melancholy and meeting her sister's eyes in the mirror. "What do you think?"

Leila's shoulders lifted and fell. "It is pretty." The way her eyes sparkled, Leila knew it was more than just *pretty*, but she felt too shy to say so.

Summer also stood. All the women were standing now. "It's spectacular."

Everyone had forgotten that Jasmine had been distracted. Nobody asked why she'd walked away.

When they got back to the house, should she tell Leila about Basma's email? If she did, Leila would tell Michael. Maybe Michael would help.

But Michael worked for the US government, and Basma's uncle was an Iraqi diplomat who worked with the Americans. Did Michael know him? Would he feel obligated to tell him Basma's plan to escape? Maybe not.

But maybe so.

Jasmine couldn't take the chance.

Anyway, Leila and Michael were going to New York with Bryan and Sophie, and after that, Michael was leaving town again. Jasmine didn't know much about what he was doing, but it was related to the terrorists he was still tracking—including her husband. She very much wished for him to find Khalid before Khalid found her. And her wish for that only added to her ever-present guilt.

She was in a family of terrorists. Married to a terrorist—the father of her unborn baby.

Was she wrong to have run away from him?

Should she have stayed? Supported a terrorist? Allowed her son to be taught to hate, or if she carried a girl, allowed her daughter to become a slave? Allowed her child to be taught about Allah instead of the One True God?

To stay or to run. Both were right, and both were wrong.

No matter what she did, she was guilty.

And now, a new guilt pressed. Because Basma needed her, and she had to find a way to help.

~

The men were already back from snowmobiling by the time Jasmine and the rest of the bridal party returned to Sam's house in Shadow Cove that afternoon. The house was large, but with everybody congregating in the living room, not nearly large enough.

When they all talked at the same time, who was listening?

Maybe that was Jasmine's job. But how was she supposed to listen to sixteen people at once?

Fading into the shadow of the Christmas tree, she used her phone to find directions to Washington, DC. The American capital was on the east coast, and Maine was as well. How far could it be?

The directions loaded, and she gasped.

Nearly six hundred miles?

Even worse, the route would take her through the cities of Boston and New York. Jasmine had only had her driver's license for a month. Could she make the drive by herself? Or would she get hopelessly lost? Or wreck Michael's car?

She needed help.

She couldn't ask Leila for advice, though. Leila would tell Michael, and Michael would not let her go, not because he didn't care about her but because he wanted to keep her safe.

He could stop her simply by taking the keys to his car.

She owed everything to Michael and his family. She lived in Michael's house and used a phone he'd provided. She worked for a business Sam owned.

She was grateful, so grateful.

But with no car of her own, limited money, and few friends, she suddenly realized she was not as free as she'd thought.

If only she could trust her sister and her future brother-in-law to help her, but her protection was their priority. They wouldn't understand what Basma meant to her, and she wouldn't be able to convince them in time to help her friend.

"Hey, sweetheart." Peggy scooted up beside her. "You're awfully quiet. Are you all right?"

"Of course." She worked to hide her turmoil. "It's just"—she gestured to the chaos—"very much."

"You want to help me get dinner on the table?"

"Yes, please."

Laughing, the older woman linked their arms and led the way.

The kitchen smelled of spices and something sweet. Jasmine should be hungry, but a few minutes later as she grated a block of cheddar cheese, her stomach churned with worry.

Maybe she could take a train to Washington. Was there a train in Portland? Or Manchester? If not a train, then surely there was a bus. There had to be a way to get to DC. But how could she help Basma and Rabie escape if she didn't have a car? If they tried to get away on foot, Basma's uncle's security would surely catch them.

She could hire a taxi to pick up her friends, but would a taxi driver help them get away?

If only Jasmine had Leila's boldness. If Leila were in charge, she'd be halfway to Washington already. She'd have a plan, and it would all work out, as things always did for Leila.

"Are you sure you're all right?" Peggy added spices to a thick, meaty stew she'd called chili. "You seem distracted."

"I am fine."

The older woman set her spoon down and faced her, leaning her hip on the counter. She studied her with narrowed eyes, and Jasmine's face warmed. Rarely did anybody pay that much attention to her. Well, except for her sister and Derrick.

He'd become such a good friend.

He'd know what to do.

Why hadn't she thought of him immediately? Of course Derrick would help her.

Peggy's eyebrows lifted. "What are you thinking?"

"How happy I am to be here."

The older woman's brows lowered, her lips pressing closed. "Mmm-hmm. I'm sure that's true, but that's not what you were thinking."

Shame—a familiar emotion—rolled over Jasmine. "I am sorry. I do not mean... Please forgive me."

Peggy rested her hand on Jasmine's arm, the contact warm and comforting and making her miss her own mother in a way she hadn't in a long time. Peggy reminded her of Mama and all the things Mama had been and could have been. And hadn't been.

Like protective.

Like loving. Toward Jasmine, anyway.

So unlike this woman, who seemed to love completely and without reservation.

"You don't owe me an apology or an explanation, sweetheart," Peggy said. "I'm a friend. If you ever want to talk about anything, you can trust me." She flicked her gaze behind her, as though to include everyone who filled the house. "You can trust us all. We're your family now. You know that, right?"

Peggy meant the words kindly, but Jasmine stepped back, feeling her smile tighten.

Family meant bonds. For most people, bonds meant security and comfort and provision. For the people in this house—even Leila—bonds were good things.

But for people like Jasmine, bonds were shackles.

She'd been a slave to her father, then to her husband.

If Jasmine didn't intervene, her friend Basma would become a slave to her brother.

The last thing Jasmine wanted was to be part of another family. At least here in the States, she was autonomous.

Peggy's eyes narrowed. "What is it?"

"Nothing." She transferred the grated cheese to a bowl and rinsed the grater in the sink. "What else can I do?"

"We're pretty much done here. Why don't you go visit—?"

"I prefer to work."

Peggy watched her for a long moment. "If you're sure."

Jasmine was thankful to be given a task. As long as she offered to help—as long as it was her choice—then she wasn't a slave.

She would never be a slave again, and if she could help it, neither would Basma.

When the meal was ready, the patriarch, Roger, called the Wright family to the kitchen. They came in laughing, joking, and jostling. The sisters-in-law and girlfriends were as different as the brothers were alike. The men were all tall and handsome, though none as handsome as Derrick, the youngest. His shoulder-length hair was curlier and messier than normal after a day of snowmobiling. His cheeks were red from the sun, and his ready smile widened when he caught Jasmine's eyes.

She smiled back. Yes, Derrick would help her.

When Roger offered a prayer of thanks for the food, she added her own silent, *please God*. She would need help from the One True God if she was going to pull this off.

The family lined up to serve themselves from the buffet on

the peninsula. The kitchen was large but didn't feel that way with all the Wrights in it.

While the rest of them filled their plates—the decibel level was louder than ever—Jasmine returned the opened food containers to the refrigerator and stacked dirty pots and pans in the sink.

"You've done enough."

The words were low but still startled her. She spun, and Derrick took a dirty cutting board from her hands and set it aside. "Didn't mean to frighten you. You've been hiding in here long enough."

"I'm not hiding."

His eyebrows hiked, and though he didn't say anything, his expression held a challenge.

"Your family is very loud."

At that, he grinned. "Can't argue with you there." He set his hand on her lower back. "Come on. I already fixed your plate."

"You didn't have to do that."

"Figured you'd do it wrong." There was humor in his tone, but he must have been serious. Why else would he have gotten dinner for her? What man would ever get dinner for a woman?

It was odd enough that the men let the women serve themselves first—opposite of the way things were done in Iraq.

But to serve a woman?

Unheard of.

Derrick led her out of the kitchen, across the hallway, and toward the formal dining room.

Jasmine had eaten in there on her first visit to Sam's house, when she and Leila had just arrived in Maine. It held a round table large enough to accommodate the twelve chairs surrounding it. The last thing she wanted was another crowd.

She paused outside the door. "Would you mind very much if we find someplace private to eat? I need to talk to you."

"Oh." His eyes brightened as if he liked that idea. He walked down the hall and peeked into the living room, then glanced back with a smile. "Grab a seat. I'll get our food."

There were two wingback chairs near the fireplace, a small table between them. She settled into one of the chairs and watched the fire flickering nearby, lifting her hands to warm them.

She loved Maine. She loved the winter, even when it was so cold she worried her fingers and toes might fall right off. She loved the snow that covered everything in a layer of purity. And she loved the indoor fireplaces that people lit for no reason, as far as she could tell, except that they were cheerful. Sam's house had a furnace, like the house where Jasmine and Leila lived. So the flames were just for fun. For kindness and coziness and comfort.

Derrick set a tray on the table between them. "Eliza grabbed the tray so I wouldn't have to make two trips."

"I should have helped. I'm sorry."

"You're fine." He sat on the other chair and picked up a bowl. "Have you ever had chili before?"

"No." She took her dish, which he'd filled with the meat stew, orange chips—Fritos, she remembered from the package—grated cheese, sour cream, and green onions.

Derrick was mixing his concoction, so she followed his lead and tasted it on her tongue. It was spicy and creamy and crunchy and salty.

He watched. "Well?"

She chewed and swallowed, considering. "It is...different."

"Different?" Did he seem disappointed? "That's it?"

"I like it." It wasn't the most delicious thing she'd eaten in Maine, but it was food, and she would be thankful.

He shook his head, though his smile said he wasn't really unhappy with her.

She forced another bite, but she was too nervous to eat.

"Did you want to talk about something specific? Or did you just miss me?" He wiggled his eyebrows up and down, and she couldn't help the laugh that escaped.

"You are a very silly man."

"Hmm." Some of his amusement seemed to fade. "Silly. That's me. What's up?"

"I need your advice." She swallowed and added, "Really, I hope for your help."

"Sure, anything." He set his bowl on the table. "What's going on?"

She did the same, then clasped her hands in her lap. What if she told him about Basma's problem and he refused to help? What if he laughed at her? What if he told Michael, and Michael demanded she stay out of it?

Though these men hadn't exercised any control over her yet, they could. They had all the power.

As usual, Jasmine was powerless.

If she kept her mouth shut, she could simply take the car and go.

But...but she didn't even like to drive on the highway to Portland. How could she make it through Boston and New York City? And even if she only took the car to the bus station or the train station, it didn't belong to her. And this family had been nothing but kind. She owed them her trust.

The most terrifying gift to give.

Derrick's lingering amusement faded, his lips tightening at the corners. "What is it, Jasmine? What's wrong?"

She had to tell him. And he had to help her. If he didn't...if he didn't, then she'd find another way. She had to.

She took a breath and decided to trust. For now. "This is between you and me, okay? You must not tell anyone."

"Sure. No problem."

"I have a friend from Baghdad, a very close friend. She and her little brother are in trouble. They're going to be in Washington, DC, for a couple of days, and they need my help getting away from their guardian."

Derrick's mouth opened. Closed.

Jasmine sipped her water—he'd added a squeeze of lemon juice, just like she liked it. How thoughtful.

She set the glass on the table and waited for the questions forming in his eyes.

"Who is this person?"

"An old friend."

"Does Leila know her?"

Why did that matter? "Basma and I didn't meet until after Leila left Iraq."

"Your friend—Basma?" She nodded, and he continued. "She's trying to take her brother away from his parents?"

"No. Their mother died of cancer, like mine. It's why we became friends—we had that in common. Her father was much older and died a few years ago. He was a kind and gentle man who adored Basma and Rabie. He arranged for them to live with his brother and sister-in-law, where they have lived ever since. But Basma has a half brother—the son of their father—who has decided he will take them to live with him from now on."

Derrick was nodding slowly. "And that's a problem because...?"

"He is evil."

Derrick sat back, eyebrows hiking. "Evil?"

"Yes."

"Based on...?"

It took Jasmine a moment to figure out that Derrick was asking for proof of her claim. And she almost supplied it. She'd heard enough stories from Basma, after all. But...

"Do you not believe me?"

"I didn't say that. I'm just... How old is this friend of yours?"

"About my age. Basma's mother got cancer when she was pregnant and died a few weeks after Rabie was born. Basma convinced her father to let her remain unmarried so she could devote her life to raising Rabie. She loves him. And he loves her. Basma is the only mother Rabie has ever known—and the only parent he has left."

"That's very noble, but I'm confused. You said she lives with a guardian, so I assumed she's a child. If she's an adult, why does she need to escape? Can't she just walk away?"

Derrick hadn't seemed slow-witted, but his question showed he wasn't as smart as she'd thought, considering he'd flown the plane that had aided in Jasmine and Leila's escape from her family.

A moment passed, and then Derrick said, "But, I mean... You *couldn't* walk away. You were trapped. Imprisoned. Are you saying this woman is in the same situation?"

"There is security that will prevent her from leaving."

"I see." Derrick scrubbed his hand across his jaw. "How old is her little brother?"

"Nine or ten years?"

"She doesn't have custody?"

"He is with her. Is this what you mean? To have custody is to own, yes?"

"She's the boy's legal guardian, right?"

"Of course not."

"Oh." His eyes scrunched in confusion. "So...her uncle is?"

"Now, they live with her uncle, and he makes decisions for them."

"But the half brother will become the boy's guardian soon?"

"Yes, and he's evil. You will not help an innocent child escape an evil man?"

"I didn't say that." Derrick straightened, scowling. "It's

just... I assume you're getting your information about this half brother from your friend. But would a judge agree?"

"What judge? There is no judge."

"I mean, if your friend were to sue for custody—"

Jasmine's burst of laughter—there was no humor in the sound—cut his words short. "You do not understand anything."

"Explain it, then."

"Her half brother is a *man*. My friend is a *woman*."

Derrick didn't react. He seemed to be waiting for her to continue, as if she hadn't already said it all.

"He doesn't have to *ask* for custody," Jasmine said. "He is a man. He can do anything he wants. He has all the rights, all the power. She has no say. The child has no say. There is no judge who will question him."

"Oh, but her father—"

"Is gone." Jasmine spoke more slowly. Maybe she was speaking too fast, though normally Derrick had no trouble with her accent. "Dari is her brother, so he has authority over her and Rabie."

"Over *her*?" Derrick sounded genuinely surprised. "A grown woman?"

"Of course."

"But she's an adult."

Jasmine threw her hands up. "She is a woman. She has no power. She only has choices if a man lets her." The problem wasn't Jasmine's accent at all. How could Derrick not see?

"Okay. Okay." He lowered his gaze and rubbed his forehead. "Sorry. It's a cultural thing, of course. It's hard for me to comprehend. It's...bizarre." He met Jasmine's eyes. "I'm not trying to be thickheaded. I just come by it naturally."

"I see that."

His lips quirked, but the smile never materialized. "Truly, Jasmine. This is very foreign to me. Can you understand that?"

She took a breath. "I think, yes."

"And what is it you're asking me to do?"

"Go with me to help her and her brother escape."

He shook his head. "Way too dangerous. What if somebody sees you? What if—?"

"She is my friend. I should let her suffer because I am afraid?"

He started to say something, stopped himself. "She's not your responsibility."

"She is, of course. She is…she is like a sister. You would do this for your brother, yes?"

"Obviously, but she's *not* your sister. And how do you know she's telling you the truth? What do you know about this brother of hers?"

"My friend would not lie. And I have met Dari. I know him." She stood and paced across the living room, asking God to help her explain. The fire flickered, the Christmas tree lights twinkled, such a contrast to her dark thoughts.

She peered out the windows at the bottom of the hillside. It was winter, but a few boats bobbed on the water, lit by colorful holiday lights that matched those in the small, secluded town of Shadow Cove.

In this place, everything was bright and cheerful and happy. How could Derrick possibly understand a man like Dari?

Her focus shifted, and she caught sight of Derrick in the reflection, watching her. She turned to face him. "Have you ever met somebody who exuded the Spirit of God? Somebody who loved the Lord so much that you could feel Him on them?"

"I'm a good judge of character, if that's what you mean. Why, do you get feelings like that about people?"

"Yes." She moved to stand with her back to the fire, enjoying the warmth after the chill that seeped through the windows. "Usually within a few minutes, I can tell if somebody is being honest or duplicitous. It is the reason that, when your brother showed up to rescue us from Iraq, I trusted him immediately. It is the reason I do not fear you and your family." At least, she usually didn't fear them, when she was thinking straight. "You are all very...clean."

His eyebrows hiked. "Uh...clean?"

"I do not know how to explain." She flipped her hands toward the family in the other room. "It is a feeling. It is just that there is a clarity, nothing muddled or twisted or ugly, you see? This house, and your brother's house, they feel clean. Like that."

"Okaaay."

"What is a place you love, a place you feel close to God? A church?"

"Oh. I see what you're saying." Derrick seemed to consider that. When he met her gaze again, he said, "In the cockpit, in the air with the clouds below me, nothing but sky all around. I realize how small I am, how big God is. Is that what you mean?"

"Yes, okay. It is a clean feeling, yes? Clear and fresh."

"I wouldn't have described it that way, but I guess."

"Now, think of a place where you were in the presence of sin."

"So like...a singles bar? Where people are drinking and hitting on women?"

The thought of him in a place like that turned inside of her, darkening her feelings for him like a swath of black across a rainbow. She returned to her chair, hoping her voice didn't reveal her surprise. "This is a place you go often?"

"What? No." His eyes widened. "Never. I mean, not never, obviously. When I was in college, you know, a couple of times—"

"Oh, I see." She couldn't help her smile. "I didn't think... Of course you would not."

"Right. Well…" He pushed his unruly hair back from his face. "A singles bar. A place like that definitely feels unclean."

"My friend's half brother carries that feeling of uncleanliness. Darkness walks with him, and fear. Basma has told me stories of things he did to her when she was small."

"Like what?"

"When she was little and he came to visit, he would go into her room at night and watch her. She would pretend to be asleep because she was afraid of him. But he would know she was awake. And he would whisper how she was worthless, that her father would be lucky to sell her to a goat farmer."

"Her brother said that?" Derrick's face twisted in disgust. "Why? Who would tell a child something like that?"

Jasmine shrugged. "Does cruelty need a reason? Even if I hadn't heard stories, I would have known. I met him once, and his evil is like the stench of manure. It is unmistakable."

Derrick stared at the fire for a few long moments before he faced her again. "Maybe this is going to sound callous, but what does it have to do with you?"

"She is my friend. She was, for a time, my only friend."

"Okay, but…is that really a reason to risk your safety? Can't she find another way?"

Her heart rate spiked.

He didn't understand anything.

And how could he, when he was surrounded by people who loved him? Even now, voices and laughter floated from the other room, all these happy, supportive people. Derrick had never known what it meant to be alone and isolated. To be abandoned and forgotten.

She pushed to her feet and backed away.

"Hey," he said, "don't do that. I'm just asking a question."

But the heat from the flames, so comforting before, felt

stifling now. "She will be imprisoned. Possibly harmed. And little Rabie will be raised to be like him."

"Why doesn't she just go to the authorities, or—?"

"What authorities?"

"I don't know. I'm not saying no, but..."

He didn't finish the statement, and he didn't have to. "You do not believe me. Or you do not trust me."

"I don't even know what you're asking me to do."

"To help my friend the way you helped me. She has a cousin in the States."

"Let's talk to Michael. I'm sure he'll—"

"No. You must not."

Derrick's eyes flashed with worry.

"I will find another way." She turned and walked out, not that she had anywhere to go. But she had to do something. Now that she was free, how could she do nothing while her friend was taken into captivity by a man like Dari?

She couldn't.

And if Derrick wouldn't help her—

She'd figure out a way to help Basma on her own.

CHAPTER FOUR

Derrick watched as Jasmine stormed toward the front door, then froze. Wise woman, considering the temperature outside. It was December in Maine—not exactly evening-stroll weather.

She swiveled and headed down the hall, away from the family and toward Sam's office and the private living area.

Derrick wandered to the foyer and stood beside the staircase, where he could intercept her if she headed for the door again, thankful for the time to figure out what to do.

He wanted to help her, of course. He'd do anything for her. But Michael had risked his life getting her out of Iraq, and the people she'd escaped were still searching for her and Leila. They were safe here in Shadow Cove. Was helping her friend really worth risking that safety?

He should talk to Michael, but Jasmine had asked him to keep what they talked about to himself. He could go against her wishes, but that would cause conflict, and if he'd learned nothing else growing up as the youngest of six hotheaded brothers, he'd learned that conflict harmed relationships, sometimes nearly irreparably.

Bryan and Grant had taught him that.

Heck, Derrick and Grant had barely had a relationship for the majority of Derrick's life—and that had been the result of someone *else's* conflict. He hoped their conversation today would help them move past that. Maybe it would.

Maybe not.

Derrick had risked a conflict that morning and lost a client.

Conflicts were like dirty bombs. They destroyed enemies and bystanders alike.

Derrick was doing everything in his power to move out of the friend zone with Jasmine—and he did not intend to move into the *don't talk to me, I can't stand you* zone.

He hated that she'd put him in this position, but she had. And the only way out of it was through conflict. Or to do what she'd asked.

Jasmine rounded the corner at the end of the hall but stopped short when she saw him. She'd slipped on her coat—a puffy thing that was probably meant to be mid-calf length but skimmed the top of her shoes. She had her purse slung over one shoulder and a set of keys dangling from the opposite hand.

He walked toward her. "You're leaving?"

She continued toward him. "It is none of your business."

"Are you going home?"

She lifted her chin and firmed her lips, and his heart thumped.

He had a bad feeling about her lack of answer. "Where are you going?"

"I am going to get my friend. I have no choice."

"To Washington, DC?" When she said nothing, he clarified with "Right now. In the dark? You're taking the car and driving ten hours? By yourself?"

"I must help—"

"What did Leila say?"

Jasmine's eye contact slipped.

"You didn't tell her? You didn't even..." He worked to gentle his voice. "Jasmine, what are you doing?"

"She would stop me."

"Of course, because this... She *should* stop you. And... Wait a minute. You don't even have a car. Whose keys are those?"

"Michael provided us this car."

"Did you ask him?"

"He told us to use it for whatever we needed, and I need to do this."

"I think he meant for you to use it around here." He tamped down his frustration. "Like to run to the grocery store. Don't *you?*"

"He didn't say that. He put no limitations on it."

They were implied, and Jasmine knew it.

This conversation was almost as ridiculous as the one they'd had earlier. But this wasn't a cultural issue. This was Jasmine sneaking around to get her way. And, sure, not for personal gain but for her friend. Even so...

It was so contrary to everything Derrick knew about her.

Which wasn't enough. Michael had warned Derrick that once he got to know her maybe he wouldn't like her so much. He'd thought the idea impossible, but...

But Michael knew things about Jasmine that Derrick didn't.

"You can't leave without telling them."

Her eyes, those big, beautiful eyes, widened and filled with fear. She moved down the hallway toward him, then stopped abruptly just a few feet away, as if she'd thought better of getting too close. As if she was afraid *of him*. "You must not tell them." Her voice held pleading. "They will stop me. Please, Derrick."

What was he supposed to say to that? If he let her go, Michael and Leila would be furious with him. But if he told them, Jasmine might never forgive him.

He couldn't live with that.

He took a breath. "You're not driving to DC by yourself tonight. It wouldn't be safe for you. And I'm not going to let you steal my brother's car—"

"It would not be stealing. He said—"

"Not telling him would be taking advantage of his kindness, and you know it."

The fierce look she tried to send his way faded. She dropped her gaze and crossed her arms.

"They would come after you. They would worry about you. It would cause all sorts of trouble, and if they found out I knew, it would cause *me* trouble."

"I have to help my friend."

"I understand." He stepped toward her, but she moved back, eyes popping wide.

He stopped. Took a breath. The last thing he wanted was to frighten her. When he'd first met her, she'd been as skittish as a rabbit. In the two months since then, she'd come to trust him, to be comfortable with him. To talk to him and laugh with him.

He wasn't going to let one conversation ruin everything they'd built.

"Helping your friend is not as simple as you're making it sound." He worked to keep his tone reasonable and kind. "But I can see that it's very important to you. Just let me think. Okay?"

At her slight nod, he considered his options.

They were few. Letting Jasmine leave by herself at night wasn't an option. Jasmine could barely drive across town—in the daylight. She would be a competent driver eventually, but she didn't have enough experience yet to make it to DC, with all the traffic between here and there, without incident.

And it sounded like getting Basma and the kid away from the aunt and uncle—had she said something about security?—

was going to take some doing. Did she really think she could do that by herself?

Obviously not. She'd asked Derrick for help.

Would Michael help if Derrick told him what was going on? Maybe. Best case scenario, he'd take care of the two Iraqis himself.

Worst case scenario? He'd refuse and prevent Jasmine from helping as well. If that happened, would Jasmine ever forgive Derrick?

Probably not.

Which left door number three, the one he'd been hurtling toward since Jasmine had first asked for his help. As if there'd ever been a question.

"My charter for this week was canceled," he said. "I'll take you."

Her eyes lit up. "You will drive me?"

"Drive?" Her joy sparked his own. "Why would we drive when I have a perfectly good jet all fueled up and ready? I'll pick you up first thing in the morning."

"If we leave tomorrow, we will get there in time? They are only here for a few days."

"Trust me. But you need to tell your sister where you're going. Maybe we can make it back in one day, but if not, we don't want her to worry."

She peered past Derrick toward the crowd still enjoying dinner in the dining room and kitchen. Then she stepped close. "They are leaving for New York at four o'clock in the morning."

Right. He'd forgotten Michael, Leila, Bryan, and Sophie were going to the city for a couple of days. Bryan had an event at some museum there, and the rest were tagging along for fun.

Derrick and Jasmine had been invited, but Derrick had had the charter scheduled.

"Why aren't you going with them?"

"I do not wish to spend the weekend with the couples and all their lovey...kissing, you know? I had already told Leila I would stay home."

"So you're thinking we leave after they do and get back before them," Derrick said, "so they don't know what we're up to?" He didn't like the idea of sneaking around.

"It is only that I think they will worry."

He let his raised eyebrows show his skepticism, and she sighed.

"It is that...I believe they would stop me. Michael and Leila are worried about my safety, and for this I am grateful. But neither of them can understand how important Basma is to me. She was my only friend for many years. I am free now. How can I not help her to also be free? It is what Leila did in Munich, is it not? To tell others about Jesus, to help them find freedom? I know that it is a risk, but some risks are worth taking. Some people are worth risking for. My sister and Michael, they might understand my desire, but they will not agree that it's worth the risk. I fear that, even if I am able to convince them, it will be too late to help my friend."

Derrick wasn't sure Jasmine had ever strung so many words together at one time.

Obviously, she felt passionate about this. And she'd asked Derrick for his help.

How could he refuse her? He'd have to figure out how to get Basma and her little brother away from the people watching her and deliver them to their cousin without risking Jasmine's security.

How would he do it? No idea.

He'd just take it step by step.

～

They soared above the clouds in Derrick's Cessna Citation, the sunrise pink and orange in the east, the sky dark and starry in the west. Trouble far below, God so close, and the woman he loved at his side...

For Derrick, this moment was perfect.

Or would have been, if she were truly his, beside him because she chose him, not because she needed his help.

Someday, though, this would be their life. Someday, when the charters were short and didn't require a copilot, she could sit beside him in the cockpit. Instead of sitting in hotel rooms by himself, waiting for clients, he could show Jasmine sights all over the country. Take her to dinner. Take her to shows.

They could go to the beach. Go skiing. Go dancing. Go... wherever they wanted.

This could be their life. Someday. Soon.

As always, this morning she wore a shapeless dress, this one denim with a wide neckline that gave him a glimpse of her defined collarbones. Flowers were embroidered at the bottom of the flared sleeves and the flowing skirt.

She dressed so differently from other women—modest, for sure. But also, it seemed as if she were trying to hide herself, her figure. Which made sense, considering the culture she'd come from. And her captivity. And the fact that she was, in fact, hiding from her family.

Even in the not-so-attractive clothes, she was lovely. Especially when she added makeup like she had today, which accentuated her nearly black eyes. The way the eyeliner tipped up at the corners brought to mind the only other Jasmine he knew of —the princess in that Disney movie.

His Jasmine was far more beautiful than the animated one, especially when she had that wonder in her eyes as she asked question after question about every button and lever, every light and display.

Each answer he gave led her to ask a follow-up question—not that he minded. He loved flying, and he loved her. This was the dream.

"You're going to be able to fly this thing by the time we land."

She laughed, the sound lighthearted. Apparently, she'd forgiven him for not jumping right on board the *let's go to DC* train. So that was something.

He still wasn't sure they were doing the right thing, but he'd spent some time on his knees the night before, praying for guidance, and all he'd felt was a compulsion to help Jasmine come to her friend's aid. Derrick wouldn't claim he felt peace about this course of action, but he didn't feel peace about *not* doing it, either. He definitely hadn't felt the Lord telling him to stop.

That must mean he should go on. Or maybe it meant he'd do anything for Jasmine, even if the thing was stupid and reckless.

Less than two hours after takeoff, they landed at Dulles, and he taxied toward the private terminal. He nodded to the cell phone she held on her lap. "Did your friend give you any more details?"

She'd found out the name of the hotel where Basma and her brother were staying—a Marriott near Embassy Row. He knew the area well, having been to DC many times. He'd suggested Basma and her brother sneak out in the middle of the night. Jasmine had emailed them before they'd taken off.

Now, she opened her phone while he followed the ground crew past private jets of every size and flavor imaginable.

"Basma and Rabie are going to a lunch today." Jasmine scrolled her email. "And then to a fancy dinner. She says guards watch the doors of their suite all night, so they will not be able to sneak away after dark. The best time, she thinks, will be in the afternoon. Her aunt will nap, her uncle will be in meetings, and she and Rabie can go to the lobby for a snack. She believes they can slip away then."

"The guards will let them go alone?"

"Maybe she thinks she can lose them?" By the way the words ticked up, Jasmine wasn't sure. "I don't believe her aunt and uncle suspect her of planning to run. I believe the guards go with them for their protection more than anything."

"Protection from what?"

Jasmine's shoulders lifted and fell. "Perhaps there are enemies here? I do not know."

"Hmm." Derrick doubted there would be an attack on the niece and nephew of an Iraqi diplomat at a hotel in DC. Maybe the aunt and uncle were paranoid. More likely, they *did* suspect that Basma planned to run.

He didn't like this. Not at all.

He was directed to a spot between an old Embraer Legacy— he'd only seen photos of that particular jet—and a Gulfstream. He powered down his Cessna. "You need help with your seatbelt?"

"I got it."

"This'll take me a minute, if you want to freshen up."

"All right." She climbed from the right seat and headed toward the cabin.

When he finished his routine, he lowered the door with the built-in airstairs, letting in a chill and the stench of exhaust and diesel fuel. Intellectually, he knew the scents were off-putting, but to him they smelled like everything he'd ever wanted.

Jasmine joined him, and he thought, *almost everything.*

Beside him, she took in the acres and acres of jets as if she gazed at the mighty Rocky Mountains. She aimed those wide eyes at him. "It is amazing, is it not? To step on in Maine and step off in a whole different place?"

He used to feel that joy at flying. Still did, sometimes. But right now, the beauty beside him overshadowed everything else. "Amazing." When the urge to pull her close nearly overwhelmed him, he cleared his throat and inhaled the chemical-tinged air.

Man, when she looked at him like that, those giant, gorgeous eyes filled with trust and wonder, it was all he could do to keep his hands to himself.

Take it slow, Wright.

Or you're gonna blow it.

He scooted past her in the small space and grabbed their bags from where he'd left them on a couple of passenger seats. They'd each packed enough for a few days, just in case, but if Basma thought they could escape this afternoon, it was possible they'd be able to fly her and her brother to wherever they needed to go and return to Maine by midnight. Not that he'd mind extending his time with Jasmine, but the sooner this task was over and she was back where she was safe, the better.

With their bags slung over his shoulder, he nodded to the stairs. "Ladies first."

It took an hour to fill out the airport's paperwork and rent a car. Finally, they were headed east for the forty-minute drive into DC beneath an overcast sky. In the passenger seat of the silver midsize sedan—he'd chosen a car that wouldn't stand out —Jasmine watched the landscape pass. "It is not very different from Maine with all the trees."

"It's warmer in Virginia, though." The high was predicted to be in the midtwenties in Portland, while it was already forty-one here and headed to the fifties.

"Less extreme," she said.

"More like the mild weather you were used to in Iraq."

She giggled. "Mild. Exactly. But...wait." Her tone shifted. "We are in Virginia?"

"Yeah. Washington, DC, borders Virginia and Maryland."

"What state is it in?"

"Neither. It's the only city in the US that isn't in a state."
He glanced at her and grinned. "Weird facts about America."

"Your country is very interesting."

Not as interesting as Iraq, considering it had been populated
since the dawn of time, literally. After all, the Garden of Eden
had been in Iraq, hadn't it? Where the Tigris and the Euphrates
met?

"Did Basma tell you what time she thought they'd get
away?"

Jasmine unlocked her phone. "She thinks the lunch will last
until two o'clock. She said perhaps three or after."

It was just past eleven, so they had some time to kill. "Hungry?" He'd brought them both cups of coffee—decaf for Jasmine,
which she preferred—and pastries from a bakery in Shadow
Cove. They'd finished the snacks hours before. "There's a diner
not far from here. It's got everything from salads to burgers—and
they serve breakfast all day, if you like that."

"How do you know this place?"

"I fly in and out of Dulles a lot. I've got clients who come to
DC a couple times a year. Also, my uncle—Dad's brother—
worked with the government in some capacity—though I think
he's employed by a defense contractor. I've brought him down
more than once."

"What did your uncle do?"

"I don't know. He never talked about his work."

"He made enough money to fly in a private jet, though."

"True." If money were the most important thing in life, and
if life were a contest, then that branch of the Wright family
would be winning. But money could only buy so much.

"Your family is very successful," Jasmine said, "and
connected, no? With people in powerful positions?"

"Michael is, I guess, and probably Uncle Gavin."

"And Sam, with his business connections. And you with yours."

"I'm a high-priced chauffeur. I might know a few powerful people, but we're not exactly on equal footing." When Jasmine said nothing, he glanced her way.

She seemed pensive, almost nervous.

"What is it?"

"Nothing."

He didn't ask again, just waited. Because it was definitely something, but if he pushed her, she'd clam up. He'd learned that the hard way.

Sure enough, after a moment, she said, "It's only...in Iraq, it was good to be connected—until the people you were connected to became the wrong people. My father worked for the government under Hussein. He secured a job after the dictator fell, but he was never able to move up in the government. And then, when the Americans left, Baba lost his job. He couldn't gain footing again. It is the reason we left Baghdad and ended up at the compound. It is the reason everything fell apart."

Derrick reached across the console and took Jasmine's hand, something he rarely allowed himself to do—though she didn't seem to mind. "This isn't Iraq. Leadership changes here frequently—the presidency every four or eight years. The Senate and House change a little every couple of years. State and local governments are changing all the time. The shifts are pretty minimal compared to what you've witnessed. You don't have to worry about anybody's connections—or lack of connections. You're safe here. You're safe with us." *With me.* He squeezed her hand and let it go.

He felt her eyes on him and caught a glimpse of admiration and something else he was afraid to name.

Was it more than friendship? Was she starting to feel a fraction of the tenderness toward him that he felt toward her?

Did he dare hope?

"The diner sounds good." Her voice was tentative. "I am hungry, but I do not have money. I already owe you so much."

"You owe me nothing. This is what friends do." And fine. He'd never flown any of his buddies hundreds of miles for free— and then bought them lunch. Or committed to helping them aid foreign nationals in escaping their guards.

He liked his buddies well enough. But he wasn't in love with any of them. For Jasmine, he'd do just about anything.

CHAPTER FIVE

The French toast was delicious—thick, eggy cinnamon-spiced bread covered with butter and warm maple syrup. But try as Jasmine might, she couldn't finish it. She was too full to eat, or perhaps just too nervous.

It hadn't been that long since she'd escaped her husband. Helping Basma and Rabie shouldn't be anything like that. They weren't in Iraq, after all. They didn't have to hide in crates and cross borders. All they had to do was get Basma and Rabie into their car and then get lost in the traffic on their way back to the airport. It should be easy. But no matter how much she tried to convince herself, the fear wouldn't leave her alone.

The restaurant Derrick had chosen was large enough to seat a hundred or more at the booths and rectangular tables, most of which had people seated around them. More congregated near the doorway, waiting. There were men in business suits or sweaters, women in designer jeans or slacks, blazers or blouses. Some carried laptop bags. Others bounced babies.

The building was old, with its concrete floors and high ceilings that showed heating ducts overhead. The table she and Derrick shared was scuffed in places, the booth well-worn. Not dirty or dingy, just comfortably broken in. The atmosphere was clean and fresh and happy and...free.

"What are you thinking?" Derrick asked.

"I like your diner."

"Food's good, right?"

"Yes, very. Though I don't think I can finish it. I'm sorry for ordering so much."

His lips twisted into a smirk. "Why are you apologizing? I suggested the French toast, remember?" He nodded toward her plate. "You sure?"

She pushed it toward him, and he traded his empty platter—he'd ordered a bacon burger and fries—and dug in.

"Worked out for me."

"Where do you put all the food?"

Food halfway to his mouth, he said, "There's always room for more."

She turned her attention to a group at a nearby table. There were four women, a little redheaded girl of about three, and a baby boy in a high chair. The girl was moving from lap to lap while the women carried on a conversation, not at all bothered by the child's restlessness. The baby concentrated on what he was eating.

A lemon slice, Jasmine realized. He'd swallowed almost the whole thing when he shuddered as if he'd just discovered how sour it was.

The women at the table laughed, and Jasmine found herself chuckling as well.

"What's funny?" Derrick asked.

She explained, and he twisted to see.

When the little girl caught his eye, Derrick waved, and she giggled and hid behind one of the women.

He turned back to Jasmine. "Cuties."

She tried to imagine herself as one of those women. Sitting

in a restaurant, enjoying a meal. Not looking over her shoulder. Not afraid.

The picture wouldn't come. No matter how far she ran, Khalid would never stop searching for her.

She would never be safe.

"What do you think?" Derrick asked. "Will Michael and Leila have kids right away?"

Jasmine tried to shake off the creeping fear. "Leila never spoke much of children when we were little. Now, I think she would discuss such things with Michael, not me. But I would guess they want children, and she is almost thirty, so perhaps it is wise not to wait."

"Women can have kids into their thirties, though, right?" By the way Derrick's brows lowered, he seemed worried.

"Yes." This was not something she wished to discuss.

"Do you want them?" He aimed his fork at the other table. "Kids?" As if she didn't know what he meant.

She nodded, sliding out of the booth. "I will find the restroom, if that's okay."

"You don't have to ask for permission." He smiled, perhaps to soften the words he'd spoken to her many times.

"Right. Sorry." She hurried away, breathing deeply to calm the sudden nausea.

She should tell him the truth. She should tell him everything. But...but how did one go about explaining her situation? What would Derrick say when he learned she was not only married but carrying a child? What would he think of a wife who'd run away from her husband? What would he think when he learned of the danger she'd put him and his family in? Because they sheltered her, and Khalid would pursue her as long as he had breath in his lungs.

How could she tell Derrick that she would never be safe?

How could he comprehend all she'd gone through, all she'd done to survive?

Leila was about to get married and start a life with Michael. Yes, the Wright family counted Jasmine as one of their own, but only out of obligation. And family obligations went both ways. When Leila was married, what would being obligated to the Wrights cost Jasmine? What would they expect of her? Demand of her?

Only Derrick had *chosen* her, not out of obligation but because he liked her. When she told him the truth, would he still choose to be friends with her? Or would he judge her?

Would he hate her?

He was such a kind, gentle man, but even kindness had limits. Would Derrick reject her? The question sent fear to her middle and moisture to her eyes.

How would he react? She wasn't ready to find out. Soon enough, her pregnancy would show, and there would be no more hiding the truth.

Until then, she would keep it to herself. Until then, she would enjoy their protection. She would enjoy Derrick's friendship. Yes, the longer she put off telling him, the worse it would be. But she couldn't bear to lose them—to lose him—before she had to.

She used the bathroom, washed her hands, and checked her reflection. She looked better than she had in Iraq. Now that she was in the US, now that the terrible sickness from her early pregnancy had passed, she felt healthier and stronger. Her dark skin had lost its yellow pallor. Her eyes were bright again, her long, straight hair silky and shiny.

She was herself again, like the Jasmine she'd been before Khalid.

But she shouldn't, if she wanted to remain hidden. She should cut her hair. She couldn't bring herself to do it, but she should try to disguise herself. She dug a hijab from her purse and wrapped it over her head, careful to tuck her hair in. Though she hated wearing the Muslim headscarf, at least it hid her long hair. Maybe she wouldn't be as recognizable.

Not that she planned to run into anybody she knew. But it was possible Basma's uncle knew Jasmine's father. If he saw her and told Baba, then Baba would tell Khalid. And Khalid would know where to search for her.

Derrick had finished the French toast and was handing their waitress money when she slid into the booth across from him. He thanked the server, then looked at Jasmine—and frowned. "Why are you wearing that?"

"I do not want to be recognized. I wish to be...blending in."

His eyebrows hiked. "Do you see any other woman here wearing a head scarf?"

She scanned the room. "But I thought, in the city—"

"Wearing that will make you stand out."

"But Michael says my hair is distinctive. And my height. I fear I will be recognized."

Derrick straightened, his brows lowering over his dark eyes. "Who are you afraid of? Is there a chance your father will be there?"

"No, but Basma's uncle probably knows him. They would have worked together for a time."

Derrick's expression turned to a scowl. "You didn't tell me that. Why didn't you...?" He blew out a breath. "Jasmine. What are we doing? This is too risky."

"I must help her. She is my friend."

"Yeah, but..." He pressed his lips together, then slid out of the booth and shrugged into his brown leather jacket—a bomber jacket, he called it. It was distinctively Derrick. "Come on."

She followed him to the exit and out into the gray day.

Halfway across the parking lot, he said, "We have a couple

of hours before your friends'll be ready. There's a mall nearby. Let's get you a better disguise." He glared at her head scarf. "Please take that off."

"You do not like it?"

He stopped and faced her. "You're beautiful no matter what you wear."

Oh. The compliment warmed her despite the winter air.

"But you don't have to wear that. You don't have to hide or be ashamed or...cover your head like some sort of...of inferior creature. And maybe that's not what it represents. I'm sure I just don't understand, but..." He pushed back his hair. Unlike his brothers, he kept it on the long side, almost reaching to his shoulders. She liked it. It was soft and touchable, a little curly, a little messy. It was lighthearted and easygoing, like he was. Though the intense expression he wore now was anything but. "Do what you want. I'm not your boss." He continued to the car and opened the passenger door.

She slid in, and while he walked around to the driver's side, she pulled her head scarf off and shoved it back in her purse. She was checking her hair in the visor mirror when he sat beside her.

He started the car engine, then sighed. "I don't mean to be a jerk. You can wear the scarf if you want."

"I thought it would be good to hide my hair."

His lips tipped up in the tiniest grin. "We'll find a better option."

Jasmine studied her reflection in the department store mirror. She and Derrick had considered a few disguises. This one had been his idea. Aside from her still distinctive long hair, she did look different.

She'd never worn a sweatsuit in her life, certainly not one like this. If she were a normal height, the hoodie—it had the word *Georgetown* imprinted across the chest—would barely reach her belly button. Fortunately, Jasmine was petite enough that even the extra-small reached the waistband of the matching navy sweatpants.

Derrick believed that she could pass for a college-aged woman. Maybe, but she felt ridiculous.

"You okay in there?" Derrick was standing outside the dressing room. "Do we need to go to the children's section?"

She picked up the humor in his voice. "Haha."

He chuckled as she joined him at the dressing room entrance.

He took her in, head to toe. "That's perfect."

"I look foolish."

"You look like you're nineteen. You look nothing like yourself."

"But my hair—"

"Easily solved." He held out a baseball cap and a fabric scrunchy.

She snatched both. "You think you are very clever."

"There's mountains of evidence."

"Silly man." Shaking her head, she turned to a triple mirror, pulled her hair through the hole in the back of the cap, and then twisted it into a bun, which she secured with the hair band.

"You look like a Georgetown coed," he said.

She met his eyes in the mirror. "What is this, a coed?"

"A female college student."

"That is a funny name." She angled this way and that, scrutinizing her reflection. This disguise would work.

"One more thing." He held out a pair of sunglasses with thick black rims.

"It is cloudy."

"I thought we could pop out the lenses. From far away, nobody'll notice. Try 'em."

She did, though with the dark shades, it was hard to make out anything.

"Perfect," he said. "If you just pull off all the tags, I'll buy everything, and then you don't have to change again."

Fifteen minutes later, they were back in the car and headed to the city.

She'd been distracted when he'd made the purchases. Now, she opened the sack he'd handed her, searching for the sunglasses, and found, along with her denim dress, another baseball cap and a red jacket. "What are these for?"

He hit the blinker and angled onto the highway. "I didn't realize before that your friend's aunt and uncle knew you. If there's any chance they might see you, I don't want you anywhere near them. So, you need to email Basma and tell her that I'll meet her and her brother and bring them to you."

"She won't agree to that."

Derrick kept talking as if she hadn't spoken. "I wanted to wear something that she'd be able to easily pick out—and that no other man would have on. Tell her to be on the lookout for a tall guy wearing a white baseball cap and a bright red nylon jacket. Then, if I have to get lost in a crowd, I can take off the jacket and hat, which'll make it easier for me to blend in."

"She will not go with you."

"Then she can go back to Iraq and live with her half brother."

"Derrick." Jasmine's voice rose. "We cannot leave them. We must help."

"That's what I'm trying to do."

"I must come with you. Basma will be afraid, and Rabie as well."

Derrick hit the blinker and then angled back off the highway, though they couldn't be anywhere near their destination. He fought traffic until they turned into a gas station packed with cars. He pulled around to the back, put the car in park, and faced her. "This is nonnegotiable."

She worked out the meaning of the long word, then crossed her arms. "You do not own me. You tell me all the time that I am free and can do what I wish."

"If that's how you want to play it, fine." His tone was calm, his expression bland, but emotion hummed beneath his words. "You can do this by yourself. I'll just head back to the airport and fly home."

"You would leave me here?" Her heart slammed against her ribcage. "Alone?"

"If you insist on putting yourself in danger, yes."

"But you cannot... How could you...? What about Basma and Rabie? They are in danger."

"They can come with me, or they can find another way out of their situation. Or they can go back to Iraq."

"That is... You are not cruel. Why would you do this?"

"Because your safety—"

"What of theirs? You would let them be harmed?"

"To protect you? In a New York minute."

"What is this? I do not understand."

He blew out a long breath, frustration showing for the first time, though she guessed it'd been there all along. "It just means...fast. Yes, I would let them be harmed if it meant keeping you safe. If it's between you and them... Maybe it's wrong. Maybe it's unfair. But..." He stared up at the ceiling, pushing his hair away from his face. "They're not my responsibility. I can't save everyone." He lowered his gaze and met her eyes. "I choose you. If it's either you or them, I choose you."

The strangest feeling spread through her chest, warmth and

affection and tenderness, stinging her eyes and muddling her thoughts.

Foolishness. Likely, he was worried what Michael would say if any harm came to her. But...no. The way Derrick looked at her, as if she really and truly mattered, made her discard that idea.

Derrick was her friend. She'd had so few of those, almost none who'd chosen her, just for her and not because she was Leila's twin.

There'd been Basma.

And now Derrick.

And nobody else.

He reached across the console and took her hand. "Don't cry, Jazz. I'm trying to protect you. Can you understand that? I want to help your friends, but not if it means putting you in danger."

She used the arm of her sweatshirt to swipe away her tears. "I do not wish to be difficult. I only worry that Basma won't go with you."

"She'll have no choice. You can take a picture of me if you want, though I don't know that that's a great idea. I mean, God forbid somebody hacks her email, we wouldn't want them to figure out who I am."

"A photo is a bad idea."

He nodded at the jacket and cap on her lap. "They're distinctive. Email her. Tell her to watch for me in those and that you'll be waiting in the car."

"What was the point of this then?" She plucked at the sweatshirt he'd insisted she buy. "Why must I be in disguise?"

"In case they see you. In case somebody happens to walk by who might recognize you. Or we're caught on camera or something. Just a precaution."

That word was new, though she understood *caution*. And *pre* usually meant before.

"Email your friend. If she refuses to come with me, tell her she'll have to find another way to her cousin's house." Derrick squeezed her hand. "You don't want your father finding you, right?"

It wasn't her father she feared. Jasmine could see Khalid's face twisted in fury. Her husband wouldn't hurt her, not until she gave birth to his heir, the only reason he'd taken her as a wife. After that, he'd kill her. Unless he wanted more children and thought she was worth the trouble of keeping around, in which case he'd lock her in a room and use her as a baby-making machine until she could no longer conceive.

And then he'd kill her.

"You're safe here, Jazz." Derrick's voice was gentle. "I just want to keep you that way, okay?"

Jasmine couldn't seem to make herself speak past the emotions jumbling inside—fear, gratitude, shame. She managed a nod.

Derrick reached into the bag for the sunglasses, popped out the plastic lenses, and handed the frames to her.

She put them on, lowered the visor, and checked her reflection in the mirror. The large, black rims distracted from her face. "It is different." She turned to him. "What do you think?"

His eyebrows hiked. He swallowed, his Adam's apple dipping in his throat. "Yeah, that's...you make those look good."

She checked her reflection again. "Smart, yes? Like a student?"

"You *are* smart, and yes, you'd fit right in on campus, no doubt. Email Basma, okay? I've got one more thing I forgot to do."

Derrick took the jacket and hat and climbed out of the car, and she emailed her friend.

Derrick went to the trunk. A moment later, he circled to the front and crouched down. She had no idea what he was doing, but the sedan moved the slightest bit.

After he'd closed the trunk, he climbed back into the car wearing the ugly jacket. He'd hidden his long hair inside the white hat. "You ready?"

"Basma must still be at lunch, but she will email back when she receives my message."

"Okay. Let's go." He shifted gears and started driving.

Soon enough, they'd be in the city. Though Jasmine had balked at the idea of staying in the car, she saw Derrick's point and appreciated his desire to protect her.

As long as Basma agreed to go with Derrick—and what options did she have?—this should be simple. Basma and Rabie would be delivered to their cousins, and then Jasmine and Derrick would be on their way home to Maine and safety.

But if Jasmine had learned anything in the last few years, she'd learned not to assume anything would be simple.

And that she was never truly safe.

CHAPTER SIX

Derrick's heart pounded like it wanted out.

He'd known Jasmine would argue when he told her his plan. But what choice had he had? Thank God she'd told him Basma's uncle was acquainted with her father. Now that Derrick knew, he couldn't allow her anywhere near the man.

But what if Jasmine had called his bluff? What if she'd tried to get out of the car, insisting she'd find her way to DC without him? Obviously, he couldn't have let her. Would the disagreement have caused a permanent rift in their relationship?

He hated confrontation. He could argue with a stranger. He could have a knock-your-block-off fight with an enemy—not that he did that on a regular basis, but he *could*.

Yet the slightest disagreement with someone he loved scared him to death.

He hated that about himself, and he had way bigger worries than his childish fears right now.

Following the car's navigation system, he wound the sedan along the narrow streets of Washington, DC.

"It is very pretty."

He hadn't been paying attention. He tried seeing the city

through her eyes. The sky was overcast and gray. The trees planted along the road were leafless, but even so, they had a stark beauty. The buildings, mostly brick, were somehow both charming and imposing. Not that there weren't ugly parts of the nation's capital, but this area was well maintained. "Someday, I'll bring you back and show you the sights. The White House and Capitol Building, the monuments."

"I would like that."

"And the Smithsonian. The Air and Space Museum is my favorite."

"That does not surprise me." Her voice held a smile, but he kept his focus on a busy traffic circle. They reached the hotel, but he continued past it, searching for a place to turn around.

Jasmine craned her neck. "I think that was it."

"I want to be on the other side of the street, in case we're followed when we leave." He pulled into a parking lot across from the hotel and backed into a space. "Did Basma email back?"

Jasmine had checked her email periodically during the drive. She did again now. "Yes. She says they just returned from lunch. She's not comfortable going with you, but she'll do it."

Derrick was careful to keep the smug expression off his face, but seriously, it wasn't as if the woman had a whole lot of choices. Jasmine seemed comfortable with the plan. She'd even used a few contractions, something she only did when she was relaxed.

"She says there's a coffee shop that opens to the sidewalk." Jasmine peered across the street. "Do you think that's it?"

An awning-covered glass door was just down from the main entrance. "That'd be convenient. She's going to go there?"

"Yes. At three fifteen to get a drink. Or near that time."

He glanced at the dashboard clock, then his watch to be sure. It was almost three now.

"Basma believes the guards will come. She worries about their ability to get away."

"We'll figure it out." They were probably just going to have to run for it. "Can you tell her where the car is parked?"

"I will email, but I don't know if she will see. She said she might not be able to check her email again without causing suspicion."

He watched the traffic passing in front of them. This was a busy road, but only two lanes, and the cars weren't moving fast. He'd parked no more than a hundred feet from the coffee shop entrance. All he had to do was get Basma and her brother out the door, across the street, and into the car. He could park right in front of the entrance, but he worried about Jasmine's face being caught on camera. Plus, he wanted to be able to drive straight to Dupont Circle, which he wouldn't be able to do if the car were facing the opposite direction.

The large, busy traffic circle was only a couple of blocks down. The silver sedan Derrick had rented would easily blend into the city's afternoon traffic. From there, he'd hit a couple more roundabouts before getting back on the highway toward Dulles.

Once he was sure he'd lost anyone who might follow, he'd find a place to stop so he could remove the old license plates he'd put on the car when they'd stopped at the gas station earlier. When he was a kid, he used to collect all manner of weird things, including memorabilia from his parents' youth, things they tried to throw out. Even now, though he had no use for the boxes of old stuff, he couldn't seem to part with them. The plates had been his mother's from college.

If the guards watching Basma and Rabie happened to get a glimpse of Derrick's rental, surely they wouldn't be able to trace them, considering the number hadn't been registered to a car in nearly half a century. And since they were from New Hampshire, they wouldn't even lead to the right state.

He'd thought the motto printed on the plate apropos for the situation...

Live free or die.

He was in favor of the first part but, God willing, nobody would have to die to get Basma and Rabie to freedom.

To be safe, Derrick had used a green marker to change one of the numbers on the license plate, turning a three into an eight. It wouldn't stand up to a close inspection, but as long as he didn't get pulled over, it should work.

Derrick watched the coffee shop entrance for a few moments, then turned to Jasmine, who was studying her phone.

Her dark skin had taken on a yellowish undertone, reminding him of how sick she'd been when he first met her.

"Is something wrong?" he asked. "Or are you just nervous?"

She faced him, and the fear in her eyes was unmistakable. "Basma said that if something goes wrong, she wants you to take Rabie. To leave her. That getting him away from Dari is more important than anything else. She says she will be able to escape her aunt and uncle more easily without him."

"I'm not doing that. I'm not taking a kid away from his guardian. Guardians—plural, because you said the uncle is actually the guardian, right?"

"Yes, yes." Jasmine sighed, clearly relieved. "Of course you cannot do that." She slid her fingers around his arm, the light touch sending energy and strength surging through him. She'd never initiated a touch between them before.

He liked it. Enough that he had to work on focusing as she spoke.

"You will get them both." Her big, liquid eyes met his, filled with earnestness and trust. "I am confident you will bring them both back." Before he could respond—and what was he supposed to say to that?—Jasmine closed those eyes and prayed, asking God to protect him and help him rescue her friends.

Derrick agreed with her prayers but didn't add to them. His thoughts were too jumbled with nerves—and her hand on his arm—to think of anything coherent.

She finished with "God go with you."

"Thank you. Keep praying." He opened his car door, but before he got out, he turned to her once more. "No matter what happens—if police come or the hotel catches fire or blows up— do not get out of this car. If I get arrested or... If anything bad or even mildly unexpected happens, drive away and call Michael. Okay?" She nodded, but he wasn't satisfied with that. "Promise me?"

A moment passed, but finally, she said, "I promise."

"Good. Be right back."

It was five past three when Derrick stepped into the coffee shop, taking in the sounds of grinding beans, steaming machines, and chattering voices. He'd hoped the place would be busy, and he wasn't disappointed. Patrons were seated at the tables—mostly women in casual clothes who wore lanyards around their necks —from a conference, he assumed. The line at the counter reached almost to the wide exit on the far end of the room that led to the lobby.

Derrick leaned against a long bar near the door and opened the email app on his phone to make it seem like he was busy.

He had no idea how to do this. Could Basma and Rabie just...leave? Could Basma tell the guards they were going for a walk? If they did, would the guards try to stop them or just casually follow? Were they suspicious of her, or were they more concerned about protecting her and Rabie from the outside world?

If Derrick could indicate to Basma where the car was, assuming she hadn't gotten Jasmine's email, she and Rabie could run for it, and he could stop the guards from following. Might hurt, and it might get him in trouble, but if he played it right, he could feign innocence. *Sorry, man. I tripped. Didn't mean to get in your way...*

Might work. Worth a shot, anyway.

He texted Jasmine to warn her.

> Slide into the driver's seat and get ready to leave. I might send them to you. When they get there, drive away, take a right, and go.

> What about you?

> Put the address of Dulles Airport in the navigation. You might need to make sure you aren't being followed. If you are, aim for roundabouts. They're all over the city—maybe Basma can help? Stop after you know you're safe and take the NH plates off the car—one in front, one in back. The real plates are underneath. There's a screwdriver in the trunk. Make sure you're out of sight—those plates aren't legal.

He should've explained what he was doing when he put them on. He added,

> I'll get an Uber and meet you there.

She responded with a thumbs-up emoji.
Okay. Good. This could work.

If it didn't, Derrick would wing it. He was pretty good at that. No pun intended.

He kept his eye on the opening to the lobby. If he were the one waiting in the car, he'd want updates, so at a quarter past, he texted Jasmine.

No sign of them yet. Nothing to worry about.

Jasmine responded with a thank-you that made him smile. When he glanced up from his phone, he realized the coffee shop was emptying, women with bags slung over their shoulders hurrying toward the lobby. It seemed their break time was over.

Within two minutes, just a few patrons remained, sitting at tables here and there. Without a crowd, this would be much harder.

You're going to have to step in here, God.

He spotted a Middle Eastern woman holding hands with a curly-haired boy, walking toward the coffee shop. Had to be them.

Derrick moved toward the counter, pretending to study the menu on the wall behind it. He felt it when the two came close, but he didn't turn their way.

"Are you in line?"

He turned at the female voice and smiled.

Basma wore a long-sleeved tan-colored dress with a matching headscarf. Though her words had been casual, fear flicked in her eyes.

The little boy wore slacks and a sweater—dressy for a kid his age, but they'd gone to a lunch of some kind, so maybe that was why. Rabie carried a bright red backpack.

"Still deciding." Derrick stepped back. "You two go ahead."

The little boy tugged on her hand, clearly not happy she wouldn't let him walk away. He said something in Arabic.

She responded, her tone sharp, and moved in front of Derrick.

He kept his voice very low, not wanting the kid to hear. "Don't look and don't react."

She didn't, which meant either she was paying close attention or she didn't hear him.

"Jasmine's across the street in a silver Honda Accord. Nod if you hear me."

Her head dipped the slightest bit.

Derrick scanned the restaurant, trying to act nonchalant.

Two men had followed her in. They wore dark suits and dress shoes and had short dark hair and beards. One stood near the lobby exit. He was about five-eight, maybe a hundred sixty pounds.

The other stood beside the door that led outside. He was bigger than his partner, just under six feet, probably one seventy. Not quite as tall as Derrick but probably about the same weight. Derrick assumed both guards were in fighting shape.

So much for plan A.

In front of him, Basma leaned down to talk to Rabie, though Derrick didn't understand a word.

When she straightened, he whispered, "I'll take care of the guard at the door. When I do, run. Don't look back, and don't wait for me. Just go."

Her shoulders stiffened, and her head dipped in a tiny nod. She stepped forward, placed their order, and paid for it.

How in the world was he going to do this? Sure, he'd had a million wrestling matches with his big brothers when he was a kid, but he wasn't exactly an MMA fighter.

Guidance, Lord?

He ordered a large Americano, a plan forming.

He'd *accidentally* spill the coffee on the guard by the door.

Keep him busy, ostensibly trying to help. That should give Basma and Rabie time to run.

What could possibly go wrong?

The answers to that question popping into his head were not helping.

Basma and Rabie got their drinks and a couple of cookies and found a table near the door.

While Derrick waited at the counter, he texted Jasmine.

> Be ready. They'll be out in a second.

> Be careful.

The barista called, "Robert?"

Derrick had given his middle name because it seemed wise not to offer the guards any real information. It wasn't like there was a manual to follow, or a step-by-step plan.

He sure could've used one of those.

At the sugar-and-creamer station, he added a packet of sugar, not quite securing the lid when he was finished. He shoved a handful of napkins in his pocket, then headed for the door, giving Basma and Rabie a friendly smile on his way.

Rabie was intent on his cookie, but Basma's eyes met his for the briefest moment. She saw. She understood.

Derrick neared the exit, nodded to the guard. "How you doing?"

Then he tripped, stumbled forward, and spilled his coffee all over the guard's shirt.

The man jumped back—toward the door—letting out a string of Arabic that Derrick guessed, by the tone, were curses.

"Ah, dude. I'm sorry. Lemme help." He grabbed him by the arm and pulled him forward, hopefully giving Basma space to get by him.

The guy tried to shake him off, but Derrick's grip was solid. He shifted the guard so he faced away from Basma and Rabie, who were already up and headed toward them. "Here, I've got some napkins—"

The other guard shouted something.

Still holding guard number one, Derrick backed up farther, pulling him with him. He ran into a chair and stumbled, pulling the guard off his feet.

The guy fell.

"Now look what I've done."

Was anybody believing this *Three Stooges* bit?

Basma reached the door and pushed outside, Rabie on her heels.

"Man, I'm such a klutz." Derrick reached down to the guy. "Here, let me help."

"Get your hand off me!" the guard shouted.

"No need to get testy." He gave the barista behind the counter a *what are you going to do?* look, trying to keep her from joining the melee or calling security.

At the door, Rabie yanked away from Basma and ran back inside, toward where they'd been sitting. A glance told Derrick he'd left his backpack.

They'd been so close!

The second guard was closing in, barking words at Basma that sounded like orders. He had a cell phone to his ear.

The first guard shook Derrick off, then shoved at the table and chairs that were hemming him in to give himself room to stand.

Wide-eyed, Basma called Rabie to come to her. She seemed afraid to return inside but was obviously unwilling to leave without him.

Backpack in hand, Rabie started for the door, then caught

sight of the guards. One on the floor, the other crossing toward them, shouting in Arabic.

The boy froze, confused. Probably terrified.

Across the street, the door to the sedan opened. Jasmine stepped out.

No.

She'd promised.

Basma's expression morphed from fear to determination. Her focus shifted from Rabie to Derrick.

For one second, she held his eye contact, and he knew what she planned.

No time to stop her. He needed to get out of there before Jasmine put herself in danger. He absolutely would not allow that.

He lifted his foot and kicked guard number one in the back, knocking the guy's wind out and earning an "Oomph." Just in case, Derrick kicked him again.

Basma shouted, "Please!" And then she barreled into guard number two, taking him by surprise.

Derrick grabbed the boy around the waist, pushed out the glass door, and ran.

CHAPTER SEVEN

Jasmine watched in horror as Derrick bolted across the street, Rabie tucked in his arms like a small child.

Where was Basma?

Jasmine opened the back door as Derrick got close.

He shouted, "Get in the car!"

She scrambled into the backseat, and Derrick tossed Rabie in beside her, then slammed the door and climbed in the driver's seat, jamming the car into drive.

It lurched forward, and he yanked the wheel to the right, knocking Rabie into the door.

The boy stared at her with wide, terrified eyes.

"It's okay, Rabie." She spoke Arabic with as soothing a tone as she could manage under the circumstances. "It's okay. Let's get your seatbelt on." She took the backpack he held tightly in his grip and dropped it on the floor, then reached across him to grab the belt.

"You too." Derrick sounded frantic—or furious. She wasn't sure which. "Now."

In the middle seat, she put her seatbelt on and then wrapped her arm around Rabie. "It's okay. It's going to be okay."

"I want Basma." He was crying, trying to twist to look behind them.

She turned as well. Lots of traffic, but a black SUV seemed to be bearing down on them. They were being followed. No wonder Derrick was angry and intent.

"What happened?" Rabie asked. "I don't understand."

Jasmine faced forward, forcing calm for his sake. "Your sister is all right." *Please, God, let it be true.* "She asked us to come and get you."

The boy looked at Jasmine for the first time.

"I knew you a long time ago. I am Yasamin. I lived next door to you. You were just a little boy the last time I saw you."

His eyes, red-rimmed from tears, narrowed. She thought he might recognize her, but he didn't say so. Tears streamed down his face. "I want my sister."

"I know, love. I know." She pulled him against her. "I do too. I love your sister as if she were my own. We will get you back to her." *Please, God, help me keep that promise.*

Derrick sped around a traffic circle, then whipped down a wide road, moving much faster than the rest of the vehicles.

His gaze kept flicking to the rearview.

Were they still being followed?

By police? Or guards?

She wanted to check, but Rabie was sobbing against her, and the last thing he needed was more stress after what had just happened.

What *had* just happened?

Derrick weaved along the city streets—seemingly randomly, though he must have a plan. He didn't say a word.

Finally, Rabie took a couple of breaths, then wiggled away and studied her again. "You used to give me rides on your back."

"Yes, you remember!"

"And you let me sip your tea, even though Basma would tell you not to."

She shrugged. "A little sugar is not such a big thing."

He didn't smile, but a tiny bit of the fear left his eyes. "Can I play with my toys? They're in my backpack."

"Of course." She reached for the bag, switching to English. "Your sister told me you've been going to the international school."

"Uh-huh." He plopped it on his lap and opened the top. He'd changed, of course, since she'd last seen him. He was tall—almost as tall as she, not that that was saying much—and lean, having lost all the chubbiness he'd had as a baby. But his hair was still curly and wild. His nose and eyes were wide with surprise on his angular face. She remembered that, when he smiled, his smile was even wider. Maybe she'd see it, eventually.

"I went to the same school when I was your age. Do you like it?"

"It's okay, I guess. I have a lot of friends, and I play soccer. Forward." His English was excellent, one of the benefits of the international school. That was where she'd learned, after all. He pulled out some kind of electronic toy, gave her a look, then dropped that one back in the bag and grabbed another one. His hands were shaking, but he seemed to be trying to hold himself together, settling a multicolored cube-shaped puzzle in his lap. "Are we going to get Basma? Those guards were really mad. I'm afraid they're going to hurt her."

The thought had her stomach twisting. "Do you think your aunt and uncle would allow that?"

He seemed to take the question seriously. "They will be angry that I'm gone. Very angry."

"Yes." Jasmine saw no point in disagreeing with the obvious. "But have you ever seen them hurt your sister? Did they ever hurt you?"

He shook his head. "Basma isn't afraid of them. It's Dari she's afraid of, our half brother. He wants us to live with him."

Jasmine took Rabie's hand. "Your sister is very afraid of him, afraid enough that she was willing to do all of this to protect you from him. She loves you very much."

His eyes filled again. "When am I going to see her?"

"I don't know, love." Jasmine pulled him close again. "Soon, I hope. Let's ask God to help." She uttered a short, simple prayer, asking God to protect Basma and reunite her with them, then kissed Rabie on his head. "Okay?"

He shrugged and started twisting the toy in his hand.

When he was distracted, she focused on Derrick. Though his gaze still flicked often to the rearview, he didn't seem nearly as worried.

"Everything all right?"

He nodded, though the action was brisk.

She leaned forward, between the seats. "You are angry with me."

"You promised to stay in the car." His words were practically growled at her.

"I saw you coming and thought—"

"You got out of the car before that, when Basma first pushed the door open."

He'd seen that? She had only wanted to make sure Basma knew where she was. "I was worried. I wasn't thinking."

"I asked for one thing."

"I had to make sure she knew—"

"What about you?" He was getting louder. "Who died and made you Joan of freaking Arc, standing there like a symbol of freedom?"

She didn't know who that was, and now didn't seem a good time to ask.

"Do you have some kind of a...a martyr complex?"

"I was only trying to help—"

"At *your* expense! You remember what I said?" He'd lowered his voice, but he might as well have yelled for all the vehemence it held. "If I had to choose between you—"

"You would choose me, but I choose them."

"I was afraid for you, for *you*. Because you got out of the car, I had no choice. My face is probably being broadcast on every news channel in the metropolitan area."

"I'm sure that's not—"

"I took a kid, Jazz. Against his will. There were guards there, trying to stop me. Maybe Basma will convince them she wanted me to take him. But her uncle is the diplomat. He's the guardian, right? What if he tells them his nephew was kidnapped? Will the police listen to your friend or her uncle? Will the police even ask her?" He scrubbed his whiskers. "Maybe I can explain all this away. But...I shouldn't have done it. I wouldn't have except I was afraid you were going to get hurt. I didn't know what you'd do." He ran his hand over his head but bumped the cap. He yanked it off and threw it on the passenger seat. "What I just did... It's a felony. If I can't explain my way out of it... And maybe I can, but maybe not. I could go to prison. Do you understand that?"

Prison?

Her stomach dropped. Surely not. Surely nobody would send him to prison.

"And here's the worst part." He met her eyes briefly in the rearview mirror, and she saw not the anger humming on his words, but fear. "So could you, Jazz. I made you an accomplice. In a felony." His lips pressed so tightly they turned white. He swallowed, shook his head. "I should never have agreed to this."

"I didn't mean—"

"I know. I know that. Just...let me process." He took a breath and blew it out. "I'm sorry. I need to think. Could you just...sit back, please?"

She wanted to press her case—she hadn't meant to cause trouble. And nobody had seen her, so he'd probably overreacted. And it wasn't kidnapping. It was a rescue mission.

Would the authorities see it that way?

She wanted to explain how she felt, to get him to understand. She wanted...she wanted him to not be angry with her. Because, what had he said? That the worst part about this was that he'd made her an accomplice? That *she* could go to prison?

How could he see that as the worst part? As if her welfare was important to him. As if...as if *she* mattered to him more than *he* did.

Which didn't make any sense at all.

She settled beside Rabie, who was still focused on his toy.

Derrick had been a good friend to her from the moment they'd met. He'd taken her places. He'd gone out of his way to spend time with her. But there were limits to friendship, at least for most people. Like committing a crime—that was a line most people wouldn't cross, even for a friend.

Yet Derrick had crossed it. To protect her.

Because he was her friend?

Or...

Oh.

Suddenly, she understood what people had been trying to tell her for weeks. Leila had encouraged her to tell Derrick about Khalid and the baby to protect his feelings.

Michael had suggested that the longer she waited to tell him, the more it was going to hurt him.

Jasmine had figured they'd meant that Derrick's feelings would be hurt because she hadn't been honest, but maybe there was more to it.

What had Sophie said the day before?

You don't think there's any chance he's interested in you?

She'd not understood what her new roommate meant. But now...

Did Derrick's feelings go beyond friendship?

Even as she allowed the question to form, the answer seemed as clear as the buildings passing outside the windows. Of course they did. Why else would he have done this?

She hadn't understood. She'd never had a man interested in her romantically. Even Khalid was only interested in her health and her ability to bear children. He barely knew her. He talked to her, of course. They'd shared a bedroom, and he liked to talk about himself and his plans, but he never expected her to respond with more than nods. He'd rarely asked her questions and never wanted her opinion. He'd never sought to understand her. She was—had always been—irrelevant.

How did Derrick not understand that?

He had done this for her because he cared for her, and she'd taken advantage of him. What a cruel, cruel trick. When he learned the truth, he would never forgive her.

And how could he have such feelings for her? He didn't know her, not really. She needed to tell him the truth about her past, her life. When she did, his feelings would change.

She'd made a terrible mess of things.

But if she hadn't, Rabie would still be in his uncle's hands. He and Basma would still be destined to go back to Iraq to live with Dari. Now that Rabie was gone, perhaps Basma could get away.

Had Jasmine saved Rabie—and, God willing, Basma—only to destroy the friendship, the feelings, or the future of the only other friend she had in the world?

CHAPTER EIGHT

Derrick checked the rearview again. Two black SUVs had been following him, courtesy no doubt of the second guard and whomever he'd called on his way across the coffee shop. The vehicles had been no more than a block behind when Derrick had first peeled out into traffic.

He'd replayed the scene in the coffee shop a thousand times.

The whole thing had happened so fast. Thirty seconds from start to finish, and just like that, Derrick had...what? Was he a kidnapper? Was he a wanted man? He had no idea.

He should've just left Rabie and run.

Stupid. But the way Basma had looked at him, with such pleading in her eyes...

He hadn't had the heart.

All well and good, except if he didn't get out of DC and deliver the kid to his cousins, they'd get caught. Rabie would end up with his psycho half brother, and Derrick and Jazz would land in prison.

God...

What? What was he supposed to ask for here? He had no idea.

At least he knew DC, a city designed to confuse with all the traffic circles everywhere. Between those and some quick turns down hard-to-see alleys, Derrick had managed to lose the SUVs.

How many security people did Basma's aunt and uncle have? And how in the world did Basma think she was going to escape now that she'd shown her hand? And if she didn't escape, then what were Derrick and Jasmine supposed to do with Rabie?

Did Jasmine know where their cousins lived or how to get in touch with them? And if not, were they supposed to just take the kid home?

Derrick should have refused this whole stupid adventure. Told her no way would he help her. And then he should've told Michael what she planned, and then he should've...flown to Florida or something, somewhere away from her and those big, beautiful brown eyes and that sweet, sweet smile.

He was an idiot. A stupid, smitten idiot.

And now he was a felon. And so was Jasmine.

And there were guards searching for them, and no doubt police, and probably FBI.

Maybe this could still work out. Maybe Basma would email Jasmine and find a way to meet them. Maybe they could pass off the kid without incident and walk away from all of this.

Right.

Maybe he should put a down payment on that bridge in Brooklyn too. And keep his eye out for the Yellow Brick Road.

He needed to call Michael. And he would, too, as soon as he had a little time to think through what he wanted to say and what to ask for. Michael had all those CIA contacts. If he couldn't help, maybe Grant knew somebody in law enforcement who could intervene. He was a detective in Coventry now, but between his time in special forces and his work as a bodyguard, he had to know people, didn't he?

Just what Derrick wanted—to beg his brothers to help him out of a jam. They would give it, but would they ever respect him again? Would they want anything to do with him?

He had to squelch an urge to punch the steering wheel. No need to scare the kid. Or Jasmine.

He checked the rearview again—no sign of the guards—then scanned the area. He'd driven far from where they'd started. The structures here weren't stately and beautiful, and the streets weren't tree lined. Instead, though the buildings might've been newer, they seemed to sag under the weight of neglect. The sidewalks were decorated with litter and filth. The few people outside seemed wilted, some sitting on steps, others lying on the sidewalk. One trudged forward, pushing a shopping cart.

Derrick drove past a small park that'd become a tent city for the homeless.

Amazing what a difference a few blocks could make.

And a few hours, apparently.

At a stoplight, Derrick turned to check on his passengers. Rabie was playing with a Rubik's Cube. Jasmine was bent over her phone.

He cleared his throat. "Any news?" He didn't add *from Basma* but figured Jasmine knew what he meant.

She shook her head, her expression so distraught he was tempted to stop the car, pull her out, and give her a long hug. Tell her it was going to be all right and promise that he'd take care of everything.

That was the kind of thinking that'd gotten him into this mess in the first place.

The light turned green, and he accelerated, driving toward a small strip mall he remembered from an earlier visit to the city. He parked behind it, catching Jasmine's eyes in the mirror. "Sit tight." And then, in case she didn't know what that meant, added, "Stay in the car."

Only after she nodded did he get out. He removed the New Hampshire license plates, scoffing at the motto. Ha. *Live free or die.*

He was going to end up behind door number three, where there were steel bars and barbed wire.

He shoved the license plates into the bottom of his duffel bag, then tossed the cheap red jacket on top. With the Virginia plates showing again, nobody should be able to pick out the nondescript car.

Back behind the wheel, he navigated toward the highway. It was after four, and traffic was heavy and only getting worse.

"Derrick?" Jasmine's voice was tentative, which made sense, considering he hadn't exactly been kind to her.

He worked to keep his voice even. "Yeah?"

"What is the plan?"

"We'll be at the airport in about forty-five minutes." They were so far backed up at an intersection that they'd probably end up sitting through two rounds of lights, so he turned to face them. "Not sure where we should go, but we'll fly somewhere."

Rabie looked up from his puzzle, eyes wide.

Derrick smiled at him, hoping it passed for natural. "How you doing?"

The kid shrugged.

"I'm Derrick. Sorry if I scared you. Have you ever been on a private jet?"

"We came here on a big plane." His English was almost as good as Jasmine's.

"Mine is small. I'll let you ride in the cockpit after we take off, if you want."

His eyes lit, though the expression didn't last. "We are going without Basma?"

Derrick let Jasmine field that.

"She will meet us as soon as she can." Jasmine managed to

be gentle but not patronizing. "She asked us to take care of you, and that's what we're trying to do. You can trust us, Rabie. I promise."

The kid focused on Derrick again as if trying to decide whether this strange man who'd snatched him away from his sister truly could be trusted.

Though traffic moved around them, Derrick didn't break his eye contact. The kid had to be traumatized.

Finally, Rabie reached for his backpack and dug out another toy, apparently satisfied, at least for now.

Jasmine relaxed against the seat and checked her phone again.

Derrick inched forward in traffic. When they reached the airport, they'd have to return the rental and then get to the terminal. By the time he finished his checklist, best case scenario, they'd be wheels up in a couple of hours. At which point, if they hadn't heard from Basma, he'd reach out to Michael and figure out what to do next.

Assuming they didn't get arrested and thrown into jail between now and then.

After Derrick found a spot in the vast rental car lot, he ordered an Uber.

"Put your game away." Jasmine's voice was tender when she spoke to Rabie.

He didn't respond, but Derrick heard the bag zipping, so he must have obeyed.

"Thank you, Rabie." To Derrick she said, "We are waiting for something?"

He caught her eye in the mirror. "We'll get out when our ride is near. You all right?"

She nodded.

"No news?"

"No, but she will reach out. The Ghazis are good people. They will not harm her."

The Ghazis. He filed the name away, not bothering to argue with her assessment, though how people who wouldn't give a grown woman her choice of where to live and with whom—who would employ guards to stop her—could be considered good, he couldn't fathom.

When the Uber driver was three minutes away, they headed toward the rental car facility. Though anxiety churned in his gut, he did his best to act confident, like he belonged. Like he did this all the time.

Which he did—renting cars, anyway. Not the kidnapping part.

He dropped the keys in the box and the suitcases into the Uber's trunk—it was a midsize Nissan—and slid into the backseat beside Rabie. Jasmine sat next to the other window.

The driver—Kyle, according to the app—couldn't be more than twenty-two. He was slight and pale with messy blond hair that made him look like he'd stepped right off a surfboard. "Signature Aviation, yeah?"

"That's it."

He angled into traffic and maneuvered away from the main terminal toward the one used for private aircraft.

Traffic was dense, as always. It seemed to take forever before, finally, Kyle left the bulk of the cars and headed for the modern building.

It wouldn't be long now. As soon as they were on the plane, they'd be safe.

"Don't stop!" Jasmine shouted.

Kyle had slowed considerably. "Ma'am, I gotta drop you—"

"Keep going," Derrick said, then to Jasmine, "What is it?"

"He is inside. There, see?" She averted her gaze while Derrick peered past her.

The automatic doors slid open as the driver passed, and Derrick saw a Middle Eastern man wearing a suit and tie. He was watching the road, and everything about him screamed *security*.

Derrick twisted to face Rabie. "Did you recognize that man?"

He shook his head, but he seemed terrified. Of Derrick? Or of the man inside the terminal?

"What you want me to do, dude?" Kyle asked.

"Can you just drive, please?" Derrick needed to think.

"I mean, I'm only gonna get paid to bring you here, so..."

Derrick wrangled his wallet out of his back pocket and pulled out two fifties. Holding them between the seats, he asked, "This enough to get us back to DC?"

The kid eyed the cash. "You got it. Where abouts?"

"They're following us!" Jasmine had twisted and was watching out the rear window. "Isn't that the car from earlier?"

Derrick turned and saw the SUV. It was a good seventy yards behind but gaining on them.

"How did they find us?" Jasmine's voice was shrill.

As if he knew. He was tempted to tell her to calm down—because that *always* worked. To Kyle, he said, "There's an extra fifty in it for you if you can lose that SUV."

"Not cops, right? I can't—"

"Not cops." He leaned forward and lowered his voice. "My friend's ex. I'm trying to help her get somewhere safe. The guy thinks he owns her and her kid. You know what I mean?"

"Gotcha. No problem." Kyle floored his little sedan, the sudden acceleration pressing Derrick back against the seat. He whipped around slower cars, never staying in the same lane more than a minute or two.

If Derrick were watching from another vehicle, he'd call the guy a maniac. He *was* a bit of a maniac, but Derrick wasn't going to complain.

Jasmine was still looking behind them. "They're falling back."

Between them, Rabie held his backpack on his lap, arms wrapped around it like it contained his most valuable possessions. His eyes were wide. Unfortunately, in the middle seat, he had a great view of Kyle's Mario Andretti driving. As if the kid wasn't scared enough.

Jasmine gave updates every few seconds.

"I think we lost... No, he's speeding up."

A moment later, "He's stuck behind a bus." And then, "He's way back there."

It seemed Kyle was losing their pursuers.

Derrick clasped Rabie's shoulder. "It's going to be okay, son."

The boy gaped at him, terror clear in his expression, and Derrick's heart cracked just a little.

This was his fault. He'd taken this child away from his sister and his aunt and uncle. He'd taken him away from his security and safety. And maybe it would be better for Rabie in the long run, but right now, the kid had every right to be terrified.

Obviously, Basma hadn't told her brother about her plan for them to escape, much less about Jasmine and Derrick. Frankly, the kid was holding it together incredibly well.

Derrick hated to think how he'd be acting if someone had snatched him away from his family when he was nine years old.

He shifted to face Rabie, lowering his voice so Kyle wouldn't hear. "I'm sure you're scared, son. If I were you, I'd be terrified. I promise that Jasmine"—he nodded toward her and switched to her Iraqi name—"Yasamin and I aren't going to hurt you. We're going to do everything we can to reunite you with your sister. Do you know what that word means? Reunite?"

His face scrunched in confusion.

"It means get back together. Your sister asked us to take you away, even if she couldn't come. Jasmine can show you her email when we're someplace safe. We are only trying to do what she asked. You understand that?"

He nodded, but his eyes filled with tears. "I want Basma."

"I know, buddy. I bet you do."

"Are we gonna get to fly on your plane?"

"Not today." Derrick leaned back and met Jasmine's eyes over Rabie's head.

She relaxed against the seat. "They're gone."

"Good." To Kyle, he said, "Nice job."

"Where should I take you?"

That was the question. It was one thing for Basma's security to guess Derrick might be headed to Dulles—as opposed to the other two major airports in the DC area—but how had they guessed they'd be headed to the private terminal?

Either the guards had virtually unlimited resources, enough to cover every terminal in the metro area—and Derrick wasn't buying that—or they'd known where they were going.

Which didn't make any sense at all.

"Jazz?" He kept his voice low and conversational. "Did you tell your friend how we were getting here this morning?"

"No."

"You're sure? No hints?"

"It was not a game of guessing. I gave no hints."

"Did you tell her we were flying, even if you didn't mention my jet?"

"Derrick, I did not tell her—"

"Did you mention Dulles?"

"I told her nothing," Jasmine snapped.

Fine. But if she didn't tell Basma, then how did the security guys know?

"Is it possible we overreacted?" she asked. "Perhaps the man inside the building was not searching for us. Perhaps the black SUV was not following us."

"You were watching him. What do you think?"

Her lips pressed together, and her gaze flicked toward the rear window. "He was also driving...like this one." She tipped her chin toward Kyle. "But not as..."

"Aggressively?"

"Yes. I think. Perhaps he is just a bad driver. Perhaps we only thought we saw something that we didn't see."

Yeah. Maybe.

Much as he didn't want Basma's people to be that far ahead of them, he hated to think he'd panicked.

It was all so convoluted and crazy.

"You guys decide where to go?" Kyle asked.

It seemed they'd lost the bad guys for now—assuming anyone had been following them in the first place. Derrick just needed to get Jasmine and Rabie somewhere safe where they could rest and regroup. He pulled his phone from his pocket. "Let me make a call."

This was Derrick's favorite hotel in the DC metro, not because it was fancy—it wasn't. But because it was close enough to the airport to get there quickly, far enough away that he could go for a jog without the constant rumble of takeoffs and landings, and affordable.

He'd been surprised to learn they had a suite available. The word *suite* made it sound much fancier than it was. One room had a kitchenette with a small table and a living area with a pull-out sofa.

Jasmine and Rabie were in the other room. The door was closed, the shower running. Derrick had insisted Rabie leave his backpack, which had nearly caused a full meltdown.

There'd been screaming and tears, but Jasmine had calmed him, speaking soothingly in Arabic. The kid hadn't relaxed until Jasmine had said to Derrick, "You aren't going to take anything or break anything, right?"

"I don't plan to." He didn't figure Rabie would miss a tracker, assuming Derrick found one. It'd occurred to him—too late, obviously—that a tracker could explain how the guards had guessed their destination.

"And you'll give it right back?" Jasmine asked.

"I promise."

"You see. It'll be all right." She'd crouched beside the boy at that point. "Go ahead and ask him. Even if he says no, he will be kind."

Rabie had blinked a couple of times, then said in a rush of words, "Can we have pizza for dinner?"

Derrick felt his answering smile. "My favorite. You like pepperoni?"

Jasmine's wide eyes and the quick shake of her head came a smidge too late. Right. Muslims didn't eat pork.

He amended quickly. "What toppings do you like?"

"Cheese and beef?"

Hamburger would work.

After they left the room, Derrick had ordered a small pie for Rabie and another for himself and Jasmine—who'd come to love pepperoni since she'd moved to Maine.

Then he clicked on the TV and found a local news channel, fearing he'd see his face plastered on the screen. But he didn't.

Nor did a Google search on his phone show any news regarding the kidnapping of the nephew of a foreign diplomat.

Come to think of it, there'd been no Amber Alerts on his phone all day.

So either Basma's uncle hadn't reported the kidnapping, or the police were keeping it quiet. Derrick prayed it was the first and not the second.

Jasmine opened the door and tossed Rabie's dirty clothes onto the corner of the couch. "Here they are."

He'd asked her to bring them out when Rabie was in the shower. "Thanks."

He searched the small slacks, sweater, underwear, and socks, sticking his hands in the pockets and feeling around all the hems and stitching, finding nothing that didn't belong.

He studied the kid's dress shoes and again found nothing out of place.

He left the pile of dirty clothes on the corner of the couch, then took the backpack and dumped the contents onto the kitchen table. There had to be a tracker or something, somewhere. How else could the guards have found them at Dulles?

If there was a tracker, he figured it wasn't a great one, or maybe it didn't work well in the congestion of the city. But once Derrick had aimed for Dulles, those watching it had made an educated guess. Derrick, Rabie, and Jasmine had stayed at the rental car place a few minutes waiting for the car, which could have given the guards time to get into position at each of the terminals.

But even that felt...implausible. Dulles was a huge airport. There'd have to be twenty guards or more to watch all the doors. Why would they bother having anybody at the private terminal —the least likely place for them to go—much less a car there at the ready?

Didn't make sense.

But Jasmine swore she hadn't told Basma about Derrick's jet.

After sorting the items in the bag, Derrick started with the clean clothes, which Jazz would want right away. A pair of pajamas, socks, and underwear had been shoved into the very bottom of the bag. He searched them like he had the dirty clothes and found nothing, then set them, along with a little baggie that contained two toothbrushes, toothpaste, and other toiletries on the edge of the couch near the door to Jasmine's room.

He texted her to tell her they were there and moved on.

There were a Rubik's Cube and a few other brain-teaser-type puzzles. He studied them, turning, twisting, and sliding the little pieces to make sure each was authentic. Seemed like normal puzzles to him.

A couple of chapter books—in English, interestingly. He flipped through them, then held them up and shook them to see if anything fell out. Aside from a bookmark in one, nothing did. He shoved it back in—wrong spot, but that was the least of his worries.

There were three drawstring fabric bags. He opened and upended one, and puzzle pieces spilled out. After running his hands among them—just regular cardboard—he felt inside the bag, then squished the fabric through his fingers, feeling for anything out of place. Nothing.

He replaced the puzzle pieces, then repeated the process with the other two bags and found more puzzle pieces but no tracker.

Three glossy eight-by-tens had to be pictures that went with the puzzles. He set them on top of the books.

He studied the handful of Matchbox cars, thinking maybe

something sinister had been attached to one, but they seemed just like the cars of his youth.

He dug through the backpack again and found one more thing in the outside pocket, an electronic game—and it had been left on.

His heart thumped. This was it. These things were notorious, weren't they? Weren't all handheld games connected to the internet these days? He clicked it off, but it was too late.

Adrenaline surged through Derrick's veins. Were the guards on their way even now? He got up and check the parking lot through the third-floor window, half expecting to see the place surrounded by black SUVs and well-dressed thugs.

But the lot was quiet. The sun had long since set, and falling rain sparkled in the glow of the streetlights. The wet pavement seemed to shine. In the distance, cars sped past on the interstate, moving at a decent clip now that rush hour was over.

Everything seemed fine.

Derrick sat on the sofa and turned the handheld video console back on. It was filled with games from his own childhood—games like Frogger and Super Mario Bros, Space Invaders and Tetris. Weird.

He found the name of the handheld system and looked it up on his phone. Seemed it was considered safe for kids specifically because it *wasn't* connected to the internet. If one wanted to plug it into a TV, it came with an actual, good old-fashioned cord.

He turned the thing over and saw the port.

Apparently, this couldn't be used as a tracker either.

Derrick searched the backpack thoroughly, checking every crevice, then moved his hands along the fabric slowly, carefully, squeezing every inch between his fingers. If there were something there, even a tiny something, he'd feel it.

He was pretty sure he would, anyway.

But he felt nothing except zippers and snaps and stitching.

Maybe they hadn't been tracked.

Which made sense. If they had been, why would the guards wait until they'd reached the airport, crawling with security? Why not come after them when they were stuck in traffic near the DC Mall? Or inching their way through the worst part of town? Assuming the guards wanted to retrieve Rabie themselves —and the lack of news made him think that was the plan—why wait?

Unless they really hadn't known where Derrick and Jasmine were.

It was good news, but it came with bad.

It meant Basma's family had enough manpower to cover every airport terminal in the metro. Derrick couldn't begin to count how many that was.

Or, even worse, they somehow knew who Derrick was.

That idea didn't bear considering.

Or he and Jasmine had panicked and the burly Arab-looking men they'd seen hadn't been following them at all.

The door between the rooms opened, and Jasmine said, "He's out of the shower and hungry. The food is coming soon?"

He checked his watch. "Fifteen minutes or so. Do you mind hanging in there with him for a little while longer? I need to call Michael."

Her eyes widened, and she stepped into the living area and closed the door. "Is that a good idea?"

"He can help us, Jazz. He knows people."

"But he will be angry, no? What if he wants us to take Rabie back?"

"The guy who risked his career—and his life—to rescue you and your sister from Iraq? You think he'd do that?"

"I don't...think so." But obviously, she wasn't sure.

"I'll feel him out and find out what he thinks we should do before I tell him where we are. I trust my brother. Completely." More than Michael could trust Derrick, it seemed, all things considered.

She looked as if she wanted to argue, then lifted the pajamas and bag of toiletries. "Can we have his toys back?"

He gathered the boy's things and shoved them into the backpack, then handed it to her. "I'll let you know when the pizza's here."

She returned to the bedroom, and Derrick pressed his brother's contact on his cell.

It went straight to voice mail.

Derrick resisted the urge to bang his phone against the wall. At the beep, he said, "Call me back ASAP. It's an emergency."

He tried a few more times, only giving up when a knock sounded on the door. He peeked through the peephole, then accepted the boxes and two-liter bottle of soda from the pimply teenager and knocked on the door between the rooms. "Dinner!"

Rabie's face was freshly scrubbed, a little red. His hair was wet and curly.

"Have a seat, buddy." Derrick pulled out a chair for him at the table, but the kid didn't move toward it.

Derrick hadn't paid attention to the superhero pattern on his PJs before. "Which is your favorite Avenger?"

The boy shrugged.

"I've always been a Spider-Man fan myself." He found plates in the small kitchen and slid a slice of the hamburger-and-cheese pie onto one. "I'd love to be able to swing from buildings like he does, wouldn't you? And scale them? That'd be so cool."

Rabie came a little closer, finally reaching the table. He sat in the chair Derrick had indicated, and Derrick set the plate in front of him.

"You like Sprite?" Derrick asked.

"Yes."

"Me, too." Derrick put ice in three glasses and poured soda. He set the drinks on the table. "Where's Jasmine?"

From the other room, she called, "I'm coming. Don't wait."

Rabie reached for his pizza, but Derrick said, "Uh-uh. Even when a lady says that, she means wait." He winked. "It's impolite to start before everybody's at the table."

"But she's just a woman."

Derrick pressed his lips closed to keep his first response from slipping out. He smiled, then leaned in like he was sharing a secret. "Women are precious and deserve respect, just like men. You should remember that if you ever want to get married."

"Ew." His face twisted in horror, and Derrick barely stifled a chuckle.

"You might change your mind one of these days."

They sat quietly for a few moments, and then Rabie said, "Ironman."

Ah. His favorite Avenger. "Ironman is wicked cool. What do you like about him?"

"He is an ordinary man, only very smart. Basma tells me I'm smart. I want to be like Ironman."

"You are smart, no question."

The boy eyed his drink. "Do I have to wait for Yasamin to sip?"

"I think it'll be okay." He sipped his own to show solidarity, and Rabie swallowed a few gulps.

Finally, Jasmine came in. Her hair was wet, and she'd changed into one of her many shapeless dresses, this one as drab as all the others she wore. Even so, she was beautiful.

Derrick stood. "Pepperoni?"

"I can get it."

But he was already in the kitchen, so she sat at the table, peering at his plate, then Rabie's. "You could have started."

Rabie rolled his eyes. "He said we had to wait for you."

Derrick set her plate in front of her. "We're learning manners."

Jasmine grinned. "He is a very polite man."

Derrick asked a blessing over their meal, and they dug in.

After half a slice, Jasmine asked, "What did Michael say?"

"I left a voice mail."

"They were going to a play tonight, right?"

Oh, yeah. His brother was in New York with Sophie and Bryan. He sort of remembered something about tickets to *Hamilton.*

After dinner, they put together one of Rabie's puzzles, and then Jasmine declared it bedtime and shooed him into the next room. Before she closed the door, she said, "Do you wish to sleep, or should I come back?"

He glanced at his watch and lifted his eyebrows. "It's eight fifteen. I think I can stay up a little longer."

"I'll come back, then, if it's okay, so he can sleep."

While she was settling Rabie down, Derrick hopped in the shower, thankful the suite had two bathrooms, and changed into his sleep pants and a T-shirt. He hadn't been back on the sofa five minutes before Jasmine tapped on the door.

"Come on in."

She did, settling on the club chair catty-corner to him. "No word from Michael?"

He checked his phone, not that he hadn't done that every few minutes since he'd left the message. "Nope."

She seemed to relax at the news. "He will get back to you when he can."

"Good thing it's not an emergency." He'd meant the words sardonically—he'd never had *more* of an emergency—but Jasmine only smiled.

"We're safe here, yes?"

"I'm worried about those guys at the airport."

"That man could have been anybody. He was probably an American businessman waiting for his wife or a partner or something. Since we escaped Iraq, I am quite paranoid."

He leaned toward her. "I don't think it's paranoia if people are actually out to get you. We call that wisdom."

Her lips tipped up at the corners as if he'd said something amusing. He wasn't trying to be funny, though. Somebody *was* after her, and he'd been a fool to take her away from the safety of Shadow Cove.

Michael was going to kill him.

"Do you want to tell me about your escape?" Derrick asked. "I'd love to know more. All I know is that Michael rescued you and Leila from your father's house and got you out of Iraq. What was it like? Probably a lot worse than today, huh? Were you afraid the whole time?"

"From the moment Michael showed up at the compound until your jet lifted off from Mytilene, I was afraid. I'm still afraid he'll find me."

Jasmine wasn't afraid right now, using all those contractions. That was the kind of thing only somebody obsessed with her might notice, which was why he'd never mentioned it.

"Your father." Derrick named the one she feared.

She looked away.

"That *is* who you're afraid of, right? Your father? Because the other guys, the ones who pursued you across Turkey, are dead." And there'd been an uncle, but he'd been arrested in Germany a few weeks before and was still in custody. Derrick didn't know much about that, just what Bryan had been free to share.

"Correct." Jasmine added a smile, but it was tight at the corners. Derrick had missed something, and by the way her expression shuttered, it was something important.

His brother's words from the morning before came back to him. *There are things you don't know... It's possible your feelings for her will change.*

No chance of that. But what didn't Derrick know?

Though she sat across from him, safe and secure, and though Michael and Leila were also safe, as Jasmine related more of the details about their escape from Iraq, through Turkey, and out of Greece, his heart thumped as if the events were happening in real time. As if she were, at that moment, being smuggled over a border in a wooden crate, then bouncing over waves in a raft.

Every moment of that, her life had been in danger. He could have lost her before he'd even met her, and that knowledge raised terror and affection he could no more squelch than explain.

When she finished her tale, he took her hands. "Sweetheart." The tender word slipped out against his will.

But she leaned close, her fresh scent—floral and intoxicating—overwhelming him.

Something surged between them. She had to feel it. It was undeniable, as if lightning had struck the ground where they stood.

It took effort to remember what he'd meant to say. When he did, he infused tenderness into his voice. "You're so strong and courageous. I'm sorry you were held captive. I'm sorry you had nobody all those years to protect you. I'm sorry you had to go through that."

Tears filled her eyes, and she leaned a little closer, so close he could feel her breath on his cheek.

There was no question that she felt what he did.

Thank You.

Maybe not to the same degree, but she had to feel something, the way she was looking at him, her gaze filled with longing and affection.

But then she blinked and straightened. "Thank you. You are a very good friend."

Whoa. What?

Could she really be so indifferent to his feelings?

No.

He wasn't buying it.

Or was this a cultural thing? Maybe he needed to be clearer, give her an opening.

"Jasmine, I—"

"I have had very few friends in my life." She pulled her hands away and stood. "In school, people wanted to be friends with Leila. She was outgoing and had lots of energy, the kind of person who drew people close, you understand?" Though Jasmine's voice was casual, her fingers were clutched together. And she'd gone back to the stilted speech pattern. She gazed around the nondescript room as if she found it fascinating. "People were drawn to her. We were a...a package deal." She looked back at him. "This is the expression, no? We came together?"

"Yup."

"When she left, I was alone. And then Mama died, and I got to know Basma. And now there is you." Jasmine wore an overbright smile and spoke with a perky tone.

Which told him everything he needed to know.

Jasmine knew exactly what Derrick had meant. And she

knew what she was doing. What she was saying. How she was ripping his heart out.

She ended with, "It means much to me to have this friendship."

A skywriter couldn't have made it clearer. He could practically see the puffy white words against a bright blue sky.

Not interested.

Apparently, committing a felony wasn't enough to get a guy out of the friend zone.

And if that didn't do it, nothing would.

CHAPTER NINE

J asmine had always been compliant and obedient. She was the good daughter, not that it had made any difference. Not that it had made her parents love her.

But because she'd been good, she'd avoided the physical abuse many women endured. Even her sister had been hit more than once during their childhood, but not Jasmine.

The only exception came on the day her father told her she was to marry Khalid.

Even though Baba had promised both her and her mother that he would never force her to marry.

Even though he had sworn he'd never allow her to be any man's second wife.

Even though he'd vowed not to give her to a man who was so old that he would leave her a young widow.

Jasmine had trusted her father. She'd trusted him enough that her words came out before she gave them thought.

"But Baba, you promised..."

When his palm struck her cheek, she'd stumbled, slammed her head against the wall, and crumpled to the cold stone floor.

The sting had been shocking, but her father's betrayal had been far, far worse.

Seeing the hurt in Derrick's expression now, Jasmine longed for the sting she'd felt that day. She deserved no better than to be crumpled in the corner. She was a betrayer and a manipulator. That she hadn't understood his feelings before was irrelevant. She should have. She should never have asked him to help her.

Not that she'd had any choice. That was the life of a slave, wasn't it? All unmet needs, no choices. All pain, no relief. All suffering, no love.

But she had Christ. Her hope was in Him.

Jesus hadn't come down and offered a divine jet to fly her to DC. He hadn't gone into the hotel to get Basma and Rabie away. Jasmine had needed Derrick.

She'd *used* Derrick.

The only way forward now was to tell Derrick the truth—or enough of it to put an end to whatever misguided feelings he held for her.

Even if the thought made her eyes sting, made her want to shrivel up and disappear.

Because she could love him. She could love Derrick, if only Baba had kept his word. If only Khalid hadn't chosen her. If only...if only she were not who she was.

Derrick turned his attention to the blank TV screen.

She slid back into the chair and prayed God would help her show him the truth. And protect his heart.

"It makes sense, of course," she said.

He faced her. "What does?"

"The fact that I've had so few friends."

He broke their eye contact again. "You're shy. I'm guessing your sister took the lead when you were kids. It's probably hard for you to make friends."

"She is the...worthy sister."

"What are you talking about?" He barked the words, then shook his head. "Sorry."

Even in anger, he was kind.

"After Leila escaped when she was eighteen, Mama got sick. I was busy taking care of her. I think that if Leila had been there..." No, she should not say that. "It was good Leila left."

Derrick's anger seemed to seep away. He faced her, his head tilting to the side. "If Leila had been there, what?"

Jasmine shrugged. "You know how you know something here"—she tapped her head—"but not here?" She tapped her chest.

"Yeah."

"It is like that. I know that Mama had cancer, and I know the cancer took her, but even so, I feel like she would have survived if Leila had been there."

"Your sister broke her heart, and that led to her death? Is that what you're saying?"

"No, no. It is that Leila is full of life and joy and energy. Mama loved her so much, and when she was gone, Mama was only left with me. And Baba, of course, but..." She wasn't sure how to say what she meant. "I do not believe she was very much in love with Baba. I believe he had let her down. And I was not worth fighting for."

Derrick's back straightened. "You were her daughter. Why would you say that?"

"It is only that I was always just 'the other one.' You know?"

"No. I have no idea what you mean."

She sighed. How could he not understand? He knew Leila. He knew her. How did he not see what was so obvious? "Once, when we were little, Leila lost her temper and broke a vase. Baba was furious. He slapped her and locked her in her room."

Derrick's mouth opened, then pressed closed. Finally, he said, "Okay."

"I was cleaning up the mess, and I was thinking that she was a troublemaker, but I was the good daughter. I was feeling proud of myself for this, you see? And then, in the other room, I heard my parents talking. Baba said, 'Nawra'—that is Leila. You know this?"

He nodded.

"'Nawra is a holy terror,' Baba said, 'and the other one is barely a shadow.'"

"'The other one.'" Derrick repeated her words in a whisper.

"You see?" Jasmine waved her hand toward him to make her point. "I am only 'the other one...a shadow.' Irrelevant."

The confusion on his face gave way to kindness. Tenderness.

He reached for her, but she popped up from the chair. "You do not understand."

"I understand your father was an idiot. I think we've established that. But your mother—"

"My mother said, 'At least she can clean up the mess.' This is me—I am the one who cleans up the mess. I am the servant."

"I stand corrected." As if to punctuate his point, Derrick pushed to his feet and faced her, so close that if it were any other man, she would have shrunken away in fear.

"Apparently," he said, "your mom was also an idiot. Sorry to speak ill of the dead, but...." He shoved his fingers through his hair and took a breath. "Sorry. I don't mean..." He took a step back, giving her space. "Your mother should have defended you, but would she have, really? Your dad doesn't sound like the nicest guy in the world. Would she have disagreed with him? Or are you saying... Do you really think your mother didn't love you?"

Jasmine went into the kitchen and filled their glasses with water. Her hands were shaking, not with fear but with the terrible truth she didn't want to discuss. Or face.

Had her mother loved her? Perhaps. But not like she'd loved Leila. Leila had brought her joy. Jasmine had brought her tea.

Leila represented freedom.

Jasmine represented slavery.

Leila was Isaac, the child of promise.

Jasmine had always been Ishmael, the child of sin and slavery.

Ironic, considering Jasmine had become Khalid's Hagar.

When she returned to the living room, Derrick had settled on the sofa again. She handed him a glass.

"Thanks." He didn't sip it, just turned it between his hands.

"She did not love me like she loved Leila." Jasmine perched on the chair and sipped the water. "This is all I'm saying. I am a different kind of person."

Derrick stared at the wall, and though his head moved up and down, she didn't take that for agreement.

He set the glass on the coffee table and shifted toward her. He took her hand, enveloping it with warmth and gentleness. "I know you don't want to hear this, but since I'm pretty sure you already know, I'm going to say it anyway."

"Please, do not."

"How your father felt about you is irrelevant." Derrick continued as if she hadn't spoken. "How your mother felt about you doesn't matter. I wasn't there, and I can't... I don't know anything about that. I know this, though. I care about you very much, and not just because you're my friend. I have strong feelings for you."

"You must not." She tried to pull away, but he held on.

"Just let me say this."

"You must not!" She tugged again, and he released his hold. "You do not understand."

"Apparently." His expression blanked. She didn't see hurt. Or pain. Or rejection. She saw...nothing.

A mask.

It broke her heart.

"You do not understand." Her voice cracked.

He faced the blank TV again. "So you said."

She stood and walked toward the kitchen, needing distance. Because everything inside her wanted to move closer to him. "You are confused." She was nearly to the table when she turned to face him. "You are here." She lifted one hand high in the air. "You are this kind of person."

He squinted. "Tall?"

"No, no." She shook her head. "Inside, I mean. Your character. Your family. Your...everything. You are this kind." She jabbed the hand she still held above her head. "You see?"

"No."

She lowered the hand to her knee. "I am this person. Low, you see?"

"Short, yeah. I noticed."

She stomped her foot and jabbed her hand again at knee level. "Listen. I am here." She lifted the hand. "You are here." She punctuated each statement with a jab of her hand. Keeping it high, she said, "Leila is here. Michael is here. All of you are here. I am"—she lowered the hand again—"here."

"Jazz, that doesn't even—"

"You be quiet now. You listen."

His eyebrows hiked. For a moment, he seemed amused, but it didn't last. He sat back and crossed his arms. "Go on, then. Explain."

"You are college. I am not college." With each explanation, she moved her hand, up and down, hoping he would finally see what she meant. "You are business owner, pilot, professional. I am cleaner. You are from good family. I am from bad family."

"Leila's from the same family you are. Why isn't she—?"

"She is different. She has always been different. Better. She escaped bad family. I only escaped because of her, you see?"

"No."

Jasmine wanted to scream in frustration. Was he being deliberately dense?

"You do not...what is word!" Her English was getting all jumbled. She was angry and frustrated, and she couldn't think. She swiped at tears, telling herself to stop her foolish crying. But how could she make herself reject this man?

And how could she not? She had no choice.

"I was with terrorists. I served terrorists. They were evil, and while they planned evil, I cooked, you see?"

She sounded ridiculous. By the time she was done, Derrick was sure to reject her. Which was what she wanted. Exactly what she wanted.

He stood, grabbed a box of tissues off an end table, and held it out to her, his expression filled with tenderness—and confusion.

She grabbed two and wiped her eyes.

"Did you choose to be there?" He perched on the arm of the sofa, giving her plenty of space. "With those terrorists?"

"It does not matter."

"It does matter, Jazz. Your choices matter very much."

Somehow, his kindness calmed her. She took a breath and leaned against the kitchen table. "There is a story in the Bible. A Canaanite woman came to Jesus and asked Him to heal her daughter. He came not for her but for the lost sheep of Israel. She appealed to Him, saying that even the dogs get the scraps. You know this story?"

Again, his eyes narrowed, only this time she wondered if he guessed where she was going. "What about it?"

"There are dogs, you see? There are people who belong and people who do not. You belong, Derrick. You and your family, you are good people. You are...chosen. I am grateful that Jesus loves even the dogs who don't belong. I know who I am."

He stared at her for a long time, and there was a moment when she thought she saw a flicker of understanding in his eyes. That tiny flicker nearly cracked her heart into a million pieces.

But then he shook his head. "I'm trying to understand, I really am. But you're not a Canaanite, and neither am I. And neither one of us is Jewish, either. We were not born as children of Abraham, but if God chose us, then we're chosen. That's how it works." Derrick walked toward her, slowly, deliberately. "God doesn't have a caste system, sweetheart."

The closer he got, the faster her heart raced. "Do not. You do not understand. Even my twin would not have come back for me. Even for her, I was not worthy."

"Leila doesn't define your worth, Jasmine."

"Mama loved Leila and died when she left. Baba loved Mama and fell apart when she died. Nobody loved me."

"God loves you. Doesn't He count?"

What she couldn't say, what she never wanted to have to say to Derrick, was the ugliest truth of all. That her father had seen her as a slave, never a daughter. And then a liability. He'd sold her to the first person willing to take her off his hands. To a man who saw her not as a beloved wife but as a concubine, a means to an end.

"I am not somebody who people love," she said. "I am not what you think. And it will not work."

He stopped a foot away from her. "You are precious and beautiful, Jasmine, and no matter how hard you try to talk me out of it, I love you."

No.

He couldn't. He couldn't possibly.

"I'm sorry if that makes you uncomfortable, but..." He shrugged. "It is what it is."

Emotion clogged her throat, but she forced words past it. "Then you are a fool." Before he could say anything else, she escaped to her bedroom.

CHAPTER TEN

Derrick stared at the closed door. It was probably a good thing there was a little boy sleeping in Jasmine's room. If not for Rabie, Derrick might storm in there and demand an explanation.

Which would be unacceptable, of course.

But, *come on.*

Her whole argument made no sense. She was unlovable because her parents had been stupid?

He obviously couldn't love her because they hadn't?

What in the world had her parents done to her to make her feel so unloved?

And what could Derrick do to prove to her how precious she was?

Could he change her mind? If he did, would she be open to him? Or was he fooling himself? Was her speech all some big, roundabout way of saying, *It's not you, it's me?*

His phone rang, the trill too loud in the silence.

He snatched it off the coffee table and swiped to answer the call.

"Just got your message," Michael said. "What's up?"

Perfect. Because he'd already been in such a great mood.

"Jasmine asked me for a favor," Derrick said, "and I...probably should have said no."

"Hmm. We all know how good you are at that." Michael sounded amused.

"Yeah, well, in this case..." Derrick explained what she'd asked—and the plan they'd come up with. "We figured it'd be easy. Just meet them at the hotel, get them in the car—"

"Wait a minute," Michael said. "Please tell me you're calling because you're having second thoughts."

"I wish."

"You're saying you did this? You're in DC? Did you get them, her friends?"

"Things didn't go exactly like we'd hoped."

"Explain."

Derrick told his brother about the botched rescue mission and the harrowing escape. "I had a feeling we might be followed, so I rented a nondescript car. I lost them in the city traffic."

There was a beat of quiet, and then Michael exploded. "Are you out of your flipping mind? What were you...?" Deep breath. "I can't believe..." Another breath. "I know exactly what happened. She batted those big eyes, and you fell all over yourself like some ridiculous smitten...flipping...kitten."

Derrick's churning frustration turned to fury. "Said the guy who disobeyed orders, flew to Iraq, and—"

"I'm a CIA agent, Derrick. I'm trained. I'm—"

"Why don't you write down everything I did wrong and go over it with me later? That'll be fun for both of us." He clamped his lips shut, took a breath. Started over. "Could we just get past the part where you tell me what a moron I am? Because I get it, all right? I get it."

Silence.

Derrick pushed his hair back. "Sorry. I'm not..." The last thing he needed was to alienate his brother. "This isn't your fault. This was all me."

"Yeah, well... I might have done the same thing, if Leila had asked me. At least you got out of there. Where are you now?"

"Hotel. We were going to fly out, but when we pulled up to the terminal, there was a guy at the door who looked like he might be a guard. We thought he was searching for us. In retrospect, I think we panicked. I can't imagine how they'd have known we'd be there—at the private terminal."

"Huh. I see what you mean."

"Then we thought someone followed us leaving Dulles, but again, we could have imagined that. Our Uber driver managed to lose the guy in the airport traffic."

"That also seems unlikely, if the person following was trained."

Maybe, under normal circumstances. But Kyle had been a little crazy.

"When we got to the hotel, I went through Rabie's clothes and backpack, just in case someone had stuck a tracker somewhere."

"Good thinking. Next time, go through the stuff before you get to the hotel. Or, better yet, just toss it all out the window. The backpack, anyway."

Next time? There wasn't going to be a *next time.* "The kid was freaked out enough. I was trying not to—"

"Better than the alternative."

True. "The point is, I didn't find anything. And if there was a tracker, wouldn't they have come already? Wouldn't they be here?"

"Probably."

"The thing is, I planned to get both of them, the brother and the sister. But I only got the kid. I've been watching the news, and there's nothing yet, but I'm afraid there's gonna be an Amber Alert or something. I'm thinking we should just go back to the airport and fly out."

"No. Stay where you are." Michael's voice had that big-brother authority Derrick used to find annoying. Right now, he was happy to have help. "Where were you headed after you got them?"

"No idea. Basma didn't tell us where her cousin lives."

"And there's been no indication they reported anything to the police?"

"Not that I can tell. I thought you might be able to learn more."

"I'll see what I can do. Sit tight until you hear from me. We need to move you someplace safe until we figure out what to do with the kid or hear from the sister. Do you know the family's name? You said they're diplomats?"

"That's what Jazz said. Last name is Ghazi."

"Ghazi? I've heard of him. Never anything bad. What about this brother she's afraid of? What's his name?"

"Dari."

A beat, then, "Did you say Dari? Dari Ghazi?" The tone of Michael's voice, surprise mixed with worry, had Derrick's heart rate ticking up.

"Yeah?"

Michael muttered under his breath something that sounded very much like a curse word Derrick hadn't heard from him since he was a teenager.

"What is it?"

"If it's who I think it is," Michael said, "then your girl-friend's right. He's dangerous. We've been on the lookout for him."

Well, that was something. At least Derrick's big heroic deed wouldn't be for nothing. Wasn't going to get him the girl, but maybe he could save two people some grief, assuming Basma could escape.

"Put Jasmine on the phone." Michael spoke the words like a command.

Now that Derrick had calmed down, he didn't want to face her again tonight. He needed to process everything that'd happened that day, and everything she'd said.

He figured Jasmine needed that too.

"Can it wait until morning?" he asked. "She's in the other room with Rabie. She's probably already in bed."

"It's important, Derrick."

"I get that. I'm just saying...a couple of hours. We just had a..." It was stupid. They were dealing with big international issues. People's lives and futures were at stake.

What difference did Derrick's feelings make in the grand scheme of things?

"You had a what?"

"Doesn't matter. The point is, she's not my girlfriend, but I can get her up if you want me to."

"Ah. Sorry, man." The big-brother do-what-I-say voice was gone, and Derrick wasn't a fan of the pity he heard now.

"It's fine."

After a long pause, Michael said, "I have plenty to keep me busy tonight. I need to figure out what's going on with the Ghazis, see what they're doing to locate you, find out if they've alerted the police or the FBI. And I'll get you a place to hole up."

"I can fly anywhere, just—"

"Don't go near your plane. If they are watching you, it'll lead them right to Portland, which is way too close to home."

If they saw the tail number, but how would they?

"Maybe you lost them," Michael continued. "Or maybe this is all a ruse to smoke out Leila and Jasmine's hiding place.

Until we figure out where to take the kid, you need a safe house."

"That's easy," Derrick said. "We can go to Uncle Gavin's cabin. I just have to get there."

"Not a bad idea. It's off the grid, but I don't want you telling Gavin you're there."

"Uh...why?"

"Or anyone else," Michael added quickly, but Derrick had the distinct impression he hadn't meant that. He'd meant their uncle, specifically.

Which was weird, but whatever.

"I know the door code," Derrick said. "He told me I was welcome to go there anytime I was in town."

"Let me find out where he is, make sure he's not around and the place is empty. And I'll check on the rest of this stuff. Keep your phone charged and your ringer on. Get some rest, but be ready to move when I call. Where are you exactly—address and room number."

"You're not going to return Rabie to his uncle, right?"

"Of course not. Why would you even ask?"

"Jasmine's worried."

"Wow. And here I thought she trusted me, but obviously, if she went to you—"

"She knew you wouldn't let her—"

"She's right about that. I'm trying to keep her and Leila alive."

"I know. I should've talked to you." Derrick yanked the cushions off the sofa bed and stacked them beneath the window. He wasn't tired, but he should at least try to sleep. "I think she's afraid that, since you work for the government, you might have to turn Rabie over."

"Tell Jasmine I've got my future-brother hat on, not my CIA-agent hat. She can trust me. And so can you."

"I never doubted it." Derrick gave his brother the address and their room number, then ended the call.

He unfolded the bed and made it with pillows and blankets he found in the closet.

He checked the locks on the door, turned off the lights, and settled between the sheets. It wasn't exactly sleep-number luxury, but he'd slept on worse.

Not that he'd be able to sleep after the longest, hardest day of his life. He'd practically kidnapped a kid, barely escaped a bunch of armed thugs, and lost his shot with the only woman he'd ever loved.

Talk about a red-letter day.

CHAPTER ELEVEN

When Derrick ended the call in the other room, Jasmine tiptoed to the bed, ashamed of her eavesdropping.

She'd learned to slink about like a mouse, making no noise and taking up as little space as possible. After she and Baba left Baghdad and moved to the compound, especially after she'd been joined to Khalid, she'd learned the wisdom of going unnoticed.

But she'd always listened, seeking to understand what the men were doing and thinking and feeling, knowing that the more she did, the more she could anticipate their demands. She'd learned to discern the emotional tenor in a room so she could slip away quickly, before anyone got angry. Before she could become a target or a scapegoat.

In this way, Jasmine had protected herself.

She hadn't felt the need to do that with Derrick before today, but now she dared not face him.

So she'd listened at the door like a spy.

Apparently, Derrick was satisfied that Michael would help them because he gave his brother the address of the hotel. She wished she knew everything Michael had said, but she had no courage to ask.

She set down her phone. Still no word from Basma. Though Jasmine felt too keyed up to sleep, she finished getting ready for bed and crawled between the sheets beside Rabie. She curled onto her side, away from him, replaying all the tender things Derrick had said to her. He'd called her courageous. He'd called her *sweetheart*.

He'd told her he loved her.

Tears wet her pillow. If only she could give in to what she felt inside. If only she could be who Derrick wanted her to be.

But she could not, and to wish it was more than foolishness. It was torturous.

She tried to give all her errant, inappropriate feelings to the Lord, though she felt herself snatching them back, one by one. Feelings were not grains of rice one could simply flick away. They clung like grime, impossible to remove without painful scrubbing and stinging bleach.

How did one bleach a soul?

Stupid, silly thoughts from a stupid, silly woman.

She flipped onto her other side, hoping a change of posture might change the direction of her mind.

Rabie's curly brown hair was a mop against the white pillow. His eyes were closed, the lashes brushing his cheeks. In sleep, his expression was peaceful and unafraid. His little hands were pressed together as if in prayer, tucked beneath his head.

He was precious. He didn't belong to her, and she only felt responsible for him because she loved Basma like a sister. Even so, Rabie was precious.

In her midsection, she felt the strangest tickle, soft as a bubble. Not painful, barely discernible.

She shifted to her back and pressed her palm against her abdomen.

She was nearly five months pregnant now. Dr. Wright—he insisted she call him Roger, but it felt wrong to do so—had told her she might start to feel it moving soon.

Was that what she'd felt? The child?

She had not wanted it. Every time Khalid had come to her, she'd silently prayed she wouldn't conceive. God had refused her—why did this surprise her?—and here she was, married, pregnant, and on the run.

Drawn to a man who was not her husband. Carrying a child she would have to give birth to and provide for and raise, all alone.

But the feeling came again, the slightest movement inside. A tiny life, making itself known.

Here I am, Mama.

Do you not love me?

Jasmine's tears started again.

Not an *it*. Not just *the child*. *Her* child. Her *baby*.

Like Rabie, Jasmine's baby had no control over who his family was or how they behaved. Like Rabie, her baby was precious.

And it was Jasmine's job to protect him. Hers, and nobody else's. Not just to protect him, but to love him.

She would not do what her parents had done. It didn't matter who her baby's father was. If she had the freedom to be in her baby's life, she'd love him.

Or her.

Let it be a girl, Lord.

A girl who resembled her, not like Khalid.

But even if the baby was a boy, and even if he looked just like his father, and even if he had many of his father's traits, he didn't have to *be* like the man who'd fathered him. He didn't have to be a terrorist. He didn't have to be evil. Those were choices, and her child could be raised to make good choices. He could be raised to know the truth and love God. He could be raised to be a good man, like Derrick and Michael and the other men in the Wright family.

If only Jasmine could stay hidden.

What was she doing here?

What foolishness had driven her so far from Shadow Cove and safety? Was this how she planned to protect her baby? By putting herself in danger?

What a fool she was.

For the first time since she'd received Basma's email, she understood the enormity of what she'd done.

With Derrick, she'd glossed over the danger that coming to DC would put her in.

She'd hardly considered her own safety. Maybe that was part of her problem, the belief that she only deserved to exist if she made everyone else's existence easier.

She'd spent her life sacrificing herself—her happiness, her freedom—to accommodate those around her. When she didn't willingly sacrifice herself, she'd learned the sacrifice was taken against her will, so why fight it? Why not just give in for the sake of safety and harmony and peace?

Right.

As if those had ever existed for her. They'd been elusive as wind until she'd reached Maine.

But she had found them in her new home—and then risked them. Why?

She would have to answer that question, someday, because knowing she'd put herself in danger to save her friend didn't bother her at all.

But now she saw what she'd refused to see before—that she might have put her sister in danger. And she certainly *had* put Derrick in danger.

And she'd risked her baby. Not that Basma and Rabie

weren't worth the risk, but she hadn't even considered the child she carried.

She turned to Rabie and saw again his incredible...preciousness. He was valuable because he *was*. It was that simple.

And so was Jasmine's child, regardless of who his father was.

Jasmine rubbed a hand over her belly. *I love you, my child. I will protect you.*

Fresh tears slid down her face. She did love him, and when she failed to do so, she would ask God to help her. He would, of course. It was His will that she love, certainly that she love her own child.

If only she could promise her child the love of a good father. But she would die before she let Khalid get his hands on her baby.

It wasn't Khalid's face that swam in her mind's eye, though. It was Derrick's.

No.

She curled up again, refusing to imagine what it would be like to be Derrick's wife, to have him as the father of her child.

Because she was a married woman. As much as she despised her husband, she'd taken a vow. And there was no undoing that.

Loud knocking pulled Jasmine from sleep.

She sat up, blinking in the light from the bathroom, which she'd left on for Rabie. Only darkness showed through a space between the curtains.

"Jasmine?" Derrick's voice coming from the other room was faint.

She slipped from the bed and cracked the door open.

On the other side, he wore his T-shirt and pajama pants, his hair sleep-tousled. "We need to go."

"What? Where?"

"Michael just called. He's sending someone to pick us up, and they'll be here in twenty minutes. He wants us to be ready. I need about five to get dressed, and then I can help you. What do you need?"

She was still trying to catch up. "Where are we going?"

"We'll talk about it in the car. How can I help?"

She glanced at the boy asleep in the bed. He hadn't stirred.

"I think we let him sleep, if you can carry him?"

"Sure, yeah. Open this door when you're dressed, and I'll grab the bags."

"All right."

Fifteen minutes later, she followed Derrick out of the hotel room, pulling her suitcase and his wheeled duffel bag. He carried Rabie, who'd barely stirred, the red backpack slung over his shoulder.

A thirty-something woman who'd introduced herself as Marie, a friend of Michael's, led the way to the elevators. She carried herself like a soldier, and if Jasmine wasn't mistaken, the bulge on her side indicated a weapon.

On the first floor, they walked through the lobby and out the sliding doors to a dark sedan waiting at the curb. Exhaust streamed from the back, puffy and white in the chilly December air.

A man standing beside the car scanned the area.

The woman waited until Derrick, Jasmine, and Rabie had loaded into the backseat.

Once they were all in and buckled, Rabie's head leaning on Jasmine's shoulder, the man and woman climbed in, and the woman drove out of the parking lot and toward the highway.

The dashboard clock read four thirty-two.

Marie said, "You both need to power down your cell phones."

"Why?" Derrick asked.

Jasmine pulled hers from her purse and did as she'd been told.

"Precaution," the man said.

Derrick seemed like he might argue, then turned his off and shoved it in his pocket. "What's the plan?"

Marie answered. "We're taking you to a house in Harper's Ferry."

He nodded as if this made perfect sense to him.

"What is this, a ferry?" Jasmine turned from the people in front to Derrick. "We will get on a boat?"

"It's a town," Derrick said. "There's a house there where we'll be safe."

"Whose house?"

He shook his head, gaze flicking to the people in front. Perhaps he didn't want them to know, though she couldn't imagine why, considering they were driving.

She remembered something she'd overheard on the call, something about a place he'd been told he could use anytime. Maybe that was where they were going.

"How far away?"

Marie answered. "Little over an hour, ma'am. Might as well try to get some rest."

Derrick relaxed against the headrest, apparently planning to do just that. Rabie was still asleep.

Jasmine figured it wouldn't hurt to try. She closed her eyes and prayed that, wherever they were going, they would be safe there.

It took Jasmine a few moments to remember where she was. She lay on the soft bed and glanced around at the room. She was not at the house in Shadow Cove or at the hotel where they'd eaten pizza the night before.

No, this was the new place.

They'd arrived just before dawn, when morning was coming but the world was still bathed in shades of black and gray.

Derrick had carried Rabie inside and laid him on the bed, then told her to rest.

She'd wanted to ask him where they were and why, but he'd gone straight into another bedroom and closed the door.

She couldn't blame him for not wanting to talk to her after their discussion the night before.

She'd slipped back into her nightgown and, despite all the strange events of the previous day and night, had fallen immediately asleep.

Now, she took in the space. It was a corner room, and the exterior walls were made of horizontal logs, brown and rustic, laid one atop the other to create this shelter. Curtains had been pushed to the side of large windows so that only gauzy fabric blocked the sunny day. The bedspread was white, like the curtains and the other furniture in the room, which included a small bureau, a shelving unit filled with books, and a rocking chair. On the wall opposite her, a stone fireplace rose to the ceiling.

The effect was simple and elegant.

A clock on her bedside table told her it was half past nine.

She gazed at the empty bed beside her and sat up with a start. Where was Rabie?

She stood too fast, then paused, holding onto the bed as a wave of dizziness passed.

A noise came from the other room, and she tiptoed to the door.

"What'd I tell you?" Derrick sounded amused.

"Can I have another one?" Rabie asked.

"You can have as many as you want."

Since they seemed to be doing fine without her, she washed her face and changed her clothes before following the voices out of the bedroom and down a narrow hallway, inhaling the scent of frying oil and something she couldn't identify.

She stepped into a space she'd learned was called a great room, which had a living area, dining area, and kitchen with no walls separating them. It was decorated much like the bedroom had been—log walls, soft white sofas and curtains. The tables were not stark white but whitish with a little brown showing here and there. Antiques, or perhaps made to seem like they were. There were more shelving units filled with books of all sizes and colors.

Off the kitchen on one side of the house, three windows angled around a casual table for six.

There was a more formal table in the dining room on the opposite side, imposing, much darker brown than the log walls, and surrounded by twelve hefty chairs, the kind she and her sister could have shared as children—and probably could still.

Overhead, the ceiling peaked at twenty feet or more. The wall closest to her was all stone with a fireplace in the center. She stepped close, letting the flames warm her back, gazing through the tall windows on both sides of the room.

Nothing but forest all around—tall pines and stark, leafless oaks and birches and maples.

There were no other houses or structures in sight.

"You're awake." Derrick pushed up from where he'd been leaning on an island in the kitchen. He wore the pajama pants and T-shirt she'd seen the night before, along with a pair of blue slippers.

On the other side of the island, Rabie, still clad in his pajamas, sat on a stool, his little legs swinging beneath him, his curls a floppy mess. White powder rimmed his mouth. Funny how similar they looked, despite their different skin color—and facial structure. It was their matching smiles, she thought.

"Yasamin, you come try this. Derrick made donuts."

"You are a baker?" She crossed the living area to the kitchen. The light wood cabinets matched the color of the log walls. The black granite countertop was dotted with sugar—or maybe it was flour—and cinnamon, she guessed, based on the scent she picked up as she neared. There were two bowls, each filled with small donuts, and beside them, plates, forks, and napkins.

On top of the stove, a black skillet held an inch or so of oil, and by the way it sizzled, it was still hot.

She stood beside Rabie but spoke to Derrick. "I did not know you baked."

"I don't." He snatched a package from the countertop behind him and held it out to her.

She took the strangely-shaped paper, the remains of some package. She read the label. "Biscuits?"

"Canned biscuits. You know, Pillsbury?"

She didn't know, so she just shrugged.

"You just stick a hole in them," he explained, "and drop them in the oil."

"They are very good," Rabie said. "He likes the ones with the cinnamon, but I prefer the white ones."

"Powdered sugar," Derrick said. "You want one?"

"They sound very healthy."

"Sure. You got your important food groups. Bread. Vegetables."

She let her surprise show on her face, her eyebrows hiking. "Where are the vegetables?"

He pointed at the skillet. "Vegetable *oil*. Duh." He winked at Rabie, who giggled.

"You are ridiculous." She shook her head, trying to keep her lips from giving away her amusement.

"Sugar comes from a plant." Derrick nodded to a glass of milk on the counter. "And there's dairy. What are we missing?"

"The healthy part, I think."

"Killjoy." To Rabie, Derrick said, "Women."

He echoed, "Yeah. Women."

They both laughed.

She had no idea how long they'd been awake, but clearly long enough to form a bond.

Derrick took a mug from beside the coffee pot behind him. "There's no decaf, but I found some herbal tea, if you'd like. It's maple-ginger."

She started to walk around the bar. "I can make it."

He turned on the electric kettle. "Have a donut, Jazz. I got it."

Jazz.

She'd never told him how much she liked it when he called her that.

Probably, when this was all over, he'd quit calling her by the nickname. He'd quit calling her altogether.

She couldn't dwell on that or she'd get emotional like she had the night before. The thought of all the things she'd said to him and her frustration when he didn't understand warmed her cheeks.

She must not think of that. And she must never think of what *he'd* said.

Using a fork, she slid two donuts, one of each flavor, onto her plate and settled on the stool beside Rabie. She cut a bite of the cinnamon donut first and ate it.

"Well?" Rabie asked in Arabic. "It's good, right? The other one's better, though."

"English, please," she said. "It's unkind to speak in a language not everyone understands."

His gaze flicked to Derrick. "Okay."

She wrapped her arm around the boy's narrow shoulders and held him close. "I'm so glad you're here." She let him go and took another small bite, enjoying the sweetness on her tongue. "It's very good."

"Try the other one," Rabie urged.

She cut a bite of the white one and ate it.

"Good, right?" he said.

Derrick was watching her.

She swallowed. "Yes, very. Very sweet. I like them both."

"You have to pick one." Rabie sounded horrified. "Which one is better?"

"Why do I have to choose? Why can I not like them both?"

He seemed to struggle for an answer, finally saying, "I don't know. Just because."

Derrick chuckled. "Everything's a competition, don't you know?" He shook his head, focus on Rabie. "She doesn't get it."

"Girls never do."

"Ha!" Derrick punctuated the point with a fork aimed at the child. "You should meet my sister-in-law. She's the most competitive person I know, and that's saying something, considering I have five brothers."

His little eyes widened. "Five?"

"I'm the youngest. When I was born, my parents knew they'd finally gotten it right and didn't have to keep trying."

Jasmine laughed, though Rabie didn't seem to understand the joke. She took another bite of the cinnamon donut, then asked Rabie, "How did you sleep?"

"I sort of remember getting here last night. When I woke up, I heard a noise and came out to see what it was. Derrick was tearing up newspaper."

Leaning against the counter, arms crossed, Derrick gave him a fond smile but didn't interrupt.

"He let me help him build the fire."

She glanced at the flames across the room. "You did a fine job."

Rabie beamed. "He even let me use the lighter."

"Have you ever done that before?" When he shook his head, she said, "I haven't either. Maybe you could help me learn?"

His little eyes brightened. "I can teach you."

Ah, the confidence of children. "We will ask Derrick to supervise so I don't burn the house down, eh?"

That brought a solemn look. "Good idea. Women need help with these things."

Derrick cleared his throat. "We all need help when we don't know how to do stuff, don't we?" The electric kettle steamed, and he poured hot water into Jasmine's mug, added a teabag, and slid it across the bar to her, along with the sugar bowl and a spoon.

"Thank you."

He nodded but kept his focus on the boy.

Rabie didn't respond, just studied him as if he couldn't quite figure him out.

Not surprising. Derrick was different from all the men she'd known in Iraq. This culture was different. This world was different.

Rabie had probably never met a man who treated women like equals. It felt foreign to her, who'd at least understood, theoretically, that such men existed in the world. In Baghdad before Iraq fell apart, she'd seen Western men, Americans and British and others. Some diplomats and businessmen, but mostly soldiers. They treated women with respect and dignity.

Rabie hadn't had that example.

She sipped the tea, added a little sugar, and sipped again. It was strange. Sweet and sharp and unexpected.

She glanced up to find Derrick watching her.

He blinked. "Uh, is it okay? You want a glass of juice?" He headed for the refrigerator, adding, "I think there's orange—"

"No, thank you. Where did the food come from?"

Derrick returned to his side of the bar. "I guess my friend"— he mouthed *Michael*—"had the people who drove us here last night pick up some groceries, enough for a couple of days."

"And he knew about the biscuit donuts you like to make?"

"Nah. I just found the cans in the fridge. Figured nobody would mind if I cooked them up." He grabbed a sponge and started wiping the counter.

"Do we have a plan?" she asked. "What happens now?"

He stopped, gaze flicking to Rabie, who was devouring another sugary donut, his fingers and mouth covered with white.

"There's a secure VPN here that you'll need to connect to."

"I don't know what this is, VPN?"

"Uh... Virtual private network?" He said the words as if he wasn't sure either. "The point is, it'll hide where we are, even if someone's monitoring, so it's safe. As soon as you finish breakfast, we'll connect and see if you've gotten an email."

From Basma, but he didn't say so.

"As soon as we get that," Derrick continued, "I'll reach out to my guy, and we'll make a plan. Okay?"

She nodded, and he started cleaning again.

"Let me do that." She slid off the stool. "You cooked. It is only fair."

"I don't mind."

"I would like to help. You have done enough."

"Fine." He tossed the sponge in the sink. "I'll get changed."

He crossed the room and disappeared into the hallway that led to the bedrooms.

For Rabie's sake, Derrick had been kind and conversed with her, but their easy friendship was gone. If Rabie weren't here, what would their relationship be?

She had ruined it.

Maybe she wouldn't be able to fix it. Maybe it was too late. She must tell him the truth, all of it. He might not forgive her for keeping the secret, but at least he would understand.

CHAPTER TWELVE

A fter a shower and some time in prayer, Derrick emerged from the bedroom. He'd started the fire as soon as he'd awakened, thinking he'd sit by it and read his Bible. That plan had been thwarted by Rabie's early wake-up. At least he and the kid had developed a rapport.

It was Jasmine's appearance that'd rattled him. She'd pulled her hair up into a ponytail that made her look years younger, and her cheeks had been pink, as if she'd just scrubbed them. She'd been beautiful and so...guarded after their conversation the night before. Everything was different now. There'd be no going back.

He'd needed some time to think and regroup and pray.

She and Rabie were sitting on the area rug at the coffee table, engaged in a game of Connect 4.

Derrick paused in the hallway, not wanting to interrupt.

And fine. Maybe he liked watching her when she wasn't on her guard. Maybe he liked seeing her interact with the child with such kindness and patience. She'd make a wonderful mother someday.

Not to *his* kid, though. She'd need to find some pathetic

man-servant she felt was as lowly as she was. Derrick half-hoped her father would show his face in Maine. What Derrick wouldn't give to teach the guy how it felt to be treated like he didn't matter. Like he was *barely a shadow.*

A wave of fury rolled over him.

God would need to deal with Jasmine's father. And teach her who she was.

Derrick had trusted God all his life. He could trust Him with his feelings—and with the woman he loved. He would try to, anyway.

Jasmine was on her knees, studying the yellow vertical game board, her long ponytail draped over one shoulder. She dropped a red game piece into place and sat back. "Your turn."

"Ha. You can't beat me." With barely a thought, Rabie played a blue piece.

Even though Derrick hadn't been in the room, they were speaking English. Had Jasmine asked him to do that? Or had they just not switched back?

"You think so?" She dropped a red disk into a slot.

He scowled and studied the game with narrowed eyes as if nothing had ever been more important, then dropped a piece in.

They went a few more turns, and then Jasmine settled back with a grin. "It seems I *can* beat you."

Derrick expected the kid to be annoyed. Sportsmanship didn't come easily to competitive nine-year-olds. With five older brothers, Derrick had learned that lesson.

Rabie stood and shouted in Arabic. Then, he swept the board and all the pieces off the coffee table—toward Jasmine.

She curled over, ducking and wrapping her arms around her middle.

Her instinct—that self-protection, as if she expected to be harmed or hit—might as well have been a punch to Derrick's gut.

What had she endured that would cause that reaction?

The pieces scattered harmlessly across the area rug and the hardwood floor.

Rabie watched until they'd all stopped moving, then straightened his shoulders, planted his feet, and crossed his arms—the perfect King-of-Siam look—and peered down his nose at her. Though Derrick didn't understand the words he spoke, his meaning was clear.

Clean it up, woman.

But she'd recovered from her instinctive fear, sitting up once again.

Her eyebrows rose. She didn't move or cower. She didn't hop to do the bidding of a child she could toss over her knee and spank. And probably should.

Well, except the kid was nearly as big as she was, so maybe it wouldn't be as simple for her as it would be for Derrick.

He was about to step in and give Rabie another lesson on how to treat women. Not just women but humans in general. The kid needed to learn how real men behaved.

But Jasmine stood slowly. She took her time brushing off her dress, then stepped closer to him. Her expression was determined, but her dark skin was sallow, as if she were sick—or afraid. "I do not answer to you, child." Her voice was strong, regardless of what she was feeling. "Pick up every piece and return them to the box."

Rabie's face turned red with fury. "I will not."

"You will."

He lowered his chin, not in humility but as if he were about to charge.

Derrick cleared his throat and stepped into the room. He didn't say anything. Didn't move any closer. Just stood there and watched.

Rabie's eyes rounded.

Jasmine's gaze flicked from Derrick to Rabie, and he guessed she was waiting for him to come to her aid. But this was her fight, not his. He gave her the slightest *go ahead* nod and crossed his arms.

She turned back to the child. "Rabie, look at me." Only when he did—reluctantly—did she continue. "When you behave unkindly, you must apologize to those you've hurt and, if possible, undo the damage you've done." She gestured to the mess. "This was a small thing, simple to fix. But you must fix it. You must apologize to me and pick up the game—every piece. If you refuse, then you will go to the bedroom and stay there until you're ready to do what I've asked."

The kid turned to Derrick. Did he think he'd get help? No chance.

Rabie seemed to realize that. He scanned the room, and his eyes lit at the sight of his red backpack, which they'd dropped on a side table the night before. He started toward it.

Derrick got there first. "Uh-uh."

Rabie froze halfway between Jasmine and Derrick.

"If you go to your room," Jasmine said behind him, "you go without your toys."

Funny how children couldn't hide their feelings. Right now, indecision played across his face. Humble himself and obey, or sit alone in the bedroom with nothing to do.

He spun, barked something in Arabic at Jasmine, and stormed into the hallway.

A moment later, the bedroom door slammed.

Jasmine's shoulders drooped, and she sat heavily on the sofa. "I should have let him win."

"He needs to learn to be a good sport." Derrick set the backpack down again. "If he acts like that when he's nine, what's he going to be like at fifteen or twenty? Or when he has a wife and kids of his own?"

Jasmine glanced at the hallway, covering her abdomen with her hand. That was the third time she'd done that since Derrick had come out from his shower.

"Are you sick? Was it the donuts?"

"What? No, no." She lowered the hand and started to stand. "I will go talk to him."

"Give him time."

"If you say so." She dropped to her knees on the floor.

"What are you doing? You told him he needed to pick those up."

"But I should—"

"It's fine."

She sat back on her heels and gestured toward the hallway. "I made a mess of that. I made a mess of this. I must do something."

"Rabie made the mess. You did exactly the right thing."

"I did?"

"Children need to be taught. You were firm and kind. I can't imagine how you could have handled it better."

The way her expression brightened, all hopeful and encouraged, had his stupid heart flip-flopping.

"You really think so?" She soaked up his words like a wilting plant did water.

"It was perfect, but now comes the hard part. You have to wait him out."

"How do you know so much about raising children?"

He shrugged. "I don't. Just watched my parents do it, I guess. And I spent time with Daniel and Camilla when Zoë and Jeremy were little. Dan was gone a lot, but Camilla ran a tight ship."

Jasmine's gaze flicked to the hallway again, then the windows.

Though the sun was shining, the air was cold—he'd learned

that when he'd gone out for wood—and wind whistled through the trees.

"You don't think he'll try to get away?" she asked. "Go out a window?"

Derrick grinned. "Even if he managed to, this place is surrounded by a fence even I couldn't scale. But there's a crazy security system. If Rabie so much as cracks a window, we'll know." He settled on the couch adjacent to her. "As long as he's busy, let's see if your friend has reached out."

Derrick had spent enough time at his uncle's cabin over the years that getting onto the VPN was second nature. He wasn't sure exactly what Uncle Gavin did before he retired, but he got the impression it was all very hush-hush, which probably explained the whole off-the-grid cabin in the woods.

Jasmine provided her information, and he logged into her email account on one of the laptops he'd found in the basement that morning. He figured his uncle wouldn't appreciate him showing Jasmine the whole top-secret-security setup down there, considering how long he'd kept it secret from Derrick, so Derrick had just grabbed the laptop and brought it upstairs.

Now, while he waited for the thing to connect, it occurred to him that maybe Michael knew exactly what Uncle Gavin did. They were both in the hush-hush business, after all. Did they work together? Probably not, or Michael would trust him.

While Derrick waited for the connection—the VPN was always slow—he said, "Michael wants to talk to you."

Jasmine winced. "He is very angry with me, no?"

"Probably more with me. He'll get over it. He's helping us, and that's what matters."

"I should call him? It is okay to turn on my phone?"

"Uh, no. I left a message for him when I woke up. He'll call us back. Last night when I talked to him, he sounded like he recognized the name of your friend's brother. Dari Ghazi, right?"

Her eyes narrowed. "Michael knows him?"

"About him, if it's the guy he thinks it is. That's why he wants to talk to you. Is that a common name?"

"Ghazi." Her head wagged from side to side. "A little, I guess. Dari, no. It is not his whole name, I think, but shortened. Like you call me Jazz."

"A nickname. For what?"

"I have only ever heard him called Dari, but I would guess Darius or Dariush. These are common names. I will ask Basma when she emails."

"Before I forget." He lowered his voice. "We need to be careful not to say anything about where we live or my family in front of Rabie. Certainly not my last name. I screwed up this morning when I mentioned how many brothers I have." He'd realized it a minute too late. "Boneheaded move on my part. Nothing else, though, okay? God forbid his brother gets him back, we don't want to lead Dari or anyone else to you and your sister."

"I understand."

"If he asks where you live, tell him all about it, but tell him it's near a big lake, not the ocean. One of the Great Lakes. Okay?"

"These are the ones in the middle of the country, on top?"

"Yup. That's them. Tell him you live in...Michigan. They both begin with M. Should be easy to remember."

"Michigan on a Great Lake."

"Exactly."

Her emails had loaded—there were just a handful, all from the same account. He turned the screen to face Jasmine.

142

She leaned in and frowned. "Nothing new." When she gazed up, her eyes were filled with fear. "What if they've hurt her? Perhaps she is not all right. What will we do?"

It was instinct, the way he reached for her hand and squeezed. He hadn't even realized he'd done it until it was too late. He let go and put more space between them. "Don't borrow trouble." Before she could ask or give him that *I don't understand what you mean* look he found adorable, he added, "Don't get ahead of yourself. Don't worry until you have more information."

"This is to borrow trouble?"

"Right. Like...you're imagining there'll be trouble in the future and taking it on now, I guess. Or at least worrying about it now." He'd never analyzed the cliché. That was one of the things he liked about being with Jasmine—the way she kept him thinking, considering his words carefully. Not just his words, though. His actions.

He enjoyed teaching her what it meant to be treated like a lady. He enjoyed opening the door for her, pulling out her chair. He enjoyed standing when she approached a table to show her respect and serving her a donut and a cup of tea. After what he'd learned the night before, he understood that she'd been treated as nothing more than a servant most of her life, and it made him want to serve her more.

He loved seeing her confused expression when she couldn't figure out what he was talking about. He loved the wonder in her eyes when she saw something she'd never imagined—like aisles and aisles of food at Walmart.

The first time he'd taken her with him to the grocery store— just to pick up a couple of things for dinner—she'd quizzed him for an hour in the produce section, wanting to know the name and flavor of all the fruits and vegetables she'd never seen before. He'd spent a hundred bucks so she could try one of everything.

Just to make her smile.

There was no smile on her face now, only a sad frown as if she guessed his thoughts. She blinked and turned away, her palm resting once again on her abdomen.

She'd been so sick when he'd first met her, given to random bouts of vomiting. It'd gone away pretty quickly. She'd been gaunt then, skin and bones, her olive skin almost greenish. But she'd put on weight since she'd come to the US. In fact, he'd even noticed the slightest paunch in her midsection when she'd worn the short sweatshirt and sweatpants the day before. Not fat—not even close—but not the flat stomach her twin sister had. He never saw Jasmine's figure, thanks to the shapeless clothes she always wore, but he'd always assumed she had the same trim figure as Leila.

He was glad she'd put on weight. She'd certainly needed it. The last thing he wanted was for her to get sick again, but maybe the stress they were under was causing her to feel ill.

"I should have fed you something healthier for breakfast. There's some fruit in there."

She yanked the hand away from her belly as if it'd been caught in a cookie jar.

Weird.

"Do you need something to settle your stomach?"

"I am not sick." She crossed her arms and glanced toward the hallway. "Should I check on him?" She looked in Derrick's direction but didn't quite meet his eyes.

What was going on?

Was she lying? Why lie about being sick?

He wanted to press her, to demand she tell him all her secrets. But they were none of his business.

"I'll check on Rabie."

She agreed, and he pushed to his feet and headed for the bedroom Jasmine and Rabie had shared the night before.

He knocked. "Mind if I come in?" Getting no answer, he pushed the door open and stepped inside.

Rabie had pulled the curtains closed. With no lights on, the room was dim and gloomy. The boy lay curled up on the bed, only his messy hair and the top of his head showing.

Derrick sat beside him and patted the little hip sticking up beneath the covers. "How you doing, buddy?"

One little shoulder moved. "I want Basma."

"I know." Derrick's heart broke for the kid. "We're doing our best to get you back to her, I promise."

Rabie didn't say anything, but it was obvious by his shaking shoulders that he was crying.

"You want to tell me what happened out there. Why'd you get so mad?"

"Girls aren't supposed to beat boys."

"Who told you that?" When he said nothing, Derrick guessed. "Do you usually beat your sister at games?"

"Uh-huh."

"Any chance she lets you win?"

Another shrug seemed the only answer he was going to get.

"Sometimes, men lose games. It doesn't matter who you lose to. It matters *how* you lose. You can be gracious—smile and say congratulations. When you get big, you'll even have to shake hands and say things like 'good game.' Even if you're frustrated or angry, you can be polite. That's how strong men behave. It is not mature or manly to throw a temper tantrum. Have you ever seen a strong man throw a temper tantrum?"

No response.

"It's pretty funny to think about, isn't it? Imagine some big, strong man lying on the floor, banging his hands and fists." Derrick smiled as he said the words, trying to be funny.

The kid didn't laugh, but maybe he stilled a little. Maybe he stopped crying.

"None of us is perfect," Derrick said. "We all mess up sometimes, which makes it easy to forgive when people are honest about their mess-ups. So the solution, when you do something you shouldn't, is just what Jasmine said. You apologize—which means saying you're sorry and asking for forgiveness—and then, if you can, you fix the mess you made. In this case, you can."

Again, no response.

He didn't have enough experience with kids to know what to do next. He hadn't been around a lot of them, just Daniel's kids, and they'd never lived nearby.

Derrick had been fifteen when Daniel and Camilla were expecting Zoë, their oldest, and he'd spent a lot of his school breaks with them that year, helping with their fixer-upper. Though Daniel was as handy as Derrick—Dad ensured his sons knew how to take care of a house and car—Daniel hadn't had much time away from the hospital in those days. The brothers between Daniel and Derrick had been too busy with high school and college—and the Army, in Grant's case—and girls and sports to help.

But Derrick had been eager to spend time with his oldest brother and new sister-in-law. Those were good days, when life was simple. He knew who he was and had been confident that his life would turn out just as he planned it.

He'd earn his pilot's license—he'd nearly earned his solo license by then—and after he finished college, he'd get a job with a charter company to gain flying hours while he saved up to buy his own plane.

And when he met the right girl, he'd fall in love, and she'd love him back.

How hard could it be?

After all, it'd worked out for Daniel.

146

Derrick had been a cocky kid, not all that different from the cocky kid lying on the bed right now.

But Daniel had done it right, and Derrick had wanted what he had. A good career, a decent place to live, and a loving wife.

Derrick could still picture Camilla, the way she oversaw the renovations of their house, turning the old place they'd bought in St. Louis into a home. She'd stand in the middle of the wreckage of one of the rooms, one hand tapping her nose, deep in thought, the other resting on her swollen abdomen protectively like...

His thoughts stilled.

He blinked in the silence, images of Jasmine flashing across his mind like a slideshow.

The nausea when he'd first met her—which had gone away so abruptly.

The rapid weight gain.

The little belly she hid under the loose clothing.

Just a few minutes before, in that instant of fear when Rabie had lost his temper, she'd curled up, protecting not her head but her abdomen.

Derrick lurched to his feet, the motion so abrupt that Rabie whipped around with wide eyes.

"Sorry, bud. You...uh..." He raked a hand through his hair. "Come out when you're ready to apologize." He didn't wait for a response, just turned and fled.

CHAPTER THIRTEEN

A door closed, and Jasmine twisted toward the hallway, expecting Derrick and Rabie to step in. Instead, Derrick passed without glancing her direction.

His door slammed.

Was he angry with Rabie or with her? Or had Michael called?

But Michael wanted to speak to her, so that couldn't be it.

Maybe Derrick had no desire to spend time with her, and for that, she couldn't blame him.

She checked the screen, but Basma still hadn't emailed.

Restless, Jasmine stood. The game pieces were still scattered on the floor, and she itched to pick them up if for no other reason than to have something to do. But she didn't. Derrick had told her she'd done the right thing with Rabie. Why give him another reason to be disappointed in her?

She'd cleaned the kitchen thoroughly already, and the house was spotless, not a speck of dust to be found. She added a log to the fire and used one of the tools beside it to get it burning, then watched as flames licked the wood, finally catching.

She wandered to the bookshelves but found nothing she wanted to read.

A long table behind the sectional caught her eye. Photographs had been artfully arranged, all of the same people at different ages, a family. There was one man, tall and dark-haired, like Derrick, though much older. He seemed familiar, somewhat like Dr. Wright—Roger, Derrick's father. Could this be a relative? Perhaps Derrick's uncle?

That made sense. Hadn't Derrick said something about an Uncle Gavin in the conversation she'd eavesdropped on the night before? This house must belong to him.

The rest of this branch of the Wright family was very different from Derrick's, though. The only one who seemed old enough to be Gavin's wife was tall with silvery-blond hair and blue eyes. There were five others, all women. Three had varying shades of blond hair, like their mother, one had brown hair, and one had dark red hair that Jasmine thought must not be natural. She found the photo she guessed was the most recent and tried to work out their ages. The one who looked the youngest was probably in her early twenties, tall and willowy. There were a number of photos of her, some on the deck of a boat, her long blond hair flying behind her with the wind. She seemed free and full of joy.

The middle three—she assumed as much, anyway—were pictured together often. Redhead, blonde, and brunette. She couldn't tell who was older or younger, only that they seemed close, always hugging or standing shoulder to shoulder, cheek to cheek, smiling at the camera.

Jasmine lifted a photo of the one who must be the oldest. She had her mother's silvery-blond hair and the slender figure of the youngest, though nobody would call her willowy. She was slender but somehow tough, like she could defend herself. Though she smiled in a few photographs, she never wore the joyful look of abandon Jasmine saw on her younger sisters' faces.

"That's Alyssa."

Jasmine jumped, swiveling toward the voice.

Derrick's gaze flicked to her stomach, and she yanked her hand away, shifting to set the photo down.

"Sorry. I was just... Sorry."

"No need to apologize. That's my cousin. Alyssa."

"She is the oldest, no?"

"How'd you know?"

Jasmine shrugged. "She just looks it."

"She's only a year older than her sister. Irish twins, Dad always called them."

"I guess it is how she holds herself," Jasmine said. "She has that protective look of an older sibling. A little tough. A little guarded."

Derrick studied the picture. "I can see that."

"This is your uncle's cabin, then. He resembles your father."

"You think?" Derrick looked at one of the photos of Gavin. "They're so different, but I guess I see what you mean." Derrick continued into the kitchen and grabbed a glass. "You want some water or tea or something? There might be some lemonade."

"Water, I guess."

He took a second glass. "Bring the computer. Let's sit in here." He nodded toward the round kitchen table by the bay windows.

She did, choosing a chair that would give her a view of the outside. The cushion was upholstered with a pretty yellow-and-blue plaid, which matched a vase of silk flowers in the center of the table.

Outside, the forest seemed to stretch forever.

"We are far from Washington, DC, here, are we not?"

Derrick set down her drink, along with a sleeve of crackers, and sat. "Sixty, seventy miles, but it feels like a long way. We're in West Virginia."

"We were in Virginia yesterday, right?"

"Right."

"These states are very small."

"They're bigger out west. We didn't get that deep into Virginia, either. Just skimmed the border."

"I see."

He nudged the crackers toward her. "I thought you might be hungry."

Thoughtful, as always. She was a little. She hadn't finished the donuts, which had been too sweet and too heavy. She took a couple of crackers and nibbled one.

He nodded to the laptop. "I guess Basma hasn't emailed?"

She glanced at the laptop, just in case, then shook her head. "Did Michael call?"

"Nope." He checked the watch he always wore, a hefty stainless steel one that had probably been expensive, not that she knew anything about men's watches. "Weird. He almost had me wake you up last night, and here it is, almost eleven, and nothing."

"He must be busy."

"I left him another message."

She took a cracker, broke it, and ate half.

"Are you pregnant?"

His question brought a gasp that had her inhaling cracker crumbs. She spluttered and coughed.

"Dang. Sorry. I shouldn't have..." He jumped up and hovered over her, his hand on her back. "What can I do? Are you okay?"

She sipped her water, coughed again. Trying to breathe. Trying to think. Because...

How in the world had Derrick guessed her secret?

"What can I do?" he asked again. "Do you need—?"

"I'm all right." Her voice was croaky and rough. She cleared her throat, sipped more water. It took a few moments, but when she thought she could talk, she tried again. "Really."

Derrick moved back to his seat. She was afraid to look at him, but when she did, his expression surprised her almost as much as his question had. In his eyes she saw not condemnation but kindness.

She felt the most amazing...tenderness. Gentleness and patience.

She couldn't bear it.

She turned away, staring out the window at the stark trees, bent by the wind. How lovely the sight would be in the summertime, all green and lush, the skeletal branches hidden by the foliage.

Even a layer of snow would add a hint of beauty. Not the ugly nakedness displayed there now.

"Jazz?"

"I was going to tell you." She forced herself to meet his eyes. "I decided last night I would tell you today."

Derrick's expression didn't waver. He held very still. Only his Adam's apple moved as he swallowed. "Do you want to tell me about it?"

She shrugged. "What is to tell? Your father says the baby is healthy."

Derrick's eyes squeezed shut. "Dad knows."

It wasn't a question, so she didn't say anything.

A moment passed, and then he said, "Michael knows."

Also not a question, but now Derrick opened his eyes and watched her.

She dipped her head.

By the way he winced, the acknowledgment had inflicted a wound.

"I did not tell him," she hurried to say. "He guessed, on your plane, on the way from Greece because I had been so sick. Even Leila hadn't realized."

Derrick rubbed his lips together, took a long breath. "That makes sense."

"And your father... I needed a doctor. I couldn't keep food down. Michael arranged for me to see him right after we arrived."

"You don't owe me an explanation."

"But you are my friend."

"I thought I was."

Tears stung, and she turned, ashamed of them. Ashamed of herself. Just...ashamed. She covered her face with her hands, wishing for a better hiding place.

The chair scraped, and she was sure Derrick was going to walk away.

But he brushed his hand over her hair. "I'm sorry, sweetheart. I shouldn't have said that." He scooted the chair closer and wrapped his arm around her shoulders. "Forgive me. Please."

"You did nothing wrong." She wiped her tears and forced her hands to her lap. He was so close that his breath warmed her cheek. "You are always kind."

He gazed beyond her, out the windows. "You can talk to me about...whatever. I'm happy to listen. If you want to talk about how it happened, or..." He seemed to struggle, then forced out, "the...father, I can—"

"I do not." She ducked out from under his arm and leaned away.

"Um... Okay. I was just wondering if maybe..." Derrick looked stricken—as if she'd slapped him. And knocked him over. And then kicked him. "Is he the reason you don't... You're

153

not...?" Derrick took a breath. "Did you love him very much? Do you—?"

"Stop." She stood and backed up. "I do not wish to talk about him. Or this. I cannot."

"I'm sorry." He shoved his fingers through his hair, and she felt terrible.

She should tell him everything. It was only shame that kept her quiet, but not telling him would make this worse.

She was a coward.

Courage, Lord. I need courage to speak. And the words to say, please. And...

"Yasamin?"

She spun at the sound of her Iraqi name.

Rabie stood in the middle of the kitchen, gaze flicking between her and Derrick. "I'm sorry I was mean." He spoke in English, adding, "I'm supposed to ask you if it's okay that I'm sorry or something." He turned to Derrick. "I forget what you said."

Derrick cleared his throat. "Yeah, uh. You say, 'Will you forgive me?' Basically, you're giving her the option to accept your apology or not."

Rabie focused on Jasmine again and spoke with great solemnity. "If I clean up the mess, will you forgive me?"

"Yes." She forced a smile, dropping to her knees. "Yes, of course I will. Can I have a hug?"

He moved into her arms, and she held on tight.

She had done this right. This one thing, with this one child who didn't belong to her. Maybe it meant she wouldn't mess up her own child too badly, the way she'd messed up her friendship with Derrick.

If she could be a good mother, maybe her child could be more like him and Leila and the rest of the Wrights. Perhaps, if she could be very, very smart and very, very wise, her child could be worthy of love.

CHAPTER FOURTEEN

After Rabie put away the game, he grabbed the Uno cards, and the three of them sat at the coffee table in front of the fire and played. Derrick tried to make conversation, and he could tell Jasmine was working at it as well, but it wasn't easy. Fortunately, the kid seemed oblivious to the tension.

Jasmine played a card, and Derrick glanced at his hand, grabbed the first yellow one he saw, and dropped it on the discard pile.

He still couldn't believe it.

She was *pregnant*.

She'd been pregnant when she'd left Iraq in October, two months before. As long as Derrick had known her. But she had to be more than two months along. Didn't morning sickness end after the first three? Not that Derrick had that much experience, but people talked about this kind of thing. Had her morning sickness ended, or had Dad given her something to make it stop?

Was morning sickness curable?

If it were, why would any woman have it?

And there'd been that tiny belly. When did a woman start showing a pregnancy? Summer was five months pregnant, maybe six, and she barely had a belly. So was Jasmine farther along? Or was it not that simple? He had no idea.

He itched to get on the laptop and do some research, but he'd agreed to play a few games of Uno. He could wait.

Besides, the answers he most needed wouldn't be found on the internet.

"Your turn," Rabie said.

Derrick saw the blue card on the pile. His only blue card was a reverse-direction, so he plopped that down, earning a scowl from the kid.

Jasmine said, "To me, yes? Yay!" She sounded overly chipper, faking it, just like he was. She played a card.

Rabie did next, and then Derrick had to draw from the pile. He'd lost count by the time he grabbed the right number, changing the color back to yellow.

He was replaying Jasmine's reaction when he'd asked if she loved the baby's father. Her lip had curled. Had that been... disgust?

Why would she be with a man who—?

"Uno!" Rabie announced.

Jasmine groaned. "Oh, no."

Derrick fanned out his cards and gave her a look. "We're in trouble."

"We must work together to defeat him."

Work together? He liked the sound of that. Would that they could work together on more than just a stupid card game.

His mind circled back to the question. Why would she be with a man who disgusted her, unless...?

Oh.

Oh, man.

Had she been...?

That had to be it. There was no other explanation that made sense, not with a woman like Jasmine. Hadn't she told him she was the obedient one? She would never have disobeyed her father by sneaking off with some guy. She would never have dishonored him that way. Which meant some man had forced himself on her.

Cold fury stole over Derrick. What kind of man would take advantage of a woman like Jasmine—tiny, defenseless, afraid.

What had Michael said back at the house a couple days before, that Derrick's feelings for her might change once he knew the truth?

If Michael thought that, then he didn't know Derrick at all.

"I win!"

Whoops. Derrick had played that all wrong. Not that he'd been paying a whit of attention. He smiled and high-fived him. "Nice going, kiddo. Good game."

Rabie beamed.

Jasmine gathered the cards and started shuffling them. It was a huge deck, and Derrick held his hand out. "Let me help."

But a phone rang. Had to be Michael.

Derrick sprang to his feet and hurried to the cordless handset he'd left in the kitchen. "Hello?"

"It's me," Michael said.

If anything, Derrick's fury only ramped up. "Hold on." He hurried into his jacket and zipped it up. He didn't need Jasmine or Rabie overhearing this conversation.

"Can you put Jasmine on?" Michael asked.

"First, you and I are going to talk." He stepped outside and slammed the door behind him. The air was aggressively cold, dry and brittle. A stiff breeze carried away the vapor of his breath as he marched across the small yard to the line of trees and stepped beneath them. They blocked most of the wind, at least. "She's pregnant."

"She finally told you."

"*You* should have told me!"

"It wasn't—"

"I'm in love with her." Derrick was shouting, but he couldn't seem to stop. All the frustration and anger and worry and...all of it, everything he couldn't unload on Jasmine burst out. "You knew, and you said nothing."

"I told her to tell—"

"What about loyalty, huh? What about brotherhood? What about—?"

"I'm loyal." Michael sounded...hurt.

Derrick didn't care. "You and your"—he swallowed a word he was shocked even came to mind—"secrets. You just love knowing things nobody else does. Does it make you feel superior?" He needed to stop. He was being irrational, throwing a temper tantrum just like Rabie had.

If he didn't stop, he'd shred their relationship. He'd say something he couldn't take back. Maybe already had.

He clamped his lips shut, swallowing the rest of the vitriol like poison.

"Are you done?" Michael's voice was even.

Derrick's fury faded. It wasn't Michael he was angry with. Not *only* Michael, anyway. "You should have told me."

"She's Leila's sister, Derrick." His words were even, holding none of the emotion Derrick had just unloaded. "She's going to be *my* sister. I'm loyal to you, but I have to be loyal to her too. I hated not being able to tell you."

Derrick stared at the ground beneath his sneakers. Dirt, dead leaves, fallen pine needles. The scent of earth and forest reminded him of home and his childhood. He leaned back against a thick oak. "You told Dad." He sounded like a pouty child.

"She needed a doctor."

"Does Mom know?"

"Not unless Jasmine told her, and I don't think she did."

So it wasn't as if they all knew. Bad enough they all knew Derrick was in love with her. How horrifying to think they'd all been waiting for him to learn this secret, watching like it was some melodrama playing out in real time.

"Leila knows, obviously," Michael added. "Sophie might know, but she lives with them, so it would make sense they'd talked about it. And I should tell you..." If Derrick didn't know his brother better, he'd say Michael sounded nervous.

Which made Derrick nervous.

"I told Bryan, a couple weeks ago."

Bryan knew? Derrick's best friend? Even *he* hadn't said anything?

He lowered his head and massaged the back of his neck with frigid fingers. This was humiliating on so many fronts.

"He was going to Europe to do that thing for me," Michael said, "and... I felt like he needed to understand how important it was to keep their whereabouts secret."

Derrick snapped his gaze up, wishing he could look Michael in the eyes, not that he ever gave away information he didn't intend to share. "What does that have to do with her being pregnant?"

"Did she tell you... How much did she tell you?"

"She hasn't told me anything. I figured it out about the pregnancy. Is that who's after her? The father? I thought the people who followed her and Leila were all killed on that boat. Well, except her dad and uncle, but you're saying—"

"Jasmine can explain."

"Just tell me!" He winced at his demanding tone. He was the brother who held everyone together, not the one who made demands and shouted accusations.

But...but this was too much.

"It's still not my place to tell her story. Put her on the phone." Michael tagged on a "please," but it wasn't a request.

"Fine." Derrick turned and headed back to the house, still angry but also...worried. "I'm sorry I said all those things." He ground out his apology, knowing he owed it, even if he didn't feel it. "I shouldn't have, and—"

"Why are *you* sorry?" Michael sounded genuinely confused. "You have every right to be ticked. I did what I had to do, but if I were you, I'd want to punch me. Not that you should try it, 'cause, you know, I'd throttle you."

"You wish." Derrick tried to match his brother's joking tone. "I didn't mean what I said, you know, about the secrets. I was just..." What? What was he? Hurt, but he wasn't going to say that. "Are we good?"

"I'm good if you are."

"I...will be. I'm just... I'll get there."

"Fair enough," Michael said.

Just like that, it was over.

Huh.

Derrick returned to the house, where Jasmine stood in the living room, waiting for him. Rabie wasn't in sight.

"I asked him to play in the bedroom for a few minutes," Jasmine said.

"Good." Derrick held out the phone. "You should probably go into the kitchen."

She took the handset and walked away, perhaps hoping for privacy.

But Derrick wasn't going to make it easy for her to keep secrets. He'd had enough of those, both from his brothers and from the woman he loved.

CHAPTER FIFTEEN

"What do you know about Dari Ghazi?" Michael asked.

Jasmine stopped near the window beside the kitchen table and gazed at the deep forest, feeling more isolated than she had since she'd escaped Iraq. She hadn't realized how much Derrick's friendship meant to her until it was gone. Yes, she had Leila and Michael, but they had each other. She was back to being barely a shadow.

This was not the time for such dreary thoughts. "I only met Dari once. He is polite and charming on the surface, but there is something about him that is like a tiger, you know? Like he is... stalking?"

"Predatory?"

"This is a good word. But also sneaky. I think, even if Basma had not told me about him, he would have made my skin crawl."

"What'd she tell you?"

"When she was a child, he used to frighten her. She said he was always kind when people were around, always well-behaved. But when nobody was watching, he found pleasure in scaring her. He did not hurt her or even touch her. But she said his presence was...like a monster? I cannot think of a good word for it."

"Menacing?"

"I do not know."

"It sort of means threatening, but maybe a little more dangerous, a little more hidden. Not that I'm Noah Webster, so—"

"Who is this Noah Webster? This is somebody I should know?"

He chuckled. "Nobody. Never mind. So Basma told you he was like that, and when you met him, you could see it?"

"Not see, but feel." Maybe Michael would think she was crazy, but she was only trying to be honest. "This makes sense to you?"

"I get that. Can you describe what he looked like?"

"It has been many years. I think he was not as tall as you and your brothers. His hair is curly. It was short then, and he had a beard. Brown eyes and thick eyebrows. He was not handsome and not ugly. He had the kind of face nobody would notice, you see?"

"Anything more specific?" Michael asked. "Take your time."

She'd never been good at recalling what people or places looked like. She'd never been one who remembered things in pictures, instead holding memories in words and scents and feelings. She closed her eyes and willed herself back to that moment in the courtyard behind Basma's house. She and Basma had been chatting while they kicked a soccer ball with Rabie—who'd been three or four at the time.

Dari had stepped outside from the house, and Basma's laughter had cut off as if clipped with a knife.

Though Dari did nothing but join the game, it felt like when a thick cloud blocks the sun, and the wind blows, and everything changes.

The air crackled with tension.

Dari and Rabie kicked the ball. Basma and Jasmine faded to the courtyard wall. Basma seemed to shrink in on herself.

When Dari tired of the game, he walked toward them and stopped a little too close to Jasmine. He didn't touch her, but she could feel his regard, the way he studied her as if she were an interesting...exhibit. Or perhaps an animal caught in a trap. There was an odd snapping and grinding in her memory.

Basma introduced her. They chatted. It was all very polite.

Even so, she'd been afraid. As soon as Dari had gone inside, Basma insisted Jasmine leave. She'd felt like a coward for abandoning her friend, but she'd done it, happy for once to return to her own house. Baba was grief-stricken and barely spoke to her, but at least he was safe.

Jasmine opened her eyes and focused on the log house around her. "He carries an arrogance, as if he is above everyone. Also, I remember that he had a cigarette lighter, not the kind you throw away, though. You know what I mean?"

"Yup."

"He would open it, light it, then close it, over and over. It is a strange thing and probably not helpful."

"It is," Michael said. "Very helpful. I'll show you a picture when I can so you can confirm it, but for now, I can tell you this. If this guy is who I think he is—and from your description, I'm almost a hundred percent sure he is—then your friend is right. He's a psychopath, and she was wise to run."

"But she is not free, right?"

"Actually... Is Derrick there? I need to give both of you an update."

She turned to call him, but he was leaning against the kitchen counter, arms crossed, watching her. "He is here."

"Can you put the phone on speaker?"

"Um...I don't know." She crossed toward Derrick. "He wants us both to hear. Is there a way?"

"Sure." He took it from her and pressed a button. "We're here."

"Is the kid nearby?"

"He's in the other room," Derrick answered.

"Okay, good," Michael said. "I managed to get a private conversation with the uncle this morning."

"You're in DC?" Derrick asked.

"Sent Leila, Bryan, and Sophie home and came straight here. I'm flying overseas later, but I wanted to put out some feelers, figure out what's going on. I went to Ghazi's hotel and managed to get a private word with him. He told me that when you showed up, Derrick, his security team thought you were up to something. They'd gotten a tip that someone might try to kidnap Basma and Rabie. That's why they were staying so close. After you and the kid took off, Basma ran the other way, and the team was... Well, I'm guessing they were confused, though Ghazi didn't say that. One of them followed her, one followed the kid. They both got away."

Jasmine asked, "She got away—?"

"—That's not what happened." Derrick spoke at the same time, adding, "There were more than two. They followed—"

"The uncle claims to have no idea who followed you."

"How can that be?" Derrick's tone was more irritated than confused. "The guard made a call. I saw him—"

"To hotel security," Michael explained. "The story checks out."

"Okay, but..." Derrick shook his head. "Even if that's true... What's the uncle doing to find them?"

That was not the right question. Frustration hummed inside Jasmine. Where was Basma? Why didn't Derrick ask that?

"Claims he's not going to search for them," Michael said. "He seemed sorry that he hadn't taken her seriously when she begged him not to make her and Rabie go live with Dari, and he'd ignored her. He was justifying himself, though, you know how you do, right? 'I didn't have any choice. He is their brother.' He actually told me to tell them—"

"Where is Basma?" Jasmine gasped and slapped a hand over her mouth. She should not have interrupted. She looked at Derrick, expecting him to scowl at her or demand she be quiet.

He reached toward her, and she couldn't help the wince. But he squeezed her wrist, the slightest touch, reassuring her with his kindness. "You're right. I got distracted."

"Sorry, sis," Michael said. "I should have led with that." Michael also didn't sound angry. And he called her *sis,* which he did sometimes, as if she were already his sister. And to him, that didn't mean control. It meant devotion and brotherly love.

She should know these men better than to expect anger from them. Even so, their kindness sent tingles to her eyes.

"Ghazi said Basma escaped, but somehow, in the melee, she dropped her phone." Michael related the information calmly. "The security guys grabbed it. They thought Ghazi could hack into it to figure out where she was going."

"Did he hack it? Maybe this is why Basma hasn't emailed. Maybe she fears he'll find her emails to me."

"Maybe," Michael said. "But he's not looking for her, or at least he claims he's not. In fact, he gave me the phone."

"He is letting her go?" Jasmine asked. "You really believe this?"

"That's what he said."

"But we were followed." Derrick turned Jasmine's way. "I'm not crazy. We *were* followed, right?"

"I think. I saw one SUV."

"You were." Michael sounded confident. "Checked the CCTV footage, and you were followed by three SUVs. I'm impressed you lost them."

"If they weren't Ghazi's men," Derrick asked, "then who were they?"

"Our guess is that Dariush suspected Basma might try to run and assigned them to watch her. The question is why. Why did he care that much if they got away?"

"They are his family." Derrick was nodding his agreement. To the phone, she said, "You do not think this is enough?"

"He wasn't close to them, right?" Michael asked. "And he hasn't lived in Iraq for years. As far as I can tell, he barely knows them. I'm not saying he doesn't care. But why does he care enough to move back to Baghdad to take responsibility for them? And to hire guards to ensure they don't get away? Do you think he loves them?"

"I do not think he is capable," she said. "Control, perhaps?"

"Maybe."

"I don't know." Derrick's lips squished together the way that told her he was considering something. "Not that I know anything about him, but wouldn't a guy like that have higher aspirations than to control his siblings? What's in it for him?"

"Exactly." Michael sounded impressed. "That's exactly what I want to know. I can't imagine Dariush Ghazi doing this unless there was something meaningful—something *valuable*—in it for him. Jasmine, how long did they live next door to you?"

"They moved in around the time when Mama got sick, but Dari didn't live there. He is much older than Basma."

"And you only met that one time." It wasn't a question, so Jasmine didn't respond. "Did he know your father?"

"He never came for tea, and Baba barely left the house in those days. Why?"

"Because Dariush Ghazi was working with your uncle. With Hasan Mahmoud."

"What?" Jasmine tried to put the pieces together in her mind. "That does not make sense. How did they know each other? I cannot imagine how that happened. I never heard his name mentioned. I never saw him at our house or at the compound."

"I don't know what to tell you." Michael's voice was flat. "If he is who I think he is, they definitely knew each other. Which makes me wonder if this—the thing Dari will get out of all of this—has something to do with you."

"No. That cannot be."

"Why not?" Michael said something else, but his words seemed to come from far away, muffled and echoing. The world was tipping and closing in.

Because if Dariush Ghazi knew Mahmoud, then he probably knew Khalid.

And if he knew Khalid, then maybe he knew Jasmine was his wife. And if that was the case...

Was Khalid behind this whole thing?

Something scraped, and then Derrick said, "Sit down, sweetheart." He urged her into a chair he'd pulled close. "Put your head between your knees."

She did what he told her, concentrating on her breathing, trying not to think about anything but the air going in and out, in and out.

"You two all right?" Michael asked.

"I'll call you back." The phone beeped, and then Derrick crouched beside her, rubbing her back. "You're okay, sweetheart. It's okay."

But it wasn't okay.

Had this whole thing been an elaborate ruse to find her?

Had Basma been in on it?

No, of course not. She would never have betrayed Jasmine. But Dari had used her, guessing Basma would reach out to Jasmine—and Jasmine would come to her aid.

Khalid was coming for her.

All that she'd done to escape him would be undone.

Because Jasmine was a fool.

CHAPTER SIXTEEN

D errick managed to get Jasmine to drink her glass of water. She didn't drink enough fluids. Or eat enough, especially if she was eating for two.

He was still trying to wrap his mind around that.

But her dark skin still had that sallow, yellowish tint to it that told him she was ill. She wouldn't take more crackers, and she clearly wasn't up for talking. "Why don't you go lie down? You're probably exhausted."

"It is all right?" She looked up at him with those big eyes. "You don't mind?"

"Of course not." He took her hand and helped her to her feet. "Come on." He led her not to the room she'd shared with Rabie but to the one where Derrick always slept when he stayed here. Queen-size bed, heavy, masculine furniture, red-and-blue plaid comforter, it was a guy's room, unlike the one where she'd slept, all gauzy and feminine.

"What if you wish to rest?"

He shoved his things into his duffel bag. "I'll take a nap on the sofa. And this way, if Rabie wants to hang in his room, he can." Derrick straightened the covers and pulled them back, wishing he'd made the bed. "In you go."

She climbed in—and it was a climb, the bed so tall he almost gave her a boost—and curled up. She seemed tiny on the large bed, barely taking up any space at all.

"Get some rest." He tucked the covers over her, then kissed her forehead. Maybe that was too familiar, but he wanted her to feel comfortable. "You're safe here."

He stepped away, but she caught his wrist with her cool fingers. "Derrick?"

He turned back, his heart thumping far too wildly for the innocent touch. "Yeah?"

"You are very sweet. If things were different..." She released her grip and curled up again, breaking their eye contact. "I wish things were different."

She did?

Why couldn't they be? What needed to change for her to return his feelings?

He wanted to ask, but she needed rest, and his lingering while she lay in his bed didn't seem like the best idea.

He grabbed his duffel and closed the door on his way out.

After checking on Rabie, who was working a puzzle on the floor in the other room, Derrick returned to the kitchen and called his brother back.

"She okay?"

"You said this was about her," Derrick said in lieu of hello. "Not about *them,* the twins, but about her. Explain."

"Talk to Jasmine."

"Does it have to do with the baby?"

"What do you think? The kid has a father."

"Who is it? Did he...? I don't understand how it happened. What about Jasmine's father and her uncle. How could they let it happen?"

"You need to talk to Jasmine," Michael said. "I've got some information about Basma's cousin. Do you want it or not?"

What Derrick wanted was to grill his brother about Jasmine and the baby and the man who'd fathered it. "Fine. What?"

"Basma said her mother has a cousin in the US. She actually has two who relocated here, but one was about twenty years older and moved away when Basma's mother was a little girl. We assume it's the other cousin Basma reached out to."

"How did you already figure all this out?"

"I've got a couple of connections." Michael's voice was deadpan, and maybe it had been a stupid question. He was in the CIA, after all. "We got a whole team on this. Everybody wants to catch Dariush Ghazi."

"What's so special about him?"

"Classified. We're still working on finding out where the cousin lives. She changed her name."

"She's in hiding too?"

"Probably not. I'm guessing she just got married. Her last known address was in the Chicago area. You're going to need to leave Gavin's house today."

"Why? We're safe here. Can't we stay until—?"

"Gavin lands in DC tomorrow."

"Is he coming here? He usually stays in the city."

"He does? How do you know that?"

"I've flown him in and out of DC a bunch of times. How do you think I have the code to this place? He almost never uses it."

"Oh. Well, I have no idea what his plans are, but—"

"I'll call him and—"

"No." Michael's voice carried a don't-fight-me-on-this ring to it. "I'd rather Gavin not know you're there. You can tell him later, but not now. All right?"

"I don't understand."

"I know." There was a sigh. "It's not that I don't trust him. I just don't know."

"He's our uncle."

"The contractor he works for—"

"*Worked* for," Derrick said. "He's retired."

"Is he?" By Michael's tone, Derrick had missed something obvious.

"Isn't he?" Though even as he asked the question, he saw what Michael meant. Uncle Gavin traveled an awful lot for a man who was retired. "He consults."

"Uh-huh. But on what, and with whom? He's doing something, and without more information, I just don't know enough to trust him."

Derrick stoked the fire and added a log. "Why would you have that kind of information?"

"You'd be surprised the things I know—or can find out, if I want to. The point is, the contractor where Gavin made most of his money is involved in some shady stuff. I don't think he'd betray you or me. But Jasmine? Leila? If he had any idea who they were, if there was something in it for him…?"

"How are you going to hide them from him?"

"I'm not. But they're going to get the same story the rest of the public gets. Leila and Jasmine are Iraqi immigrants who've been living in Germany for years. But if he sees Jasmine and Rabie… I just don't want him digging."

"He's Dad's brother, man. Do you really think—?"

"I'm just telling you what's what, bro. I trust our cousins. I mean, we can't tell them the truth, but I trust them."

"How magnanimous of you."

"You get a thesaurus for your birthday?" Michael was trying to make a joke, but Derrick wasn't amused.

He started pacing. He hadn't had a workout in days, and all

this sitting and worrying was grating on his nerves. He stalked from one end of the long great room to the other. "I think you've been a spy too long. If you distrust your own uncle—"

"I'll have a car delivered this afternoon."

"A car?" Derrick stopped in the middle of the living area. "We just need a ride back to the airport. We can fly anywhere you want us to go."

"No flying. I think those guys at the airport were waiting for you."

"How?" This was news. New...news. He started moving again. "How could you possibly—?"

"Security footage," Michael said. "There was a guy just inside the door. When you drove by, he ran out and jumped into an SUV waiting at the curb."

"It was at the curb?" Derrick hadn't seen where the car came from, but... "That doesn't make sense. How could he possibly have known—?"

"I don't know." Michael sounded worried. "I don't know, and I don't like it. I sent Leila and Sophie to stay with Mom and Dad, just to be on the safe side. But if those guys knew who you were and where you lived, there'd be people in Shadow Cove already, and there aren't. As far as I can tell, it's safe. We fudged the records at the airport, so your tail number isn't recorded properly right now, but if somebody saw you head to the plane, if somebody saw what plane you got into—"

"They could see its history, see where I'm based. I get that. But still... How do you know Shadow Cove is safe? You're not even there."

"I've got people watching. You think I'd ever leave home if I wasn't sure? There's a reason I keep telling Leila and Jasmine to stay close."

"Who?" How many people did Michael have...watching? Who were these people?

"I've made friends with local law enforcement and hired some security."

"Did you come into money I don't know about?"

"Sam's helping. He insisted. You know how he is."

Oh. Their brother had made a fortune in his business, and he was generous with it.

"The point is," Michael said, "I know what's going on in town. If there were strangers hanging around, I'd know it. It's safe."

"Except Leila isn't there."

"Well...I'm almost positive. Until this blows over, and until I'm back there, I want her to hide."

This was all too much for Derrick. He wanted to go back to when their lives were simple, before terrorists were more than just an over-there kind of problem.

In other words, about three months before. Except if they went back, he wouldn't know Jasmine.

He wouldn't trade knowing her for anything.

"Fine," Derrick said. "But I can't leave my plane at Dulles forever."

"Could Bryan pick it up for you?"

Like it was a car with an extra set of keys.

But...yeah. Maybe, as if his brother had nothing better to do than fly to DC. "I'll ask."

"Good. Okay, along with the car, you'll get ID, a clean credit card, and a couple of burner phones. I don't want you and Jasmine turning your personal phones on at all. Just use the burners. Travel after dark and try to avoid cameras. I assume the cousin is still in the Chicago area, so go that direction until you hear differently. Wear a baseball cap. Keep Jasmine and the kid in the car as much as possible. When they have to get out to use the bathroom or whatever, get them caps, too, and make sure she hides that hair. Try to choose small, independent gas stations and restaurants, which are less likely to have surveillance cameras. Don't take the most direct route, in case they guess where you're headed. Start out going west and then turn north."

"How could they guess Chicago?"

"How many people could Basma know in the States? If they follow the logic we're following, then they could learn what we've learned."

That made sense.

"One more thing," Michael said. "We think Dariush might have accessed the email address Jasmine and her friend used, which is how he was prepared for the escape attempt. We're monitoring it, hoping he'll access it again. If he does, we might be able to catch him. You need to let Jasmine know that if any messages pop up, she can't answer them."

"But what about Basma? How will—?"

"We'll take care of her. We've got a lot of people working on this, and we're very good at it. Trust me."

Easy for Michael to say. He didn't have a distraught pregnant woman and a scared little boy to take care of.

Derrick hated this. He hated all of it.

Man, if he could go back to the other night when Jasmine asked him for his help, he'd tell her absolutely not and immediately alert Michael.

If he'd known then what he knew now...

But he hadn't. And if not for this, when would Jasmine have told him about the baby? When she needed a ride to the hospital to give birth?

Too late to go back. They were in the middle of it now. He just needed to keep Rabie and Jasmine safe all the way to the other side.

An hour later, Derrick knocked on Rabie's door, then peeked inside. "You hungry?"

The kid hopped down from the bed. "Where's Yasamin?"

"She's taking a nap. You like macaroni and cheese?" He'd prepared the box already, so the answer better be yes.

Walking in front of Derrick toward the kitchen, Rabie shrugged. "I have never had it."

Derrick couldn't imagine a life without mac and cheese, although it might be a healthier life.

In the kitchen, he dolloped a spoonful onto Rabie's plate, put one onto his own, added a couple of carrot sticks and celery sticks to each of them, and carried them to the kitchen table.

Rabie sat where Jasmine had earlier. Derrick half expected him to turn up his nose at the vegetables, but Rabie grabbed a celery stick first, munching until it was gone.

Derrick snatched the plastic bag of veggies before he sat. "I'm going to say grace." He bowed his head without waiting for a reply. "Thank You, Father, for bringing us safely to this place. Take us to our next stop. Please keep Basma safe and bring her and Rabie back together soon. And bless this yummy food. In Jesus's name, amen."

When he looked up, Rabie was watching him through squinted eyes. "I do not pray to Jesus."

"You can pray to whomever you want." Derrick speared a forkful of macaroni. "I pray to Jesus because He saved me."

The kid seemed like he wanted to say something, but after a moment, he turned his attention to the food, wary.

"Just try it," Derrick said. "If you don't like it, I'll make you something else."

"It looks squishy."

Derrick ate his bite and swallowed. "Tastes squishy too." He winked.

Rabie put a single macaroni on his fork and tasted it with his tongue.

Derrick looked down so the kid wouldn't see his smile.

When he glanced up, Rabie had eaten the bite. "Well?"

"It is okay."

Apparently, good enough to eat because Rabie scooped up a generous amount and shoved it in his mouth.

They ate and talked about school and soccer—Derrick had played for a couple of years as a kid, so they had that in common. When they'd polished off the meal, Derrick found a package of peanut butter cookies in the pantry and plopped it on the table. "Since you ate all your vegetables..."

Rabie's eyes rounded. He shoved his hand into the package and came out with three.

He reminded Derrick so much of himself as a kid.

He bit a cookie, enjoying the crunchy sweetness. When he'd polished it off, he said, "What do you think about your brother, Dari?"

Rabie wiped crumbs from his lips with the back of his hand. "He is fun. He sends me puzzles and tells me they will make me smart."

"You're already pretty smart," Derrick said, "but I bet they help with thinking skills."

Shrugging, Rabie ate another cookie.

"Do you see him very much?"

"Not in a while." Rabie spoke with food in his mouth, then swallowed. "We talk on the phone. He tells me all the things we'll do together when we live with him."

"Do you want to live with him?"

At that, Rabie gazed out the window. His little face, so open a moment before, clouded. "I want to live with him, and I want to live with Basma, but Basma does not want to live with him."

He faced Derrick again. "But she does not know. She is only a..." His words trailed.

"A woman?" Derrick guessed.

He shrugged.

"She has a brain," Derrick said, "just like you do. Why do you think she doesn't want to live with him?"

"She says he's not kind, but he's always been kind to me."

"Hmm. Is Basma a bad judge of character?"

By the way the kid blinked and then narrowed his eyes, he didn't understand what Derrick was asking.

"Is she good at choosing friends? Does she usually like good people and dislike bad people?"

"She likes my friends, and they are nice."

Such a simple way of seeing the world. It made Derrick want to smile, but he kept his expression neutral. "Does she lie to you a lot?"

He sat back, clearly affronted. "She does not lie to me."

"So why don't you trust her judgment about Dari? She's older, and she knows him better than you do. Maybe she knows something you don't know."

Rabie took a fourth cookie, but before taking a bite, he said, "Maybe I know something she doesn't know. Maybe Dari is nice, and Basma is wrong."

"Hmm. That's possible. It's just as likely—I'd say even *more* likely, that she knows something you don't." Not that it mattered what Rabie wanted—he was nine years old—but Derrick hated to think he thought his sister was taking something away from him by escaping from his brother.

On the upside, at least Dari had been kinder to his brother than he had to his sister.

After lunch, they played countless games of Sorry!, Uno, and Connect 4. They were in the middle of Monopoly when tires crunched on the gravel driveway. Derrick walked to the window.

Two cars parked in front of the house. The driver of the first —a dark sedan the very definition of *nondescript*—climbed out carrying a cardboard box. She was tall, blond, and very familiar.

Derrick went to the door and pulled it open. "Hey, Alyssa. I didn't expect to see you here."

She stepped into the house and gave him a quick hug. "Considering this is my dad's place, I'd say you're the unexpected one."

"Good point." He backed into the kitchen and gave her a once-over. She had golden-brown eyes and high cheekbones and, despite the run-of-the-mill descriptors, somehow had the bearing of a warrior. She was the tallest of the Wright women at about five-eight, slender, but unlike her sisters, nobody would call her skinny. She was the kind of woman who could take a guy out with a left hook and walk away, brushing lint off her pants.

"Sounds like you've gotten yourself into a pickle," she said.

"Michael called you?"

"He's unbelievable, that brother of yours. If he ever calls without starting the conversation with, 'Hey, I need a favor,' I'll probably drop dead from shock."

News to Derrick. He'd had no idea Michael and Alyssa ever talked, much less that she did favors for him. What kind of things did she do for a CIA agent? Deliver cars, for one, but he figured that wasn't her raison d'être.

"Were you meeting him here?" Derrick asked, then clarified with, "Your dad?"

"No, no. I was in DC for something else. Just lucky for your brother." She handed Derrick the box. It was heavier than he'd expected.

"Lucky for me, I think." He set the box on the kitchen

counter and peeked inside. Along with a Maryland driver's license bearing Derrick's photo beside a fake name, a credit card under the same name, and two cell phones and chargers, there was a Smith & Wesson 9mm semi-auto, a box of bullets, and a holster, like he was some sort of Old West outlaw.

Which was, he had to admit, a little cool.

"Did you do all this?" he asked Alyssa.

"Don't know what all's in there, and after grabbing it from the sketchy guy your brother hooked me up with, I don't want to." She dug a set of keys from her pocket and tossed it to him. "Michael says it's clean and should get you where you're going."

"What does that mean, it's clean?"

She moved past him and pulled a couple water bottles from the fridge. "You know Michael. There's no telling what he ever means."

Derrick was starting to get the feeling Alyssa knew his brother better than he did.

She opened one of the bottles and was tipping it to her lips when she froze, looking into the living area. She lifted a hand. "Hey there, kiddo. How you doing?"

Rabie said, "Hi," but didn't leave his spot by the game board.

Alyssa peered at Derrick, one eyebrow raised.

"Long story."

"I bet." She put the cap back on the water bottle. "I'll let you get on with it. You'll be back for the party?"

He'd forgotten about the Christmas gathering with Gavin's family, which they were celebrating earlier than usual this year because Daniel and his family had to fly home soon. They'd come up to help for the whole wedding-gown-shopping thing— and to help with the Christmas tree, which the guys had put up at camp the previous week.

"We'll be there." Derrick hoped, and not just because he hated to miss the annual get-together.

He really, really wanted Jasmine safe in Maine again.

If Alyssa wondered who he meant by *we,* she didn't ask. "All right. See you soon." She headed out, calling, "Be careful," over her shoulder.

That was the plan—to be careful and to get everyone out of this crazy situation alive and well. The sooner, the better.

CHAPTER SEVENTEEN

Despite the hours of sleep Jasmine had gotten that afternoon, she yawned, trying to keep Derrick from hearing.

But of course he did, shooting her a look from the driver's seat. "Feel free to close your eyes."

"It is"—she glanced at the clock on the dashboard—"six thirty. I'm not tired."

"Mmm-hmm." He wasn't convinced, and by the amusement in his expression, he wasn't irritated with her, either.

"You're the one who needs rest."

"I'm fine."

So he said. But when she'd emerged from the bedroom and her nap, she'd found Derrick sound asleep on the sofa, Rabie curled up with his video game on one of the chairs.

"You two are like little babies," the child had said. "I don't need naps anymore."

"You weren't up half the night." Jasmine had ruffled his hair on the way to the kitchen in a quest for a snack.

Derrick hadn't slept long, and when he woke, he broke the

news that they had to leave. She was sorry to say goodbye to the cabin, a safe shelter, but she'd packed her things, and as soon as the sun went down, they piled into the waiting sedan and began the long trek down the mountain.

Finally, the dark and winding road from the cabin ended at a busy highway, this one with streetlights and businesses.

In the backseat, Rabie said, "What road is this?"

Derrick took a right. "A bigger one."

"What kind of a car are we in?"

"A Chevy Malibu." Derrick gave Jasmine a quick grin.

"What does the G on the license plate mean?"

"I didn't even notice it," he said. "I think that means it's a government car."

"How did you get a government car?"

"A friend let me borrow it."

"Where are we going?"

"Rabie." Jasmine turned to face him. "Must you ask so many questions?"

He didn't respond, his gaze catching on all the lights and glitter outside the windows. Greenery and red ribbon wound around lampposts that lined the road. The doors and windows of the downtown shops were decorated with wreaths and fake snow and brightly colored ornaments. A sign had been suspended over the road announcing a holiday festival and parade.

They passed a park where a Christmas tree that rose three stories high twinkled with lights that reflected off a circle of ice, where people skated.

Jasmine searched the dashboard for the outside temperature but didn't see it displayed. "I didn't realize it was so cold here."

Derrick had stopped at a light and followed her gaze. "The temperatures are milder than where I grew up. I'm guessing they have a machine that keeps it frozen."

"Have you ever done that, Derrick?" Rabie asked.

"All the time with my brothers when we were kids. There was a pond on our property, and we used to clear the snow off it. We didn't do it like that, though—orderly, skating in circles."

"What did you do?" Rabie asked.

"Ice skating was more of a contact sport with us. We played hockey or had races or just...knocked each other over."

On all that hard ice? With freezing water beneath? The thought of it made Jasmine shiver. "Sounds dangerous."

Derrick shook his head, catching Rabie's eye in the rearview mirror. "Girls."

He giggled. "I would like to try skating. I would be very good."

"Maybe you'll get to." Derrick followed the traffic, leaving the little park behind.

"Is all of America so cold?" Rabie sounded excited by the prospect, though Jasmine couldn't imagine why. She liked the cold, but she was eager for summertime. Derrick had assured her that it did warm up in Maine for a few months every year.

"There are all different climates in the US." Derrick followed the map, turning at the next light. "Depends where you live."

"Where did you grow up?"

"Michigan." The untruth rolled off his tongue as if he'd practiced.

"I want to live somewhere I can skate," Rabie said. "Maybe we will live in Michigan."

Derrick picked up speed as they left the little town behind. "There are ice skating rinks all over the country, even in warm climates. They're just indoors. Maybe you'll get to learn to skate."

The road narrowed to two lanes lined with homes. Most of them were decorated for Christmas. Elegant nativity scenes and giant blow-up snowmen in the deep yards. Glittering reindeer munched grass, and colorful balls hung from trees. There were lights everywhere—steady and flashing and twinkling. They passed one house that had so many, it was nearly blinding. And she could swear she heard Christmas music coming through the windows.

In the backseat, Rabie was taking it all in. She hadn't been in America so long that it was normal to her, either.

"This is all because of Christmas?" he asked.

"Yeah." Derrick's tone was almost...embarrassed. "We go a little overboard."

"I think I would like Christmas."

"Oh, yes," Jasmine said. "I helped put up the tree at Derrick's family's house last weekend. It is a big, beautiful home, and the tree is six meters tall."

"Inside?" Rabie sounded awed.

She twisted to face him. "A real tree they took off their property, an island they own."

Derrick flashed Jasmine a warning look. "On Lake Huron."

Right. She must be careful about what she disclosed to the child. "Even with so many people, it took all day to decorate the tree and put up all the decorations. And then we had a feast and ate cookies and played games. And this is only one of the traditions. Next, there will be a party with aunts and uncle and cousins."

"How many people will be there?" Rabie asked.

Derrick had to think about that. "Probably...about twenty, maybe twenty-five? Depends how many of the cousins can make it."

"And they all fit at this house?"

He shrugged. "It's a big house."

"They will go back to the island for Christmas." She glanced at Derrick. "Yes?"

"You, too." Was he annoyed with her? "Unless you have other plans."

"I do not assume."

It was a moment before Derrick shook off his irritation. "It's a wonder anybody in our family gets any work done in December with all our trips up to camp. And back home, Mom's always trying to get us to go caroling." He rolled his eyes.

"What is caroling?" she asked. "I have not heard of this."

"It's when you walk from house to house and sing Christmas songs on people's doorsteps."

"That's weird," Rabie said.

"No kidding. But then we go back to the house, and Mom feeds us. So, you know, there's always food."

"And presents?" Rabie asked. "I have heard of many presents."

"This I have also heard," Jasmine said.

"Yeah, presents." His tone was solemn. It was a moment before he spoke again. "Sometimes, all the decorations and presents get in the way of the real meaning of Christmas, though. Basically, it's a huge birthday party for Jesus. I think we forget that."

"And does the food get in the way?" she asked.

"Oh, no." He shot her a grin. "The food is the most important part."

They left the residential area and its lights behind, entering a world of darkness and trees.

Twenty minutes passed before they turned onto another well-lit road, this one much less charming than the last.

Rabie piped up again. "Where are we now?"

"Still in West Virginia."

"Where are we going?"

Derrick chuckled. "We're headed to the interstate."

"But to where?" He was practically wailing with the whine.

"When we know," Jasmine said, "we will tell you."

"I know what you need." Derrick's voice took on a teasing tone. "Dinner. What sounds good? There's everything a boy could want." He nodded to the brightly lit fast-food restaurants that lined both sides of the road ahead.

There were too many options, most of which Rabie wasn't familiar with. Derrick ended up parking at the back of a strip mall lot and summing up the menus at all the different places and offering his personal opinion about each one.

Finally, Rabie chose Bojangles, a restaurant she'd never heard of that Derrick had described as "a Southern place with fried chicken."

The last thing she needed after the heavy breakfast donuts.

They used the drive-through to pick up fried chicken sandwiches and french fries for the boys and a grilled sandwich and coleslaw for her, along with three iced teas. Hers was so sweet that she dumped half out the window and filled the cup with water from one of the bottles they'd brought from the cabin.

Sitting in another dark parking lot, they ate their meals and then icing-topped, berry-filled biscuits Derrick had insisted they try.

The man could put away more calories in a meal than she could eat in a week. Rabie tried to keep up with him as if it were a competition, and she didn't miss how he watched the man, seeking to emulate him, seeking his approval.

Somehow, Derrick had connected with Rabie, gaining his trust. Considering how they'd met... Considering Rabie had every reason *not* to trust Derrick, it was impressive.

But then, Derrick was a good man, and his goodness shined through. She and Rabie both were fortunate to have found such a friend.

She'd already known that, of course. But as they spent time

together, as she got to know him even better, she was more and more aware of what she would lose when this was all over.

His friendship and everything else they could have been to one another.

After they finished their dinners, Jasmine collected the empty bags and cups and tossed them in a trash can.

Derrick maneuvered the car back onto the road, and a few minutes later, he angled onto I-70. He'd found a classical music station, and between that, her full stomach, and the low hum of the road beneath their feet, she found herself yawning again.

Rabie played on his video game in the back until, after a couple of hours, Jasmine decided it was time for him to sleep. "Put that away and close your eyes. You need to get some rest."

"I'm not tired."

"Even so." She twisted. "Put it away or I will take it."

He scowled but shoved the game into his backpack.

After another hour of driving, she turned to find him curled up with the blanket and pillow they'd borrowed from the cabin.

"How's he doing?" Derrick asked, voice low.

She watched another moment, seeing nothing but the steady movement of his breathing, then faced forward again. "He's asleep."

"Poor kid. This has got to be hard for him."

"I cannot imagine."

Derrick checked the rearview and lowered his voice even more. "I talked to him about his brother. Rabie likes him. Which is good, I guess. I'm glad Dari treated him better than he treated Basma, but we should be careful what we say about him. My... guy thinks the email address was compromised."

Michael, he meant. "You called him back?" And then the more important part of what he'd said registered. "Compromised? What do you mean?"

"He thinks that's how Dari's men knew we'd be there."

"How will Basma reach us?"

"He says he's got it under control." By the way Derrick's lips pulled to one side, he had no idea what Michael planned to do. "Apparently, they have ways of finding people." He seemed to force a smile. "We just have to trust him."

"This I have done and will keep doing. I only wish we knew more."

"You and me both." He filled her in on everything else his brother had told him, including their destination. They were heading toward Chicago for now but might have to change that when Michael called on one of the burner phones and gave them a more specific destination. There were two phones on the console between the seats, one of which was connected to the car's navigation system.

"So until we hear from him," she said, "we keep driving?"

"That's the plan." Derrick reached toward her as he'd done so many times. She'd loved how he would take her hand and hold it. His touch was always gentle and warm and comforting. But now he pulled back, wiping his palm on his jeans as if he'd meant to do that from the start. He drove a few miles in silence, nothing but unfamiliar music playing in the background.

She hated the tension between them. It was time to tell him everything.

"You would like to know about the father?"

His gaze snapped to hers but didn't hold. He focused on the road, cleared his throat. "Yeah. Obviously. I mean, if you want to talk about it."

"I don't, but I want you to know, so I must."

He angled up and checked the rearview mirror.

She looked as well. Rabie hadn't moved.

"I, uh..." Derrick glanced her way. "I was thinking maybe someone... The way you reacted, maybe it wasn't your choice." He winced, shook his head. "I don't know how to ask this without just...asking."

She guessed at the assumption he'd made, that she'd been assaulted. "It is not what you think." She almost wished it were. Then she could claim innocence.

"Oh." Now, he squinted like he was trying to figure that out. "Okay."

"After Leila left and Mama died, it was only Baba and me. We were in Baghdad. He had worked for the government, but he had been away from work so much because of Mama's illness that he lost his position. I think perhaps they wanted him to go. It was an excuse, maybe? Money was not a problem—Baba has money. We could have left the city. There was our family compound, but his parents are dead, and other family have moved on or... They no longer associate with Baba. It is Hasan they do not wish to associate with. They knew of Hasan's connection to Saddam and terrorists.

"Baba and Hasan were close, but Hasan didn't go to the compound anymore, so it was as empty and as lonely as the house in Baghdad. Mama's parents, they did not wish to see him and cut him away."

"Cut him out?"

"Yes, yes. They blamed Baba for her death, I think, and did not approve of him. I don't know what they knew. Perhaps Mama told them about Hasan? Anyway, we could not go there."

"What about you?"

"What about me?"

"They're your grandparents. Didn't they want to see you?"

"I do not matter."

Derrick scowled. "Not true, but go on."

191

That was the thing about Derrick. He didn't see Jasmine for who she truly was. After this story, maybe he finally would.

"Baba had no purpose, you understand? No job, no family. He had no reason to leave the house. Some days, I could not coax him out of bed. I could not get him to eat."

"He was depressed."

"Yes. I feared he might follow Mama to the grave. And then Uncle Hasan came and saw how he was. He offered for us to go to the compound of his friend, where he was spending much time. He said that we wouldn't be alone there. I didn't want to go because of Basma. Baba had forbidden me to leave, but when he was in bed, I would sneak away to her house. We would sit in her courtyard. If Baba called me, I could hear and hurry back as if I had never left. In Basma, I had a friend and companionship. But Baba was fading, and if he died, I didn't know what would become of me. There was only Hasan, and to live with Hasan alone would be worse than to live with Hasan and Baba, you see? I thought Baba would protect me."

"You *thought* he would?" Derrick shot her a look. "What does that mean?"

She was getting there. "This person who owned the compound, he was a friend of Baba's, and I had met him. He was an old man, even older than Hasan and Baba, as old as my grandfather. His name meant nothing to me. If I had under-stood... Not that it mattered what I wanted, only that I think I would feel better about what happened."

She was taking her time telling the story. They weren't in a hurry, after all. And the longer it took to get to the end, the longer she could put it off.

They'd left the city—whatever city that had been—behind. Aside from the occasional orange lights above the divided high-way, there was darkness. She wondered what the countryside was like. Perhaps hilly and beautiful, like Maine and the place they'd just left. But for all she knew, it was barren and ugly. In the darkness, it was impossible to tell. It could be...anything.

That was the problem with darkness. One never knew what lurked until it was too late.

"What happened, Jazz?"

"I didn't understand what they planned."

Derrick's lips pressed together, but he didn't ask again. She was thankful they were in the car and thankful for the darkness. At least she didn't have to face him.

"Basma set up the email so we could keep in touch. And then Baba and I moved to the compound. I had imagined a family, you know? Women and children and grandchildren, as our compound had been when I was a girl. But when we arrived, it was only Hasan and Khalid, the man who owned it."

"Just you and those three men?" Derrick clarified. "But you were related to two of them, and one was an old man, so..."

"Khalid's wife had been unable to bear children, and he wished for a second wife to give him a child."

"Oh." Derrick swallowed. "She died? He was a widower?"

"No. She is alive. She prefers to stay in Tikrit near her family. They have a house there where Khalid spends most of his time. He is only at the compound for planning their...operations, you see? Khalid and Hasan are part of an organization that has people in cities in Europe. Your...person calls them cells."

"Terror cells," he clarified.

"Yes. They would make plans at the compound, and then Khalid would return to his wife in Tikrit."

"Okay." Derrick drew the word out, clearly confused.

She needed to stop stalling.

"Baba made a deal. Actually, Hasan made it, but Baba went along. Hasan worried for Baba and wanted to bring him to the compound. They are twins, like Leila and me, and they do love

193

one another. I believe Baba is the only one Hasan is capable of loving. Hasan wanted what was best for his brother. I was only..." She swallowed, unsure what to name herself. A pawn? A trinket? She sat up and told herself to tell the story. *Give me courage, Lord.* This was hard, even harder than she'd imagined. "They decided I would marry Khalid, become his second wife, to provide him with an heir."

There.

It was done. The words were out and could not be taken back.

Derrick's jaw tightened. On the steering wheel, his hands clenched, his knuckles turning white.

A long time passed before he said, "You're married."

"Yes."

"You're some man's *second wife?*"

"Yes."

"Your *father* married you off to some grandfather. Some... pervert"—his voice was rising—"so you could—"

"Shh. Please. I don't wish for Rabie to hear."

Derrick clamped his mouth shut.

"It is done," she said. "Sometimes, in our culture, when a man has no heirs and is able to provide for two wives, then—"

"You agreed to this?"

His question had irritation filling her voice. "Sometimes, Derrick Wright, you are very dimwitted."

He blew out a breath. "Of course you didn't agree. Of course. I'm sorry. It was a stupid... But that man... Your husband..." Derrick jabbed his fingers into his hair and pulled. "He was with you, and you're carrying his kid, his *heir*..." The word held malice. "If he comes after you, I'll kill him."

A terrible, awful part of her would like that very, very much. Because then she would be free.

But Khalid was her husband. She should feel something for

him besides this hatred that simmered inside. What she felt was wrong. She knew that. God commanded wives to respect their husbands. She had prayed many times for God to help her do that, to even love Khalid, but how could she love a man who planned such evil and cruelty?

Perhaps if he'd treated her as anything but a toy and an incubator for his child, she might. Good women loved their terrorist husbands not because they were terrorists but because they were loved in return. But Khalid didn't love Jasmine. He didn't even know her. He'd never tried to know her, had never treated her like anything more than a slave.

She was accustomed to that from her father, from her uncle, from others in her life. She'd rarely been treated as more than a slave.

But from the man who shared her bed? The man who thought he owned her body and could do with it as he pleased?

She loathed him.

There were days that, if not for her faith in Christ, she'd have put a blade through his heart. Even if it meant her own death. And after she learned she was carrying his child, she'd longed for her own death. She'd longed for the child's.

It was wrong. She knew it was wrong. Sinful. Horrible. Evil. But those feelings would not go away, no matter how hard she prayed.

Some days, she believed God had rescued her from Khalid.

Some days, she wondered if she'd compounded her sin by running from her husband. What was the greater sin? To disobey her husband and run? Or to raise a child to become a killer?

Derrick reached across the space and took Jasmine's hand. "It's not real, you know."

Had she been so lost in her own thoughts that she'd missed something? "What is not real?"

"The marriage, of course."

"What do you mean?"

"He was already married to someone else. He's a bigamist. That nullifies it."

"No, it—"

"And it wasn't your choice. If you don't agree, it doesn't count."

"Marriage is not a game, Derrick. You don't get to...to make up rules and declare they are true. You don't get to decide the rules at all."

"It doesn't count, Jazz." He sounded vehement, almost angry. "You're not really married."

She pulled her hand back. "I do not know what you mean."

"He's not your husband. You're not his wife."

"These are the rules according to Derrick, I think. Not according to God."

He glared at her. "Do you *want* to be married to him?"

"It matters not what I want. I *am* married to him."

"No, you're not. Marriage is between one man and one woman. Read Genesis."

"Was it not in Genesis that Jacob married Leah and Rachel? Were they not both his wives?"

"That's not... They knew what they were getting into."

"As did I."

"You had no choice."

"I had a choice."

"What do you mean?" His jaw dropped, and even from the side, she read in his expression. Horror.

She'd expected it. She'd known it would come. Even so, her heart splintered and cracked, knowing that the way Derrick had seen her and the love he'd felt for her were gone. Gone forever.

"Are you telling me that you could have refused and didn't?"

She crossed her arms and gazed out the window, watching the darkness slip past.

"Please explain," he said. "I don't understand."

"I do not owe you an explanation."

"Just answer the question." He was yelling at her, even if his voice was a whisper. "Did you want to marry him or not?"

"Did I want to?" Her head whipped back toward Derrick. "I wanted to not be harmed. I wanted my father to be well, not dishonored. I wanted to stay alive."

"So you had to."

"I made a choice."

"With a gun to your head."

"Gun? There was no—"

"It's a...metaphor, Jazz. It means... If your choices were get married or die, it wasn't a real choice. You really think God would hold you to that?"

"He held Jacob to it, did He not? Jacob married Leah against his will. He didn't know who he slept with that night. When morning came, it was not Rachel. Jacob didn't wake up and claim it didn't...count." She used his word, then lowered her voice until it was barely audible. "They had been intimate. It was valid."

"But it was..." Derrick was breathing hard as if they were engaged in a physical fight. "You were forced to marry him. You were forced into his bed."

"I. Was. Not."

She had gone willingly to her husband's bed. It mattered not that she hadn't wanted to. It mattered not that she'd closed her eyes and prayed it would be over soon. Or that Khalid would not be able to do it, or that he would die of a heart attack before he finished. It mattered not that she'd begged God to prevent his seed from planting inside her.

Go willingly to bed or be forced there—and bring dishonor

to her father and pain to herself. Why would she have chosen that?

She'd been trapped in the middle of the desert with no help and no chance of escape.

Now, she was married to Khalid Qasim, and nothing Derrick or anybody else said would change that.

CHAPTER EIGHTEEN

Jasmine's words echoed in Derrick's head.

I was not.

She was wrong.

She hadn't chosen that old man to be her husband, so she had been forced. Which meant the marriage didn't count. Or it definitely *shouldn't* count. Because she was meant for Derrick, not for that...that disgusting old man.

How could he convince her?

Even if he succeeded, would she ever truly agree with him, or would she always think of herself as being married to a terrorist half a world away?

That wasn't the real question.

Derrick didn't want to consider the real question, but it was right there, hovering like a storm cloud.

Was Jasmine right? Was her marriage valid?

God, is that how You see it?

Couldn't be. No way.

And he didn't think that because of what Jasmine had claimed—that he was living by the rules according to Derrick.

No court in America would declare her married to a man who had another wife.

Who cared that she hadn't lived in America when she'd married? She did now, so...

So what?

He could practically hear her argument in his head. *The rules according to America are no more valid than the rules according to Derrick. It is God's rules that matter.*

Sure. But if she'd follow America's rules, then she wouldn't be married. Then Derrick could marry her and be her husband and...

Be her kid's father? Would he do that?

Beside him, Jasmine sat with her arms crossed, staring out the far window. In the glow of the dashboard lights, moisture sparkled on her cheeks.

He'd made her cry.

Yeah, well... She should've told him a lot sooner than this. About the baby and the husband and all of it. Because now he was in love with her, and it was too late to go back.

What did she expect? Was he supposed to agree that she was married? Just...give up and go along with her crazy...

What? Crazy what?

Desire to honor God?

Was that really so crazy?

He loved that about her. He loved how dedicated she was to the Lord. He loved her humility and gentleness and kindness. He loved how she always put others above herself.

Despite all the hardship she'd endured, he'd never heard her rail against God. He'd never even heard her complain. She just laid out facts as facts, never posing the old why-me questions, never acting as if she felt she deserved better. She'd been a victim, but she didn't see herself as one, and she certainly didn't have a victim mentality.

Jasmine was tiny and vulnerable. She was quiet and shy. But she was the strongest woman he'd ever known, and he loved her with everything inside him.

So yes. Yes, he would happily adopt and raise her child as his own, and he didn't care that the birth father was a terrorist, a perverted grandfather who might as well have bought and paid for her as if she were no more valuable than a...trinket he could buy at the bazaar alongside a bottle of olive oil.

If Derrick ever had the chance, he'd put an end to their sham of a marriage with a well-placed bullet. He thought of the gun holstered to his hip right now. He could do it. He was a good shot. Not a sharpshooter like Bryan, but he could hit a target. All those years hunting with his brothers.

So what that he'd never had the stomach to kill a deer.

Deer were beautiful and innocent.

Khalid-the-grandfather-slash-terrorist was anything but, and Derrick wouldn't hesitate to kill the man.

And if that landed him in prison, so be it.

Really?

He swallowed the question posed by his conscience...or maybe his God.

Would he really set out to kill a man to get what he wanted?

Yes.

No.

Maybe.

He didn't know. He longed to be given the opportunity, but in some small part of his mind—or perhaps it was his spirit—he hoped he never would. Because how could he live with himself?

Lord, what am I supposed to do with this? Can You convince her, please, that she's not really married?

God didn't answer. Or, if He did, Derrick discounted the words that filled his mind—that quiet *Isn't she?* Because God couldn't possibly agree with Jasmine.

And if He did...

Whatever.

Derrick didn't have any answers tonight, and his mind was playing tricks on him. What he knew, what he'd known from the first moment he laid eyes on Jasmine, was that she was the woman for him.

Which meant that God would work it out. Somehow.

Derrick had to believe that.

He just had no idea how it could possibly happen.

"Would you like me to drive?" Jasmine asked.

"I'm fine." His words were sharp. He wasn't angry at her, just at...at everything.

He cleared his throat and tried again. "Sorry. I'm awake. I can drive for a while." Wasn't as if he'd be able to sleep now.

"But the traffic is little," she said, "so it would be good for me. To do driving? And I had a long rest."

When she was upset, her English suffered.

He infused his voice with gentleness. "Close your eyes, sweetheart. If I get tired, I'll wake you up."

They'd brought some extra pillows and blankets from the cabin, and she tucked a pillow between her head and the window and pulled a blanket up.

He eased it over her shoulder, then brushed her hair back from her face, enjoying the warmth of her, the feel of her.

She was all he wanted.

And yet, he needed to face the truth.

That somehow...he was going to have to let her go.

CHAPTER NINETEEN

Jasmine hadn't thought she'd be able to sleep. The conversation with Derrick had been frustrating—and confusing. Derrick had been angry, but not for long. He'd returned to the kind man he'd always been.

In telling him her terrible secret, had she put some of her burden on him? Because, when she was finished, and when he'd touched her so gently and called her sweetheart, she'd felt unburdened in a way she hadn't in months. Perhaps years.

Nothing had changed, of course. She was still the wife of Khalid Qasim, still carrying his heir. But now that Derrick knew the secret, she could tell the rest of his family.

Derrick hadn't rejected her. He still wanted her, though it seemed impossible. And she found that nobody else's opinion mattered to her at all, not compared to his.

With the pillow beneath her head and the warm blanket Derrick had tucked around her, she closed her eyes and fell asleep.

"Hey, bud. You okay?"

Derrick's words, spoken softly beside her, pulled her back to consciousness.

"I need to go to the bathroom," Rabie said.

They'd been driving a long time, and Jasmine needed to stop as well.

"Okay," Derrick said. "We'll find you one."

The faint dings told her Rabie was playing on his video game.

She sat up and stretched, glancing at the clock. It was after midnight, meaning she'd slept for over an hour.

Derrick ignored an exit that seemed it would have been a good place. She spied many gas stations and restaurants right off the highway.

"Would there not have been bathrooms there?" she asked, twisting to look as they zoomed past.

"Hey, sleepyhead. Did you get a good nap?"

She yawned. "I can drive, if you wish. But I also need to use the restroom, please."

"I need to find someplace a little less crowded."

It was another few minutes before he exited the highway and parked on the side of a small, remote gas station. "You two stay here. I need to see if they sell baseball caps, just in case there are cameras."

"But I need to go!" Rabie whined in the backseat.

"Rabie," she snapped. "Do not argue. You can wait." She met Derrick's eyes and let a little pleading fill her voice. "You will hurry, I'm sure."

"I promise." Leaving the car running, Derrick jogged inside.

Rabie returned his focus to his game, and Jasmine closed her eyes. She ought to help Derrick with the driving so he could sleep, but she felt sluggish and drowsy. Perhaps she should ask him to buy her something caffeinated. She rarely indulged in drinks with...

A door jerked opened. Derrick, already?

But Rabie gasped.

She spun in time to see his legs yanked out of the car, his feet kicking furiously.

"Rabie!" She reached for him as if she could pull him back. But he was gone.

Her door flew open.

A hand clamped on her mouth, and a man leaned in, his thick arm wrapping around her waist. He pulled her from the car.

She grabbed the door handle and hung on, kicking behind her, aiming for something, anything to make the man loosen his hold. She whipped her head back and forth, desperate to free her mouth. To breathe. To scream.

"Let go!" He spoke Arabic, his words a growl in her ear. "Yasamin! Let it go."

Her name in his mouth only made her hold onto the car tighter.

His hand loosened from her mouth.

She gasped.

But a sharp jab to her midsection cut off her scream.

Her grip slipped, and the man dragged her away.

CHAPTER TWENTY

The small and slightly dingy store was empty—not even an employee in sight. Derrick found a display of trucker hats and snatched a couple at random. He glanced at the many snack options but decided to let Jasmine and Rabie use the bathroom first and then pick out what they wanted.

Approaching the register, he called, "Hello?"

"Be right with ya." A woman came in from the back hauling a cardboard box twice as wide as she was. "Sorry 'bout the wait. Workin' on stockin' the shelves." With her deep Southern accent, she made *shelves* a two-syllable word.

After dumping the box at the end of an aisle, she moved behind the counter. She seemed barely old enough to have a job. What was she doing working the all-night shift at a place like this? All alone, it seemed.

She rang up the hats, and he handed her cash. "The bathrooms are unlocked? My family's in the car."

"Help yourself. You need a sack for your things?"

"No, thanks." He took his change, pushed out the door, and rounded the building.

He froze at the corner. It took a half second to get a read on the situation.

A man was dragging Jasmine away from the car, one hand over her mouth, the other around her waist. She was fighting, dragging her feet, trying everything to keep him from taking her.

Another guy nearly had Rabie to an SUV half-hidden behind the store. But he'd stopped to watch the other man wrangle Jasmine. Maybe he thought it was funny, the way she struggled. Maybe he thought his thug-buddy would need help.

Rabie was pummeling the man's back with his fists, but the guy wore a thick jacket, and the kid's punches were having no effect.

Derrick didn't think. Didn't say a word.

He dropped the hats, yanked the handgun from the holster, aimed at the thigh of the man holding the boy, and fired.

The guy went down, dumping Rabie on the concrete.

Derrick aimed at the other thug, who'd let up his grip on Jasmine to reach for a weapon.

She ducked away, and Derrick fired, hitting him in the chest.

He staggered backward and fell, his gun bouncing beside him.

Jasmine hurried toward Rabie.

"Get in the car!" Derrick started toward the boy as Jasmine ran to the sedan.

The first thug turned over, handgun raised.

An instant before he got a shot off, Derrick ducked behind a trash can against the building, bumping against something sharp. He ignored the pain in his side and squeezed the trigger. His bullet missed. Crouching, he set his feet, peeked around the can. The guy was aiming elsewhere—toward Jasmine? Rabie? Their car?

Derrick didn't wait to find out. He lined up his shot and fired.

The guy flopped back on the pavement. Dead?

He didn't know.

Rabie stood unmoving a few feet from the waiting SUV, eyes wide, jaw dropped in a soundless scream.

That was the strangest thing about the whole situation. Except for the echo of gunshots, all was quiet.

The clerk didn't come outside. No sirens rang in the distance.

In the movies, there'd be music and sound effects.

But the world had gone silent.

Derrick bolted toward Rabie, scooped him up, and turned toward the car.

Jasmine was behind the wheel. She backed out of the spot and braked hard.

He dove into the passenger seat, the kid on his lap, and slammed the door.

She hit the gas and drove toward the interstate.

"Go east," he said. "Turn left, under the highway, then back the way we came."

She didn't respond, just did what he said. Not that he had any idea what he was doing. Just going on instinct now. That was all that had been—instinct.

"You hurt?" he asked her.

She shook her head. Maybe she wasn't hurt, but she was definitely terrified. Traumatized.

"You sure?" At her nod, he said, "Get off at the next exit." There'd been a couple between the busy, brightly-lit one and the one where they'd stopped.

He just needed a second to think. To breathe. To figure out what to do.

He turned his attention to the kid, who was way too big to be sitting on his lap. "How about you, buddy? You okay?"

Rabie babbled something in Arabic.

Jasmine responded, also in Arabic.

So helpful.

Derrick felt moisture on his jeans. Was Rabie bleeding?

And then Derrick noted the scent of urine. Oh.

The kid had warned him he had a full bladder. Now, he was probably embarrassed. Derrick wasn't sure how to play it and decided best to pretend he didn't notice.

"You were wicked brave," he said. "Those guys were huge."

Rabie backed away, shaking his head. Then, his eyes popped wide. "You are hurt!"

"I'm fine, buddy. I'm fine."

But Rabie touched Derrick just below the armpit, and...

He sucked in a breath. Yikes!

What in the...? He saw a small hole in his sweatshirt—and a dark stain that had to be blood.

That sting he'd felt had been a...bullet?

"What?" Jasmine was barely going the speed limit. "Do we need a hospital? What happened?"

"Can you pick up the pace?"

"What is a pace?" she asked. "Where is—?"

"Go faster!" he snapped. "I just shot two people. I'd rather not get arrested."

"Oh, sorry." She pressed down on the gas.

"You were hit!" Rabie's voice was too loud and too close.

Now that he'd pointed it out, holy smokes, it smarted.

"It's nothing." He managed to grind out the words. "Crawl in the back, bud."

Rabie did, barely missing using Derrick's wound as a foothold.

When he was buckled in, Derrick lifted his sweatshirt and checked. The bullet had grazed him. Blood dripped from a gash on his side a couple inches below his armpit—and beside his heart.

They'd need a first-aid kit, but it could've been so much worse. He bunched his sweatshirt and pressed it against the wound, holding it in place with his upper arm. With his free hand, he grabbed one of the phones and dialed Michael.

When his brother answered, his voice was too loud over the car's speaker. "Everything okay?"

"They found us." Derrick turned down the volume. "I was inside buying hats. I managed to..." He could see it, the men falling. Not moving. *Don't think about it.* "I shot them. Two men at a gas station just west of Wheeling, West Virginia."

"Are you all right?"

"I was... I'm fine." Nausea worked its way up his throat.

"He was shot." Jasmine's voice was weirdly calm.

"What!" Unlike Michael, whose shout had Derrick cringing.

"I'm fine. It grazed me. I just...I don't know what we should do. Go to the police, or—"

"No. No, absolutely not." Michael took a breath. "Where are you now?"

Jasmine was angling off the highway.

"We're on I-70 about ten miles west of Wheeling, just stopping to breathe. Jasmine's okay." He looked at her. "Right? You're okay? He didn't hurt you too badly?"

"I am unhurt."

Derrick twisted to Rabie, wincing again at the shocking sting in his side. "And you? He didn't hurt you, did he?"

The boy shook his head.

But Derrick barely noticed, his focus pulled to headlights.

A black SUV angled down the off-ramp after them.

He faced forward again. "There's someone behind us."

Jasmine checked the mirror. "How? They were down? How could they have—?"

"I don't know!" Derrick searched the darkness ahead. They needed to get back on the highway, but where was the onramp?

No time to find it.

"Don't stop at the stop sign." There was nothing but forest all around. "Just take a left and gun it."

She did, and Derrick braced himself to keep from slamming into the door.

"Where are you exactly?" Michael asked.

Derrick zoomed out on the phone's map. There was nothing anywhere nearby. Nothing but this lonely stretch of two-lane road that went for miles in both directions.

The on-ramp had been in the other direction.

"Derrick!" Michael said. "Where?"

He told his brother the highway.

"Okay. I'll see what I can do."

But Michael wasn't going to be able to get them out of this.

"Hit the gas, Jazz." Derrick should be the one behind the wheel. "Go as fast as you dare."

"But I'm not a good—"

"You have no choice."

She did as he said, leaning over the steering wheel as if that might help. The road twisted and turned, and Derrick needed to know—had to know for certain—if the driver of the SUV was really following them.

Was it thugs behind them, or just a family who happened to live in this direction?

He prayed for the second.

But no matter how fast Jasmine moved on the winding road,

the SUV was still there, the glow of its headlights bouncing off trees behind them.

"Rabie, move to the other side." Derrick's voice was unnaturally calm.

"What are you doing?" Michael asked through the speakers. "Just give me a second. There's got to be a place—"

"Be quiet, Michael. There's no time."

His brother stopped talking.

"Put your seatbelt on, son." Derrick heard a click, then launched his too-tall body over the seat, trying—and failing—to keep a grunt of pain from escaping.

"What are you doing?" Jasmine's voice was too high and too loud in the small car.

Derrick took a couple of deep breaths, waiting for the pain to pass.

He'd brought the phone with him and now studied the map.

"Jazz, you're going to have to turn the car around, fast. As fast as you can. There's no time for a three-point turn. You understand?"

She nodded, hands white-knuckled on the wheel—ten and two, just like he'd taught her.

She'd only learned to drive a couple of months before. *Please, God. Guide the car.*

"There's a left turn up ahead. You can use it to give you a little more space. I don't want you take the left. Just do a U-turn. You have to do it in one shot. It doesn't matter if you go off the road. Just don't crash. As soon as you're facing the other way, flip the lights off."

Michael said, "What are you—?"

"Quiet!"

Again, Michael fell silent, though it had to be killing him.

Her voice shook. "I can't do it."

"Think about it, Jazz. Why was he taking you? Why *you*?"

He only gave her a moment to ponder that, but he'd already worked it out.

Dari shouldn't care about getting Jasmine. He should have left her. Why risk it?

The thugs could've taken Rabie and been gone. Jasmine had been the one slowing them down, putting up a fight.

"You want him to catch you?" Derrick asked. "There are obviously more of them than us. We're outmanned and outgunned. And I'm injured. This is our shot. Can you do it or not? Because if you can't..." Then he had no idea what to do.

"I will. I will do it."

Derrick twisted. The headlights glowed. "Gun it. Go as fast as you dare. I'll tell you when the road is coming. As soon as you're turned around, flip the lights off. You see where the dial is, on the dash on your left?"

A pause, then, "Yes."

"Okay. Whenever you're ready."

She floored the accelerator, and the headlights behind faded.

He watched the map. "Coming up... About ten seconds."

"I see it." She took her foot off the gas, then shouted, "Hold on!"

Like some sort of stunt-car driver, she barely braked before she whipped the car into a tire-squealing turn, using the narrow —too narrow—road to give her a little bit more space.

The car bumped off the road, slid.

For a split second, Derrick was sure they were going to crash and die.

And then, she straightened the wheel.

He was already lowering his window, calling, "Lights!"

They went out.

"Rabie, on the floor. As soon as you see them, Jazz, hit the gas and get as low as you can." Derrick leaned out the window.

Headlights glowed up ahead, and then the SUV came around a bend.

Derrick aimed at the front passenger tire and fired.

The SUV jerked toward the narrow shoulder.

Jasmine hit the gas.

"Duck!"

The rear window was going down. Derrick aimed that way and fired, then shot out the rear left tire. He aimed at the gas tank and squeezed the trigger again, but the gun clicked.

He stifled a curse, shouted, "Go, go!"

Rabie climbed back up and peeked out the back window.

Derrick launched himself over the kid as gunshots sounded from behind.

Jasmine sped toward the highway.

And then, aside from the engine noise, all was quiet.

He sat up, collapsed against the seat back. Pressed his hand to the wound that suddenly throbbed again. Took a few deep breaths.

"Everyone all right?" He rolled up the window, slowly comprehending the cold, cold air.

Jasmine said nothing.

Rabie seemed too stunned to speak.

"Jazz?"

"Yes, yes, I think so. I think..." She checked the mirror. "There is no one there."

Somehow, they'd gotten out of it. They were all three safe and alive and...

"Good-flipping-night!" Michael's voice was way too loud over the speaker. "You just took ten years off my life! What did you...? What just...?"

"We lost them," Derrick said. "Can't figure out where they came from. We left two guys down. The SUV at the gas station didn't follow us. If there'd been anyone in it..."

There couldn't have been. They'd have returned fire or at least given chase right away. They'd have snatched Rabie for sure, wouldn't they?

"Must've been a different vehicle," Michael said. "Maybe another group coming to meet the guys you took out."

Maybe. "Anyway, we lost them, thanks to Jasmine's wicked skills at the wheel. Right now, that's what matters. Could you direct us to somewhere safe? And tell me how in the world they found us."

"Been thinking about that," Michael said, "and there's only one logical answer. You obviously missed something in your search. Toss the kid's backpack and everything that was in it. Now."

Rabie's eyes rounded and filled with tears that probably would've broken Derrick's heart under any other circumstances. But his side was throbbing, his hands vibrating with tension, and his ears ringing with the echo of gunshots. He could have lost Jasmine tonight. He could have lost them both.

And it would've been his fault because he'd missed something. And he'd been too soft-hearted to do what he should've done when he'd first gotten the kid.

"Sorry, son." He grabbed the backpack and tossed it out the window.

Rabie twisted, watching the backpack get smaller and smaller on the lonely road behind them.

"Was there anything else?" He directed the question to Rabie, searching the pockets on the backs of the seats. "Anything you stashed—?"

"Those things were mine!"

He found no toys. "Jasmine?" He worked to keep his voice even. "Are any of his things in your bag?"

"He carried them all. He insisted."

"Okay, good." He ruffled the kid's hair, but Rabie ducked away. "I'll buy you whatever games and puzzles you want."

"There were gifts from my brother in there."

"Yeah?" Derrick's irritation spiked. "Those men who nearly kidnapped you? Who nearly kidnapped *Jasmine*? Those thugs were also *gifts* from your brother. I think I've dealt with all the *gifts* from Dari Ghazi I can handle."

Rabie turned to the window and crossed his arms.

Right back at ya, kid.

And yeah, he was being a jerk.

But at the moment, he didn't care.

CHAPTER TWENTY-ONE

Jasmine drove a few miles on the interstate, then took another dark exit and pulled the car over. She was trembling, and she needed a bathroom, and she desperately wanted Derrick to take her spot behind the wheel. But she caught his face in the rearview and knew he was in much worse shape than she was. Pale and wincing in pain, there was no way he should be driving.

She stayed where she was. "Move to the passenger seat, please."

He didn't argue, which gave her more confidence that she'd made the right decision. Even though he'd taught her to drive, he teased her about her caution behind the wheel. Once she'd earned her license, he'd taken over the driving whenever they were together.

He settled into the passenger seat without a word.

Little though she wanted to, she trudged into the forest and emptied her bladder. They couldn't risk stopping at a gas station anytime soon, but she couldn't hold out any longer or Rabie wouldn't be the only one who'd soiled his clothes.

A few minutes later, she eased back onto the interstate

toward Wheeling. Michael had said to go that direction and continue to Pittsburgh. Fortunately, it was not far, only sixty miles, if the sign was accurate. The display in the dashboard told her they had seventy-five miles remaining before the gas tank would be empty, so she hoped Michael would find a hotel on this side of the city.

She was surprised to find that Pittsburgh was so close. Was it not in another state entirely?

How many states would they drive through today? A tiny, curious part of her wished it were daylight. If Khalid found her and took her back to Iraq, this would be her only opportunity to tour America. She hated that she was only seeing darkness.

In the back, Rabie's arms were crossed. He stared out the window. She didn't miss the glint of tears on his cheeks.

There was nothing she could say to make this better for him. He didn't know his brother like Basma did. He would simply have to trust that Basma knew what was best. If he couldn't be convinced of that, then he'd grow bitter and angry toward her.

Perhaps he would end up like his brother anyway.

And all of this would have been for nothing.

Jasmine should've stayed out of it. She should've stayed in Maine. What foolishness had driven her to this? Love for Basma, yes. But Michael could have helped her friend. And would have, probably, if she'd asked him to. But instead of taking the risk that he might refuse her, she'd not only put herself in danger, but she'd risked her unborn baby's life. And Derrick's life.

She could still feel the warmth of that terrible man's breath on her cheek when he'd spoken to her.

Yasamin.

She hadn't thought about what it meant at the time, only that she couldn't let him take her.

But she had to think about it now. Derrick was right. There had to be a reason Dari would have Jasmine kidnapped.

If he was acquainted with Hasan, then he was likely acquainted with Khalid.

Were they working together? Was he seeking favor? Or did Dari intend to use her as a bargaining chip? A hostage? Did he plan to sell her back to her husband?

No matter how it might have happened, Jasmine would have been returned to Khalid.

Thank You, Most High God, for delivering me. Again. And for keeping us safe. Forgive me for my foolishness. Please, protect us.

She hadn't put an address into the navigation system. She followed signs toward Pittsburgh, glancing at Derrick in the passenger seat.

His eyes were squeezed shut, his hand pressing the sweatshirt against his wound.

Even thinking of it—what had happened, what could have happened—turned her stomach. "Perhaps we should find a pharmacy."

"No." The word was clipped. "Just drive until Michael calls back."

"But it needs to be cleaned."

"I don't want to go to jail tonight."

This she understood. But the wound could get infected, and then they would have to go to the hospital, no? And then, more likely jail.

But she didn't argue, just drove, willing the phone to ring.

They'd driven through the small town of Wheeling and were ten or fifteen miles past it before it finally did.

Derrick barely reacted to the shocking trill in the silent car.

She pressed the phone icon on the steering wheel. "Hello?"

Derrick straightened a little.

"You guys okay?" Michael asked. "No issues? No more lurking SUVs?"

Derrick responded with, "We're fine."

"We are in need of antibiotics and bandages and a safe place to rest. Your brother is pale and sick."

She could practically feel him glaring at her.

Well, it was true, whether he wanted to admit it or not.

"I'm looking now," Michael said. "You're driving, sis?"

"We have just passed into Pennsylvania."

"Perfect. We're making calls about the shooting, telling the locals it's a federal matter, that we've got it under control—national security and all that. But it'll take some time, so don't get stopped."

"We won't get stopped for speeding." Derrick attempted to add a little humor to that remark.

"He is teasing about my driving."

"Better too slow than too fast," Michael said. "Bro, can you make it another forty-five minutes? I got you a motel in the city, the kind of place that won't ask a lot of questions."

"I can do it," Derrick said. "You all right to drive that far?"

"Yes," she said. "We must have a pharmacy."

"I found one. I want you to check in, get Derrick and Rabie settled, and then go to the pharmacy alone."

"No." Derrick sat up straighter. "She's not going alone."

"Can you do it, sis?" Apparently, Michael was ignoring Derrick.

So she did the same. "I will, yes."

"I'll text all the information. Let me know as soon as you get there." Michael ended the call.

"You're not going alone." Derrick was practically grumbling beside her.

"This is the first I have seen you injured. Are you grouchy when you're sick, too, or only when you're in pain?"

"I'm not grouchy. I'm trying to keep you alive."

"As I am doing. And to keep you out of jail. This you also want, yes?"

"I'm just saying—"

"I do not think it has to be one or the other, me or you. Your brother says I will be safe, and I trust him."

She wasn't sure if Derrick agreed or had simply lost his energy, but he didn't argue further. After he put the address to the hotel into the navigation system, he pulled the blanket over himself, tucked the pillow beneath his head, and closed his eyes.

In the back, Rabie wasn't asleep, just staring out at the darkness.

Jasmine turned the music back on—still the same classical station, so it must be satellite radio. She focused on the sounds, trying not to let the memories of all that had happened—and could have happened—distract her.

Right now, all she had to do was reach the motel without incident and get Derrick and Rabie inside. Then she'd go to the pharmacy. Then she'd tend Derrick's wound and soothe Rabie.

What had Derrick said? That she shouldn't borrow trouble? It was like what Jesus said as well, that each day had enough trouble of its own.

This night had been filled with it. And soon the sun would rise on a new day.

Perhaps...perhaps they would find Basma, locate her cousin, and deliver Rabie.

Perhaps before the sun set again, they would go home.

She could only pray that God would make it happen.

Jasmine returned to the motel and parked on the side opposite from their room, as Michael had directed. If the police—or, God

221

forbid, Dari's men—located them here, they might be able to escape out the back and reach the car before they were found.

It seemed farfetched to her, but Michael's ideas were usually good.

She'd figured out how to use the burner phone's map and had added the other phone's number to it, in case she needed to call Derrick. She'd mastered her own phone, but it was powered down and tucked in her suitcase. Not that she'd be missing a lot of calls, but she was certain that at least her sister had tried to reach her.

After her visit to the pharmacy, she understood why Michael hadn't been afraid for her to go by herself. Though she hadn't seen many people while she was out, a number of those she had seen were Middle Eastern, and the clerk had been as well—he'd even spoken Arabic. Nobody had given Jasmine a second glance as she'd bought and paid for the items. She'd gotten the first-aid supplies as well as drinks and snacks. She'd found a deck of Uno cards, a puzzle, and a small backpack for Rabie. Then she'd discovered the store had a small collection of clothes. She'd chosen a package of boy's underwear, a package of socks, two pairs of sweatpants and two sweatshirts. Since he'd soiled one outfit and the other had gone out the window, he'd need something to wear.

Perhaps she could cheer him up a little.

The motel rooms opened to the outside adjacent to the parking lot. The exterior walls were whitish, the paint peeling. Most of the rooms were quiet—it was nearly three o'clock in the morning. Music thumped from one, and she picked up the sounds of men talking and women giggling.

How authentic was the giggling, though? Did those women want to be there? Were they paid to pretend, or forced to?

Slavery looked different here than it had in Iraq, but it existed everywhere. She'd seen the news reports and heard

Leila's and Sophie's stories about what happened to many refugees, how their dreams of freedom turned to nightmares.

She hurried past the music, not wanting anything to do with those inside, and reached their room. She slid the keycard into the slot and pushed the door open.

The space was dim, only lit by an overhead light outside the bathroom on the far side. It smelled of dampness and old onions, though it was tidy enough.

Derrick lay on top of the covers on the closer bed. He'd changed into his pajama pants but hadn't peeled off the blood-soaked sweatshirt. The room was chilly, but his face sparkled with a sheen of moisture. He pushed himself up onto his elbow. "Any problems?"

"All is well. Please rest. I'll be right there."

She half expected him to argue, but he fell back against the pillows.

Rabie stepped out of the bathroom, and the scent of shampoo and soap wafted out with him—an improvement. His hair dripped, and he had a towel wrapped around his waist.

Her suitcase was open on the floor in front of the closet. She hadn't opened it when she'd rolled it in earlier, and Derrick wouldn't have done that.

"Did you need something?" she asked Rabie.

"I was trying to find something to wear."

"Next time, please don't go through my things without asking." She smiled to soften the reproof, crossing the room toward him. "A shower was a good idea. It will help you relax. I bought you a treat."

She held out the bag that had the things she'd bought for him, and he took it and dug around inside. He pulled out the little cream-filled chocolate cake, his eyes slightly brighter than before.

"You deserve chocolate, no?"

That almost brought a grin. "I think yes." His gaze flicked to Derrick. "Does *he* get one?"

"I don't think he's up for it, but I bought him one for later." She moved a little closer and lowered her voice. "He risked his life to save you, Rabie. You should be thankful."

"He threw my stuff away."

"Yes." She nodded, keeping her expression solemn. "Are your things more important than his life? His safety?"

Rabie's shoulders lifted and fell.

"You are tired. Please, put on some clothes, eat your cake, and then brush your teeth." She stepped into the steamy bathroom, grabbed a bath towel, and backed out again. "And then we sleep, okay?"

Rabie took the clothes she'd bought into the bathroom and closed the door.

Jasmine moved to the bed opposite Derrick and opened all the packages she'd bought.

His skin was pale as paper, his eyes bloodshot as he watched her warily.

"Take off your sweatshirt, please."

"You're finally coming around to my way of thinking."

She tipped her head to one side. What did he mean?

"Trying to have your way with me?" His lips quirked at the corners. "Very unseemly."

Her cheeks warmed. He was teasing her. She lifted the brown bottle. "This will sting. How much it will sting"—she lifted her eyebrows—"this will depend on you."

He winced. "I take it all back." He pushed himself into a sitting position and worked his shirt up, his face contorting in pain.

She held the sleeve so he could pull his arm free, then tugged it over his head.

"Not that I mind you undressing me," he said, "but this isn't how I imagined this would go."

She would ignore his remarks. Perhaps they were his way of dealing with the pain. And she didn't want to think about Derrick imagining...anything. Because his shirt was off now, and his chest drew her gaze. Smooth except a little hair that crawled up from his pajama pants toward his belly button. She'd known he was strong, but she hadn't imagined such defined muscles.

His body was...perfect.

Jasmine forced her gaze away, turning on the bedside lamps. She spread the bath towel on the bed behind him. "Lie down and face away, please."

He did, lifting his arm over his head so she could access the wound.

His hair fell toward the bed, exposing his neck, his ear. His skin was light compared to hers, stretching tight over muscles that rippled as he held himself steady.

She was thankful he was facing away from her and didn't see her staring. It was all she could do to keep herself from reaching out and running her fingertips between his shoulder blades.

The only man she'd ever seen without his shirt on was her husband—wrinkled and hairy and pudgy. How were Khalid and Derrick even the same species?

Derrick was beautiful inside and out.

"Is it that bad?" His voice was low and rumbling.

"No. It's..." She shook herself and swallowed. The gash was about ten centimeters long and one centimeter wide, running from his front to his back. It was ugly and red and still seeping blood. "You washed it?"

"Yes, Nurse Ratched. I rinsed it, just like you said."

"Who is this Ratched?" Jasmine got the gauze and tape ready, then opened the brown bottle.

"She's from a movie."

"She is a good nurse?"

He chuckled. "She's a nightmare. It was a joke. She's nothing like you."

"Hmm. We will see." She tried a joking tone as well. "Hold still." She tipped the bottle and squeezed liquid over the wound.

He sucked air through his teeth, his muscles tightening.

As if her own body felt the pain, her stomach flopped. "It is to clean," she said. "I am sorry for the pain. Michael said gunshots infect easily."

"Yup." The word was clipped. "It's fine."

She capped the bottle and set it on the table.

Behind her, the bed shifted. Rabie climbing in.

She pressed the gauze to the wound, then taped it snug. "I am finished."

Derrick eased onto his back and sat up. "Let's do *that* again soon."

"We must clean it at least twice a day."

He groaned. "I was being sarcastic."

Rabie laughed.

Derrick leaned forward. "You think that's funny?" He was smiling.

"I thought you would cry like a girl."

"Only manly crying for me."

"Ha. No such thing."

Jasmine gathered all the first-aid supplies and returned them to the plastic bag. "You two are like little boys. And it is time for all the little boys to go to sleep."

"Aw, do we have to?" The whine came from Derrick, the silly man.

She reached to flick off the light between the beds, but he stopped her with an upraised hand and leaned past her to face Rabie again.

"Hey, son?"

"What?" Rabie sounded annoyed again,

"I had no choice about your backpack, so I'm not going to apologize for that. I am sorry I had to do it, though. And I'm sorry I wasn't more patient. Will you forgive me?"

Rabie's eyes widened, then narrowed as if he were trying to figure Derrick out.

Derrick's expression held nothing but sincere regret.

After a few beats, Rabie nestled under the covers. "I guess." The words were faint, but it was something.

"Thank you, son." Derrick nodded at the lamp, letting out a very loud, very put-upon sigh. "I guess if you say, we gotta go to sleep."

She flicked the light off, then leaned down and kissed Derrick on the forehead like she might a child.

But he wasn't a child, and she should not have done that.

In the glow coming from the bathroom, she watched his eyebrows hike. He caught her hand and held on, gazing at her in that way he had, his expression filled with tenderness. "You were amazing tonight."

"You saved me, Derrick. I owe you everything."

It seemed like he wanted to say something else, but after a moment, he released her hand.

She kissed Rabie good-night and escaped to the bathroom.

CHAPTER TWENTY-TWO

Derrick 's eyes were closed when Jasmine emerged from the bathroom a few minutes after she'd practically run in.

He'd managed to get his T-shirt on, and then he'd crawled between the sheets, exhausted. But he couldn't sleep. Too many images. Men with guns and Jasmine being dragged across the parking lot and shooting at SUVs.

And he swore he could still feel her lips on his forehead.

He didn't mind focusing on that memory.

Her kiss had been so natural, as if she did it every day. He wished...

He wished for more than a kiss on the head.

He wished for things he couldn't have.

"Are you awake?" Her voice was barely a whisper.

He opened his eyes.

She stood over him, a silhouette with the light spilling from the bathroom behind her. She'd changed into the pink pajamas he'd seen when he'd woken her the night before. Considering the shapeless dresses she always wore, he'd figured her for the flannel-nightgown type, but as usual, she'd surprised him. These were cute and shapely and...

He cleared his throat. "I'm awake."

She held out a glass of water. "I forgot to give you Tylenol. You wish to take them?"

"Yes, please." He pushed himself up, trying very hard not to let pain show in his expression.

How could a little scrape hurt so bad?

Well, maybe it was more than a *little* scrape. He'd been shot. Did it count that the bullet hadn't actually gone inside him? What were the rules for these things?

Not that it was a competition, but had any of his brothers ever been shot? Grant, probably, with all his military experience, but what about the rest of them? Derrick rarely had bragging rights over his brothers, but maybe...

"Why are you smiling?" Jasmine asked.

"Never mind." He opened his hand, and she dropped a couple of tablets into his palm. "Just two? Could I have a couple more?"

"The package says—"

"Let's walk on the wild side, shall we?"

With a wary expression, she got him two more pills, and he swallowed all four with a gulp of water.

Rabie hadn't stirred in the other bed. His breathing was even—not loud enough to be considered a snore, but close.

"You must be exhausted," he said.

"And you." But even after she took the empty glass, she didn't move away from his bedside.

"Rough day. Probably about the worst day I've ever had."

Her head moved up and down slowly, but she said, "I have had worse."

He didn't want to think about that. He didn't want to think

about all the terrible, terrible days Jasmine had endured in her life.

Maybe she was thinking about them, though. Was that shiny glint on her cheeks…a tear? "What is it, Jazz?" He tried to push himself up, but it hurt too much. "What's wrong?"

"Nothing." She swiped her fingers beneath her eyes and turned down the covers on her side of the bed she would share with Rabie. "It has been a long day."

He patted the space beside him. "Do you want to talk? There are extra blankets in the closet. Maybe you could just curl up with me for a minute."

She didn't turn back to him. Of course she'd refuse him. He didn't even know why he'd asked.

But then she grabbed a blanket and climbed onto the other side of his bed. "It is okay, if I stay on top?"

"Of course." His voice was suddenly husky. He shouldn't have offered if he couldn't handle it. He *could* handle it, though. For Jasmine, he would do anything.

"Khalid is going to find me." She rested her head on the other pillow and pulled the blanket over herself. "If you hadn't come out of the store when you did… I am afraid."

"I know, sweetheart." Derrick shifted and tucked her against his good side.

She curled into him. "I should not, but only for a moment."

"Sometimes, you just need a hug."

Her only response was the slightest…trembling.

She was sobbing.

Dang. He was trying to help, but he'd made it worse. He didn't know what he'd said, or what he should say, so he just held her and let her tears soak the blankets that separated them.

And hoped Rabie had been wrong about all crying being girlie, because his own eyes prickled. He was tired and in pain and…and he'd almost lost her.

What if she'd been taken? What would he have done? Would he have ever found her again?

A few minutes passed before she settled, her breathing evening out. For a moment, he thought she'd fallen asleep. But then she sighed. "I'm sorry."

"For what? I'm sorry. I wish I knew how to help. What to say or..."

She shook her head. "It was this I needed. Just this."

This...what?

She cuddled back in beside him.

Oh. "Hug-starved?"

"It would seem so." Her words were light. But a moment later, she spoke again. "For years, I was not hugged. Barely touched, and never with affection."

Derrick worked to keep his reaction calm. "That's awful."

"At the compound, it was only Baba, Hasan, and Khalid. Baba doesn't feel anything toward me. Nor Hasan. Khalid's touch was not... I should not speak of such things. Forgive me."

Yeah. He didn't want to hear about that. He already wanted to kill the guy. No need to add fuel to that fire. But... "If you ever want to talk about it, I'll listen."

Because, if it would make her feel better, he could handle the torture.

She was silent for a few moments. "Mama was very affectionate. And Leila. Even Basma and I would hold hands or sit close when we grieved or shared stories. Rabie was little then and always wanted me to play with him. It's silly that it should matter so much. It is friendship to touch sometimes, no?"

Derrick wasn't sure about that. He and his friends weren't exactly huggers, but they high-fived and slapped each other on the back. And Derrick had his brothers, and his sisters-in-law, and his mother, who hugged everybody, even if she'd seen them an hour before. Even if she'd just met them.

He'd never thought much about physical affection because he'd never lacked it.

"People need affection." He kept his voice at a whisper. "That you were denied such a basic human need..." From her father, her uncle, her *husband*. These men who should've protected and loved her had denied her. They'd treated her like property.

"Is it so important?"

"They say that a baby, even if he's fed and physically cared for, if he isn't held, will wither and die. So yeah. It's that important."

Jasmine stiffened. "Who would do that? Did the Nurse Ratched?"

"No." Derrick kissed her head. "She was a character in a movie, but people did do it. Real people. Cruel, horrible people who didn't understand the value of the human beings they experimented on. That's the problem, isn't it? When we forget to value people?"

Her head moved, a nod. "That is how I felt. Like I had no value. Like I was withering away. When Leila came, I was willing to risk anything to escape, even my own death—even your brother's death. I was, in that moment, like them—not valuing life. I had nothing to lose."

"I'm so sorry." He wished he could think of something... better to say. His words were pathetic, but what else did he have?

"You are sweet."

"You are incredibly valuable and precious and I..." *love you.* He swallowed that truth. "I think you're amazing and brave and strong, and you're going to be a wonderful mom."

She was. He had no doubt. But until she changed how she felt about her marriage, he needed to respect her choices. He needed to keep his feelings to himself.

She said nothing for a long time, just lay there, her tiny body somehow a perfect fit beside his long one.

He had no idea how much time had passed when she spoke again. "I wasn't alone, though, all that time. God was with me. I felt His presence."

"Mmm." Derrick was drifting off. "He never leaves us or forsakes us."

"He gave me hope when there was no hope." She yawned. "There was always eternity."

Eternity. Eternity would be beautiful and painless and amazing, and maybe it would be a little like the feel of Jasmine pressed right beside him, warm and alive, breathing steadily. Safe.

Derrick woke to the sound of raised voices, but he had no idea what they were saying.

He opened his eyes. Bright light peeked around the edges of the pulled curtains, where Jasmine stood between his bed and the window. She still wore those pajamas. Her long silky hair was sleep-tousled. She blinked as if she were just waking up.

Behind Derrick, Rabie babbled angrily—Arabic, of course. By the way Jasmine's shoulders stiffened, she didn't like what the kid had to say.

Derrick sat up, remembering the gash in his side a little too late. "What's going on?"

Jasmine's gaze flicked to him but didn't hold. "I fell asleep."

"Mmm. Me too."

Rabie said something, and Jasmine's dark skin flushed.

Ignoring the pain—it was better today, thank heavens—Derrick turned over, flipped the covers back, and swung his feet to the floor. "What is he saying?"

"It does not matter," Jasmine said.

Derrick faced Rabie, who stood at the end of his bed wearing sweatpants and a sweatshirt, curly hair sticking out everywhere, arms crossed in that *King-of-Siam* stance he liked.

"What did you say?" Derrick asked

He straightened his back. "I said the truth. She is just as Dari said American women are. A whore."

Derrick stood and crossed the room—fast.

Rabie backed against the wall, eyes widening.

Yeah, you should be scared, you little brat.

Derrick lowered himself all the way down to the punk's level and got in his face. "You want to repeat that?"

Rabie blinked.

"Go ahead. Say it again."

"Derrick, it is okay." She stood behind him, her voice somehow kind despite what the kid had said.

"It's *not* okay."

The starch went out of Rabie's spine. His bottom lip trembled. He was scared and sad and...and maybe Derrick had over-reacted.

Jasmine slipped her hand around his arm. "He is only parroting what he's been told. And I should not have—"

"Don't." Derrick straightened and took a step back and a breath, needing a little calm. "Don't act like you did anything wrong, Jasmine." To Rabie, he said, "Jasmine and I are friends. We were talking, and we fell asleep. And we don't owe you an explanation or a defense. Apologize to her. Now."

He muttered something in Arabic.

"That will not do," she said.

Good for her.

"Try again," Derrick said. "In English."

The kid stared at the floor. "I'm sorry."

"Look her in the eyes. And don't forget the second part, the part where you ask her to forgive you."

Rabie glared at Derrick, then turned to Jasmine. "I am sorry. Will you please forgive me?"

That was as close to a real apology as a red Skittle was to a fresh strawberry.

But Jasmine said, "I will."

Derrick crossed his arms. "It's fine if you're still mad at me, kid. Don't take it out on her, got it?"

He shrugged.

"Uh-uh," Derrick said. "I want to hear, 'Yes, sir.'"

He parroted the words. "Yes, sir."

"You will be kind whether you feel like it or not. You understand?"

"Yes, sir."

Amazing how much vitriol a nine-year-old could put into two syllables.

Derrick turned to Jasmine. "You okay?"

"Of course." But by the sadness in her expression, she wasn't, not even close. She moved past them into the bathroom.

Great way to start a day.

It was after ten—a good thing. They'd all needed the sleep.

They didn't talk much as they got cleaned up. Derrick was running out of fresh clothes and suspected Jasmine was as well. She'd changed into a dark gray dress that reached to her ankles and could double as a single-man tent. At least she wouldn't have to spend a lot of money on maternity clothes.

Oh. Huh. Maybe that explained her fashion choices.

She'd apparently grabbed a few things for Rabie at the store the night before. He wore a navy sweatshirt and gray sweatpants. Not exactly haute couture, but they would keep him warm, anyway. The kid didn't even have a coat.

After Derrick's shower, Jasmine tortured him with the

hydrogen peroxide again, then put another bandage on his wound. It was past noon by the time they were ready.

Not that they had anywhere to go.

The night before, Michael had told them to sit tight until they heard from him. Derrick had called his brother that morning, but he hadn't answered, only texted back saying he was working on it and to stay out of sight.

Which meant being stuck in that tiny room with a beautiful —and embarrassed, Derrick guessed—woman and a sullen kid.

Fun for everyone.

He ordered a pizza and a family-sized salad for lunch, which they ate sitting on their separate beds while they watched a superhero movie.

After that, they played a few rounds of Uno, and Derrick even let Rabie win the second one, hoping it would shift the kid's mood.

It did, a little.

The sun was sinking on what seemed like a beautiful day outside when the burner finally rang. Derrick swung his long legs off the end of the bed where he'd been sitting cross-legged, teaching Rabie and Jasmine how to play gin rummy—the tiny room didn't have a table or any chairs—and grabbed the phone from the bedside table. He saw the familiar number and answered with, "Please, tell me you have a plan."

"Going a little crazy, are you?" Michael sounded amused.

"You have no idea."

"How are you feeling?"

"I'm fine. We're all fine."

"How about the wound?"

Derrick turned to find that Rabie had gone to the bathroom. Jasmine was watching Derrick.

"Don't worry," he said. "Jasmine's been having all sorts of fun pouring salt into it."

Her jaw dropped, and amusement danced in her eyes. "Not *much* fun," she said. "Only the proper amount of fun."

Michael must've heard because he laughed. "She's hilarious when she lets her guard down. It doesn't happen very often."

It did with Derrick. Or it had, before this...adventure.

Not that he wanted to kill the mood, but he needed to know... "What about the guys at the parking lot?"

"One's dead."

Oh.

Wow.

Derrick had killed a man. Actually killed him.

He, who'd never taken a shot at a deer, had killed a human being.

"The other's critically wounded," Michael continued. "We got someone at the hospital to take him into custody if he wakes up, but it's not looking good."

Maybe Derrick had killed two men.

"You with me?"

"Yup." Derrick couldn't seem to force anything else out of his mouth.

"Couple things about that." His brother's tone softened the slightest. "First, it was them or Jasmine and Rabie. You didn't have a choice."

"I know."

"Second, even though that's true, I haven't found it helps much. You gotta talk to someone about it when you get back, process it. Otherwise, it'll either eat you up or make you callous."

"You mean like a counselor?"

"Exactly. Bryan's doing it. He could give you a name, and you two could even talk to each other."

"Bryan? Did he...?" Derrick's brother had told him a little

ROBIN PATCHEN

about what had gone down in Germany a couple of weeks ago, but he hadn't shared that much.

"Talk to him," Michael said. "Tell him I said it's okay to tell you. The point is, it *should* bother you. If it didn't, that would be a problem. Okay?"

"Yeah, thanks."

"And also, nice shooting. I'm impressed."

That didn't help, at all. "About that plan?"

"Not only do I have one, but I have good news. Put me on speaker, would you? They'll want to hear this."

He pressed the button and, dropping the phone on the bed, called, "Rabie? Come here for a sec."

The kid came out of the bathroom.

"He's here," Derrick said.

"Hey, buddy." Michael's voice was loud over the speaker. "Guess what." When the kid didn't say anything, Michael continued. "We found your sister."

His eyes popped wide. He climbed onto the bed and spoke to the phone. "Is she okay?"

"Aside from how worried she is about you, she's fine. When my friends told her you were safe, she started bawling."

"Girls." Rabie shook his head like the thought disgusted him.

Derrick pretended not to see the moisture in his eyes.

Jasmine covered her mouth, not bothering to hide her own tears. "Where is she?"

"She's with my friends," Michael said. "They're going to escort her to meet her cousin. You guys will meet them there tomorrow morning."

Rabie's face was brighter than Derrick had ever seen it. "We will see Basma tomorrow?"

Jasmine nodded and pulled him into a hug. "Thank you." She aimed her words at the phone. "Thank you so much."

238

"Of course. But sis, next time—"

"There will not be one," she said. "Never again. I promise."

"Hmm. Okay. Leila had a long message she wanted me to pass along with lots of…suggestions for you."

Sniffing, Jasmine swiped her fingers under her eyes. "She is very angry with me?"

"More scared than angry," he said. "She wants to call you, but I won't give her the number, just in case."

In case what? In case Dari caught up with them again? How would he?

Derrick didn't want to think about that.

"I don't want any links to her," Michael continued. "You understand."

"Yes, yes." Jasmine was nodding as if Michael could see her. "I can guess what she wants to say anyway. Tell her that I love her too."

"I'll do it. Derrick, take me off speaker, and I'll give you the details."

He did, heading toward the window. He eased the curtain aside and peeked out at the growing darkness, lowering his voice. "No luck locating Dariush?"

"No hits on the email at all. The guy's slipperier than ice."

"I don't understand something. Last night, those thugs were trying to manhandle Jasmine and Rabie into the SUV. The thing is, they were both armed. Why didn't they just use the guns to force them to go?"

"Probably the same reason your crazy stunt worked— shooting at the car. That's what you did, right?"

"Shot a couple of tires. I tried to hit the gas tank, but I ran out of ammo."

"Rookie mistake. Always reload after a shootout."

"Thanks, Rambo." Derrick deadpanned his voice. "I'll remember that next time."

"Not that what you did couldn't have worked, but did they shoot back?"

"Yeah, but..." Come to think of it, they didn't try that hard to hit anything. No windows broke. Not that Derrick had looked, but he didn't think the car had been damaged at all. "They didn't hit anything."

"Maybe it would've worked, then." Did Michael sound impressed? "You've got good instincts, obviously. I think you missed your calling."

"You gotta be nuts to want this kind of stress in your life."

Michael chuckled. "You're not wrong, bro. To answer your question, I'm guessing they were told that Jasmine and Rabie weren't to be harmed. They shot at you, but they weren't going to risk hurting either one of them—that would've defeated the purpose, right?"

"True, but the threat of being shot would have gotten them into the car faster. The only reason I had any shot at stopping them was that Jasmine fought so hard." Derrick could still see the way she thrashed and struggled, digging her heels into the ground. Maybe motivated by fear, but he had to believe at least a little of that came from her hope that, if she held out long enough, Derrick would rescue her.

"Dari probably told them not to use guns," Michael said. "If they shot at the car, they were probably desperate. You did great."

"Hardly. I was scared spitless."

"If you hadn't been, I'd be worried. I would've been scared too."

That made Derrick feel a little better. "You seem concerned that they're going to find us." Derrick was sure to keep his voice low so Jasmine and Rabie wouldn't hear. "How could they?"

"You guys should be safe."

"Then why can't Jazz and Leila talk? What aren't you telling me?"

"What are you talking about?" Michael sounded more puzzled than annoyed.

Maybe it was the sting of the gunshot wound. Or the lack of sleep. Or the sheer...strangeness of the previous few days, but Derrick didn't know what to think. "Dari's men found us. Twice."

"Yeah. The kid's backpack—"

"If it was that, then why didn't they find us sooner? Why not at Gavin's cabin?"

"There's no Wi-Fi there."

"Why not at the hotel before that?"

"I don't know. Maybe he didn't have anybody he could send."

"The guys who were at the airport could've—"

"I don't know," Michael snapped. "I'm not in the guy's head. It's weird."

It was more than weird. It didn't make sense. None of it made sense. Derrick hated to suggest the idea that presented itself, but he had to, even if it ticked his brother off. "Is there any chance somebody on your end is feeding him information?"

"No. None."

"But what if—"

"Seriously?" Michael's voice didn't rise with anger but lowered so that Derrick had to strain to hear him. "Do you seriously not trust me?"

"That's not what I'm saying. Maybe somebody else, somebody you work with—"

"I didn't know where you were last night."

"The car has a navigation system. If somebody knew what we were driving—"

"They'd be there now. The car is with you, isn't it?"

His brother made a point. But... "They could be waiting for us. The car isn't parked outside our room."

"They're not there, Derrick. You're being paranoid." Michael exhaled audibly. "There isn't some big government conspiracy going on here. You're my brother. She's my bride's twin. You really think I'm going to take any chances with your lives?"

"Then how did they find us?"

"It had to be the backpack or something inside it." Michael seemed convinced. "Maybe the tracker they had with the kid's stuff isn't very good. Maybe it has to have a great signal or something, and that's why they didn't catch up with you before. Maybe Dari's having personnel issues. There's no telling. But now that you don't have the backpack, you really should be safe."

Should be didn't feel good enough. But Michael had gotten them this far.

"Okay, fine. What's the plan?"

CHAPTER TWENTY-THREE

This was the riskiest part of the plan, but Michael wanted them to head to the airport in Pittsburgh, thinking that if somehow Dari's men tracked their car down later, maybe they would assume Jasmine and Rabie had gotten on a flight.

So, after Derrick pulled the car away from the motel where they'd spent the day, Jasmine couldn't help checking the road behind them, certain she'd see a black SUV on their tail.

As far as she could tell, nobody followed.

In the backseat, Rabie clutched his new bag to his chest as if terrified Derrick would try to pry it away and throw it out the window. Despite all Derrick had done for him, Rabie hadn't forgiven him.

They didn't talk while Derrick followed the signs and then drove into an airport parking garage. They remained quiet as they grabbed their bags and made their way to meet the shuttle that would take them to the off-site car rental facility.

It was after eleven at night by the time he plugged their destination into the Toyota sedan's navigation system.

"This is all it will take?" She double-checked the arrival

time on their latest car's screen. "Only six hours to New York City."

"Sounds right."

New York was another state she'd never seen—and still wouldn't because of the darkness. "We will be early, no?" They weren't supposed to meet Basma and her cousin until eight o'clock in the morning, when the train station would be packed with people. But the map told her they'd arrive in the city a couple of hours before that.

"There'll be traffic, and we'll need to find a place to park. We can get some breakfast. That'll kill some time."

"What is the plan exactly?"

Derrick's eyes flicked to the rearview mirror, and he shook his head.

She twisted and saw Rabie was staring out the window, wide awake. She reached back and patted his leg. "I think you should try to sleep."

He didn't bother to look at her. The joy at hearing that Basma was going to meet him had faded, leaving him sullen again. Or perhaps afraid something would go wrong. "I'm not tired."

"You want to be well-rested when you see your sister, no?" One of the blankets they'd brought from the cabin had been shoved onto the floor at his feet. Jasmine tried to drape it over Rabie, though she couldn't reach him to do it well. "The pillow is there too. Get comfortable. If you sleep, the time will pass faster."

He seemed about to argue but, after a moment, did as she directed, cuddling the cheap bag she'd bought him like a stuffed animal.

"You can put your backpack down. Nobody's going to touch it."

He sent a narrow-eyed glare at the back of Derrick's head

but dropped the bag on the floor.

She smiled at him. "In the morning we'll get breakfast. Do you like pancakes with maple syrup?"

He shrugged.

"You will. Trust me. And then we'll see Basma, okay?"

That brought a slight softening of his features. She couldn't blame Rabie for his worry. He'd been through so much.

"Where are we going now?" he asked.

"New York City!" She infused the words with enthusiasm.

His eyes widened. "To the Statue of Liberty?"

"I don't think to that place, but perhaps Basma can take you another time."

"Then where exactly?"

She waited for Derrick to answer, but he didn't, just kept driving.

"We'll see when we get there. Please, get some sleep." She grabbed the other blanket, the one she'd folded and placed at her own feet, and covered herself. "I'm going to rest too."

That seemed to mollify him. He closed his eyes and settled against the door.

She did the same, and they drove in silence for a long time, nothing but the sound of the classical music playing softly over the speakers.

She tried not to fall asleep. Derrick hadn't had any more sleep than she had, and he'd been injured. She should probably help keep him awake. When she hadn't heard anything from the backseat in a half hour, she peeked.

"He out?" Derrick asked.

"I think so." She kept her voice low. "Why don't you want him to know where we're going?"

"It's stupid, but..." Derrick glanced at her. "I was thinking about all the questions he was asking when we left the cabin about what kind of car we were driving and the license plate and where we were going, and I just..." His shoulders lifted and fell. "There's no way he could have been in contact with Dari, right? But what if the thing that alerted his brother wasn't a tracker? What if it was some kind of a transmitter, and the guy was hearing what Rabie was saying? Or even listening to us?"

"You think he was telling Dari where we were? You think he wants his brother to find us?"

"I don't know. Maybe. He likes Dari, and he doesn't put a lot of stock in his sister's opinion."

He wouldn't, especially if Dari had fed him lies about her.

"Even if there'd been some kind of...transmitter"—Derrick seemed uncomfortable even suggesting the word—"it's gone now, lying by the side of the road in West Virginia." But by the worry in his eyes, he wasn't convinced. "It doesn't make sense. Rabie didn't have a phone or any way to contact him. Michael's probably right and there was a tracker, and it just wasn't very good." Derrick tapped the wheel. "If that's the case, how did they catch up to us so fast at that gas station—in the middle of nowhere? They must've been following us for a while. I just hadn't noticed." He checked his rearview mirror, then shook his head. "They could be back there right now for all I know." By the way his lips pressed closed, he wasn't happy about the thought.

"You couldn't have known. None of this is your fault." His hand rested lightly on the gear shift, and she slid her palm over it.

He weaved their fingers together, then dropped their joined hands on his knee. "I'm glad you think so."

"Every second vehicle on the road is an SUV, and most of them are dark. For all we know, they've switched to another kind of car altogether. Why this whole...flock of SUVs?"

That brought a grin. "Fleet?"

"This is the word?"

"For cars, yeah. If they attacked riding giant geese, *flock* would work."

The image made her smile. "You are a silly man."

"Hmm. Just how I always wanted to be described." He was joking, but by the way his amusement faded, he wasn't *only* joking.

Perhaps men preferred not to be referred to as *silly*.

His voice was serious when he continued. "I just want to get Rabie back to his sister and get you home before anything else goes wrong. This whole thing has been...bizarre."

"I'm sorry I got you into it."

"I could've said no." He squeezed her hand. "I'm sorry I didn't talk you out of it. I'm sorry I couldn't keep you two safe."

"How could you have seen any of this coming?"

"Michael would have." The way he grumbled the words made her smile. Then he muttered, "I doubt he's ever been described as *silly*."

That was probably true. Michael was intense. She loved her future brother-in-law, but she could never be with a man like him, a man who took the world so seriously. She much preferred the one who sat beside her, who appreciated good things, who focused on joy, not darkness. Who laughed and wanted others to laugh with him. Derrick valued peace over conflict and war. Derrick was simply...happy. She'd known so few truly happy people in her life. To her, his happiness, his joy, was magnetic.

She'd spent enough of her life with hate- and anger-filled men, whose laughter was cruel and whose smiles were sinister.

Not that Michael was like that. But he wasn't light or joyful like Derrick was.

And also... "Your brother is not perfect. Even with all his training, he makes mistakes." Jasmine and Leila had nearly been returned to Iraq because Michael had let his guard down. "You should be less hard on yourself. To spend time with, I prefer you. Even now, with all this happening, I prefer you."

That brightened Derrick's expression.

She shouldn't have said that.

Even if it was true, she shouldn't have said it. She added, "He will be my brother, but you are my friend."

"Right." Derrick's smile faded, and he slid his hand away. "I'm glad."

She wasn't sure what to say, and silence stretched between them. Before, back in Maine, their friendship had been easy and comfortable, never tense as it was now.

Would they be able to return to the way it had been, or was it ruined forever?

"So, um..." Derrick sounded as tentative as she felt. "You seem to know a lot about the Bible. You had one, I guess? In Iraq?"

"Oh, yes." This was a safe subject and one of her favorites. "When Leila and I gave our lives to Christ, the father in the family that led us to Him gave us each Arabic Bibles."

"You must've kept it hidden."

"I did, for all those years. It was easy in Baghdad. Baba never came into my room. After Khalid, it was more difficult, but I hid it at the very bottom of a chest, and he never suspected me of anything. He never found it. I don't think...I don't think he ever considered that I had thoughts, like a human being, you see? It would never have occurred to him that I would have something that would matter, something worth keeping secret."

"Sounds like a keeper, that one."

"Oh, yes. He was like Don Joo-an."

Derrick laughed. "Don Juan."

"That's not how it's spelled."

"Spanish name."

"I see. But it was the correct usage, yes? I read it somewhere, a man was described like this, a charmer, no? A ladies' man?"

"You got the name. You even nailed the sarcastic tone. Nicely done."

His compliment brought a flush of pleasure. Not that she should aspire to sarcasm, but it was hard enough to be amusing in Arabic, much less in an unfamiliar language. She used to be funny, when she was a child. Back when life was easy. She was always the shy twin, and perhaps for that reason, people were even more surprised when she would say something to make them laugh.

"What if he had?" Derrick's tone was serious again. "Found the Bible?"

"Oh." She shrugged, though Derrick didn't see. "He probably would have killed me, at least before he knew I was expecting."

"What a risk."

"Perhaps, for some. But I was desperate to be free in whatever way God chose for it to happen—through escape or death. I would have taken either."

Derrick winced. "That's..." He lifted his hand like he was going to reach for her, then gripped the steering wheel. "I'm sorry."

"'To live is Christ, to die is gain,' no?"

Derrick didn't respond, but a muscle twitched in his cheek, which told her he didn't like that answer.

"The Bible was my only friend. In Baghdad, after Mama died, I would read for hours and hours. It was my comfort. At the compound, if Khalid was away, I would read all night long. When he was there, I didn't dare take it out, but he was with Salwa often."

"Salwa is...?"

"His beloved wife."

"Oh."

Even in the darkness of the car, she could see the scowl that crossed Derrick's face.

"And sometimes"—she hurried to add—"he would go on trips. He is the one who found Leila in Germany. He knew who she was because—"

"You're identical."

"Yes. He recognized her immediately."

"Makes sense."

Derrick grew quiet, but Jasmine longed to prolong the conversation, to keep things from getting awkward again. Jasmine and Derrick had discussed their faith often enough, so this felt like a safe topic.

"Michael has several Bibles on a bookshelf in his living room, which he said I could look at. It is fascinating, all the English translations and how different they are—and also how similar, yes? And there is a book with the original Hebrew and Greek words and their definitions, and how they are used in different places in the Scripture. Also a book with archaeology and history, and some commentaries with people's opinions about every verse in the Bible. Do you have these things as well?"

"I have a couple books like that, yeah."

"Do you study these? Do you find them helpful?"

"I don't use them as often as I should, I guess."

"There were things I couldn't understand before—historical events, for instance, about Israel and the world at the time of the Scripture. Michael's resources have opened my eyes to the stories in a new way. But other things in those books I'm not sure the purpose of. Why have a man interpret Scripture when God will do it if only you ask Him?"

"Just for a different perspective, I guess."

"But another perspective is better than God's?"

"You've never found God to be silent? To not give you insights?"

"No. Have you?"

"Sometimes. Maybe I'm just in too much of a hurry."

Ah, yes. It seemed to her that Americans were always in a hurry. "How many Bibles do you have?"

He considered the question a moment. "Probably…seven or eight, more if I count the ones I've had since I was a kid."

"This is amazing, to have so many."

"Especially when you consider that I use the Bible app on my phone most of the time."

"This I like, to have it always with me, as you have always had. You must know so much, being able to study whenever you wish, to go to church and study with others."

"I don't know. From all the conversations you and I have had, I think you know more than I do. I have all the access I want, but I never had to fight for it like you do."

She considered that. "To have to fight for it is good?"

"When you became a believer, you knew what it might cost you. When I became a believer, everyone celebrated me. I had nothing to hide, nothing to worry about. Yeah, maybe some kids at school made fun of me sometimes, but really, what did I care about that?"

"You had all the freedom to study the Bible and didn't."

"I did, I just didn't treasure it like you did."

"I see, yes." She thought about the leather-bound book she'd loved, its pages worn, her handwritten notes in the margins. She never would have dared writing in it if not for the kind man who'd given it to her. He'd encouraged her to not only make notes but to date them so that, years later, she could remember what the Lord had taught her during different seasons.

Though Jasmine had bought a new Bible in Maine, that first, treasured Bible was lost to her forever. She'd had no choice but to leave it behind. It was the only thing she missed about her home.

Had Khalid found it? If so, what did he think? That it had corrupted her?

If he thought that, then he was a fool, and that was no surprise to her. His eyes had been darkened by lies and deception. He didn't know better, and she prayed he would, someday. That he and Baba and Uncle Hasan would someday understand the truth.

At least, when she was her best self, she prayed for them.

Mostly, she prayed Khalid would never find her.

Jasmine was relieved when Derrick exited the highway.

"We need gas," he explained. "And I could use some caffeine."

She twisted to see Rabie sitting up and stretching. "Do you need to use the bathroom?"

"Where are we?" His words came out on a yawn.

"About halfway there." Derrick shot her a look she figured was meant to remind her not to tell him anything more detailed than that.

Inside the brightly lit gas station, he accompanied Rabie into the men's room and was waiting outside the ladies' room door when she emerged. "You need anything?"

"Maybe some water."

He grabbed two bottles of water and one of Coke. After he paid for them, they all returned to the car together. It seemed Derrick didn't intend for them to split up for even a second this time around—and she certainly wasn't complaining.

She and Rabie climbed into the car while he filled the tank.

"Are you excited to see your sister?" Jasmine asked him.

"Uh-huh."

No matter how hard Jasmine had tried, Rabie hadn't warmed up to her again after catching her on the bed with Derrick.

"Can I talk to you about what happened this morning?"

His narrow shoulders lifted and fell.

"I know you have heard that men and women who are not married should not sleep together, yes?" At his nod, she continued. "This is true. There is more to that—what men and women are not to do in bed—than what happened between Derrick and me last night."

"I know." He crossed his arms. "I'm not a baby."

She did her best not to smile. "Then you understand that Derrick was under the covers, and I was under a different blanket on top of his covers. You see? We were not together in that way."

"You should not have been..."

The door opened, and Derrick climbed in. "You guys ready?" When he saw them, his eyebrows draw together. "What's wrong?"

"Rabie and I are discussing what happened last night."

"Why?" By his tone, Derrick still felt it wasn't the kid's business.

"Because it looked unseemly, and we are not to give even the appearance of sin, is that not true? I believe we gave the appearance of sin, so we ought to explain. It's about holiness."

Derrick's mouth snapped shut. He shifted into gear and started driving.

Jasmine turned her attention to Rabie again. "You are correct, Rabie. I should not have been there. We gave the impression that we had done something wrong, and it made you feel uncomfortable, which I did not wish to do. So, I want to explain now that I was only beside Derrick because I was sad and frightened after what happened, and he wanted to comfort me. We were talking, and we fell asleep. That is all. There was nothing else. Do you understand?"

Rabie's gaze flicked from her to the back of Derrick's head. He nodded.

"Will you forgive me for making you feel uncomfortable?"

His little lips quirked, and he straightened, triumphant. "I will. Now, I have forgiven you both for something."

"Does that mean you win?" She asked the question, even though it made no sense to her.

"Of course."

Beside her, Derrick chuckled. "Okay, bud. Back to sleep. We have three more hours."

He didn't argue this time, just pulled the blanket up over himself and tucked in. Within minutes, he was out.

After a few miles, Derrick asked, "What did you mean, holiness? If we did nothing wrong, how was it about holiness?"

"To be holy is to be set apart, no? To be set apart for God, but also to look set apart to the culture. To Rabie last night, we looked as if we had sinned. I didn't wish for him to believe that about us. It's even more important when you think of what his brother tells him about all American women. I think many in America don't understand, but in my country, and I think in much of the world, people believe all Americans are Christians."

"Really? Why?"

"Perhaps because most countries do not have so much... difference? Different cultures and religions?"

"Diversity?"

"Yes, this is right. When Dari says American women are all, you know—"

"I remember."

"What he's saying is that *Christian* women are like that. He believes Christians have loose morals. All Christians are evil and impure. You see? I didn't wish for him to believe that. He needs to understand that what his brother says is not correct. Also, I didn't want him to hold a grudge against me or to think you and I had done something we hadn't done. It felt wrong not to explain."

He grunted. "I guess I was being a little stubborn."

"A little?"

His quick grin didn't hold. A few minutes later, he said, "Can I ask...?" But his words faded.

When he didn't finish, she prompted with, "Ask what?"

"If you don't want to talk about this, I get it. And if it's none of my business, then I get that too. Just tell me, and I'll shut up."

She twisted to check on Rabie, but he hadn't moved. "Okay."

"I get that you feel married."

Irritation spiked. "I *am* married."

"Right. That's what... I'm just... If you'd been married in America, and he was married to someone else, it wouldn't be legal."

"I was not married in America."

"I know. It's just weird to me for a man to have two wives. I'm trying to say that I get it, sort of. How you feel. Or I'm trying to. You and Khalid were intimate, and you're carrying his child. If you weren't married, then what would that mean for you? You'd be like one of those women with loose morals. So I get it. You're married." The last two words came out with a defeated breath. He took another, then started again. "Did he ever hurt you? Physically?"

Jasmine flashed back to too many moments at the compound, moments she preferred not to remember. "He did not hit me."

"That's a carefully worded answer. What does it mean?"

ROBIN PATCHEN

"I would prefer not to discuss this."

"Jazz, come on. Just tell me."

Had he not just said she didn't have to talk about it if she didn't want to? And yet, here he insisted she talk about it.

His hands tightened on the wheel, but after a moment, he said, "Fine. He didn't *hit you,* but I'm guessing he did hurt you."

"It is not unusual in my country. He would grab me sometimes or push me if I didn't move fast enough. Nothing terrible."

"In America, that would be considered abuse, and that's grounds for divorce. Not that you need grounds here—you can divorce for any reason at all, but as a Christian... I'm just saying, God wouldn't ask you to stay with a man who hurt you."

"I do not understand what you're saying."

"If you don't think the fact that he has another wife is good enough reason to divorce him, then abuse definitely is. I don't know the legalities of it. We'd need a good lawyer to figure out how to go about it, considering Khalid lives in Iraq. But the point is—"

"You're saying I should divorce him?"

"Of course. It's the simplest solution."

"Why?"

"What do you mean, why? Because... Do you *want* to be married to him?"

"That is irrelevant. I am married to him."

"But you don't have to be. In America, the law is set up—"

"I do not live by the law of America."

"This is your home now. This is where you're going to spend your life, right? You have to obey the law of the land."

"Yes, you're right. Like in the Book of Romans, of course." Jasmine was trying to understand what Derrick was saying. "But first, I obey a higher law."

"I know that." His volume ticked higher. "I'm just saying—"

"Please, do not wake Rabie."

He raked a hand through his hair and took a breath. "Sorry." Though he spoke more quietly, his words carried just as much frustration. "Don't you want to be free of him? Why wouldn't you?"

"Free? Is that what I would be?"

"Of course."

"You think he would stop pursuing me if I divorced him? He would stop searching for his child?"

"If Khalid came for the baby, you'd have legal recourse. You would have full custody. You could seek protection. If you petition the court with all the facts—about his other wife, about the abuse—they wouldn't consider Khalid a fit parent. He wouldn't have any legal right to take him."

Ah. "So for protection, you think I should do this. But custody will not make a difference to Khalid. He will not accept the law of America."

"Well, right. But if you're hidden, as long as he can't find you..."

"Then what does it matter?" She shifted and pulled her knee up on the seat to better face Derrick. "I do not understand. If a divorce wouldn't protect me, then what would be the point?"

"You would be free of him. Don't you want that?"

"How would I be free? I think...I think this freedom you talk about is different from the freedom I seek. I am already free."

"You're hiding. You're pregnant, and you're about to raise a kid by yourself."

"But that would not change if I—"

"I'm talking about the freedom to decide your own future, Jazz." He glanced her way, then reached for her like he'd done so many times. His palm was warm over the back of her hands, and she reveled in his gentle grip. "If you divorce Khalid, you can get married, for real, to a man of your choosing. You can..."

Derrick's Adam's apple dipped as he swallowed. His voice was lower when he continued. "We could be together. *I* could be your husband. *I* could be your baby's father. You don't have to be alone."

"Oh." Her cheeks warmed. Her whole body flushed with his words, with what he was saying.

Derrick wanted to be with her. He wanted to *marry* her.

This good, good man wanted her.

If only things could be different. But they could not, and they would not. And they were not.

No matter how she wished it.

"I guess you're not there yet." He must've misinterpreted her silence. "I think, if you let yourself consider it, let yourself see me as more than a friend, you'll see that this is a good option." He lifted her hand to his mouth, then pressed a kiss to the backs of her fingers.

The slight touch sent pleasure shivering across her skin.

She pulled away and crossed her arms.

He exhaled. "If you'd just give me a chance. That's all I'm saying. I'm all-in here. I would... There's nothing I want more than to be with you. But even if... Even if you don't want me, wouldn't you like to be free of Khalid? Wouldn't you like the freedom to make that choice?"

His simple kiss to her hand—had he even realized he'd done it—had thrown her off-kilter, as if the whole world were tipping to one side, and she couldn't keep her balance.

She needed to think. She took a few breaths, trying to work out what to say. What she must say. "In America, you see freedom as the ability to do anything."

"I'm not talking about America, sweetheart. I'm talking about you and me."

She continued as if he hadn't spoken. "Here, you are free if you can go where you want and do what you want. You are free if you have money to buy what looks pretty in the store. People wear whatever clothes they choose, even if they are immodest or even ridiculous. They can eat and drink anything, whether it is healthy or will make them fat or will make them drunk. There are few rules, and even the rules that do exist—some rules that have existed since the beginning of time—your society wants to tear down. And they call this freedom, no?"

"That's not what I'm talking about." Derrick's words came out hard. "You were forced to marry a man you didn't choose, a man who has another wife, a man who imprisoned you and who'll no doubt hurt you—maybe *more* than hurt you—if he catches up with you. That breaks some old-as-time rules, doesn't it? I'm pretty sure Adam and Eve chose each other. How could you possibly want to stay married to him? I mean, fine, in America maybe we take the whole freedom thing too far, but come on." She didn't miss the anger in his eyes. "How can you not want to separate yourself from him?"

"You ask the wrong question. The true question is, will I be free if I do what you suggest. I say I am already free because true freedom isn't the ability to do what I want. True freedom comes from doing what God says. True freedom is in walking with Him, is it not?"

Derrick didn't say anything, but his jaw tightened. She had a feeling he was setting himself against her words.

She wished she could do that. Part of her wished she believed as he did. How much easier it would be if she thought ending her marriage were as simple as signing a legal document. That she could hire a lawyer to draw up papers, and then she could do as she wished.

But she didn't believe that.

"I think..." She paused to try to put her thoughts into words. "I think that America is blessed to have so many who believe in Jesus. And God has blessed this country. There are good churches here. There are amazing people here—people like you and your family. I have never known such generosity as I do in America. So I do not wish to criticize, but I think in some ways, American Christians have forgotten the holiness of God. You see your laws and think that, as long as you call something acceptable, it *is* acceptable. But to divorce Khalid because of these things you mentioned—that is an American way of thinking. It is...how do I say? Not to think of eternity but only to think of this life, as if this life is all that matters."

"Temporal." Derrick's single word was flat, emotionless.

"Yes, like temporary. That's all this is, temporary. There is so much happiness in America, and this is good and nice—if it is real. But it is also bad because it gives the idea that happiness here, on earth, is the point. But this is not what the Bible teaches. Jesus said we would have suffering—"

"But why do you want to if you don't have to?"

"I am married." Now it was *her* voice getting too loud.

"You already left him, Jazz. You've already walked out on your marriage. Why not make it official? I mean, aren't you supposed to honor your husband? Respect him? Wasn't running away from him sin? How do you decide which ones are acceptable and which aren't?"

"But I was—"

"And as long as you've gone halfway with it, why not finish? Why not just—?"

"If you ask me a question," she snapped, "then you listen for my answer."

He clamped his lips shut.

"You know Rahab?"

"Not personally."

She ignored his sarcasm. "In the Bible, in the book of Joshua, the prostitute who—"

"I know who she is." The words were cold. "I might not stay up all night reading my Bible, but I'm not ignorant."

"I did not mean... I do not wish to argue, only to explain."

"Sorry." He waved a hand toward her. "Go on, then. Explain."

"Rahab was in an impossible position, a position she did not choose. The Israelite spies were at her home, and when the city officials came, she had to make a decision. She could betray the spies and tell the truth, or she could protect the spies and lie. Either way, there was good, and there was sin. To betray God's people was sin. But to lie was sin also. There was no sinless path. You see?"

Perhaps Derrick knew where Jasmine was going because he didn't say a word.

"I was in a position like Rahab. To stay with a man who was married to another woman, who was a terrorist, who would have raised our son to be a terrorist like himself, or our daughter to be a slave like me. To raise our child to hate the One True God and to love a false god—this is sin, no?"

She paused to give Derrick the opportunity to argue, but still, he said nothing.

"But to dishonor my husband was also sin. I had to choose. Maybe my choice was wrong, but my hope was to honor God the way Rahab honored God. In Jericho, Rahab was a prostitute, but with the people of God, she was redeemed. This was my prayer, that my life could be redeemed. That away from my husband and my father, I could raise my child to matter, the way Rahab's child mattered. An ancestor of Christ, yes? This I studied, and this I prayed. That my child could grow up as His child. You see?"

Derrick's head dipped and rose, though by the tightness in his jaw, the admission cost him something.

"Do you think I chose wrong?"

"No." He swallowed. "No, you did the right thing." He didn't look at her.

She hated this. She hated hurting Derrick. It felt like her heart was shattering into a million pieces.

She'd known, when she married Khalid, that she was forfeiting the marriage God might have had for her—if she were a different kind of person, born into a different culture, a different world. She hadn't had a choice, but she'd grieved what she knew she'd never have—to the degree that she'd understood.

But she hadn't understood.

How could she have? She'd never known a man—not well, anyway— who was truly devoted to his wife. She'd never seen a man lay himself down for a woman like Christ did for the church.

She'd never had a man want her, desire her, or even notice her.

She hadn't experienced true love.

Even after she'd come to America and seen how the Wright men loved their women, she hadn't really processed that she could have been one of those women. She'd always felt...separate. As if she could never have been worthy.

But now she understood what she never had before.

Derrick knew her. He knew her like nobody had ever known her. After a decade's separation from her twin, Jasmine thought Derrick knew her even better than Leila.

And he loved her.

And it was wrong, and she shouldn't, and she would need to ask God to forgive her and help her overcome her feelings, but she loved him too.

She loved him like she had never known she could love a man.

For the first time, she understood what she'd sacrificed when she'd made that vow to Khalid.

"You won't do it." Derrick wasn't asking a question. The words were more a statement of fact. "You won't divorce him."

"If I thought it would protect my child, I would consider it." Tears stung her eyes and made her voice high. She cleared her throat, but that wouldn't help. There was no hiding the truth from Derrick. "To marry another man though..." She took a breath. Once it was said, it would be done. "I cannot. I did not wish to make the vow to Khalid, but I did make it. I am his wife, and I cannot undo that. No matter how much I wish I could."

CHAPTER TWENTY-FOUR

There was nothing left to say.

Derrick had waited his whole life for Jasmine.

And he couldn't have her.

It was as simple as that.

She'd grown quiet after their talk, messing around on one of the burner phones for a while, then eventually falling asleep, leaving him with his thoughts, which turned darker than the starless, predawn sky.

If he hunted down Khalid and killed him, then Jasmine would be safe.

As he drove steadily east, Derrick considered all the ways he could do it. Michael could help him find the guy. They could set a trap.

Derrick couldn't tell his brother what he planned, of course. Michael wouldn't approve.

But Derrick had killed two men already—the second had died of the gunshot wound earlier in the day.

What was one more? If anybody deserved to die, it was Khalid.

If he was dead, then Jasmine would be free.

SHELTERING YOU

But would Derrick?

Killing those men to protect Jasmine and Rabie was one thing. Killing Qasim in cold blood—so he could marry the man's wife? That was a different thing altogether. And no matter how he tried to justify it, that was his true motivation.

A real David and Bathsheba situation. Well, at least Jasmine wasn't pregnant with Derrick's kid. No, she carried that terrorist's spawn.

Spawn?

The word felt like sawdust in his mouth.

She carried a *baby*. An innocent child, regardless of who his father was.

Derrick really needed to change the direction of his thoughts.

Finally, the sun lightened the horizon ahead, and though the traffic was moving at a good clip, there were sure a lot of folks headed to New York City at five thirty in the morning, especially this close to Christmas.

He followed the line of cars down into the Lincoln Tunnel. He'd never been a fan of tunnels. Put him at thirty thousand feet in the air anytime, but knowing there were thousands of pounds of saltwater just a handful of yards above his head gave him the heebie-jeebies.

He smiled at the childish expression.

But there was nothing childish about where his mind had gone for the last hour. Not that he'd ever actually do it. Well, he wouldn't plan it and execute it. He wasn't exactly the premeditated-murder type.

Unless he knew he could get away with it. And then, maybe. He could envision it. And there was a small, terrible part of him that wanted to see the man's face, watch him...

He shook himself. What was he doing? What was he *thinking*?

265

Was this the kind of man he was?

No. *No.*

He wasn't a killer.

Cars made their way through the tunnel, their headlights and taillights reflecting off the shiny walls, giving the long, narrow space an almost cheerful feel.

All the cheer in the world didn't take away from the fact that they were in a tunnel. Without all the artificial light, they'd be in pure darkness.

And there was just a little too much truth in that. Because Derrick had followed his thoughts just like he'd followed the traffic, right into hell.

Lord, Forgive me. I didn't actually commit murder, but it's probably not okay to plot it, either.

Probably? Right.

I want to be holy like Jasmine is. No, like You are. And, to be honest, I'm not there. I like thinking about killing him. It keeps my mind off the things I don't want to think about. So... I want to want to...be holy. I know Jasmine and I can't be together. He sighed, hating this. Hating it. *If there's ever a chance, I want to be worthy of her. And worthy of You. Please fix my want-to.*

Weird prayer, but God knew what he meant, even if he couldn't quite figure out how to put it into words.

By the time Derrick's car emerged from the tunnel, the sun was peeking over the horizon, barely visible between Manhattan's skyscrapers. And Derrick was able to focus his thoughts on what would happen next.

He followed the map to their destination, then searched for a parking garage, finally finding one that would cost slightly less than his right arm.

It was probably all the tight turning as he searched for a space that woke Rabie and Jasmine.

"We are here?" Rabie asked.

"We're in New York." Derrick put some enthusiasm into his voice. "You hungry?"

"Starved."

Derrick parked, climbed out, and opened Rabie's door. "Bring all your stuff. We'll go straight to meet your sister after this."

Rabie climbed out and shoved his arms through the backpack straps while Jasmine walked around the car to join them.

They rode the elevator down. When they emerged onto East 45th, Rabie froze, gazing up at the buildings all around. He said something in Arabic, and Jasmine laughed.

"You're right, it is amazing."

Derrick always felt a little overwhelmed in this city, with the buildings and people and cars and beeping. As if that weren't chaos enough, Christmas wreaths and bows and lights and trees seemed to adorn every available space. The city had exploded with holiday decor. Music played from who-knew-where, and a Santa standing on the sidewalk across the street was jingling a bell.

"So many people!" Rabie looked from her to Derrick. "Can we go to the Empire State Building?"

"Maybe we can see it," he said, "but we can't go to the top. It doesn't open for tours until later."

Jasmine gave him a curious look. "You checked?"

"Thought he might like it. None of the cool tourist stuff opens early enough, unfortunately."

They found a restaurant and ordered. After taking their time to eat, they joined the throng of pedestrians and made their way to the Empire State Building. Derrick enjoyed watching Rabie and Jasmine take in the art deco structure. He'd spent a lot of time in Manhattan, since it was one of the more common destinations for his business-minded clients. Not that he always came into the city. More often than not, he found a hotel in

Jersey near Teterboro Airport and hung out. He'd spent a whole lot of time in hotels by himself over the years. And going to movies by himself. Shopping, jogging, and taking in sights by himself.

Which was fine. He liked his life.

This morning, though, he was enjoying seeing Manhattan from the perspective of people who'd never been there before. Not just people, but these people. Rabie, with his open-mouthed surprise, and Jasmine...though Jasmine was more reserved than usual. She'd shown more wonder when he'd taken her to Super Target than she did seeing the skyscraper.

Perhaps their conversation had affected her like it had him. It wasn't very nice, but a small part of him hoped so. He'd practically proposed to her. He'd hate to think she could discard that —discard him—so easily.

They headed back the way they'd come, Rabie chattering all the way. A couple of hours in New York, and he'd decided he was going to live there and build an even taller building and live on the very top floor, and wouldn't that be amazing?

Derrick and Jasmine nodded at all the right spots. He couldn't speak for her, but he was thankful the kid didn't seem to expect any actual feedback because, as they neared their destination, his heart rate ticked up, his eyes catching on everybody who glanced their direction.

Was Dari here? Was he looking for them?

But they stepped into Grand Central Station at quarter till eight without incident, and even Jasmine was wide-eyed as she gazed at the main concourse. People scurried in all directions, their voices and clatter echoing off the tile floor and walls. Images of the constellations in the zodiac stretched across the green arched ceiling that towered overhead. Today, there were extra lights along the edges, thanks to the coming holiday.

"It's so big," Rabie said.

"Amazing," Jasmine added.

Rabie looked around. "My sister is here?"

Derrick glanced at the iconic clock that stood above the information deck in the middle of the space. If the stories were true and it was a minute fast, then they were right on time. "Come on." He took Jasmine's hand so they wouldn't get separated—and he wouldn't think how perfect it felt in his. She held Rabie's, and Derrick led them past the harried travelers to the market at the far end of the blocks-long building.

He'd never been in here before, and as soon as they stepped inside, he knew he'd been wise to avoid it. The space was narrow—or felt narrow, anyway, with all the vendors lined on either side. Everything a person could want. Baskets overflowing with brightly colored produce. Racks of sweatshirts and hats and keychains—and more food, packaged and fresh and prepared. So many colors and flavors. It was a cacophony of sounds...and sights and smells. Was that a thing? A cacophony of smells?

He was glad for his height as he peered above heads, searching for the shop Michael had told him about. He almost missed it because the place was decked out in red and green and looked more like the kind of place you'd buy a Christmas ornament than a box of candy.

"Over here." He tugged Jasmine's hand. "Come on."

They made it to the chocolatier, and he found a spot at the end of the glass case. "You two pick something out. Take your time."

Jasmine gave him a narrow-eyed glance but did as he'd asked, perusing the selections with Rabie.

Derrick hadn't shared the plan with her because he hadn't wanted the kid to know. Paranoid? No question, but the last thing he wanted was for any more of Dari's thugs to show up. Not that Rabie could've alerted his brother but...

Yeah. Definitely paranoid.

At least he wasn't alone in that.

A man about six inches shorter than Derrick approached, Hispanic with a beard and mustache. He nodded at Derrick. "You ready for Christmas?"

The secret phrase Michael had told him to expect, like he was some sort of spy.

Relieved he wouldn't be making this handoff alone, Derrick gave him the expected answer. "Got a little more shopping to do."

"Me, too," Michael's friend said. "Saw some good stuff near the door."

Which Derrick figured meant Basma was on her way.

"I'll check it out."

The man moved along but stopped on the opposite side of the candy shop.

Jasmine told a clerk what items she wanted while Derrick kept his gaze on the people moving past the many stalls.

There were a handful of women who wore hijabs, most traveling in packs or with men or children. Derrick studied their faces. He hadn't gotten a long look at Basma, but he thought he'd recognize her.

But when he caught sight of Rabie's sister, she wasn't wearing a hijab or a headscarf but a knit cap, a worn wool coat, and blue jeans.

She saw him, and then her gaze skimmed past him, and her face lit up. She seemed as if she wanted to break into a run. She didn't, though, just continued at the same pace.

Derrick didn't miss the tears in her eyes when she walked by him. She reached Rabie and tapped his shoulder.

The boy turned, and Basma dropped to her knees and opened her arms.

Rabie stepped in, and they held onto each other for a long, long time.

Over their heads, Jasmine caught Derrick's eyes, and in her expression, he saw gratitude and tenderness and...

And things he couldn't bear.

Basma stood and hugged Jasmine. They spoke quietly and quickly, their Arabic remarks lost on him as the Hispanic man approached.

Jasmine handed her friend a piece of paper, which the woman shoved in her pocket before hugging her again.

What was that? Derrick wanted to find out, but Basma turned to him and took his hand in both of hers. "Thank you." She squeezed. "I cannot say how much I thank you."

"I'm just glad you're safe. My friend here is going to take you to the train to meet your cousin." He nodded to the shorter man.

Jasmine hugged Rabie goodbye, speaking to him in Arabic. He smiled at her before focusing on Derrick. He seemed unsure what to say.

Derrick lifted his hand for a high-five. "We did it."

Grinning, the kid smacked it hard. He turned away, then turned back and, almost like he was embarrassed, said, "Thanks."

"Happy to do it. Take care of your sister." He winked. "And treat her right."

Basma took Rabie's hand, and they followed the other man back into the Grand Central concourse, disappearing into the crowd.

And just like that, it was over.

Soon enough, Derrick and Jasmine would be in Maine. Safe and sound. Which was what he'd wanted, more than anything. Except it wasn't just this adventure that had ended.

It was also the end of Derrick's hope for a future with the woman he loved.

CHAPTER TWENTY-FIVE

Jasmine should feel nothing but relief at having delivered Rabie safely to Basma. And she *was* relieved. Thank God He'd kept them safe and reunited them.

But things had forever changed between her and Derrick.

It was too loud in the concourse and on the street to talk. In the parking garage elevator, she asked, "Basma's cousin lives in New York? You never said."

"I don't know." He leaned against the opposite wall, the car moving slowly and dinging with each floor. They were alone going up. "She took the train in this morning, and they'll head back to...wherever. I saw you hand her a note. What was it?"

"A new email address. I set it up this morning so we can stay in touch."

He straightened. "What? Why would you—?"

"Otherwise, I would never speak to her again." Jasmine turned toward the doors as they reached the proper floor. "I won't tell her where I live. I won't take risks. But she is still my friend."

"I don't like it."

Which was why she hadn't told him in advance.

The doors opened, and they passed a throng of people waiting to go down.

Nearing the car, she said, "I can drive, if you like."

Derrick shot her what might be considered a smile—by someone who didn't know him. "New York drivers would eat you alive."

"I can do it. I had a good teacher."

He didn't react to the compliment. "I got it. Thanks, though."

He clicked the button to unlock the doors. Often, in the past, he would open her door for her, but he walked straight to the driver's side and climbed in.

He put an address in the navigation system while she buckled her seatbelt.

"How long will it take?"

He backed out of the space. "Five, five and a half hours, depending on traffic."

That would give them time to talk. Perhaps they could find a way to restore their friendship. Was it too much to ask that they be friends again?

Perhaps it would be kinder to let it go, let *him* go. But the thought of losing him...

She couldn't bear it.

Was it selfish to want to stay close? Knowing how he felt about her? How she felt about him?

She would need to ask God how to proceed.

Derrick was winding down the narrow aisles toward the exit when one of the burner phones rang, too loud through the speakers.

They reached for the volume at the same time, and their fingers touched.

Derrick yanked his hand back as if she'd scorched him.

Doing her best to hide her sadness, she adjusted it lower while he pressed the button on the steering wheel.

"It went fine," he said. "No problems."

"Good." Michael sounded relieved. "Jasmine listening?"

"I'm here."

"I got a call this morning, and... There's no reason for you to worry, but I wanted to let you know..."

Oh, no.

"Khalid Qasim's face was picked up on a camera at a Metro station—that's the subway in DC—a couple of days ago."

Her hand flew up, covering her mouth. "He was there when we were?"

"We don't know when he got there," Michael said, "but if I had to guess—"

"Where is he now?" Derrick was squeezing the steering wheel.

"No idea."

"How did this happen?" He sounded furious, as if it were Michael's fault.

"No idea. We're trying to figure out how he got into the country. The border's porous, he could've just walked across."

Derrick paid the parking fee, turned onto the busy road, then pulled over. He shifted into park, glaring at the dashboard as if his brother were right there.

"I'm waiting for a call back from a contact in Mexico, who might be able to shed some light on that, not that it matters how he got here. The point is—"

"Can't be a coincidence." Derrick looked her way, his expression grim. "That he was in DC."

"I don't believe in coincidences." Michael sighed. "Sorry, sis, but I don't think there's any doubt now. He and Dari Ghazi are working together. I think this was all about smoking you out."

She lowered her head and covered her face with her hands.

She was such a fool. Khalid had set a trap for her, and she'd walked right into it. Or almost had. She had escaped only because of Derrick's quick thinking and Michael's help. Otherwise, Khalid would have her. She would be back in Iraq. Captive. She would never have another opportunity to escape.

Derrick asked, "Any more good news for us?"

"Bryan said he's been trying to reach you but you aren't answering. Did I give him the wrong number?"

Derrick grabbed the cell he'd left on the console, tapped the screen, and lifted it to his ear. "What does he want?"

Jasmine didn't hear Michael's answer now. He must've disconnected from Bluetooth.

"Fine," Derrick said. "If he can work it out... Yeah, I will." He ended the call, tossed the phone, and shifted into traffic.

"Is Bryan okay?"

"Yup." Derrick focused on the map and the busy street.

The city passed outside the window, and Jasmine told herself to take everything in. She might never be back to New York. If Khalid caught up with her...

She couldn't think about that.

At least she was getting to see this in the daylight. Funny, though. Unlike where they'd been the last few days, this city would be just as pretty, if not more so, at night. Greenery draped around doorframes, and wreaths decorated lampposts. Store window displays were alive with movement and color and lights.

"The decorations are beautiful. Is it always so festive at Christmastime?"

"Lots of tourists this time of year."

"I'm glad Leila got to see it. I wonder if they had fun. Did Michael say?"

"Nope." Derrick stopped at a light, his fingers drumming a rhythm on the steering wheel.

"What is your favorite thing about Christmas?"

"I don't know," he said. "The food, I guess."

"What kind of food? What are you most eager for?"

He shrugged. "Mom's roast."

She thought of a handful of follow-up questions, but obviously, Derrick didn't want to talk.

The burner phone rang again, though not through the speakers.

Derrick snatched it and answered. "Yeah?"

His lips pressed closed.

Her heart rate kicked up. Was something wrong?

"Fine," he said. "We'll have to return the car... Less than an hour, probably... Fine." He ended the call.

"What is it?"

"Bryan's at Teterboro."

"What is...Teterboro?"

Derrick pulled over and changed the address in the car's navigation. "It's an airport. He picked up the Cessna this morning and flew in. That's why he was trying to reach me."

"We will fly home?"

Derrick angled back onto the road. "Yeah. Well, not home. We're going straight to camp. I guess your sister packed you a bag, and Bryan packed one for me. Everyone's headed up there today for the big family party tomorrow."

She'd known about the party, an early Christmas celebration. All the Wrights would be there, including their extended family. She realized now... "This includes the family that owns the cabin where we stayed? They are coming?"

"Yup."

"I am to go as well?"

"Of course." He sounded surprised by the question. "Why wouldn't you?"

"I am not family. I knew Leila would, but—"

"You're family, Jasmine."

For the first time, he didn't seem pleased by the prospect.

"I can go home, Derrick. If you would prefer—"

"Just...don't. It's... I want you to go." He took a breath and blew it out. "Sorry. I'm not mad at you. I'm tired, that's all."

"It's good, then, that you don't have to drive all the way home."

"Yup."

He should be happy to be rid of her sooner. But by the tightness in his jaw, the little muscle twitching in his cheek, he wasn't happy at all that Bryan had flown in.

So much for her hope that they could rebuild their friendship on the drive home. She gave up trying to make conversation, and they finished the drive in silence. After dropping off the rental car, they made their way to the private terminal at the airport.

As soon as they stepped inside, Bryan spotted them and crossed toward them, leaning on his cane. "You made it."

Hauling both their bags, Derrick barely glanced at him as he passed. "Are we ready?"

If Bryan was surprised by Derrick's attitude, he didn't react. He gave Jasmine a quick side-hug. "Glad you're here."

"Thank you for coming."

"Of course. Come on."

They followed Derrick across the pavement to the small plane. She couldn't help remembering the other two times she'd been on his jet. The first, she'd practically run up the stairs, terrified Khalid would catch up to her. At the top, Derrick had met her, smiling in that welcoming way he had. She'd known Michael a little, and she'd met Bryan already. They both had short hair, trimmed beards, tidy clothes. They were serious and intense.

Derrick had surprised her. Shoulder-length, unruly hair,

beard slightly longer, wide smile. Though she'd never met him, he'd felt instantly familiar. Most men made her nervous. Most men made her want to shrink away, to hide, but Derrick had felt like an old friend. Even then, after everything they'd been through, he was...happy. Just genuinely happy.

She'd never known anyone like him. She'd liked him from the first moment. And in their time together, she'd only grown to like him more.

The second time on his plane had been Monday. Had it only been four days? He'd insisted she sit in the cockpit with him. When she'd worried she'd push a button or press a lever and cause them to crash, he'd laughed, the sound lighthearted and full of joy.

"Don't worry, sweetheart. I got you."

Now, he stood at the bottom of the steps, lips pressed closed, nearly white.

When she approached, he managed a tight "After you."

"Thanks."

She climbed the steps, sat in the first forward-facing seat, and stared out the window to hide her tears.

CHAPTER TWENTY-SIX

Derrick was on the second step from the bottom, but Bryan's low, "Dude," had him turning his head to face his older brother. His closest, not just in age but in everything.

Bryan was his best friend. Had been, anyway.

"What?"

"It's just..." He raked a hand over his short hair. "I wanted to tell you. It's been killing me—about the baby and the...husband, but Michael—"

"Don't." His tight hold on self-control snapped, and he descended so fast that Bryan took a step back. Derrick got in his face. "Michael keeps secrets. It's what he does. It's not what I do. It's not what you do. At least it wasn't."

Bryan blinked. "He told me about it because I was doing that thing for him in Germany. It was a national security—"

"This has nothing to do with national security. I'm your brother, and you knew..." Emotion—stupid, embarrassing emotion—bubbled up inside. He swallowed, swallowed everything he'd planned to say. "You should have told me."

"He's *also* my brother." Bryan didn't back down. If

anything, he stood taller. "It wasn't my place to tell you. It was Jasmine's."

Derrick looked at the jet's window. Thanks to the bright morning light, he couldn't see inside, but he had a feeling she was watching.

"I guess you had to betray someone. You chose me." He spun and climbed the stairs.

"Derrick."

At the top, he glanced back. Bryan remained on the tarmac, hurt and confusion in his expression. Because Derrick was always the guy to let offenses go. He was always the guy to get over it and move on.

Not this time.

"I'm going to sleep. Try not to crash my plane."

Derrick's heart was pounding, his hands sweating. Stupid. Who cared if he'd just yelled at his brother? Bryan had betrayed him. Derrick owed him nothing.

He aimed for the back, needing space and privacy. But of course his gaze landed on Jasmine before he passed.

She didn't even glance his way as she swiped her fingertips beneath her eyes.

Great. He'd wrecked his relationship with his brother and he'd made the woman he loved cry. And it wasn't even eleven o'clock in the morning.

What a banner-freaking-day this was turning out to be.

He adjusted the cabin temperature, making it a little warmer for his always-chilly...*not* girlfriend, grabbed two bottles of water, and walked back to her seat, holding one out. "You okay?"

She took it, nodding. "Are you?"

"You remember how to recline the seat?"

"Yes."

"Good." He grabbed a couple of blankets and pillows from a storage bin and handed her one of each. "I'm going to get some rest."

He didn't wait for a response, just made his way to the back and collapsed. He wasn't going to think about it. Any of it.

He shoved the pillow against the window and closed his eyes.

The engine powered up. A few minutes later, Bryan taxied to the runway.

Derrick hadn't realized how angry he was at his brother until he'd heard his voice earlier, and then it all just...rolled over him.

If Bryan had told him Jasmine was married and expecting a kid, then he could have protected himself. He wouldn't have gotten his hopes up. He wouldn't have had such...expectations. He could've guarded his heart.

He should've done that anyway. But he'd always been an all-in guy, especially where relationships were concerned, where *people* were concerned. He'd been like that with his brothers, trying to fix everything that broke. Everything *they* broke. It hadn't been Derrick's fault when Grant talked Bryan into going down to the dock at camp so Grant could show off by climbing up the cliff. Derrick hadn't been there when Bryan decided to follow him up. He hadn't been there when Bryan lost his grip and fell onto the rocky ground below.

Derrick had been in bed with a fever. If not for that, maybe he could've stopped it, stopped the whole tragedy from happening.

But he'd been a five-year-old kid.

Sheesh, Grant and Bryan had only been nine and seven.

Derrick could still hear the helicopter that air-lifted Bryan to the hospital. He'd been too young to understand how badly his brother was injured. It had never occurred to him that Bryan might die, though of course he knew now how serious those injuries had been. Bryan had been fortunate to end up with nothing worse than a crushed ankle. He should've been thankful.

But he'd been bitter. It wasn't the fall that'd wrecked their family. It wasn't the helicopter or the hospital stays or the medical bills or the years of physical therapy.

It had been Bryan's bitterness.

The Cessna picked up speed, racing down the runway, then lifted gently off the ground. Derrick watched the earth fall away.

Derrick had tried, back then. God knew he'd tried to fix it. To help. But Bryan had blamed Grant, and as soon as Grant was old enough, he enlisted in the Army, getting as far away from the family as he could. No matter what Derrick did, the brothers had divided—Bryan against Grant, everybody else against Bryan. Derrick had taken Bryan's side not because he was right but because he was alone.

All he'd wanted then, all he'd ever wanted, was for everyone to be at peace. He'd spent his entire life trying to bring harmony to their family.

Finally, all the brothers were friends again. Everybody was happy.

Except Derrick. All that stupid peacemaking had gotten him nothing. Nothing but betrayed.

He reclined the seat until it was practically flat. He hadn't slept all night, and the night before hadn't exactly been restful. His stupid wound was aching. His eyes were scratchy with fatigue.

He tried to get comfortable. But this wasn't where he was supposed to be on his plane. He should be in the cockpit, flying. Or at least in the right-hand seat, acting as Bryan's copilot.

Lord, help me rest. I just need to rest.

But God was silent. Of course. Because why would God give Derrick anything? All he'd done was try to follow Him all his life. Try to keep their family together. Try to be everything to everyone. Why should he deserve rest or peace or...anything?

He punched the leather seat beneath him as if it were to blame for all his troubles.

It's all about everybody else.

Exactly.

His whole life, he'd tried to make everybody but himself happy. That was his problem.

A Bible verse he'd learned when he was a kid popped into his brain. He couldn't remember the whole thing. Something about pleasing men or pleasing God.

Derrick had spent his life trying to please God. There was that whole passage in James about being a peacemaker. *Those who sow in peace raise a harvest of righteousness.* That one he remembered. It was one of his life verses.

So why didn't he feel like God was pleased?

His goal had always been to make peace, to please God.

Obviously.

Right?

He started counting backward from five hundred, his sure-fire way to fall asleep. There was nothing more boring than numbers.

But he hadn't gotten past four-ninety when more of that other verse came to him.

For am I now seeking the approval of man, or of God...? If I were still trying to please man, I would not be a servant of Christ.

Ugh.

Derrick definitely didn't want to think about this.

But now that he was, he had to admit the truth. Maybe he'd spent his life as a peacemaker because he wanted the people around him to like him. To appreciate him. To want to be with him. He wanted peace for himself, not for God. He wanted peace because anything other than peace made him feel... anxious.

And there was a manly admission. He could imagine what his tough-as-nails brothers would say if he ever admitted that.

But the truth was, his peacemaking was and always had been about Derrick.

Not God.

Meaning...he hadn't been behaving as a servant of Christ.

He pressed the button to raise the seat, leaned forward, and dropped his head into his hands. *Is that true, Lord? Have I made all of this about me?*

The emotion he'd worked so hard to keep at bay leaked from his eyes now. He was too tired for these deep thoughts and deep feelings.

God didn't respond. Derrick had expected a little condemnation, a little *Duh, you finally figured it out, you moron.*

But that wouldn't be God's voice.

All Derrick felt was a gentle Presence and overwhelming love.

I'm sorry. Forgive me.

And He did. Of course. Always.

Derrick rested in that for a few minutes.

Not that he was over his anger toward Bryan. He'd try, though. He needed to get there.

He would, eventually.

But Jasmine... *Lord, what do I do?*

He hated the answer.

She was married. He disagreed with her decision to stay married, but what kind of man would he be if he pressured her to divorce? Pressured her to do something she felt in her heart was sin?

That was not the kind of man he was.

Where did that leave him?

How do I please You in this, Lord?

He closed his eyes and waited for the answer. When it came, he accepted it. He didn't like it, but he didn't argue.

It wasn't about him. If he loved Jasmine—and he did, with all his heart—he needed to do what was best for her.

Which meant letting her go.

CHAPTER TWENTY-SEVEN

Jasmine stared out the window at the blue sky above and the green world so far below. It was lovely now, but in the distance to the west, thick clouds stretched to the horizon. She didn't need to check a weather app to know the obvious—a storm was coming.

She tried not to be offended that Derrick had hardly spoken to her. He was angry with his brother. She hadn't needed to hear what he was saying to know that. She had no idea why, though.

At least Bryan had tried to be kind when he'd stepped onto the plane earlier, giving her a tight smile before turning to the cockpit.

They'd been in the air for half an hour when Derrick came forward and nodded to the seat facing hers. "Mind if I sit?"

"Please." He did and opened his mouth, but she spoke first. "Can I say one thing? And then I will never bring it up again."

"You can say anything to me." His words were kind, and his smile, though slight, seemed genuine. Perhaps he'd left his anger at the airport, or maybe in the clouds behind them.

"I have not had much experience with these things." She

thought back to the question Sophie had asked her at the bridal shop on Sunday. "I have never had a man who was interested in me."

"Romantically?"

"Okay, yes." Or in any way, but she didn't say so.

"Obviously, Iraqi men are all blind and dumb." Derrick's lips ticked up at the corners, amusement in his eyes.

It gave her hope that maybe, eventually, they could be friends again. Not like before, but in a new way.

"If I had known that you felt something for me, I would've told you about Khalid and the baby. I should have. You were right about that. You were—you *are* my friend, and I should have told you. I thought you would judge me or see me differently if you knew the truth. I understand now that it would have been good if you had seen me differently. I did not mean for you to hope for things that could not be."

"I know."

His kindness brought tears to her eyes. "I would never hurt you. It is the last thing I want."

He leaned forward and held out his hand. He didn't take hers, but the way it sat between them, it felt like an offer.

She slipped hers into it.

"I understand. You're far too kind for that, Jasmine."

He gazed out the window, and she studied his straight nose and strong chin. He was handsome, but what she felt for him went so much deeper than his attractive features. What she felt for him she'd never known she could feel for a man.

She would need God's help getting past it, or she would have to be the one to end their friendship. The thought of that broke her heart all over again.

"All morning." He faced her again. "In the back of my mind, I've been trying to figure out how to talk you out of what you believe about your marriage, to try to make you see it how I see it. But the last few minutes, I've been praying, and even though I'm not convinced you're right, I know *you* are—convinced of it, I mean—and if I talked you into divorcing Khalid, I'd be talking you into doing something you believe in your heart is sin. Which would be a sin—on both of our parts. And that would be no way to start a life together." He squeezed her hand, then let it go and sat back. "I hate it. I wish things were different, but short of hunting down your husband and killing him..." By the serious tone and lack of smile, he wasn't entirely joking. "I don't see a way forward for us."

She'd known that already. So why did fresh tears fill her eyes?

He pulled a wad of tissue from his jeans pocket and handed it to her. "I saw, earlier... You seemed upset, so I grabbed some toilet paper. I should start carrying a handkerchief like my dad does."

She dabbed her eyes. "Thank you."

"If all I can be to you is a brother, then that's what I'll be. I'll be your brother, and I'll be your baby's favorite uncle. I'll be the coolest freaking uncle your baby could ever have and the best brother you can imagine until...until something changes. Or forever. Whatever...whatever you want, that's what I'll be. Okay?"

"A brother?"

"Yeah, sis. A brother."

Sis. Like what Michael called her. She tried to smile, and though her lips stretched wide, she doubted he was buying it. "We will be friends?"

"Friends." He reached toward her again, only this time, they shook hands, sealing their deal.

And what was left of her heart crumbled into pieces.

CHAPTER TWENTY-EIGHT

Derrick wasn't in the mood for this. Not even a little.

He'd done the right thing with Jasmine. Now he felt wrung out and exhausted, and all he wanted to do was avoid everybody.

But the cold drizzle had waylaid their bonfire, his favorite tradition. He'd looked forward to it, thinking that, in the firelight, nobody would be able to pick up his disappointment and his anger and...all his feelings.

But they were trapped inside.

Leaning on his pool cue, he stared out the window into the darkness. The crescent moon was mostly hidden behind thick clouds, along with all the stars that usually shone so brightly here on the island off the coast of Maine.

There were no city lights for those clouds to reflect so far north, just the churning Atlantic that stretched as far as he could see.

Derrick strained to hear the women, who were upstairs preparing for tomorrow's party. Mom's voice was easy to distinguish as she gave directions on how to prepare all the family's favorite foods. Before he'd come down, he'd spied cans of artichokes, so she'd be making the dip he loved. He'd seen the fixings for that Mexican seven-layer thing Camilla had introduced a few years earlier. He'd seen slices of meats and various cheeses, along with jars of olives and nuts and other yummy things, all laid out near a big wooden board, and Leila and Jasmine were working on some kind of Middle Eastern chicken skewer things.

The family had put up the tree and decorated the house the weekend before—back when Derrick had been certain of his future with Jasmine—so the whole place was an explosion of Christmas.

Last Derrick saw, though, the living room had been covered with boxes and serving trays and paper products.

He'd offered to stay up there and help the women—an excuse to avoid spending time with his brothers. He could cook. He could set tables and wash dishes. But Mom had shooed him to the basement game room. "Go play. It's so much harder to talk about you when you're in the room."

She thought she was *so* funny, but they probably were talking about him. Despite his productive conversations with the Lord and Jasmine on the flight that morning, he'd been grumpy all day. Even a long nap and a shower hadn't improved his mood.

He'd had a quick, private word with Leila.

He'd hardly spoken to Bryan.

The rest of his brothers probably hadn't noticed, but Mom never missed a thing.

At the pool table, Daniel was taking his sweet time lining up his shot.

Sam and Grant were in the middle of a game of table tennis, the rhythmic sound of the little ball hitting the paddles and table was interrupted by occasional grunts and cheers.

Sam was the best ping-pong player of the brothers, but Grant was close, and he was intense tonight.

Well, Grant was always intense.

On the other side of the room, Levi was standing on a chair, bouncing, watching the ball go back and forth as if his attention were the only thing keeping it in the air. He was rooting for his father, and whenever Sam scored, the kid reacted as if he'd hit the game-winning home run in the World Series.

Bryan stood with Daniel's son, Jeremy, near a high table at the edge of the room. They were both waiting to take on the winners.

The only brother missing was Michael. Dad had taken the boat to the mainland to pick him up. The morning's rain had tapered to a drizzle, and it wasn't too windy. They shouldn't have any trouble getting here.

"Your shot," Daniel said.

Derrick grabbed the little cube of chalk and rubbed it against the end of his stick, studying the table. He was shooting stripes, his brother solids, and if his count was right, Daniel had only sunk one.

Whereas only four striped balls remained. "Do we need to go over the rules again? You're supposed to sink the balls that are all one color."

Glancing up from his phone, Jeremy laughed.

Daniel held his pool stick like the staff of Moses. Always so grown-up, or maybe it just seemed that way to Derrick, since his brother was fourteen years older and had gray hair and even a few wrinkles—well-earned, considering all he'd been through. "While some of us were hanging out in pool halls, others went to med school and raised a family."

"Pool halls. Yeah, that was it." Derrick had learned to play right there in that basement, him against his brothers.

He lined up his shot and sank one, setting up another.

Daniel focused on Jeremy. "Let this be a lesson to you, son. Don't waste your life. Focus on what's important."

"Yeah, Uncle Derrick's such a loser," Jeremy deadpanned. "You've still just got that one jet, right?" He shook his head. "So disappointing."

Derrick felt a smile spreading, probably his first of the night. In Daniel's defense—not that Derrick would make it for him—they hadn't gotten the pool table until after the oldest Wright brother had left for college.

"Ha!" Sam, obviously the victor at the other table, plopped the paddle down and high-fived his son. "That is how it's done."

"Yay, Daddy!" The little boy launched himself into Sam's arms.

Grant grunted, but he couldn't hide his grin, watching the father and son, so happy. And why not? He'd have his own kid soon enough.

Not that Derrick was jealous. Nope. He was perfectly happy. He had his business. He didn't need a family.

He sank two more balls.

"Nice shot," Bryan said.

Everybody seemed to wait for Derrick to respond. But he didn't.

Sam cleared his throat. "You ready to lose, Bry?"

"Sure."

The little white ball started its pinging and ponging.

Derrick sank another shot, and all that was left was the eight ball.

He was lining it up when the slider at the back of the room opened, letting in cold, moist air, along with Michael and Dad, who shook out of giant yellow slickers dripping with rainwater, then shrugged out of their parkas. They hung the outerwear on the hooks by the door.

The others stopped what they were doing to greet the second-oldest brother and ask about the ride from shore.

Choppy, Derrick gathered. Wet. In other words, winter in the North Atlantic.

Derrick sank the eight ball.

"Good game." Daniel returned from giving Michael a back-slapping hug and leaned his pool cue against the wall.

Derrick walked around the table, gathering the balls from the pockets.

"I'm glad you're okay." Michael plopped a hand on his shoulder, keeping his voice low. "How's the wound?"

It hurt, but he was ignoring it. Derrick shook his brother off. "It's fine."

Michael stepped back, hands raised in surrender as if Derrick had attacked. Which...whatever.

He was being a jerk. Couldn't seem to stop, though. He racked the balls. "Who's up?"

The room was too quiet. Even Levi had stopped his constant stream of chatter.

Derrick straightened. They were all looking at him—his brothers, his dad, his nephews. "What?"

"What's your problem?" Sam glanced from Michael to Bryan and back to Derrick. "What's going on?"

"Nothing." He shoved the pool stick on the stand. "I'm going up. I need some sleep."

Confused, Daniel checked his watch.

Bryan said, "It's eight fifteen."

Derrick glared at his brother. "It's been a long day."

His father moved across the room toward him. Dad, with his white hair and gentle smile, and that concern in his eyes. He reached out and gripped Derrick's forearm. "What's going on, son?"

"Nothing."

But Dad wasn't taking that answer. And they were all watching him. And he was tired, and angry, and...

Jealous.

It was stupid.

Bryan stepped toward him. "It's my fault. I'll go."

"It's *my* fault." Michael said the words to Bryan, then turned to Derrick. "I shouldn't have told him, and I shouldn't have expected him not to tell you. If you're gonna be mad at anyone, be mad at me."

"It wasn't your story or his." Derrick ground out the words.

Jasmine should have told him. He'd managed to forgive her. He needed to forgive his brothers too.

His problem wasn't that nobody had *told* him.

The problem was that she was married and having a kid. And it couldn't be undone.

But she hadn't told the rest of the family yet, so nobody else in the room had any idea what they were talking about. He wasn't about to spill the beans.

"I'll get over it." He focused on Bryan, then turned to Michael. "It's fine."

Neither of them said anything.

Nobody said anything. If Derrick weren't the angry one, *he'd* say something. He'd let them off the hook. Fill the silence, break the tension, make everybody feel better. That was Derrick's job, and apparently nobody else in this stupid family had a clue how to do it. They were just standing there, staring at him.

"What? I said it's fine. Go back to your game."

"I have no idea what's going on," Sam said, "but I don't think it's fine."

"Yeah, well... You wouldn't understand. You have him." He

gestured to Levi, the adoring little boy with his cute blond curls and dimples. "You have Eliza. And Grant has Summer and a kid on the way. And Daniel has Camilla and an amazing family." Stupid emotion. Derrick tipped his head to the ceiling and shook the tears back. He shouldn't have come down. He should've stayed in his room and slept.

Michael said, "Bro—"

"It's fine. It's fine I'm alone. It was just easier when I wasn't alone...by myself, that's all. But you're gonna get married, and I'm happy for you." He looked at Bryan. "And you. You get your beautiful..." He thought of Bryan's nickname for Sophie and blurted, "Princess bride."

His brothers stared at him as if he'd grown a second head and three more arms. Like they didn't know who he was. And he felt like an idiot. And then...

"Maw-wige." The word came out in a perfect imitation of the priest in *The Princess Bride*. Surprising, and even more so because it came from Grant. "Maw-wige is what bwings us to-ge-tha too-day."

Derrick gaped at his brother—the quiet one. The tough one.

Grant's lips twitched at the corners. He shrugged. "What? It's a classic."

That did it for Derrick.

All of it just...hit him. His idiotic behavior. The absurdity of the moment.

He laughed.

It took a second for the rest of them to join, watching him like maybe it was a trick or something. But they couldn't hold it in very long. Even little Levi, who couldn't possibly understand what was so funny, giggled uncontrollably.

The whole thing was...ridiculous. And hilarious.

Derrick was so tired and so...he didn't know what else...that when tears streamed from his eyes, he wasn't sure if they were tears from laughing or all the other things that he'd been feeling that day, and it didn't matter. His brothers weren't perfect. But they were his, and if all he ever got to be was a son and a brother and an uncle, well...

It was a good life.

He'd find a way to live with it.

CHAPTER TWENTY-NINE

J asmine must've fallen asleep.

Embarrassed, she sat up and stretched, thankful for the clean clothes Leila had brought her from home. She'd showered and changed into a fresh dress—this one dark blue— after they arrived at the island that afternoon.

Nobody seemed to mind that Jasmine had nodded off. In fact, somebody had draped an afghan over her.

The women were seated in the beautiful living room on sofas and chairs facing the fireplace. The flames from earlier were now mere flickers and glowing coals. The room still held the scent of wood smoke that was coming to smell like home.

She'd been here the weekend before, but it felt different this time. Like a fortress, a hiding place. Even though she'd suggested to Derrick that perhaps she shouldn't come, she couldn't imagine having been left alone in Shadow Cove, without the protection of these friends who meant so much to her.

The boat ride over had been choppy, and poor Leila had sat beside her, holding her hand with such a tight grip that, even hours later, it still ached. On Leila's other side, Michael had held her other hand, whispering promises in her ear.

Leila feared water. Summer feared boats.

Jasmine feared Khalid. But here, on this island, she felt safe. As safe as she'd felt since before she'd gotten that email almost a week before.

She checked the time on her phone. Almost two o'clock in the morning? Yet, though others yawned, nobody seemed ready to go to bed.

Eliza was telling a story about her childhood, and though Jasmine had missed most of it, when she finished, the rest of the ladies smiled.

"My childhood wasn't like that," Summer said. "But this little one"—her hand rested on her growing belly—"is going to have it so much better."

"Is...*he*?" Peggy threw out the question as a guess.

Summer just shrugged. "Or she."

The older woman scowled. Family rumor had it that Summer and Grant knew the baby's gender but hadn't shared it yet. Maybe they had some big surprise planned. Maybe they wanted it to be private, just between the two of them.

To have someone to share secrets with... Jasmine envied her that. She wouldn't complain, though. God had been good to her. She was here, wasn't she? And safe.

Her child, boy or girl, was going to have this kind of freedom. Jasmine would see to it, no matter the cost. Her child would know the One True God and walk with Him. Her child would know joy.

In the corner, the twenty-foot Christmas tree sparkled, seeming all the brighter because of the darkness beyond the windows that made up the entire wall. The Wrights didn't bother with curtains or shades. Their island was private and far from the mainland—and the house so high on the cliff—that they didn't worry about strangers peeking inside.

The world outside sparkled. Was it snowing?

They'd said the rain might turn to snow, but she hadn't really believed it. She'd never seen snow. She watched it fall lazily, occasionally blowing in the breeze. It was mesmerizing.

With Peggy in charge, they'd gotten most of the food prepared for the party the next day. Roger's brother, his wife, and their daughters would be here around eleven. As far as she knew, nobody else was coming, though there was enough food to feed a small Iraqi village—with plenty to spare. There would be a game that included the exchange of gifts, something called a Yankee Swap. Apparently, everyone picked a present, but someone else might steal it. It was all very confusing, but her friends had promised they'd explain what she needed to do when it was her turn. When she'd worried that she hadn't brought anything, Eliza had assured her she had taken care of it.

This family...that was exactly what they did. They took care of each other, and her. And Leila. And she felt certain that, when the time came, they would help take care of her little one. Derrick would be an uncle, like he'd said, but he wouldn't be the only one. There would be six Wright uncles and five Wright aunts and even Wright grandparents.

Almost four months before, when Jasmine had finally admitted the terrible truth to herself—that she was pregnant, that she would give birth to Khalid's child—she'd imagined a thousand futures for herself and her baby. Never could she have imagined this.

Across the room, Peggy caught Jasmine's eyes and smiled at her. She didn't say anything, didn't expect anything. Just gave her that *I'm glad you're here* smile.

Jasmine could trust this family. This family was nothing like the one she'd left in Iraq. She didn't have to fear Peggy and

Roger. She didn't have to worry that one of the brothers was going to take advantage of her or sell her or marry her off to pay a debt. She didn't have to worry they'd decide to make her a servant or a slave. She was safe here, with these people. How she'd ever thought differently, she couldn't fathom.

Leila crossed toward her, seeming almost...worried. Why, though? On the ride from the airport to the marina that afternoon, Jasmine had told her everything that had happened since she and Derrick had left. And they'd spent the entire day together.

"Can I talk to you for a second?" Leila asked.

Jasmine draped the blanket across the back of the chair and scooted over to give her sister space. "Is something wrong?"

Settling beside her on the club chair, Leila angled toward her. "Derrick said something to me earlier, and I wanted to talk to you about it." She kept her voice low enough that nobody else could hear, not that it would matter if they did because her sister had switched to Arabic. Something she almost never did, certainly not when they were surrounded by Americans.

Jasmine's stomach churned with fear. "What is it?"

Leila took Jasmine's hands and leaned in close. "I wanted to go back for you, Jasmine."

Oh.

Derrick must've told her what Jasmine had said at the hotel.

"I would have found a way. I don't know how, but I was always thinking about you. I never forgot about you." Leila leaned her forehead against Jasmine's.

Jasmine's eyes filled.

"I prayed for you every single day." Leila's voice crackled with emotion. "Not an hour went by that you weren't on my mind. You were worthy of the risk. You have always had my love and my devotion. Always. I didn't have a way to rescue you. But I prayed every night that God would reunite us, that He would bring you to safety." She leaned away and met Jasmine's eyes. "I'm sorry you ever doubted that."

Jasmine hugged her sister, the weight of her insecurities melting away. "I shouldn't have doubted it. I should've known better—known *you* better. You begged me to escape with you. I was a fool for staying."

Leila backed away, holding Jasmine's shoulders. "You stayed with Mama. You were the good daughter. Our parents were the fools for not seeing that. But I see it, sister. I see how amazing you are."

Jasmine smiled at her twin. "We are as different as we are the same, and we are both created by God, and both worthy in His eyes."

Leila settled in beside her on the small chair, wiping her tears.

Jasmine's phone vibrated an email. It had to be from Basma, the only person with her address. She must be messaging to tell Jasmine that she and Rabie had made it back to her cousin's house, wherever that was. Jasmine tapped the icon and read the message.

Then, with a growing sense of dread, she sat up and read it again.

Was she dreaming?

Was this a nightmare?

One line stood out.

...confessed everything. He told him everything he learned. He gave him your phone number. If Khalid has a way to track it...

Jasmine stood suddenly, almost tripping over her sister's feet. She managed to catch herself on the arm of the chair.

"What's wrong?" Leila stood beside her. "What is it?"

"It was Rabie."

Leila's eyes widened.

The other women quieted, watching.

"What's this?" Peggy looked between the twins. "Who is—?"

"Where's Derrick?" Jasmine asked.

"Downstairs," Peggy said. "They're playing..."

The rest of her words were lost as Jasmine swiveled and rushed to the door that led to the basement. She ran down, gripping the railing for fear she'd trip and fall and not have the chance to warn him.

The guys were standing around, talking. Visiting. Having fun. When she stumbled into the game room, they turned her way.

She searched their faces, all so similar, until she saw the man she needed.

Derrick stepped toward her. "What happened?"

"You were right. It was Rabie. His toy, the electric one. When it was gone, he used my phone, the one I had turned off. It was in the suitcase." She remembered seeing her suitcase open in the hotel room. He'd found the phone, powered it up. "He sent Dari a message."

Michael moved close. "What are you saying?"

But she couldn't tear her eyes away from Derrick.

"How do you know?" he asked.

She held her cell out to him, and he read the email.

Michael read over his shoulder.

Grant pushed past the others. "What's going on?"

Derrick handed him the cell but focused on Jasmine. In his eyes, she saw love and devotion and determination...and raw terror.

"Who is Dari?" Grant lowered the phone and peered at Jasmine. "Who is this...Qasim?"

All the men were facing her now. Daniel, Sam, Roger, and Jeremy looked as confused as they were worried.

Grant looked fierce.

Michael and Bryan were quiet, giving her the chance to tell the story.

This wasn't how she wanted to do this, but it didn't matter now. Nothing mattered. She'd put these people in danger, these people who'd protected her and given her a home.

Derrick stepped to her side and held her hand, turning to face his family.

"Khalid Qasim is my husband." Jasmine swallowed and, so they would understand, placed her free hand on her stomach. "He is the father of my child."

"He's found her," Derrick said. "And he's coming."

CHAPTER THIRTY

"Start at the beginning."

They'd all gathered in the living room with the beautiful floor-to-ceiling windows that Derrick had always appreciated. But they left nothing but a half inch of glass between a murderous terrorist and the woman he loved. "We don't have time for this." He usually didn't argue with Grant. And with his brother in warrior mode—arms crossed, expression deadly serious—he was at his most intimidating. But was this really the time to share all the details? "We need to prepare."

"And to do that, I need to know what we're up against."

Derrick pointed to the windows. "We're not safe here."

"We are, for now," Michael said.

They'd pushed the furniture to the perimeter of the room, and most of the family was seated on the floor in front of the fireplace where, if an enemy were to fire a bullet from the ground below, nobody would be hit.

Derrick, Michael, and Grant stood with their backs to the dwindling fire.

Only Jasmine wasn't seated. She'd refused to settle with the others, instead hovering near the kitchen island. If Derrick guessed correctly, she was debating whether she should stay or bolt out the back door.

The question was, why? Because she was afraid Khalid would catch up with her?

More likely, she was afraid he'd hurt one of the people here in his quest to find her.

Initially, Leila had gone to stand with her, but Michael had insisted—practically dragged her—into the living room and settled her there. "They won't know you from Jasmine," Michael had said. "You're in as much danger as she is."

Derrick had tried to get Jasmine to join her sister, but she'd absolutely, adamantly refused to budge from her spot, saying something about how she couldn't sit still, though half the words had been in Arabic, so he'd had to guess at her meaning.

He was considering throwing her over his shoulder and dumping her on the floor.

Daniel stepped up from the basement with two rifles under his arms, two pairs of binoculars, and a couple boxes of ammo. "I only found a few walkie-talkies." He dropped his finds on a couch and yanked the old communication devices from a jacket pocket, then tossed one to Grant, who snatched it out of the air.

Bryan pushed off the wall and snatched a rifle and ammunition. "I'll head to the attic. I'll let you know if I see any boats approaching from the east and south." Bryan climbed the stairs.

"I'll cross to the north side of the island." Grabbing the other rifle, Daniel turned to his father. "That deer blind still there?"

Seated with his back to the end of a sofa, Mom at his side, Dad was all business, like everyone else. Even though he knew very little about what was happening, he asked no questions, trusting his sons. "Reinforced it this summer."

"That'll give me a view of the water north and west. If anybody approaches, we'll see them." Daniel gave both Camilla and Zoë, his twenty-one-year-old daughter, a quick kiss and mussed Jeremy's hair. Then, he grabbed the other walkie-talkie and headed toward the door, squeezing Jasmine's arm on his way, whispering something in her ear before he donned his coat and stepped outside.

"The rest of us need to get into position," Derrick said. "We need to do something." *He* needed to do something.

"We're working out a plan." Michael was too calm. "They'll keep an eye out and tell us—"

"What if Khalid's already here?" He couldn't help his demanding tone. "We just sent Daniel out there—"

"They're not here." Standing beside him, Grant's hand clamped on his shoulder. "Dad's got cameras monitoring the north dock."

Dad nodded to an iPad on the floor by his feet. "There's been no activity, son."

Most of the island sat high above the ocean, steep cliff walls protecting the land. If not for the rain and snow, it was possible enemies could land anywhere and climb. But it was highly unlikely Khalid and his men were prepared to scale slippery cliffs during a snowstorm.

"We know what we're doing." Grant looked past Derrick at Michael. "We need to work together."

Derrick wanted that, of course. He needed to pace, though, feeling too antsy to stand still. With everyone gathered, there wasn't enough room.

They'd turned off most of the lights in the house right after Jasmine had shown him the email, so the large space felt dim and creepy. Qasim and his men might not have landed yet, but they could be watching from a boat. No sense leading them right to their target.

Michael quickly explained to his family about how Jasmine had been forced to marry, how she'd run away, how her husband wanted his kid.

How Derrick and Jasmine had gone to DC to try to help an old friend of hers.

"Because I'm a fool," Jasmine said from the far side of the room.

Everyone turned her direction.

"Dari never cared about finding Rabie and Basma. It was all to find me."

Yeah. That was what the email had said. According to Rabie, though Dari had said he'd retrieve him eventually, promising to buy him gifts and take him fun places, he'd never asked about where he and Basma were going. And he hadn't asked him to get in touch with him after they relocated. All his questions had been about Derrick and Jasmine.

Basma had told Rabie the truth about Dari and his cruelty during the train ride to her cousin's house, at which point, Rabie had confessed everything. He'd admitted his electronic game had been rigged, that he'd been communicating with Dari through it. He hadn't had access to the game at the hotel in DC, and he hadn't known where he was at Gavin's cabin, which explained why Qasim's men hadn't caught up with them sooner.

But when he could, Rabie had answered all of Dari's questions and passed along their whereabouts. That was how the thugs had caught up with them at the gas station.

And what else had Rabie learned? Derrick's first name, and that his contact, Michael, was also his brother, which Derrick and Jasmine had said they weren't going to tell him but had accidentally let slip.

And that Derrick owned a jet.

That wouldn't have been enough. Not nearly enough.

But the kid was clever.

Jasmine's cell phone had been in her suitcase. The night she'd gone to the pharmacy, Rabie had found it and powered it up. After Derrick had thrown the backpack out the window—including the game Rabie had used to communicate—he'd been furious.

So he'd texted Dari from her phone and shared all her contacts—all the Wrights' full names and phone numbers—with all those Maine area codes.

If that was all he had, it would probably be enough to track them down—but it might not.

As if following Derrick's line of thought, Sam asked, "How could they find us here, though? At camp?"

"Dariush is connected." Michael's gaze flicked to Sophie, seated on the floor.

All the color leached from her pale skin. "It's not...it can't be the Dariush from Germany?"

"It is." Michael's tone was grim. "It's him."

Derrick focused on Bryan's future bride. "What are you talking about? You know him?"

"He was one of the guys who..."

"Dariush Ghazi, a.k.a. Dariush Shahin." Michael took a breath and blew it out. "We've been searching for him, but he's slippery. And he knows people." He met Grant's eyes. "We have to assume he's already pinged her phone."

"Even if he didn't, we told Rabie where we'd be." Derrick thought back to the conversation they'd had in the car after leaving Uncle Gavin's cabin. "We told him the island was on Lake Huron. But Rabie knew about the house on the island, even about the party. He knows...everything. If Qasim checks real estate records, he'll be able to find this place."

Qasim was out there, getting closer every minute.

"What about the police? What did they say?" Mom's eyes flicked from Derrick to Grant to Michael. She scooted closer to Dad, and he wrapped his arm around her and held her close.

Summer was seated cross-legged at the edge of the group.

"Local police don't have any boats running tonight. Got a call in to the Coast Guard, but I haven't heard back. The guy I talked to didn't give me a lot of hope. The storm's stronger farther south. He didn't think there were any vessels this far north, certainly none equipped for battle."

What Derrick feared...

They were on their own.

"So Qasim and his people know we're all here." Grant paced toward the windows, then turned to face the family. "They'll come prepared. What they don't know is that we've been warned. They don't know we're trained—and we'll be waiting for them." The thought seemed to amuse him because his lips did that twitch thing. His gaze flicked to Dad. "We'll need all the weapons and ammo you have."

"I'll go with you." Sam popped up from the floor and held a hand out to their father to help him up.

They went downstairs to the gun safe.

"We need the rest of the walkie-talkies." Michael leaned down and held a hand out to their mom. "Can you find those?"

"There's a box around here somewhere." She let him pull her to her feet. "Somebody will need to find batteries."

"I'll do it." Eliza stood, and then everyone started standing, moving, talking.

Everyone wanted to help.

Derrick's gaze flicked to the kitchen, where Jasmine had backed toward the door that led to the porch.

He caught her eyes, and she froze.

From there, steps led down to the wide lawn that spanned to the waist-high rock wall, the only thing between the property and the steep cliff. Below that were the dock, the boathouse, and the churning Atlantic.

The island had no roads, just dirt paths leading to the family's favorite and most visited places. A stream with a little swimming hole. A tree they used to love climbing when they were kids. A grove of Christmas trees.

There were no cars, just a couple of golf carts they used to transport things from the sea-level dock on the far side, things that were too heavy or too cumbersome to maneuver up the cliff.

Two boats bobbed in the boathouse below, but the keys were here. And the steps leading down to it would be snow-covered and slick.

Jasmine wouldn't know how to drive the boats anyway, even if she could find the keys. Even if she could find her way back to the mainland.

While the rest of Derrick's family talked, Derrick walked toward Jasmine, stopping just short of her. "What are you thinking?"

Her eyes were wide and filled with tears. "I cannot put your family in danger."

"You're part of our family, Jazz."

"I am not. And if they wanted me before, I am sure they do not want me now. People could die."

"We've got this. You just need to—"

"I could go down to the dock and wait—"

"No!" He hadn't meant to shout, but obviously, he had because the voices in the other room quieted.

She took a step back as if he'd scared her. Well, too bad.

He was tired of her...her *I don't deserve your help* nonsense. He reached for her hand, but she snatched it back.

"Fine, then." He scooped her into his arms—he'd hefted luggage heavier than she was—and carried her into the living room, where he unceremoniously dumped her on one of the couches. "She thinks we'll be safer if she leaves." He addressed the room at large.

He heard a gasp. Probably Leila.

Grant cleared his throat. "It's too late for that, and it's not necessary." He nodded to the other couch, which was already covered in weapons. "We've got this."

She blinked at the guns. Her gaze scanned the people watching her from above and landed on Dad, who'd just come back. "I did not mean for this to happen."

"Of course you didn't." His smile was kind, like Dad always was. "We knew you and Leila were in danger, that people were after you. We knew what we were getting into when we welcomed you into our family. You're worth protecting."

Derrick had always loved his father. But he didn't think he'd ever loved and respected him more.

Tears filled Jasmine's eyes.

Derrick ran a hand over her silky hair. "You're here for a reason."

"That's right." Grant looked around at the gathered group, and unlike Derrick, when he focused on Jasmine again, he did smile. "God knew what He was doing when He brought you to us."

As terrified as Derrick was, not for himself but for the people he loved, he knew Grant was right.

God had a plan for this—for all of it.

One way or another, He'd bring them through.

"You believe that?" Grant asked.

Jasmine looked around, and Derrick followed her gaze. Nobody seemed angry or frustrated. His family smiled at her. Leila sat beside her and wrapped her in a hug. From her seat on the floor, Sophie grabbed her hand.

Jasmine's eyes filled, and she nodded. "Yes. I believe you're right. I'm here for a reason."

Before anyone could respond, Daniel's voice carried through the walkie-talkie, and Grant snatched it up, taking it to the windows. He must've turned the volume down, though, because Derrick could hardly hear.

"Say that again." Grant stared out at the dark night. The snow was still falling, and a half inch had accumulated on the deck that wrapped around three sides of the house. In the window's reflection, he looked worried.

"...a forty-footer, at least. Half a mile out." Daniel's voice was faint, a little scratchy. "Four motorized rafts. I count eight on each. Wait... They just dropped another one."

"How far?"

"The first one is landing now. More are coming."

"Toward the dock?"

"Yup."

"Are you well hidden?"

"They won't find me."

"Okay. Do not engage. Repeat, do *not* engage."

"I'm just supposed to sit here and do nothing?"

"Keep me updated on the numbers. Once they hit ground, stay low and be quiet. That includes the walkie-talkie—no volume until you're safe. I'll get back to you. Copy?"

"Copy."

Grant turned and met Derrick's eyes.

Derrick was doing the math. Five boats. Eight men on each.

"That's a lot of men."

"We got this." But Grant's expression held no amusement now. "We just have to be smart. You want to stay close to Jasmine?"

"Definitely."

"Okay. This is about Jasmine, and she's your... Well, you love her, so you get a say."

He did love her, married or not. And he'd protect her with his life, if that was what it came down to.

"You can't be with her, though. I've gotta put Summer..." His brother swallowed, his gaze flicking to his wife. Summer was fierce and competent. But also pregnant. It seemed to take effort for Grant to force his gaze back to Derrick. "You can stay at the house. Michael tells me you're a good shot. You and Sam will be here, in this room, the last line of defense. If you do that, it means you stay inside unless I tell you otherwise. You trust the people outside and upstairs to do their job. Your job is to stop anyone who breaches the doors. Agreed?"

"I can do that."

"Good." Grant turned to the group. "Quiet." His voice was deep, the single word loud and commanding, and amazingly, everyone stopped talking and focused on him.

"From now until this is over, you're all combat soldiers, and I'm the general, which means you do as I say without question. Got it?"

There might've been some raised eyebrows, but when Michael nodded, the movement quick and his expression grim, the rest fell into line.

Derrick was not sorry at all that his brother was taking charge. Thank God Grant was here and knew what he was doing. Derrick wouldn't have a clue how to protect Jasmine by himself.

"All right," Grant said, "here's the plan."

CHAPTER THIRTY-ONE

This was all Jasmine's fault.

She'd done exactly the wrong things, over and over. Because she'd dragged Derrick into her foolishness, he was in danger. Leila was in danger.

Jeremy and Zoë, two sweet young people Jasmine barely knew, were in danger.

Four-year-old Levi would celebrate a birthday in a few days —if he lived to see it.

Derrick's parents, who'd welcomed her and treated her like a daughter, might not survive.

His brothers and sisters-in-law and Sophie. All of them were in danger because of Jasmine.

She sat on the couch where Derrick had put her, barely able to process what was happening.

Grant was giving orders.

Sam was checking weapons against boxes of ammo, then doling them out to the men and most of the women.

Peggy jogged down the stairs, calling, "Found it." She set a cardboard box on one of the chairs. "Eliza, did you find batteries?"

Eliza carried in a box from the kitchen. "You have enough to power a city."

"For such a time as this," Peggy said with a wry grin.

How could they smile? How could they joke?

They set to work powering up the little black communication things. Someone had given them a strange, childish name, but Jasmine couldn't remember it.

Derrick stood a few feet away from her, peering out the window through binoculars, though he kept looking at her, probably making sure she was still there.

She'd considered running. Maybe to do so would be noble, to protect this family by sacrificing herself. But would it work? Or would there be a battle anyway?

Roger had said her life was worth fighting for.

A year before, maybe even a week before, she might've scoffed at the idea. But now... He was right.

Christ had died for her. She must be valuable.

Her child definitely was.

She wouldn't sacrifice herself or her future. She wouldn't sacrifice the baby she carried. Did that make her selfish?

No.

Because Jesus would leave the ninety-nine to save the one. To Him, every life mattered. It wasn't about weighing the worth of one against the worth of many. They were all precious and too valuable to measure.

If she tried to sacrifice her own life to protect these new friends, she'd only prove how little she trusted God.

But she *did* trust Him.

If God chose to take one of His children home tonight...?

She didn't want to consider it. All she knew was that she'd spent years studying His Word, learning from Him. Now, it was time to prove that she believed.

After giving the binoculars to his father, who watched out

the window, Derrick approached, holding out one of the little black things to her. "Take a walkie-talkie."

She did. It was black, a little smaller than a cell phone but thicker, with a big button on the side and a speaker on the front. "How does it work?"

Derrick took it back and twisted a knob on one side. Nothing came through but static. "That's the volume. When you want to talk, you press this button and hold it down." He indicated the big one on the side. "Then you have to remember to take your finger off it when you're done talking or you won't hear a response." He handed it back to her. "Give it a try."

She looked from it to him. "Why do we not just use cell phones?"

"Grant's worried Khalid will be able to track us through them."

"Oh." She pulled hers from her pocket. "I should shut mine off."

"No, don't." Grant must've been listening because he stepped toward them. "Keep it on. We don't want them to know we're onto them. Plus, if they are tracking it, we want them to come straight here."

"It is...bait?"

Derrick shot his brother a glare that showed what he thought about that, but Grant either didn't see or ignored it. "If you have to evacuate the house, leave the phone behind." When she nodded, he turned to speak to Michael.

Derrick seemed like he wanted to say something to his brother, but after a moment, he shook his head and focused on her. "Our cells only work here because we have Wi-Fi, which runs off the satellite. If we lose power, we lose the signal. It'd be easy enough to disable the generator. Walkie-talkies are old technology. They don't rely on any of that. They're how we communicated before we had cell phone coverage out here." He nodded to it. "Go ahead and try it."

"What should I say?"

"Ask if there are any updates."

She felt foolish but pressed the button and said, "Hello? Are there updates?"

A scratchy voice said, "Who's that?"

"Jasmine."

"It's Bryan. All clear up here."

"Eight boats now." That sounded like Daniel. "The men are holding in the woods."

"How many?" Grant asked.

"I'd say fifty."

Jasmine's horror must've shown.

"It's okay, sweetheart." Derrick settled beside her on the couch and took the walkie-talkie, turning the volume down. "They have numbers, and they think they have the element of surprise, but they're wrong. We'll be surprising them. We have the high ground. We have Grant and Michael to strategize and fight—which is saying something."

"This I know." She'd seen Michael in action. He was a man who liked to control everything, but he'd willingly handed the reins to Grant, proving how much respect he must have for Grant's abilities. She had no doubt both men were fierce warriors.

"Bryan can shoot the button off a jacket from a thousand yards," Derrick said. "And Dad taught him everything he knows. Daniel, Sam, and I can hold our own in a fight."

She'd witnessed Derrick's abilities. He'd already saved her life once.

"Summer's a trained bodyguard," he continued. "Mom knows how to handle a gun, and Camilla and Eliza have learned to shoot. Michael's been working with Leila, who feels comfortable enough to try. Trust me. We've got this."

She did trust him, of course. She trusted all of them. But a stray bullet could end a life. How would she live with that?

"If anyone comes"—Derrick handed back the walkie-talkie — "or if you see anything or hear anything or think of anything we need to know, don't hesitate to contact me. Us, I mean."

"You will not be with me?"

Grant had given assignments to the rest of the men. The women who were comfortable with guns would be at upstairs windows, watching, shooting if necessary. The rest of the women—her, Sophie, and Leila—along with the two young people and Levi, would stay out of the way.

Because Grant hadn't given Derrick an assignment, Jasmine had assumed that meant he'd be with her.

"Sam and I will be on this floor making sure nobody gets up those stairs." He leaned over and kissed her on the forehead. "Oh." His eyes widened. "Sorry. I shouldn't have..." He pushed himself up, giving her a tight smile. "It's going to be fine."

She reached out and took his hand. "You do not apologize to me, not for anything. And I wish you to know..." She shouldn't say it. It would do no good. But if he were to die, or if she were to die or be taken... Or perhaps one of his family members would die, and his feelings for her would change...

Maybe this would be her only chance.

All around, there was chaos. The women had gathered coats and hats and gloves and boots, for what purpose, Jasmine didn't know.

Men placed other gear onto the table. Fire extinguishers and flashlights and backpacks and first-aid kits. They were preparing for every possible contingency. Nobody was paying any attention to Derrick and her.

He looked at her on the sofa, his face softening into that kind, gentle expression she'd seen so often.

"I never knew men like you existed. If I had known... I-I don't think I could have changed anything, but I would have tried. I would have tried to wait for you."

He sat again, took her hand, and leaned in. His kiss to her cheek was so light and tender that it felt like a warm breeze. "I love you, too, sweetheart." The words were a whisper in her ear. "No matter what happens, that's never going to change."

Before she could formulate a response, he stood. She thought he'd return to the window, but Sam stood there now.

Derrick went to the kitchen and took up a position inside the door, focus beyond the window to the long patio.

Already waiting for the first enemies to arrive.

She couldn't stand to see him there, in danger, for her.

It wouldn't be long before she was told exactly where to go and with whom. Until then, she'd pray. She slid to her knees and bent her face to the floor, asking for the Lord's protection and guidance and help. No matter how prepared they were, they were one family against an army.

They needed God on their side.

She didn't know how long she stayed like that before someone touched her back.

"Come on, Jazz." Sophie's voice pulled her from the haze.

She sat up.

"You all right?"

"Yes. Only praying."

Sophie nodded to the other sofa, piled high with outer gear. "They want us to take our coats upstairs with us, just in case."

She found hers, which had gloves in the pockets.

"Grab a hat," Derrick called from the other room. "If you have to go out, hide your hair."

She selected a red knit cap and put it in a pocket of her winter coat.

"We're going upstairs to one of the bedrooms." Sophie had her own coat draped over her arm.

Jasmine turned to Derrick, wanting to say...something. Or perhaps just to see him again. He still stood by the far door. He wore jeans and his bomber jacket. His hair was messy, disheveled after he'd pushed it back a thousand times, a common gesture when he was worried. His gaze was on her. "Go on."

"Be safe. Please."

"I will." He flicked a gaze outside then walked toward her. He grabbed the walkie-talkie off the sofa, which she'd forgotten. "Can I trust you to do the same? No running away? Because that won't work, you know. And then we'll have to get you back, which will put us all in jeopardy."

"I understand." And she did. All that time in prayer, the Lord had given her peace about where she was. These were His people, and He was using them for a purpose. "I trust all of us in God's hands. I won't go to Khalid. I promise."

"Okay. Good." He held the walkie-talkie out to her.

As she took it, it crackled, and then Daniel's voice came through. "They're on the move. Going quiet."

Derrick stepped close, kissed her cheek. "I'll see you soon."

Sophie's hand slid around her arm. "Come on."

Most of the women had already gone up. Aside from her and Sophie, only Summer remained. She and Grant seemed to be having some kind of argument.

"This is ridiculous." Summer's voice was low but vehement. "You know I'm capable—"

"That's why I'm assigning you to guard Jasmine." Grant had that all-business tone he'd used with everyone. "That's your job."

"Grant."

"Summer." He groaned, and for the first time, Jasmine saw a trace of fear in the warrior's eyes. "Your job is to guard her"—he nodded toward Jasmine, but he didn't take his eyes off his wife—"and her." His hand pressed to Summer's expanding middle. "Please." That last word came out imploring.

Sophie tugged Jasmine's arm, and she shook out of her stupor. She should not be staring. She should not be watching the private moment.

She followed Sophie and the flashlight she carried up the stairs. The hallway was dark, but faint light carried out from a few of the rooms—there were three on each side—and from the steps that had been lowered from the ceiling at the far end.

Sophie led the way into the first bedroom. This one faced the back of the house, away from the sea. In the glow of the narrow flashlight beam, she saw two twin beds.

Jasmine wasn't surprised when Summer followed her in. "Climb onto the beds, but if I tell you to get down, get on the floor." She closed the door, locked it, then went to the window. "Turn off the flashlight."

Sophie did, and the room was shrouded in darkness, no light except what filtered in from outside. It wasn't much, just enough to show Summer's baby bump as she stood in front of it —and to glint off the handgun she held.

"You might as well get comfortable," she said. "We're going to be here for a while."

Sophie shifted on the other bed, but Jasmine didn't want to get comfortable while people she loved put themselves in danger. She slid into her jacket—it was cold thanks to the open window. "I'm so sorry for all of this."

She wasn't sure what she expected, but she definitely didn't expect the tough bodyguard to chuckle.

That had Sophie asking, "What's funny?"

"Nothing. It's just that, a couple of years ago... It's a really long story, but there was this guy who was the relative of a client we were guarding. I knew him, and I knew he was up to no good, and like an idiot, I followed him. By myself, without alerting Grant, who was my partner at the time. The thug knew I was following him, though. I made myself a target. Anyway, it all got way out of control, and I could've gotten myself killed. And, in the end, not only myself but Grant. And Bryan."

"Bryan?" Sophie said. "How did that happen?"

"Like I said, long story. He was incredibly brave. And Grant was...amazing. The point is, I didn't get us into that on purpose any more than you did this on purpose, Jasmine. I worked as a bodyguard for a long time, and my sister and I were kidnapped once, and... Well, suffice it to say, I've been involved in some weird situations, and here's what I've learned: When bad guys do bad things, they're responsible for the things they do. Maybe you made a mistake, but that doesn't make you responsible for anything your so-called husband does. Or your friend's brother or...any of those people. You can only take responsibility for yourself."

"I am responsible for going to DC and for dragging Derrick along with me."

"Ha," Sophie said. "I'm guessing you didn't exactly have to *drag* him."

"He is very kind."

"Kind?" Sophie asked. "He's in love."

"According to Grant, he's a smitten kitten." Summer laughed. "I think if you'd asked him to fly you to the moon, he'd have fitted rockets to his jet."

These two were not nearly as afraid as Jasmine. Or perhaps they used humor to make themselves feel less so. "Did everybody know about Derrick's feelings?"

"Everybody but you." Sophie's tone was gentle. "I'm glad he finally confessed."

"Perhaps he is not, though, now that he knows about Khalid."

Neither of them seemed to know what to say about that, and silence settled.

"What's the plan?" Sophie asked a few minutes later.

Summer answered. "We want Qasim's men to believe they've succeeded in taking us by surprise. They'll creep through the woods. Grant and Michael will approach from the sides. Daniel will follow from behind. There's a tree they used to climb, I guess, so he's going to go up that. His job is to report what he sees and to stop anybody getting away with Jasmine—or any of us."

"And Grant and Michael?" Jasmine asked. "What is their job?"

"To confuse. Make the enemy believe they're outgunned and outflanked. We want them to give up and run. If necessary, Grant and Michael will take out as many as they can from the sides. Bryan and Roger will focus on the woods near the house, and Eliza, Camilla, Leila, and I will watch for enemies who get close to the house. If a few manage to breach a door, Sam and Derrick will stop them."

The thought brought terror, which escaped on a gasp.

"Don't worry," Summer said. "Grant doesn't think anyone will get that far. We have the element of surprise, the high ground, and cover. We shouldn't have any trouble pushing them back. Hopefully, they'll figure that out and run long before they get here."

Maybe the others would, but Khalid? If he was in charge, he'd let every man die for him. He wouldn't care who perished if it meant getting his only child back.

A staticky sound filled the room.

"Movement in the woods." That was Bryan's voice. "They're here."

"Hold." Even speaking in a whisper, Grant sounded commanding, fully confident in the role of general. "Thirty seconds. Let them get closer."

Time dripped slowly. Slowly.

And then, Grant said, "Now."

The first bullet was fired, and gunshots exploded all around.

Huddled in coat and hat, Jasmine gripped Sophie's hand. They'd moved to sit beside each other seconds after the first gunshot. Now, they prayed aloud, their words more gibberish than logical pleas. But God knew what they meant. He understood.

Firing every few moments, Summer had already emptied her handgun and reloaded. Cold air wafted through the open window, carrying the scent of snow and gunpowder. She seemed calm, as if everything were going as planned.

At unexpected moments, one of the men would shout a warning or an update, but mostly, the walkie-talkie was quiet, everyone too busy fighting enemies to keep the rest apprised of what was going on.

Please, God. Please protect us.

Jasmine's cell phone vibrated in her pocket. Probably an email from Basma, wanting an update. Except it continued to vibrate. A phone call?

Very few people had her phone number, and all of them were busy at the moment.

She pulled the phone out and checked the screen.

"Who is it?" Sophie asked.

"I don't know."

"Telemarketer?"

"Must be."

The vibrating stopped but started again a few seconds later. The same number.

She had a very bad feeling about that.

Sophie's gaze flicked from the phone to Jasmine's face. "Maybe you should answer, just in case."

At the window, Summer seemed unaware, her focus on the forest outside.

Jasmine swiped to answer and lifted the phone to her ear.

"Did you really think you could escape me?" Khalid spoke the words in Arabic, his deep voice like a blow to her chest.

Sophie's eyes widened. She looked from the phone to Jasmine, then stood and hurried to Summer, speaking quietly.

Jasmine blocked her free ear with a finger so she could hear over the gunfire. "I did escape you." Like Khalid, she spoke in Arabic. "I am here, am I not?"

"As am I." By the gunfire that carried through her cell phone, Khalid was close. Not in the line of fire, though. Knowing him, he was waiting somewhere safe. "I have a hundred soldiers."

A hundred?

Did he exaggerate? Or had the Wrights miscalculated?

"They are prepared to kill every man, woman, and child who stands between you and me," Khalid said. "But you can end this. Come to me, now."

"I-I cannot. They won't let me leave. They'll stop me."

Sophie was still whispering to Summer, probably translating everything Jasmine said.

"You will go out from the bottom floor. There is a door on the south side that opens near the forest. Exit there and walk straight ahead. My men will bring you to me."

"They'll see. They'll stop me."

"We will kill anyone who tries."

"I don't... I won't be able to get away."

"We'll provide a distraction. When we do, run. Do not hesitate. The sooner you obey me, the fewer people will die."

"What distraction? What are you planning?"

But the line beeped, and he was gone.

Sophie watched her.

Summer glanced her way. "Don't even think—"

"I will not sacrifice myself."

Summer nodded to the walkie-talkie. "Tell everyone exactly what he said." She smiled. "Time to set ourselves a trap."

CHAPTER THIRTY-TWO

Derrick itched to join the fight.

His brothers were putting their lives on the line while he did nothing but stare out the back door at the empty patio.

"One got through!" Michael called.

The boom of gunfire, then Grant's low, "Got him."

"Watch out, Mike," Daniel yelled. "Watch out!"

Silence stretched for seconds. A minute. Felt like an hour. Then Michael spoke, sounding out of breath. "He's down. Thanks, bro."

What had happened? Derrick wanted a play-by-play, as if his brothers had nothing else to do.

He twisted toward Sam, who was watching out the windows on the other side of the room, glancing back to the door that led up from the basement, just in case.

"You see anything?"

"Just flashes," Sam said. "Nobody's gotten through."

"Good, good." Derrick didn't want those guys anywhere near Jasmine or all the women and kids in this house. Truth be told, he didn't want them near his brothers, either.

Grant's plan was working. God willing, any second, Khalid and his men would turn tail and run.

"I got a call." Jasmine's voice on the walkie-talkie had Derrick jolting. "It was Khalid."

"What!" His shocked response was lost as everyone else reacted.

"Quiet, everyone," Grant commanded. Then, "What did he say exactly?"

Jasmine explained what the terrorist had dictated she do.

"He didn't explain the distraction?" Grant asked.

"No."

"Okay." Grant acted like this was no big deal. Just another day at the office. "Stand by."

Stand by?

Derrick was supposed to just...do nothing? Fat chance.

He pressed the button on his walkie-talkie. "Let me go out there, Grant. I'll surprise him."

"Stay where you are. Be ready for that distraction."

He glared at the walkie-talkie as if Grant could see him, then called, "Sam, trade places with me."

If they switched places, Derrick could easily slip down the stairs and *meet* Khalid beneath the patio himself.

"Not a chance," Sam said.

"If she tries to go out—"

"I'll stop her. Don't worry."

But Khalid was so close.

"They're coming over the cliff!" Dad's shout had Derrick peering through the darkness, but all he could see was the dark patio and the railing. He couldn't see the yard between the house and the cliff or any men who might be coming that way.

A gunshot echoed from upstairs. Then another. And another.

What was happening?

"From the dock?" Grant yelled. "How'd they get—?"

"Up the stairs." Dad's voice, frantic a moment ago, was calm now. After a pause and a couple of gunshots, Dad continued. "Black boats, black clothes. Black water. Didn't see 'em."

"Shoot on sight," Grant said, all business.

"We're trying!" That was Leila, and unlike Dad, she sounded terrified. "There're too many!"

"You're doing great, hon," Dad said. "Take your time. Line up your shots."

"You've got this, sweetheart." Michael was calm as could be. "You guys are doing great. Stop as many as you can. Derrick and Sam will get anyone who makes it by you."

Derrick itched to step onto the patio. If he could pick enemies off as they crossed the lawn, he could stop them before they reached the house.

But he knew his job. It was not to go meet Khalid. It was not to kill the man who would take Jasmine away but to protect everybody in this house.

Help me, God. Equip me for this.

He stepped away from the glass and aimed. Ready.

Across the room, Sam's focus was on the door that came up from the basement. Maybe he should've been downstairs, but Grant had wanted someone watching from the higher windows.

If more men were coming, then the Wrights didn't have enough manpower. Not nearly enough.

But nobody came. Maybe Dad, Bryan, and the women upstairs had it under control. If the men coming up the cliff were meant to be the distraction, then they'd handled it.

"You see that?" Bryan's voice held a hint of panic. "They've got some sort of a—"

"Take cover!" Summer shouted.

A low whistle.

Glass shattered—upstairs.
An explosion rocked the house.

CHAPTER THIRTY-THREE

The boom was deafening.

"No!" Jasmine lunged for the door. Her shout was loud in her head but muffled in her ears. Where had the bomb hit? Was Leila hurt? Peggy? One of the children?

Please, God. Please...

Another explosion. And another.

Sophie grabbed her arm.

Behind her, in the pale light coming from outside, Summer pointed to their feet.

Jasmine wanted to check on the others, but Sophie yanked her to the floor.

In the strange and muffled silence, a high-pitched whistle was unmistakable.

Summer dove on top of Jasmine and Sophie, knocking them to the hard floor.

Jasmine banged her shoulder and elbow, but everything felt numb in the surreal world.

The next explosion was so close that her hair lifted. She squeezed her eyes closed, but blinding light pierced her eyelids.

Smoke filled the space, thick and heavy. She inhaled an

acrid chemical scent and coughed, sure she'd never get another clean breath. She pulled the knit hat from her pocket and covered her mouth and nose, breathing through it.

Summer rolled off them and crawled toward the doorway.

Somehow, despite the bomb, the bedroom seemed undamaged. There was no debris from fallen walls. The bed beside her felt intact. No flames brightened the darkness, and she felt no heat.

What kind of a bomb did no damage?

Summer peered into the hallway, then pointed. "Downstairs. Stay low." Her words were clear, though faint, as if they'd been shouted from far away. But Jasmine's hearing was already coming back.

Heeding her instructions, Sophie started for the hallway.

Before Jasmine could follow, Summer got in her face and shouted, making herself heard. "Stay away from windows. Don't go anywhere alone. Understand me?"

Jasmine nodded, and Summer returned to the window.

What was she doing? She wasn't coming?

No. Summer was back at her perch, firing, determined to keep up the fight, to defend the house and the people in it.

Protect her, Lord. Protect her child.

Jasmine couldn't fight. She'd never fired a gun in her life. But she could care for the wounded.

The hallway was pitch black. Though Sophie had only been a few feet ahead of her, she was lost in the haze of smoke and darkness.

Jasmine crawled back to the bed, snatched the flashlight, and flicked it on.

Thank God the smoke rose to the ceiling. In the hallway, if she stayed low, she could breathe. It was cold enough that she pulled the hat on her head, shoving her hair inside it, before swinging the light toward the stairs.

Sophie was gesturing her forward.

She swung the flashlight in the other direction and caught sight of someone crawling toward her from farther down the hallway. Leila!

Jasmine lit the way between them. "Are you all right?"

"I think...." Leila said something else, but she didn't catch it. The faint, hazy light showed a gash on her twin's forehead and a line of blood dripping from it.

"You're hurt!"

"Only a little. Peggy told me to..." The rest of her words were lost as she twisted to look behind.

"I'll get her. Go with Sophie." Jasmine pointed to where their friend waited. "She's hurt. Help her!"

Sophie called, "Come on. Hurry."

Leila grabbed Jasmine's wrist. "Come."

"I'll be right behind you." And she would, soon. But first, she'd see if anyone needed help. Leila wanted to keep Jasmine safe, but what about Camilla and Eliza?

Bryan and Roger had been in the attic. Were they all right?

Where were Zoë and Jeremy and Levi? They were children —well, one of them was, anyway. But they might be hurt.

Jasmine's ears were clearing, picking up the sound of gunfire. The attack was still on, and most of the adults in this house were involved. Leila had been shooting from one of the windows, but with her injury, Peggy must've insisted she get downstairs.

Was Peggy searching for her family? Or at a window, taking out targets?

Jasmine wasn't going anywhere until she knew if anyone needed help.

Leila followed Sophie, and Jasmine aimed the flashlight the other way.

These bombs had been all lights and smoke and sound, but

they hadn't done much damage. Except Leila had been hurt. How had that happened?

This...this was the distraction Khalid had told her about. She was supposed to go now to meet him.

Derrick and his brothers would take care of Khalid. While they did, she would take care of the people they loved.

Movement in the flashlight beam showed Eliza walking, bent low, with her five-year-old hanging onto her octopus-style.

"Are you okay?" Eliza called.

"Yes. Sophie and Leila are downstairs. Follow them."

Eliza didn't argue, just took Levi to safety.

"Go," a woman's voice said. Camilla?

Jasmine headed toward the room farther down and across the hall.

"But, Mom, you need to—!"

"Don't argue with me."

Zoë crawled into the hallway and saw Jasmine. "I can't get her to come." The twenty-something sounded on the verge of tears.

"It's okay. She'll be okay." Jasmine prayed it was true. "Hurry, hurry." She aimed the flashlight toward the stairs. "Where is your brother?"

"He went to the attic."

"I'll find him. Go."

Zoë opened her mouth like she wanted to argue.

Camilla was at the window, peering out. She aimed, fired.

Jasmine gripped the young woman's wrist. "Your mother needs to know you're safe so she can focus on what she's doing. The best you can do is go downstairs."

Camilla glanced back and gave Jasmine a grateful smile.

"I love you, Mom." Zoë gave her mother a final look, then crawled toward the stairs.

"I can't find Levi!" Peggy's frantic shout came from the end of the hall.

"He's with Eliza," Jasmine shouted over the gunfire. "They've gone down."

"Oh, thank God." The older woman crawled closer but stopped, coughing. Hacking. "I have to make sure"—she coughed—"Roger and Bryan..." Again, her words were cut off with coughing.

"I'll check on them," Jasmine said.

"And Jeremy!" Camilla yelled. "He went to the attic—"

"I'll see to them." Jasmine aimed the flashlight toward the stairs. "Go, Peggy. Join the others. We've got this."

Peggy started that direction, then stopped. "But you should —" Hacking coughs kept her from finishing.

"I'll come when I know everyone is all right," Jasmine said. "Go. Please."

From the top of the staircase, Zoë called, "Please, Nana. Please, come on."

The older woman joined her granddaughter.

After they started down, Jasmine continued to the ladder that had been lowered from a hatch in the attic and climbed up.

She poked her head through the opening and looked around. Though smoke rose from the ground floor, this area had avoided damage. Boxes and furniture had been pushed to one side. "Is everyone all right up here?"

Bryan glanced from his spot at a window facing the rear of the house but didn't lower the rifle aimed outside. "Grant told us to stay put."

At a window nearby, Jeremy was pale but unhurt. "Did you see my mom and Zoë?"

Before she could answer, Roger asked, "Is anyone hurt?" He was on the opposite side of the attic, also aiming a rifle. The gun was out of place in the gentle man's hands.

She answered Jeremy first. "Your mother and sister are fine." Turning her attention to the older man, she added, "Peggy was coughing, and Leila has a cut on her head, but it didn't seem serious. Otherwise, we are okay."

"You're sure?" Roger's gaze flicked to his grandson. "Jeremy can take over for me."

She hated to think of the teenager shooting anybody, even if he was capable. "I think Peggy needed fresh air, and Leila's cut wasn't deep. Summer and Camilla are in position. The rest have gone to the first floor. I'll let you know if you're needed."

He seemed torn but stayed in position. "All right. Thanks."

Jasmine headed down the ladder to the second story. She was on her way to the staircase when that telltale whistle had her diving onto the hardwood and covering her head.

The explosion came from the south side of the house, facing the water.

Camilla screamed.

Smoke filled the space, thicker as Jasmine crawled toward the bedroom where she'd left her friend. "Are you all right? Camilla?"

But there was no answer.

CHAPTER THIRTY-FOUR

The latest boom came from right on top of Derrick.

Followed by a scream. Camilla?

Jasmine shouted. She was upstairs, dealing with it.

These things weren't bombs but flash-bangs, intended to create chaos but do little to no damage.

That was what Grant had said through the walkie-talkie, and Derrick figured he knew what he was talking about.

Still, he itched to run up there, to make sure everyone was all right. Which was exactly what the terrorists wanted. He stayed at the door, waiting for someone to breach it.

So far, so good.

Gunshots still came from above, a constant barrage.

How many people were out there? What was their plan?

Sophie had come downstairs with Leila. Then Eliza and Levi.

Zoë and Mom had followed.

Per Michael's instructions, Sam had sent them all into the basement. With the explosions, it would be safer down there. Three of the four walls were built partially or completely into the hillside, where the only access came from the bulkhead doors on either side. The fourth wall had windows and a sliding glass door, but because it was beneath the patio, it was somewhat protected.

The women would take cover in the storage room in the back. They were armed, should anybody get in. They should be safe there.

Grant had talked about keeping all the women in the basement from the start, and Derrick had been all-in on that suggestion. Ultimately, Grant had decided he wanted their help fending off the attack.

Obviously, he hadn't counted on the terrorists bringing rocket launchers.

Upstairs, Derrick assumed Summer was still shooting, as were Dad and Bryan in the attic. What was Jeremy doing? Couldn't he help his mother?

Jasmine needed to get into the basement. Now.

"Hold your position." Grant had maintained his calm demeanor, as if nothing had surprised him. "Mike and Dan, you have the north. I'll be in position to intercept Khalid in thirty seconds."

"Got it," Michael said.

"In position," Daniel said.

A moment passed, and then Jasmine spoke. "Camilla is hurt." She sounded slightly panicked.

"Hurt? How?" That was Daniel, of course.

"I think she's..."

"I'm fine." Camilla spoke over her, her voice coming from a distance away. "It's nothing. I'll be back at the window in just a sec."

The scrape of furniture sounded over Derrick's head.

He wanted to go up there, to check. And to drag Jasmine downstairs and hide her in the storage room, where she'd be safe. Safer, at least, than...

"He's got a launcher!" Dad shouted. "Down, do—"

Another explosion. Did that hit the attic?

"Dad! Bryan!" Sam sounded like Derrick felt—terrified. "What happened?"

Had that been another flash-bang? Or something else?

"Came from the south." Dad sounded out of breath. "We're okay. We're not going to be able to hold them off."

"Derrick." Grant sounded, for the first time, a little...ruffled. "I want you on the patio. Stay low, shoot through the slats. Take out the one with the launcher. As soon as you do, move. Stay out there and take out any enemies you see. Whatever you do, don't let anybody into the house."

"On it." Thank God, Derrick was finally joining the fight.

"Good, Sam, you're gonna..."

Derrick lowered the volume on the walkie-talkie and shoved it in his pocket. He crouched low, opened the kitchen door, and stepped out into the cold, cold night.

The snow that covered everything gave the world a strangely luminous glow.

Even so, he paused to let his eyes adjust. The patio tables were covered for the winter with weatherproof fabric. The chairs were stacked near the house, also covered. Everything had an inch of powdery snow on top.

The briny scent of the ocean mixed with a chemical stench from the flash-bangs. Normally, he'd hear little but the surf against the rocks at the bottom of the cliff, but gunshots reverberated in the night. Dad and Bryan had recovered, apparently.

Derrick peeked through the slats in the patio searching, searching.

There. A man clad in dark clothes was silhouetted against the sky. The apparatus he held was long like a rifle, but its barrel was far too thick.

Derrick aimed and fired.

The man went down.

Derrick shifted a few feet along the patio seconds before a bullet splintered the wood where he'd just stood. It'd come from near the stairs at the top of the cliff.

Derrick waited for the man to show himself again. When he did, Derrick fired. Hit him.

Scooted along the deck a few yards.

Looked for another enemy. One came from the woods on the west. Derrick lined him up and fired and moved. He kept at it. They didn't stop. He wouldn't either.

The sky turned from black to gray as the sun inched toward the horizon. Morning was coming. This couldn't last forever. There would be an end to it.

With each bullet he fired, he prayed God would protect his family and all those they loved.

He lined up another shot and squeezed the trigger, but the chamber was empty. He leaned back on his haunches to reload.

Heard rustling, then a chuckle. "It was just a matter of time." The words were whispered with a thick Arabic accent.

Derrick dove to the side, expecting a gunshot in his ear. But it didn't come.

The man tackled him. An arm came down, hard.

Pain exploded on Derrick's temple. Then a second time.

Derrick's face smacked on the hard wood deck. The world spun, his head pounded.

The man bent over him, his hot breath in Derrick's face.

"Everything you have done, she will be punished for. I will let you live with that." He stood, kicked Derrick in the back, forcing air from his lungs, then stepped into the house.

CHAPTER THIRTY-FIVE

"Go. I'm fine."

A few minutes had passed since Jasmine had helped Camilla to a chair in front of the window. Now, she stood back from the room's second window, watching. Though she couldn't see him, Derrick was out there now, shooting terrorists.

In harm's way.

"I will stay—"

"You heard Grant," Camilla said. "He wants you in the basement."

He'd told her that through the walkie-talkie a moment before.

"I know but—"

"I'm all right." The older woman sounded exasperated. "You're as bad as Zoë. Go, please."

There hadn't been another flash-bang, as Grant called them.

Jasmine didn't want to leave, not while her friends were in danger, but she had promised to do what Grant said. "Be careful." She headed to the hallway and down the stairs and was halfway to the door that led to the basement when she heard it.

The voice that turned her blood cold.

"I knew you wouldn't come."

Terror rose from her midsection and clogged in her throat, blocking a scream that tried to claw its way out.

Slowly, reluctantly, she turned toward him, the man she most dreaded. The man she despised.

Khalid.

He stalked toward her from the kitchen, then stopped a few feet away. He wore the garb of a soldier—camouflage pants, coat, and hat.

She'd always thought of him as an old man. Balding. Wrinkled. Weak.

But he seemed powerful now, as if strengthened by the prospect of all the evil he'd done. He aimed a gun at her.

"I knew you would tell the men who are protecting you where you were to meet me, and they would set a trap. And now, they are there. And I am here, with you."

Voices carried up from the basement. Her sister and some of her friends were safe. She knew that much. If nothing else, if she left with Khalid, at least nobody else would get hurt.

"You will come with me," Khalid said, "or I will direct my people to kill every single one of them. You understand?"

Could he, though? Were his people winning? She thought not. The Wrights were strong and capable, much more so than he'd anticipated. His men were being killed, one by one.

But Khalid wouldn't care about that. He'd let them all die to get what he wanted.

Her feet felt leaden. She couldn't move. Even if she could, what would she do? Her gaze flicked to the doorway that led downstairs. Khalid wouldn't shoot her. He wouldn't risk harming his child.

She could run. She could try.

He must've guessed her intention because he closed the

---

distance between them and grabbed her, yanking her toward the door. She nearly tripped, but he held her up.

"Keep your feet, you useless, pathetic little mouse." His words, spoken in Arabic, held nothing but malice. "You put all these people between us. You thought they could protect you." He propelled her outside. The storm had passed. Snow covered everything, shimmering in the pale light of dawn. The waves crashed into rocks below, steady as time. Interrupted by occasional gunshots.

Beautiful and terrible.

There was a strange lump on the patio, a dark form.

In...a brown jacket?

No. No!

She gasped. It couldn't be.

Derrick. Oh, Derrick.

"Move!" Khalid dragged her away.

She would have panicked or collapsed if she hadn't seen the slightest vapor rising from Derrick's face. He was breathing. He was alive.

Khalid pushed her to the stairs and down to the snowy yard.

As soon as their feet touched the ground, he said, "Now."

She had no idea what he meant. But then...

An explosion shook the air. Glass exploded over her head.

Someone screamed.

A wave of heat followed.

A scream.

Shouts.

The other bombs had been harmless.

But this...this had been real.

He'd bombed the house. Her friends.

Bombed them.

Khalid pushed her across the snow-covered grass toward the top of the metal staircase that led to the dock below.

"Did you really think you could escape me?" His voice held scorn. "You're just a silly little mouse. A coward."

Was that what she was? She wasn't the one hurling bombs at innocent people.

How dare he? How dare he presume to know anything about her? How dare he presume to take lives given by God?

They were just feet from the top of the cliff when she stopped and pulled away from him. "A coward? Is that what I am? Your silly little second wife? Good for nothing but birthing your children?"

"No more of this foolishness." His tiny black eyes flashed. "You are *my* wife. You will come with me." He pointed toward the metal railing. "Go, now. Go down and get in the boat."

She had had enough. She'd been afraid of him. She'd submitted to him. She'd cowered before him.

No more.

Perhaps she'd lost her mind, or perhaps she'd finally, finally found herself. But no matter what this man did to her, she would not obey him. The truth of it, of who she was—and who she wasn't—raised a laugh inside of her. She didn't stifle it but let it out. "If I'm such a coward, how did I end up here?"

He scoffed. "Your sister's friend—"

"And how did he know where to find us?"

"She told him—"

"How do you think she did that, locked in a bedroom? No, Leila didn't call him. *I* called him. Your silly little wife used *your* phone, Khalid. *I* gave him our coordinates. *I* told him how many men guarded the compound. And when he came, *I* went with him. I did that because I'm such a cowardly little mouse."

Flames reflected off his glasses. The house was *on fire*. And everyone in it was probably busy fighting that fire. Or tending to the injured.

Or fighting terrorists.

But she didn't care. She wasn't going with this disgusting old man, not unless he dragged her, and she would fight him every step.

"You knew how *happy* I was," she spat. "How deliriously happy I was. So happy that you wired that pathetic little building you called a *home* in your pathetic little compound with an alarm to sound if I went outside the pathetic little walls. You knew I might try to escape, to run away, even through the desert, even to my death! This is how happy I was with you."

"Your happiness?" Khalid scoffed that she would speak about something so insignificant, gesturing with his handgun toward the steps. "You are mine. That child you carry is mine. Your *happiness* does not matter. Go down the steps and get into the boat, or I will hurt you. As long as the baby isn't harmed, I don't care what happens to you."

"*I* care what happens to me." She'd switched to English. "My God cares what happens to me."

"Your god is who I say he is." Khalid moved toward her, but she stepped back, keeping space between them.

Movement in the forest behind him caught her eyes. Someone was there. Friend or foe, she didn't know. And it didn't matter.

Whether that was a Wright or a terrorist, she wasn't alone. She'd never been alone. She stood to her full height—all five feet of her—and glared at the man who called himself her husband. "You think you own me, but you are wrong. You are wrong about everything. I am a Christian."

His eyes widened, and he froze. Halted by his shock?

Perhaps.

But she thought of Elisha and the horses and chariots of fire surrounding him as he faced his enemies.

Maybe Khalid sensed what Elisha had known. What Jasmine knew. That her God was far stronger than his.

"I belong to the One True God. I am not, nor have I ever been, yours. Look around you, Khalid."

She paused to give him the opportunity, not allowing her eyes to drift to the figure crossing the snowy ground toward them. A terrorist would make himself known to Khalid.

Meaning it had to be a Wright. Had to be.

"You see where we are." Her voice caught at the wonder of it. "Where I am. In Maine, thousands of miles from Iraq. A coward would still be trapped in your pathetic little compound in the middle of nowhere, in a dry and desolate land, not surrounded by this beauty. I'd still be trapped with a man I despise. I'm here because I'm brave, and because I'm loved by my God and my friends. I am not your slave, and I *will not* go with you."

"You're a fool." Khalid shook himself out of the temporary stupor. "I'll shoot out your knee and then you'll never run again." His words were matter-of-fact. "Not from me. Not anywhere."

She yanked off her hat, shook out her hair—refusing to hide anymore—and pushed her shoulders back. "I dare you to try it."

He scoffed and lifted the gun.

"Drop it, Qasim." Michael stood twenty feet behind him, his weapon aimed at Khalid's head. "Your men are on the run. The ones still alive, that is. And you're surrounded."

Khalid glared at her. She glanced at the house.

There were no flames now.

Derrick was moving toward them across the snow-covered grass.

Aiming his handgun, he was fierce and determined.

"It's over, Qasim," Michael said. "Drop it."

"Now." That was Grant's voice. He was behind her.

There were no more gunshots. All was quiet as they waited.

347

Khalid didn't bother glancing at any of the men, just glared at her.

"If you wish to survive for your *beloved* wife," Jasmine said, "you will do as they say."

CHAPTER THIRTY-SIX

Try it. Come on.

The sky grew brighter in the east. Cold wind blew off the Atlantic, but Derrick didn't feel the chill.

Smoke rose from the house he and his family had built.

The woman he loved stood a yard from the man who would've whisked her away forever. The man who would've destroyed their home and killed the people who mattered most to him in the world.

Do it.

Derrick knew it was wrong to hope Qasim would defy Michael's order. But he did hope it.

If Khalid's gun so much as twitched, Derrick would shoot him.

His head throbbed, but the pain was nothing, nothing compared to the satisfaction of seeing this man defeated.

You should've killed me when you had the chance, Qasim. Live with that.

His finger itched to squeeze the trigger.

Michael and Grant kept their distance, but Derrick didn't care. He moved in, keeping the terrorist's head in his sights.

Come on, you pile of...cow dung. Do it.

But Khalid hadn't lived so many years—and the guy had more wrinkles than the prunes he ate for breakfast—by being stupid.

He tossed his handgun to the side, maybe afraid Jasmine would grab it and finish him off.

Derrick managed to stifle his frustration and the string of words that wanted to escape.

"On your knees!" Michael shouted. "Hands behind your head."

The glare Qasim gave Jasmine could've left a bruise. He took a step toward her, saying something in Arabic Derrick didn't understand.

She didn't back down. Just stood her ground against this man who'd abused her.

Derrick had never loved her so much.

And he'd never so badly wanted to commit murder.

"Now!" Michael said.

Qasim pressed his hands to the back of his head.

Rapid gunfire saturated the morning air.

The terrorist dropped to his knees. Then, fell forward, *splat.* The snow stained red.

Derrick hardly registered what was happening, just ran.

Grant shouted, "Down, down!"

Derrick was already diving. He wrapped Jasmine in his arms, bringing her to the ground with him, taking their weight on his shoulder and hip. He rolled over her, protecting her with his body.

Another volley of gunshots.

Jasmine stared up at him with wide, terrified eyes. "What's happening?"

"I don't know." Not much, anyway. Someone had a machine gun, shooting from a boat, he guessed.

The staccato rhythm stopped, leaving nothing but silence. Slowly, other sounds drifted in. The surf crashing against the cliff below. The distant call of a seagull.

Jasmine's quick breaths, the most beautiful sound of all.

"There!" Dad's shout came over the walkie-talkies.

Derrick angled up and saw the back of a boat as it sped away.

Michael yelled, "Can you stop him? Bryan?"

A rifle shot was followed by two more.

"He's too far," Bryan finally said through the walkie-talkie. "I could've gotten him if not for the waves."

Michael uttered a curse.

Beneath Derrick, Jasmine squirmed.

He was crushing her and angled off. "Sorry, sweetheart. Are you okay?"

"I think so." She rolled to her side as if to stand. "What is happening?"

"Stay down. Let's find out what's going on."

She did, shivering beside him. She'd taken her hair down, standing brave and strong against her tyrant husband, and long silky tendrils lay across the trodden snow. Her skin was flushed from cold, and dark smudges lined her red-rimmed eyes. But her expression held a mixture of fear and wonder.

She was here, safe and alive.

The most beautiful woman in the world.

He wrapped his free arm around her and crushed her to his chest. "Thank God. Thank God."

As soon as Qasim and Jasmine had disappeared down the steps from the patio, he'd grabbed his walkie-talkie, but the explosion had cut off his words.

There'd been screams and shouts of "Fire! Fire!"

He had no idea what had happened inside. Only that it'd taken precious seconds to get through on the walkie-talkie with

ROBIN PATCHEN

everyone asking questions and trying to figure out what was going on.

"Qasim has her!" Derrick had said the words over and over, all the while, standing, trying to get his bearings despite the dizziness caused by the blows to his head.

He'd watched her walk across the grass. Watched her stop and refuse to go another foot.

Finally, Grant had said, "Quiet. Everyone. Derrick, repeat."

"Qasim has her. They're headed to the cliff."

If she hadn't stopped, they'd have been motoring away before Derrick and his brothers closed in. By the time they got the keys to the boat and set out to follow, they could easily have lost them. There were so many inlets in this sea—in Maine and all the way up the coast into Canada.

She could've been lost forever.

He inhaled her scent, breathed in the very aliveness, the *there*ness of her. "You were so brave."

She backed up so she could see him. "I remembered I have God on my side, and you and your family. And I think...I think even Khalid knew it, at the end. That no matter how many men he'd brought, he was outmatched."

Outmatched, maybe. But things could have gone very differently.

"...satellites over my location?" Michael was saying.

Derrick angled and saw his brother walking toward the cliff, on the phone with someone. "There's a speedboat headed east-north-east. One person. He just killed a terror suspect and tried to kill the man's wife."

Whoa.

Had some of those bullets been meant for Jasmine?

"Nova Scotia or somewhere in Canada would be my guess." Michael listened, then said, "Get back to me."

He was standing, so it must be safe.

Derrick sat up and helped Jasmine do the same. "Are you all right? Did I hurt you? Did he?"

"I'm not hurt. Who was that?"

"No idea." He twisted to where Grant was leaning over Khalid. "Is Qasim...?" Derrick was afraid to ask the question. Afraid to hope. "How is he?"

Grant stood. "Dead."

"What?" Jasmine pushed to her knees, gazing out at the water. "You're sure? Is it safe?"

"Shooter's long gone." Grant scooped up Qasim's weapon, looking at Derrick. "Quick thinking, getting her down. I couldn't have gotten there in time."

Derrick swallowed the image his brother's words raised inside him. Had that man really been trying to shoot her?

Jasmine's hand snaked around his arm. "I wasn't thinking, but you...you saved my life. Again."

"Maybe." He cleared his throat of sudden emotion. "Just instinct."

"Good instincts," Grant said.

Derrick wasn't ready to process that or...any of this. He stood, trying to hide the dizziness caused by the sudden motion, then helped Jasmine up, keeping a hold of her hand even after she gained her feet. "How are you, really?"

"I thought you were dead."

"Just a little woozy. It took me a few seconds to get my wits back. By the time I did, the door opened, and I wanted him to think I was out, that I wasn't a threat."

Her head dipped, but her gaze flicked to the man lying in a pool of bloodstained snow.

Grant was there, his focus on the terrorist's handgun. "Huh." He closed the chamber and shoved it in his waistband. "Guy had guts, I'll give him that."

"What do you mean?" Derrick asked.

"Gun's empty. He was out of bullets."

Oh. *Oh.*

That explained why Khalid had knocked him over the head instead of shooting him.

"You mean he couldn't have shot me?" Jasmine asked.

"He figured you'd just go with him, the arrogant little rat." Grant grinned. "You probably gave him the shock of his life."

Jasmine didn't smile, though. "He is dead? He is really dead?"

"He can't hurt you now." Grant moved out of the way. "See for yourself."

"No, no. It is..." Her head shook, then her whole body shook, trembling, quaking. She swayed, her skin turning that yellowish tint that told Derrick she was not all right.

Ignoring his headache and praying he wouldn't get dizzy again, he scooped her into his arms. "It's okay, sweetheart. You're okay."

"But the house." She must've just remembered what happened before because she suddenly sounded panicked. "Who is hurt? Is Leila...? There was an explosion!"

"I think it's okay. Let's find out." He carried her across the lawn to the door that led to the basement. It slid open as they approached.

Leila stood in the opening. "Yasamin! Thank God."

Derrick set her on her feet, and she fell into her twin's arms. They hugged, then backed up to see each other, studying one another with identical gazes.

"Are you okay?" They both asked the question at the same time, then both answered with, "I'm fine." They smiled identical smiles.

"As long as you're both sure." Mom shoved past Derrick and hugged Jasmine. "Thank God you're all right. What happened? Derrick said a man had you? It was your husband?"

"Yes. He somehow—"

"It's a long story," Derrick said. "We'll explain everything. How's everyone here?"

"It could have been worse." She focused on Jasmine again. "Thank you for making sure everyone was safe."

"I'm so sorry, so sorry this happened." Jasmine seemed shaky and ill. "Is anyone hurt?"

"Camilla has a sprained ankle." Mom shooed him away, and she and Leila urged Jasmine toward the chairs against the wall. "Summer is a little banged up."

"Summer what?" Grant had followed Derrick and Jasmine inside. Now, he nudged Derrick out of the way. "Where is she?"

"Upstairs with Dad," Mom said.

Grant was already making his way past Sophie, Zoë, Camilla, and Eliza, who stood between the ping-pong table and the pool table, though they parted to give him space to pass.

Levi was playing the Ms. Pac-Man game against the wall as if all were right with the world. Thank heavens somebody had turned its volume way down. Derrick wasn't sure he could stand the mechanical munching sounds at that moment.

When Grant had reached the stairs, Derrick leaned close to his mother, lowering his voice. "Is Summer okay? Really? And the baby?"

Mom shrugged, her smile tight. "Dad's with her. She said she saw the guy aiming the launcher thing and dove under the bed. It hit..." Mom shook her head, and the tears she was trying to hold back dripped. "Hit the house next to the window where she'd been standing. Blew a big hole in the wall. But she's tough. Jeremy scrambled down in seconds."

Derrick was confused. He'd taken out the guy with the launcher.

Maybe there'd been two launchers. Must've been. And that made sense because they'd hit the back of the house and the front, and Michael or Grant would've seen and stopped anyone trying to move past the house with it.

"What about the fire?" Derrick asked. "Caused by the explosion?"

"No. Summer said one of them threw a... What do you call it? Named like a mixed drink?"

"A Molotov cocktail?"

"Yeah, that's what she said. The guy launched it through the hole created by the explosion, and it lit the northeast room, where Summer was, then rolled into the hallway and the room across, where Camilla was."

Derrick imagined the horrifying scene.

"Jeremy grabbed one of the fire extinguishers and put it out. Those rooms will need to be rebuilt, but Jeremy kept the fire from spreading and got Summer and his mom out of there. By then, I guess Bryan had taken care of that...person." Mom's lips pinched, though with the thought of her son killing a man or the thought of a firebomb aimed at her family, Derrick wasn't sure. He'd guess the second.

"But you think Summer's all right?"

"Dad said so, and he *is* a doctor." She gave Derrick a *don't ask silly questions* look. "Anyway, after that, the rest of the terrorists ran. At least that's what Bryan told me. What happened with you guys?"

"We'll tell you everything, soon." Derrick turned to check on Jasmine. She was sitting at one of the game tables near the back door with her sister, safe and unhurt.

Michael had come in and was on the phone a few feet away. Catching Derrick's eye, he held up a *hold-on* finger, spoke into the cell phone, then shoved it in his pocket.

"It is over, right?" Derrick walked toward him. "Qasim's men are gone?"

"We think so, but Grant and I will sweep the woods to make sure."

"I'll go with you. Summer was hurt."

Michael's brows lowered. "How bad?"

"Dad's with her."

Mom had come up behind Derrick. "She has a little bump on the head, but there's no reason to believe the baby's been harmed. Is it safe to go back upstairs?" At Michael's nod, she clapped her hands to get everyone's attention. "Who needs coffee?"

A chorus of *I dos* and *Yes, pleases* came from the room.

And then Levi popped in with, "Can I have a donut, Nana? I'm starved."

Derrick wasn't the only one to chuckle, and it felt good.

Good to laugh. Good to breathe.

It was over. Somehow, it was really and truly over.

The next few hours were a whirlwind.

Derrick and Michael swept the woods for terrorists and found a handful of wounded men who hadn't made it back to the boats to escape. The enemies were disarmed, given medical attention—Daniel was brought in for that—and then turned over to the police, who showed up about thirty minutes after all the excitement was over.

The police had alerted the fire department, who'd sent someone over from the mainland to ensure the fire was completely out.

Except for Levi, every member of the Wright family was questioned about what happened—not shocking, considering the number of dead bodies. But they'd been attacked. It wasn't as if Khalid's men had given the Wrights any choice but to defend themselves.

When Michael's team landed at the dock a couple of hours after the police, flashing IDs and dropping names—it didn't hurt that they worked directly for the president—the local cops stepped aside.

Finally, after all the questions were answered and everyone felt certain the island was safe from imminent terror threats, Derrick helped Daniel, Jeremy, and Sam close up the hole in the second story and board up all the broken windows.

Perched on an aluminum ladder leaning against the exterior wall, Derrick nailed a piece of plywood securely to a window frame, trying not to think about the stench that carried from inside. Charred wood, of course. Ammonia from the fire extinguishers. And a sharp, pungent odor produced by all the other stuff that'd burned. And the flash-bangs.

Would they ever get the stink out?

He hadn't gone upstairs inside the house, but the view from the ladder was enough to give him a sense of what it'd been like.

A bomb.

Someone had *bombed* his family's vacation home. And then hurled a Molotov cocktail through it.

Camilla had sprained her ankle. Dad and Bryan had been shooting terrorists. Summer had been trapped under a bed, trying not to burn to death.

He hated to think what might've happened if they hadn't had the fire extinguishers close by. Fortunately, Mom and Dad had always kept plenty on hand, just in case. Considering the closest first responders were a boat ride away, they'd prepared for every emergency they could imagine.

They'd never imagined terrorists.

But they'd been prepared for a fire.

Even the fire extinguishers would've been useless if not for

Jeremy, who'd been quick to grab them and get the fire out. The teenager was a hero.

Everybody had helped, whether firing weapons or protecting the weak or just being there, not panicking. Offering moral support.

Derrick had always known he had a good family, despite the conflicts and broken relationships. He'd lived his life in fear that he would do something or say something that might harm his family. He'd walked on proverbial eggshells, afraid of offending. Afraid of breaking bonds that felt as fragile as glass.

He pulled a nail from his pocket and hammered it into the wood.

Fragile?

Nobody in his right mind would consider the Wrights fragile.

They were strong. And not just physically, though that was certainly true. But his family was strong as a unit. Together. No matter what happened. And he realized, looking back...

They always had been.

Even the years Grant had been gone and Bryan had been bitter, if anything had threatened them, they'd have come together. They'd always loved each other. And they always would.

Derrick reached for another nail, nearly fumbled the hammer.

"Be careful," Daniel called from below. "Wouldn't it be ironic if, after everything, I was killed by a hammer to the head?"

"Not funny, man." But Derrick grinned at his oldest brother, who held onto the extension ladder as if it might spontaneously tip over. Once they'd gotten the plywood in place, this wasn't really a two-man job, so Daniel was just standing on the ground, watching him.

Derrick chuckled to himself, thinking of how he'd yelled at his brothers the night before. A week ago, he'd never have dared talk to them that way. He'd have been too afraid they'd never forgive him.

Now, he knew his family was far from breakable. Their bonds weren't glass but iron, and nothing could shatter them.

Nothing.

He finished with the plywood, climbed down to get the tarp from his brother, and worked on nailing it in place.

Dad had a multitude of tarps. When you lived on an island, you had to have everything you might ever need on hand. Dad had been an Eagle Scout once upon a time.

Be prepared.

Sadly, no plastic tarps or half-inch pieces of plywood were going to keep out the chilly Maine winter or the frigid wind blowing off the North Atlantic. Most of the house was undamaged, but a couple of rooms on the second floor needed major work. Derrick would lend a hand, and he figured his brothers would as well, when they had time. They'd build this place back, better than ever. Probably even add some cabins like Mom and Dad had originally planned to do. There'd be more kids coming along soon enough. And it wouldn't be long before Zoë and Jeremy would marry and start the next generation of Wrights. Now that Daniel and his family were moving back to Maine, their kids would be around a lot more often.

The Wrights would keep this island and their house on it, despite what they'd just endured.

The storm had moved out, leaving a blue sky dotted with puffy white clouds. The pines and oaks and birches that stretched across the island swayed in the cold wind whipping off the water.

The forest had settled as if nothing unusual had happened.

One would never know the violence that had taken place a few hours before.

The house held scars, though, bullet holes and pockmarks that riddled the siding. But none of the Wrights had been shot.

It was crazy, really, how well they'd come through that. A testament to Grant's planning and his and Michael's skills as warriors and Bryan's shooting and...

God.

Derrick and his loved ones were safe. Every single one of them.

The truth of it had moisture filling his eyes.

Thank You.

Only God could've done this.

He finished nailing the tarp in place and descended the ladder, passing more bullet holes as he went down. How in the world was Dad going to explain this to the insurance company?

We were attacked by terrorists.

No, seriously...

"What are you grinning about?" Daniel asked when Derrick joined him on the ground.

"Just wondering if we're going to end up in one of those 'strangest homeowner's insurance claims' commercials."

Daniel chuckled, lowering the extension ladder. "Let's hope not. The Wrights have had enough excitement for all our lifetimes, if you ask me."

That was the truth.

They hefted the ladder across the lawn on trampled snow toward the storage barn at the rear of the property.

They'd been through enough trouble, all of them. And yet, somehow, they'd survived—more than survived.

Grant and Summer would be parents soon. Dad had thoroughly examined Summer and pronounced her fit, except for the bump on her head and some bruises.

Daniel and Camilla had their beautiful, healthy grown children.

Sam and Eliza had Levi. Though they hadn't made an announcement, Derrick guessed by the weight Eliza had put on that she was expecting.

Michael and Leila would be married in the spring, and though it wasn't official, Bryan and his princess bride wouldn't be far behind.

And there was Jasmine.

She was free of her husband. Free to marry.

Derrick had hardly let himself consider what it meant.

Was it wrong to celebrate the man's death? Maybe.

But Derrick hadn't shot him. He'd wanted to, God help him. But he hadn't done it. He'd left his future in God's hands, and... Well, God had let the guy die.

Whoever had shot him...that was an issue for Michael and his people to figure out. Definitely not Derrick's problem.

Considering everything Qasim had done, Derrick wouldn't be shedding a tear for the terrorist.

After stowing the ladder, Derrick followed his big brother up the stairs to the patio, his gaze catching on the bloodstained snow on the far side of the yard.

Khalid's body was gone, along with all the others, driven on the family's carts across the island to the north docks, where they were loaded up and taken back to the mainland. Derrick had no idea what Michael's team would do with them now. Probably ID them if they could, figure out if they were US citizens or immigrants—legal or not. Maybe they'd try to work backward and figure out how the men had ended up working for Khalid.

Maybe the wounded combatants would be able to help with that.

None of that was Derrick's problem.

The sun was shining, the snow evaporating. Soon enough, all traces of the terrorists would fade into the land again, as if they'd never been there at all.

Derrick followed his brother into the kitchen, which was filled with the most glorious scents he could imagine. Meat and roasting vegetables and cinnamon and chocolate. Dishes covered every surface, the food hidden by layers of aluminum foil.

Flames danced in the fireplace on the far side of the great room, where the Christmas tree towered to the ceiling. Somehow, the wall of windows had remained undamaged. Amazing.

"...should hold for now," Daniel was saying.

With him, Bryan, Jeremy, Mom, and Dad congregated around the giant island, all busy getting out all the food they'd prepared for today's party. Someone had called Uncle Gavin and the rest of the other Wright family to cancel the party, but the food would need to be eaten, the sooner the better, as far as Derrick was concerned.

He'd managed to gulp half a cup of coffee and swallow a donut that morning before the police showed up, but then he'd gotten pulled into all the things that needed to be done.

"It won't keep out the cold." Jeremy held a sleeve of crackers in one hand, four of them in the other, ready to chow down. The eighteen-year-old looked ravenous. He shoved a cracker in his mouth, then spoke around it. "At least rain and snow won't get inside."

"You were a great help today." Daniel squeezed his son's shoulder. "And last night. I'm so proud of you."

Jeremy rolled his eyes, but that didn't hide his pleasure at his dad's words.

"Where is everyone?" Derrick asked.

"Grant and Summer are in one of the rooms upstairs." Dad's lips quirked at the corners. "It's hard to believe the worrier he is right now after the warrior he was last night."

"I thought you said Summer's fine." Derrick glanced from his father to Daniel, the other doctor in the family.

"Just needs to rest, like all of us." Dad shook his head, pretending exasperation he obviously didn't feel. "Grant refused to leave the bedroom until she fell asleep."

Derrick was about to ask about Jasmine when voices had him focusing on the stairs. Camilla, Zoë, and Sophie came down, covered in a fine film of white dust. Camilla was leaning heavily on the handrail and using the vacuum cleaner with her other hand like a walking stick. Zoë wore a face mask, probably a holdover from the pandemic, and held a bucket and cleaning supplies, and Sophie had an armful of sheets and blankets.

Daniel hurried toward his wife. "What are you doing, love? You're supposed to stay off your ankle."

"It already feels better." Camilla handed him the vacuum. "That probably needs to be wiped down before we put it away. Fire extinguisher dust gets on everything."

"So I see." He set the vacuum aside and brushed dust out of her hair. "You wore a mask, right?"

"Yes, doctor." She lifted her wrist, where a mask dangled.

"We told her to rest. She's a stubborn one." Sophie continued toward the stairs that led to the basement. "We'll need to wash all the bedding."

Bryan grabbed her load. "I'll take it, hon."

"Get those started," Mom called after him, taking the cleaning supplies from Zoë. "We want to get it all finished before we leave, which we'll do right after lunch."

Her mention of lunch was greeted with a chorus of yesses and amens.

Nobody heard Derrick's stomach growling, but it was on board with that.

Where was Jasmine, though?

Movement on the far side of the room caught his attention as Jasmine pushed up from the sofa. She tossed away a blanket and unfolded her legs.

Dad leaned close and lowered his voice. "I tried to get her to go upstairs to rest, too, but she refused. I don't know why." But his expression told Derrick he had a good guess—and it had everything to do with him.

Derrick pretended not to see as he crossed the room. "How you doing?"

She stretched like a cat awakened from a nap. "I'm good." But the word faded on a yawn.

"More hungry than tired?" Her eyes lit, and he grinned. "Mom said something about food."

He held his hand out, and she took it and stood, keeping her hand in his as if it belonged right there. Which it did.

Dad let out a high-pitched whistle, calling the family to gather, and those not already there made their way to the first floor, even Summer, who preceded Grant.

"Honey." Grant followed her. "Let me bring you a plate in bed. You can rest—"

"That's enough." Summer's voice was loud as she rounded on her husband and jabbed her finger into his chest. "I'm hungry. I'm rested, and I'm fine. If you suggest I go back to bed one more time, I'm going to punch you. Got it?"

Conversation stopped.

Nobody breathed.

And then Grant chuckled, kissed her on the forehead, and peered over her head at Dad. "You're right. She's fine."

Which made everybody laugh.

Even Dad, but his smile didn't last long. He cleared his

throat and turned to Michael, who'd come in from outside a moment before. "Your brother wants to talk to us before we eat."

Michael stepped into the room and took Leila's hand.

The whole family was there, watching him. Waiting.

"Sorry. Mom said lunch would be another five minutes or so." Michael looked at her, and she nodded. He scanned the family until he saw Jasmine. "I thought you might want to know what we learned."

She squeezed Derrick's hand. "Yes, please."

"Most of the men we caught aren't talking, but one of them is young and in the mood to chat. He's homegrown." Michael's lips pressed closed in his trademark smirk, and he shook his head. "Guy's from Ohio. Born and raised. Part of a terror cell that was called up. His had about twenty men. He didn't know about the other cells until they all met last night. There were ninety of them from all different places. Qasim activated them all up just for this."

Derrick slipped his hand around Jasmine's waist and pulled her close, needing the connection and figuring she did too.

All those men, all that trouble. Just to get her back.

"Any word on the man in the boat?" Grant asked.

Michael focused on Sophie. "Dariush Ghazi was spotted in Portland yesterday afternoon. Our theory is that he either rented or stole a boat. We're working on confirming that."

Sophie's skin paled to match day-old snow.

"Why would he shoot Khalid?" Bryan asked.

"I'm guessing he knew too much."

"About what?" Derrick looked from Bryan to Sophie to Michael. "I don't understand. How does all of this go together?"

"We're not sure yet," Michael said. "We know Dariush knew you." He nodded to Jasmine, and then to Leila beside him. "So he must've recognized you. Maybe he'd heard Jasmine had a twin or just put it together?"

Leila's head tipped to the side. "Perhaps that is how Qasim found me in Munich. Perhaps Dariush alerted him."

"But why?" Jasmine asked. "He is the kind of man who is always working for gain. He must have had a reason."

Michael shrugged. "When we find him, we'll ask him. That's all I know for now."

"But we're safe?" Dad clarified. "It's over?"

"Yeah." Michael looked from Leila to Jasmine. "There's nobody else."

"But what about..." Derrick hated to ask the question, but he wouldn't be able to rest if he didn't. He held Jasmine tightly against his side. "What about their father?"

Michael's lips pressed closed, and his gaze flicked from Leila to Jasmine.

She was the one who answered. "Baba does not have the resources to find us. He went along with his brother and the others, but he was not in charge. You agree, sister?"

Leila nodded. "You knew him better than I did at the end. I trust your judgment."

"I think we are safe from Baba." Jasmine squeezed Derrick's hand. "It is over."

The room seemed to take a collective breath.

"Well." Mom obviously didn't know how to segue from that to normalcy. In her defense, what reasonable person would? "Now that that's settled...the food is ready."

Dad cleared his throat. "Let's hold hands for the blessing."

They circled up, the whole crowd of them. Derrick's five brothers, their wives and future wives, Zoë, Jeremy, Levi, Mom, and Dad.

Derrick held onto Jasmine's hand, and it all just...hit him. What had happened.

What could have happened.

What they'd gone through, not just today but over the past few months.

How much they could have lost. How much they had gained.

How good, how incredibly good, their God was.

Apparently, Derrick wasn't the only one who had these thoughts because he saw a lot of moisture around the circle, mostly on the faces of the women. His brothers held their heads up, like they could shake the tears back inside.

"Well, God." Dad swallowed hard, scanning the room. "I don't think there are words big enough for this moment. *Thank You* doesn't cover it. You did this. You saved us and..." He took a breath and blew it out. "We owe You...everything."

Derrick kissed the top of Jasmine's head, and she looked up at him with more wonder than even she'd ever held before.

And for the first time, he figured his expression mirrored hers.

Dad seemed at a loss. The rest of them were just nodding along, sniffing. Smiling and crying. He and his brothers pretending not to cry.

Then Daniel said, "I think that covers it. Amen."

The room chorused, "Amen."

They filled their plates and talked and laughed and stoked the fire and gathered at the oversize dining room table in the shadow of the Christmas tree and ate.

And all the while, Derrick couldn't keep from watching the beautiful woman who was safe and healthy and maybe, God willing, might someday be his.

An hour later, Derrick crossed the yard from the cliff. He'd helped haul luggage to the dock. Even with both speedboats here, it would take a couple of trips to get everyone back to the mainland. Dad had headed across the choppy water with Mom, Grant, Summer, Bryan, and Sophie in his boat. Michael followed with Daniel, Camilla, Zoë, and Jeremy in the other.

The sun was already dipping in the west. It would be fully dark by the time Dad and Michael would be back to collect the rest of them. Not that it mattered. Traveling the few miles over the choppy water would be a piece of cake after the danger they'd endured.

Derrick climbed to the patio and crossed to the kitchen door. It opened before he reached it.

Jasmine must've showered because her hair was damp, hanging over her shoulder, her face scrubbed and glowing in the pale evening light. She wore a red dress that didn't manage to hide her beautiful shape. She'd slipped into a jacket and a pair of fuzzy boots. Had she been about to go in search of him? She smiled, the expression so open and fresh that he stopped where he was, just to look at her.

He'd rarely seen her so unguarded. So...happy.

"Well? Are you coming?" Her head tilted, and her voice held teasing. "I think your father would say heat doesn't grow on trees, no?"

Wow. The way she gazed at him was heating far more than the outside air.

Derrick's *inside* was getting pretty warm.

"Though I think, when you build a fire, heat does grow on trees." She grinned. "This is kidding, yes? This thing your father always says?" And then she laughed as if she'd just gotten Dad's stupid joke, and it was the funniest thing she'd ever heard.

Derrick couldn't stand it, not for one more second.

He crossed the space, pulled her outside and into his arms.

"Oh." Her eyes were wide, but she wasn't afraid. Just surprised and...pleased.

She was so perfect, right there, tucked against him. Tiny and vulnerable and strong and amazing and everything he'd ever wanted.

"You're not married anymore." And why was his voice so husky?

"This is true." Her words were barely a whisper.

He held her eye contact. "Are there any...rules I need to know about? With the mourning? The whole...widow thing?"

"For a beloved husband, yes. But for Khalid?" Her head shifted back and forth, the gesture slight as if she didn't want to move—as if she didn't want to risk breaking their connection.

He dipped his head and inhaled her scent, shampoo and Christmas and everything he'd ever wanted. He yearned to taste her. He wanted her lips against his. But he would give her time. He wouldn't force himself on her the way Qasim had. He wouldn't pressure her. He had all the time in the world, even if his body was telling him differently.

But she rose to her tiptoes and touched her lips to his, the slightest pressure.

He was almost afraid to move. *Slow. Take it slow.*

He tried. Honestly, he tried.

She started it.

When her lips moved, he responded in kind. At least, he hoped it was *in kind*. He wasn't completely sure.

Her mouth opened, and he had no choice but to dive in. To explore. To claim this woman he loved. This woman he would love until his last breath.

CHAPTER THIRTY-SEVEN

As a schoolgirl, Jasmine had dreamed of her first kiss. She'd expected it to be romantic and beautiful.

And then it had come from Khalid, and it had been ugly and hard.

She'd hated it. She'd hated every kiss he'd ever given her.

Though she had never said so, Khalid must have discerned how she felt—or maybe he'd felt disloyal to his beloved wife—because he had stopped kissing Jasmine. The things they did were intimate—and she'd loathed his every touch—but there was something even more intimate about kissing.

Or intimate in a different way. Which didn't make sense to her.

Or hadn't, until now.

Now, beneath the towering forest, with the scent of smoke rising through the chimney and the waves crashing so close, Jasmine felt drawn to Derrick in a way she'd never felt drawn to another man.

His arms around her, his warmth enveloping her, she'd known he wanted to kiss her. She'd closed the distance because she'd wanted him to know that she was open to a relationship with him. She loved him. And with Khalid gone, she could be with him.

She'd felt alive in his arms. She'd felt safe and protected.

She hadn't *wanted* to kiss him. She'd only wanted him to know she was available to him.

And yet...

And yet, when his lips had met hers...

Oh.

Oh.

This was what a kiss was meant to be.

This soft touch. This wondrous exploring. This promise of more.

Derrick's mouth was gentle and warm.

He held her against him, shielding her from the wind as he'd shielded her from the evil that had tracked her down. This man had protected her and guarded her and loved her. He'd loved her so well.

And now he proved to her that she'd never really been kissed at all. Perhaps the other things she'd done with Khalid could also be different with Derrick.

Of course.

Of course everything would be different with Derrick. He didn't want to use her. He wanted to love her.

He *did* love her.

She felt it in the way his lips moved against hers. In the way his hand pressed against the small of her back. In the way his fingers weaved into her hair.

His touch sparked feelings she'd never experienced, making her want things she'd never wanted. Was this what it meant to love a man? To want to be with him?

To be free. To be *free.*

To truly love was to be free to say no. And to say yes. And yes. And yes.

Derrick ended the kiss, crushing her against his chest. His jacket was unbuttoned, his heart beating against her ear. He groaned, the sound coming from deep inside.

"Jasmine."

"Hmm..."

"I love you."

She leaned back, lifted her hand, and pressed it against his soft beard. "I love you."

He smiled that sweet, happy smile. "Marry me."

Surprise zinged through her, and she stepped back automatically, but Derrick didn't loosen his grip.

"Don't. Don't leave." His smile faded. "We can wait, if you—"

"I do not—"

"I get it. You're not ready. There's no rush. We can wait. I was only...I love you, and I felt—"

She pressed her hand over his mouth. "Perhaps you should let me answer, hmm?"

His brows lowered. He didn't argue, just nodded.

"I do not wish to wait. If you are willing, I would prefer we are married before my child is born. I want him or her to have a father. To have you, if you are sure."

A little bubble of movement in her belly...

Her baby approved. Her baby would know this man, this good, good man. He—or she—would call him Baba.

No. Dad. Or, as Levi called Sam...

Daddy.

Derrick's eyes filled with sweet tears. "That's a yes? You're saying yes? You'll marry me?"

"You love me. I love you. And if we marry, we can do the kissing all the time, no?"

Laughing, he wrapped her in his arms, lifted her off her feet, and spun her in a circle. And then, he was kissing her a second time, and if her feet never hit the ground again, she would be happy.

CHAPTER THIRTY-EIGHT

"I'm happy for you. Seriously."

Derrick laughed at Michael, who'd ground out the words through clenched teeth. "Sure you are." Hiding his grin, he turned away from his brother, facing the full-length mirror somebody'd propped against the wall in Sam's den. He didn't miss Michael's scowl in the reflection.

Dad was leaning against the far wall, arms crossed, hiding his own grin but not getting involved.

When Derrick and Jasmine had chosen to marry just a couple weeks after he proposed—the Saturday between Christmas and New Year's—he'd figured he'd be wearing his best suit for the ceremony. Okay, fine, his *only* suit. He'd just hoped Leila and Sophie would be able to talk Jasmine into getting a more fitted dress than the potato-sack-shaped things she usually wore.

Not that he minded, obviously. He'd fallen in love with the woman inside those shapeless dresses, but he did hope to persuade her during their lifelong marriage that it would be all right to show her figure every now and then.

He adjusted his tie, then smoothed the vest beneath his

tuxedo jacket. He'd been directed to wear this, which meant surely Jasmine had found something better than a slightly fancier potato sack for the small ceremony his family had put together.

His tie was straight. His hair was combed back from his face. He'd offered to get it cut for the wedding, but Jasmine had asked him not to. She liked it long. And he liked the way she played with it, her slender fingers brushing against the skin on his neck. They'd spent almost every waking moment together for the past two weeks, eating and laughing and planning and just...being. Watching television and reading books and talking about their days. He'd taken her to his condo, a tiny two-bedroom on the outskirts of Shadow Cove. She'd never been there, and he'd worried she'd be disappointed. It wasn't as nice as Michael's house, where she'd been living, with its three bedrooms and two bathrooms. And it was a pale comparison to Sam's house, this palatial home with all the space and windows and ocean views. Derrick's condo was a tiny place that shared walls with neighbors and had a pathetic little yard.

He'd been embarrassed as he'd watched her take it in, afraid he'd see disappointment on her face. He should've known better.

She'd been delighted. "This whole place is yours?"

"Ours."

She'd launched herself into his arms and kissed him.

She'd gone from reticent to enthusiastic about kissing, but that day, alone in the house they'd share, nobody looking over their shoulders...

Oh boy.

He'd practically run out the door into the cold December morning, leaving a very confused, slightly hurt Jasmine behind. Hurt until he'd explained, and then she'd blushed and gotten all shy and...

Why anybody waited months for their weddings, Derrick would never understand. As far as he was concerned, the ceremony couldn't happen fast enough. And did they really have to stay here and entertain guests afterward? Because he could think of a few better things to do.

"You okay over there, bro?" Bryan was seated on one of Sam's leather sofas, his bum leg propped on the coffee table.

"I'm fine."

"'Cause your face is a little flushed. Thinking about anything in particular?"

Derrick glared at him. "Thinking I should've asked Grant to be my best man. Less talking."

Bryan just laughed.

"Be nice, son." Dad used his *behave yourself* voice. He and Bryan both wore dark gray tuxes, like Derrick's, though while his tie was the same dark gray as his suit, theirs were pale blue.

As if it had decided to coordinate with Jasmine's color scheme, the sky beyond the wall of windows was also pale blue, the sun not quite at its zenith. Fresh snow covered everything in a few inches of powder, making the hillside between Sam's house and the Atlantic below fresh and pure.

Perfect for Derrick's bride.

Bryan pushed himself up and leaned on his cane. "Michael might not say so, but I'm not afraid to admit that I'm a little annoyed."

Michael leaned against the door, crossing his arms. Funny how similar he was to their father, who stood in almost the exact same posture just a few feet away. Michael wasn't in the wedding party—only Leila and Bryan would stand up with Jasmine and Derrick—but he'd donned a suit for the occasion.

Glaring at Bryan, Michael said. "You and Sophie just met. I've been with Leila for a year, and we aren't getting married for months. She wanted to put it off so Jasmine wouldn't be pregnant at the wedding. Which was fine, but now the maid of honor's gonna be a matron, and my baby brother's beating me to the altar."

"As long as you're not annoyed," Derrick said.

"Shut up."

Dad shook his head, Bryan laughed, and Michael, though he was trying very hard to play the part of the irritated brother, couldn't completely hide his smile.

"Do you guys need anything?" he finally asked. "Mom wanted me to make sure there were no pre-wedding jitters."

Derrick turned, anxiety spiking. "No jitters here. Why? Is Jasmine—?"

"She's fine." He crossed the room and clamped his hand on Derrick's shoulder, eyes twinkling. "I heard her tell Leila the clock has never moved so slowly."

Derrick couldn't stop his grin.

Michael gave him a quick hug, slapping him on the back. "You got a good one, bro." He stepped away and checked his watch. "T minus fifteen. As soon as you hear the music, get in place. You remember everything you need to do?"

"It's just the family. It's not that complicated."

Michael was chuckling as he walked out.

Derrick glared at the closed door, then turned to Dad and Bryan. "You'd think we were performing for the president or something."

"Son." Dad peered at him over his glasses. "This is the most important day of your life—and your bride's. Don't screw it up."

Yeah. Dad was right. "I'm not going to. Not the wedding. And not the marriage."

"That's my boy." Dad squeezed his forearm. "I'm sure your mother is looking for me. You boys good in here?" At Derrick's nod, he said, "I'll see you out there."

The door closed behind him, and Derrick checked his watch. Just a few more minutes.

Bryan perched on the arm of the sofa while Derrick settled in one of the club chairs.

"You're gonna be a husband," Bryan said. "And in a few months, a father. Are you ready for that?"

Derrick had blurted his marriage proposal before he'd really thought about it. Yeah, he'd planned to marry Jasmine almost from the first second he'd met her. But a baby? One that wasn't his?

There hadn't been a lot of time to process—or pray about—that.

He'd spent a lot of time in prayer after he'd proposed. Hours on his knees, asking God for guidance. Because if he wasn't up for the job, or this wasn't God's plan for his life, then he needed to back out now, before it was too late.

As much as he wanted Jasmine, and as much as it would hurt both of them, he wasn't about to make a promise he couldn't keep.

The more time he spent in prayer, the more certain he was of his path.

"The kid's not going to look like me," he said, "or have Wright blood in her veins. But she's mine."

"She?" Bryan's eyebrows lifted.

"Yeah." Derrick hoped she'd resemble his beautiful bride. "We found out a couple days ago. I wasn't supposed to tell anyone. We're gonna do the whole gender reveal thing after the honeymoon."

"A cousin for Grant's little girl."

They'd learned that news on Christmas when Summer and Grant had presented a snow-white cake that, when cut, had spilled pink M&M's all over the table.

Bryan was grinning. "Your secret's safe with me."

"It doesn't matter who her biological father is. She'll be *my* daughter. She's meant to be my daughter. She *is* my daughter." He considered his brother's question again. "Am I ready?"

The music started—a CD playing over Sam's sound system because they hadn't been able to find a single suitable musician available on two weeks' notice in the middle of the holiday season.

Derrick popped to his feet. "Can you ever be ready for something like this?"

Bryan pushed off from his perch. "I suppose if you thought you were ready, that would only prove arrogance."

Maybe. Derrick didn't know if he was supposed to feel confident or terrified or what.

All he felt was eager to make Jasmine his wife.

As he followed Bryan down the hall, he inhaled the scent of flowers. Jasmine. Sweet and strong, just like the woman who'd chosen the name when she'd escaped her past.

One side of the formal living room was open to the foyer. The Christmas tree towered in the corner, and beside it, a low fire flickered in the fireplace. Flower arrangements in blues and whites draped from stands that had been placed around the seating area. Bows made of puffy white fabric adorned every surface, and a white carpet stretched down the aisle created by the chairs.

Derrick had no idea how his family had pulled this off so quickly. At first, he'd thought it was silly to have a fancy wedding with only a few weeks' notice, but now, seeing the beauty of it, he understood.

They'd all pitched in, these people he loved so much, to honor him and his bride. They'd always loved him so well, and they'd already made Jasmine one of them.

Mom and his brothers and their wives, girlfriends, and kids were seated in the first few rows. Besides Jasmine and her twin

SHELTERING YOU

sister, only Eliza and Levi were missing, but they'd come soon enough.

Behind Derrick's immediate family, Uncle Gavin sat at the end of the row beside his oldest daughter, Alyssa, and Aunt Evelyn. Funny how similar Alyssa and Evelyn were with their long silvery-blond hair, though Evelyn's was more silver than blond these days. The rest of the sisters sat in the row behind them. Delaney, Brooklynn, and Cecelia were bent over one of their phones. Kenzie, the youngest, seemed not to mind that her sisters paid her no attention. She caught Derrick's eyes and smiled.

In the next row of seats back, Logan sat with his girlfriend, Darcy, who'd come as his date. Or were they engaged now? If not, they would be soon enough. Logan was the caterer for the retreat center where Leila and Jasmine worked, and both he and Darcy had gone out of their way to make the twins feel welcome in Shadow Cove.

Derrick nodded to them and the other guests, who were all beaming at him.

His heart rate spiked for the first time all morning. These must be the jitters everyone kept asking about.

He took his place between the minister and Bryan. And waited.

Finally, Levi came down the stairs and around the corner, holding a little black pillow with the fake rings. The ones Derrick and Jasmine had chosen were safely tucked in Bryan's pocket. Eliza guided the now five-year-old, whispering in his ear, and he practically skipped down the aisle toward Derrick.

The kid was so cute in his tiny tuxedo and those little blond curls, and Derrick stifled the urge to muss his hair.

He sat beside his dad, and Eliza scooted down the outside edge of the aisle and settled on his other side. They were the perfect little family.

381

Leila came next, pretty in a shimmery pale-blue dress. Funny how everyone said the twins were identical. They were, but Derrick could tell them apart in an instant. Leila was pretty, of course. But she was not his beloved. As she passed him to take her place on the opposite side of the minister, his almost sister-in-law gave him a smile that said, *just you wait.*

Finally, the music changed.

And then, there was Jasmine, on his father's arm.

Holy moly.

Somehow, in a couple of weeks, she'd found a gown. Pure white and...gorgeous. Above the bodice, the lace rose to just below her neck and stretched down her arms, showing off her gorgeous dark skin. It flowed out from her waist in a wide skirt and trailed behind her. It was beautiful and modest and absolutely, perfectly Jasmine.

She was...

Wow. Just...

Wow.

He swallowed, swallowed again. Swiped moisture from his eyes to keep her image from blurring. This was a picture he never wanted to forget.

This...this woman. He was *marrying* this woman.

She gave him a shy smile. Her eyes were bigger, her lips redder. Her cheekbones higher. Her black hair was in some sort of updo with little bits curling down by her face. Her veil hung behind her like...like a halo.

And okay, maybe he was going too far, but he didn't care. He saw what he saw. Beautiful, holy, pure, and perfect.

His bride.

She walked slowly, and he savored every moment.

When she reached him, Dad kissed her on the cheek and stepped back.

Derrick took her hands.

"Who gives this woman in marriage?" the minister asked.

Leila, her twin and her best friend, answered. "My sister owns herself, chooses for herself, and gives herself, and I stand with her in her choice."

The minister knew enough of her story to offer a nod and a supportive smile. "Let's pray."

Derrick tried to focus on the words, but his eyes kept catching on Jasmine's, and she kept smiling at him, and he kept smiling at her.

They spoke vows. They exchanged rings.

And then, "You may kiss the bride."

Derrick wrapped her in his arms and did just that, a sweet, tender promise of forever.

Around them, the room erupted in cheers.

Reluctantly, he started to release her, but she clung to him.

Worried something was wrong, he held her tightly and whispered, "Are you all right?"

"All right?" She backed up, pressing her hands to his face, seeming delightfully confused. "I am much better than all right. I am yours."

"Yes, you're mine." He smiled down at his bride. She was small in stature and huge in courage. She was everything he'd ever wanted. "And I'm yours. Forever."

EPILOGUE

Dariush Ghazi stared out the window across the water. On a clear day like this, he could just glimpse the state of Maine from the second floor of the house he'd found on the southern tip of Nova Scotia, a deserted cabin in a deserted town in the middle of nowhere.

Nobody would find him here.

It was the last Saturday of December, and people with brains—and choices—stayed far from this part of the world at this time of year, when snow piled up and wind whipped off the dark ocean water.

This was a summer retreat, though why anybody would choose to stay here even in the warm months, he couldn't imagine. Did they not know there were places with clear, blue water and sunny skies? Had they never heard of the Mediterranean? The Caribbean? Even Florida had to be better than this.

This was a godforsaken place. Or would be, if there were a god.

Dariush had been trapped in Canada ever since he'd barely escaped the bullets that'd come too close that cold and terrible morning. The morning his plans had been thwarted. Again.

The day Khalid Qasim, the old fool, had almost surrendered to the Americans, the only thing he could not do.

Dariush had shot him, of course. In his fury, he'd tried to kill the man's pathetic little wife, who carried his pathetic spawn. But the woman lived. Yasamin, now Jasmine. Her twin sister also lived. Leila French, née Nawra Farad.

The curly-haired blonde from Munich, Sophia Chapman, lived.

And all those Wright brothers lived. All in Maine.

Dariush hadn't known the lame one who'd saved the blonde in Germany was related to the one with Khalid's wife, nor had he realized before this trip the man he'd seen from afar in Mytilene, the one who'd rescued Nawra and killed Waleed, was related to the others.

He hadn't put it together until he'd seen them all through his binoculars the day of the failed attack.

Rabie had told him that Derrick was one of six brothers. Dariush had their names now. And their images and the images of their women and children.

He could exact revenge if he wanted to.

But Khalid was dead. Waleed was dead. Hasan was in custody. Fortunately, he had never known Dariush's true goal, or his plans would be ruined.

Khalid had known, though. Dariush hadn't had a choice. They'd made a deal—the whereabouts of his pretty little wife for the name of the Russian.

Which was why Khalid had had to die.

Dariush's mission wasn't about the petty plans of petty people out to serve their petty gods.

He could pretend faith when it served his purpose. He could kneel on a mat and touch his forehead to the floor. He could recite words in a cathedral. He could feign worship in a synagogue.

He could play the part of loving brother. He could play the part of devoted son.

Dariush Ghazi could be whatever the moment dictated.

What he could not be, *would* not be, was defeated. And yet, here he was, in a drafty cabin in Nova Scotia. All his plans ruined, the people he'd planned to use, dead.

He stalked away from the window and into the sad little brown kitchen, all wood siding and linoleum. He flicked the top of his lighter open, sparked the flame, and snapped it closed, over and over.

Thinking. Thinking.

He was safe here, for now.

Infuriating as the snow was, Dariush's footprints, which had led from the back door of this house to the deserted store down the road and all the nearby cabins, were hidden beneath the fresh powder. He'd helped himself to provisions—food and supplies and everything he needed to stay alive and accomplish his goals.

He'd ransacked all the homes and found a decent computer and an old cell phone—couldn't risk using his own, of course. There was no Wi-Fi in this house, but there was cell service here, so he'd connected the phone to a plan using one of his many aliases and then used his hotspot to connect the laptop.

While he waited until it was safe to travel again, he did research.

He gazed at the website he'd found a few days earlier. Alyssa Wright, cousin to Derrick and Michael and the rest of those brothers.

An interesting family, these Wrights. Dariush had had enough run-ins with the men and didn't relish facing them again. But women...

Women were a different story.

Alyssa's father, Gavin, had worked for a government

contractor and had contacts in the US government and other high-ranking officials around the world. It seemed Alyssa did some work for Daddy on the side, as well as for her cousin, Michael, the CIA agent.

Thanks to his own connections, Dariush had learned many things he wasn't meant to know.

Alyssa Wright's website claimed she was an investigator, but he dug, and some of the treasures he unearthed told a different story altogether.

He sat back and flicked his lighter, enjoying the flashes of light, quickly snuffed out.

Yes, he had a feeling about this woman.

He'd lie low...for now. And then, when it was safe to move, he'd connect with Alyssa Wright.

Through her, he'd get what he needed, one way or another.

The End...

For now, but I couldn't resist writing one more chapter, and you're going to love it. Download the bonus epilogue to find out what happens next. You can get it at https://www. subscribepage.com/sheltering-you. If you have trouble downloading it, click the little "need help" button on the top right of the Bookfunnel download page or reach out to me at https:// robinpatchen.com/connect/, and I'll see if I can help.

Okay, now the end... Sort of.

Because Dariush is still out there, and he's after something. The Wright brothers have thwarted him three times—in *Finding You, Sheltering You,* and even in *Rescuing You,* though he wasn't on their radar then. But he's got a new plan, and this time, he's set his sights on Derrick's cousin, the oldest Wright sister, to achieve his goal.

Don't miss the fifth book in the Wright Heroes of Maine series, *Protecting You,* featuring Alyssa Wright. Turn the page for a sneak peek of *Protecting You.*

~

Before that, revisit Nutfield in a Christmas novella collection, featuring *Sleigh Bells and Stalkers*, a brand-new Nutfield story, releasing this November. *Christmas in Nutfield* will contain at least two Christmas novellas, and you won't want to miss it.

~

And in October, the second edition of *Finding Amanda* will release. Fully updated with a brand-new cover and brand-new content, you won't want to miss this one.

Now, turn the page for more about *Protecting You,* Wright Heroes of Maine book 5. (Cover and back cover copy coming soon.)

An excerpt from *PROTECTING YOU*

"I'm not sure I can do it."

"Of course you can, Alyssa."

Her name on his lips was like a worm slithering down her spine. What was it about this guy?

He pulled a piece of paper from his jacket pocket and held it across the table. "Go ahead."

It was a check. She stared at the number. All those zeroes. This one job would cover months of expenses. The guy was creepy, but she needed the money. She stuck out her right hand. "We have a deal."

They shook, and despite all those zeroes, when she caught the brief but unmistakable triumph that crossed his face, she had to stifle a shudder. "I look forward to—"

"Darling!"

The voice twinged her memory, familiar enough that she couldn't help looking toward the person who'd spoken it, though she was certainly nobody's darling.

A man stopped beside their table. "Sorry I'm early. I couldn't wait to see you and took a chance you'd be done." He bent toward Alyssa, his back to Charles, and kissed her cheek.

Gideon Todd? What in the world?

He whispered, "Trust me. Go with it." His words were more breathed than spoken, sending shivers down her spine, which annoyed her almost as much as the interruption.

What was happening?...

Don't miss *Protecting You,* coming this winter and featuring a familiar and deadly villain and an elaborate (fake relationship) scheme to uncover his secrets. You're going to love it.

ALSO BY ROBIN PATCHEN

The Nutfield Saga

Convenient Lies

Twisted Lies

Generous Lies

Innocent Lies

Beautiful Lies

Legacy Rejected

Legacy Restored

Legacy Reclaimed

Legacy Redeemed

Christmas in Nutfield

Amanda Series

Chasing Amanda

Finding Amanda

ABOUT ROBIN PATCHEN

Robin Patchen is a *USA Today* bestselling and award-winning author of Christian romantic suspense. She grew up in a small town in New Hampshire, the setting of her Coventry Saga books, and then headed to Boston to earn a journalism degree. After college, working in marketing and public relations, she discovered how much she loathed the nine-to-five ball and chain. She started writing her first novel while she home-schooled her three children. The novel was dreadful, but her passion for storytelling didn't wane. Thankfully, as her children grew, so did her skill. Now that her kids are adults, she has more time to play with the lives of fictional heroes and heroines, wreaking havoc and working magic to give her characters happy endings. When she's not writing, she's editing or reading, proving that most of her life revolves around the twenty-six letters of the alphabet.

Made in the USA
Coppell, TX
24 September 2024